BETTY
NEELS

Matilda's Wedding
& Nanny by Chance

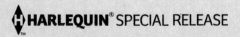

HARLEQUIN® SPECIAL RELEASE

ISBN-13: 978-1-335-04502-7

Matilda's Wedding & Nanny by Chance

Copyright © 2018 by Harlequin Books S.A.

The publisher acknowledges the copyright holder of the individual works as follows:

Recycling programs for this product may not exist in your area.

Matilda's Wedding
Copyright © 1999 by Betty Neels

Nanny by Chance
Copyright © 1998 by Betty Neels

This edition published by arrangement with Harlequin Books S.A.

For questions and comments about the quality of this book, please contact us at CustomerService@Harlequin.com.

® and TM are trademarks of Harlequin Enterprises Limited or its corporate affiliates. Trademarks indicated with ® are registered in the United States Patent and Trademark Office, the Canadian Intellectual Property Office and in other countries.

Printed in U.S.A.

CONTENTS

Romance readers around the world were sad to note the passing of **Betty Neels** in June 2001. Her career spanned thirty years, and she continued to write into her ninetieth year. To her millions of fans, Betty epitomized the romance writer, and yet she began writing almost by accident. She had retired from nursing, but her inquiring mind still sought stimulation. Her new career was born when she heard a lady in her local library bemoaning the lack of good romance novels. Betty's first book, *Sister Peters in Amsterdam*, was published in 1969, and she eventually completed 134 books. Her novels offer a reassuring warmth that was very much a part of her own personality. She was a wonderful writer, and she is greatly missed. Her spirit and genuine talent live on in all her stories.

MATILDA'S WEDDING

Chapter 1

Dr Lovell looked across his desk to the girl sitting in front of it. She would have to do, he supposed; none of the other applicants had been suitable. No one, of course, could replace the estimable Miss Brimble who had been with him for several years before leaving reluctantly to return home and nurse an aged parent, but this girl, with her mediocre features and quiet voice, was hardly likely to upset the even tenor of his life. There was nothing about her appearance to distract him from his work; her mousy hair was in a smooth French pleat, her small nose was discreetly powdered, and if she wore lipstick it wasn't evident. And her clothes were the kind which were never remembered... She was, in fact, suitable.

Matilda Paige, aware that she was being studied, watched the man on the other side of the desk in her turn. A very large man, in his thirties, she guessed. Handsome, with a commanding nose and a thin mouth and hooded eyes and dark hair streaked with silver. She had no intention of being intimidated by him but she thought that anyone timid might be. A calm, quiet girl by nature, she saw no reason to stand in awe of him. Besides, since the moment she had set eyes on him, not half an hour ago, she had fallen in love with him...

'You are prepared to start work on Monday, Miss Paige?'

Matilda said yes, of course, and wished that he would smile. Probably he was tired or hadn't had time for a proper breakfast that morning. That he had a good house-keeper she had already found out for herself, whose brother did the gardening and odd jobs. She had also discovered that he was engaged. A haughty piece, Mrs Simpkins at the village shop had said—been to stay accompanied by her brother once or twice, hadn't liked the village at all and said so.

'Rude,' Mrs Simpkins had said. 'Them as should know better should mind their manners; grumbled 'cos I didn't 'ave some fancy cheese they wanted. Well, what's good enough for the doctor should be good enough for them. 'E's a nice man, none better, just as 'is dad was a good man, too. A pity 'e ever took up with that young woman of 'is.'

Matilda, sitting primly on the other side of his desk, heartily agreed with Mrs Simpkins. All's fair in love, she reflected, and got up when he gave his watch a brief glance.

Dr Lovell got up too; his manners were nice… She bade him a brisk goodbye as he opened the surgery door for her and then, shepherded by his practice nurse, left the house.

It was a pleasant old house in the centre of the village. Queen Anne, red-bricked with massive iron railings protecting it from the narrow main street. Lovells had lived there for generations, she had been told, father passing on his profession to son, and this particular twentieth-century son was, from all accounts, acknowledged to be quite brilliant. He had refused offers of important posts in London and preferred to remain at his old home, working as a GP.

Matilda walked briskly down the street, smiling rather shyly at one or two of the passers-by, still feeling that she didn't belong. The village was a large one, deep in rural Somerset, and as yet had escaped the attention of developers wanting to buy land and build houses, probably because it lay well away from a main road, astride a tangle of narrow country lanes. Because of that, inhabitants of Much Winterlow were slow to accept newcomers. Not that there was anything about the Reverend Mr Paige, his wife and daughter to which they could take exception. Upon his retirement owing to ill health, her father had been offered by an old friend the tenancy of the small house at the very end of the village and he had accepted gratefully. After the rambling vicarage he had lived in for many years, he found the place cramped but the surroundings were delightful and quiet and he would be able to continue writing his book…

Matilda could see her new home now as she came to the end of the last of the cottages in the main street. There was a field or two, ploughed up in readiness for the spring next year, and the house, facing the road—square and hardly worth a second glance, built a hundred years or so earlier as home for the agent of the big estate close by and then later left empty, to be rented out from time to time. Her mother had burst into tears when she had first seen it but Matilda had pointed out that they were fortunate to have been offered it at a rent her father could afford. She'd added cheerfully, 'It may look like a brick box but there's no reason why we shouldn't have a pretty garden.'

Her mother had said coldly, 'You are always so sensible, Matilda.'

It was a good thing that she was, for her mother had no intention of making the best of a bad job; she had led a pleasant enough life where her husband had been rural dean; true, the house had been too big and if it hadn't been for Matilda living at home and taking most of the household chores onto her shoulders there would have been little time to play the role of vicar's wife. A role Mrs Paige had fulfilled very well, liking the social status it gave her in the small abbey town. But now she was forced to live in this village in a poky house with barely enough to live on...

Matilda pushed open the garden gate and went up the brick path to the front door. The garden was woefully neglected; she would be able to do something about that while the evenings were still light.

She opened the door, calling, 'It's me,' as she did so, and, since no one replied, opened the door on the left of the narrow hallway.

Her father was at his desk, writing, but he looked up as she went in.

'Matilda—it isn't lunchtime, surely? I am just about to...'

She dropped a kiss on his grey head. He was a mild-looking man, kind-hearted, devoted to his wife and to her, content with whatever life should offer him, unworried as to where the money would come from to pay their way. He hadn't wanted to retire but when it had become a vital necessity he had accepted the change in his circumstances with a good grace, accepted the offer of this house from an old friend and settled down happily enough to write.

That his wife was by no means as content as he was was a worry, but he assumed that, given time, she would settle down to their new life. Matilda had given him no worries; she had accepted everything without demur, only declaring that if possible she would find a job.

When she had left school she had taken a course in shorthand and typing, learned how to use a computer and simple bookkeeping. She had never had the chance to use these skills, for her mother had needed her at home, but now, several years later, she was glad that she would be able to augment her father's pension. It had been a lucky chance that Mrs Simpkins had mentioned that the doctor needed a receptionist...

She left her father with the promise of bringing him a cup of coffee and went in search of her mother.

Mrs Paige was upstairs in her bedroom, sitting before her dressing table, peering at her face. She had been a pretty girl but the prettiness was marred by a discontented mouth and a frown. She turned away as Matilda went in.

'The nearest decent hairdresser is in Taunton—miles away. Whatever am I going to do?' She cast Matilda a cross look. 'It's all very well for you; you're such a plain girl, it doesn't really matter...'

Matilda sat down on the bed and looked at her mother; she loved her, of course, but there were times when she had to admit that she was selfish and spoilt. Hardly Mrs Paige's fault—she had been an only child of doting parents and her husband had indulged her every whim to the best of his ability and Matilda had been sent away to boarding-school so that she had never been close to her daughter.

And Matilda had accepted it all: her father's vague affection, her mother's lack of interest, her life at the vicarage, helping Sunday school, the Mother's Union, the annual bazaar, the whist drives… But now that was all over.

'I've got the job at the doctor's,' she said. 'Part-time, mornings and evenings, so I'll have plenty of time to do the housework.'

'How much is he paying you? I can't manage on your father's pension and I haven't a farthing myself.'

When Matilda told her she said, 'That's not much…'

'It's the going rate, Mother.'

'Oh, well, it will be better than nothing—and you won't need much for yourself.'

'No. Most of it must go for the housekeeping; there might be enough for you to have help in the house once or twice a week.'

'Well, if you are working for most of the day I shall need someone.' Her mother smiled suddenly. 'And poor little me? Am I to have something too? Just enough so that I can look like a rural dean's wife and not some poverty-stricken housewife.'

'Yes, Mother, we'll work something out without disturbing Father.'

'Splendid, dear.' Her mother was all smiles now. 'Let me have your wages each week and I'll see that they are put to good use.'

'I think I shall put them straight into Father's account at the bank and just keep out enough for you and me.'

Her mother turned back to the mirror. 'You always have been selfish, Matilda, wanting your own way. When I think of all I have done for you…'

Matilda had heard it all before. She said now, 'Don't worry, Mother, there will be enough over for you.'

She went across the small landing to her own room, where she sat down on her bed and did sums on the back of an envelope. She was well aware of the inadequacies of her father's pension; if they lived carefully there was just enough to live on and pay the bills; anything extra had to be paid for from his small capital—smaller still now with the expense of his illness and their move.

He had received a cheque from his parishioners when he had left the vicarage, but a good deal of that had been swallowed up by carpets and curtains and having the functional bathroom turned into one in which Mrs Paige could bear to be in. The bathroom as it was had been adequate, but her father loved his wife, could see no fault in her, and since she'd wanted a new bathroom she had had it…

He was an unworldly man, content with his lot, seeing only the best in other people; he was also impractical, forgetful and a dreamer, never happier than when he could sit quietly with his books or writing. Matilda loved him dearly and, although his heart attack had led to his retirement and coming to live in straitened circumstances, she had welcomed it since it meant that he could live a quiet life. Now she had a job and could help financially she had no doubt that once her mother had got over her disappointment they would be happy enough.

She went downstairs to the small kitchen to make coffee, and while the kettle boiled she looked round her. It was a rather bare room with an old-fashioned dresser against one wall, an elderly gas cooker and the new washing machine her mother had insisted on. The table in its centre was solid and square—they had brought it with them from the vicarage—and there were four ladder-backed chairs round it. By the small window was a shabby armchair, occupied by the family cat, Rastus. Once she had a little money, decided Matilda, she would paint the walls a pale sunshine-yellow, and a pretty tablecloth and a bowl of bulbs would work wonders...

She carried the coffee into the living room and found her mother there. 'I'll take Father his,' Matilda suggested, and she crossed the hall to the small, rather dark room behind the kitchen, rather grandly called the study. It was very untidy, with piles of books on the floor awaiting bookshelves, and more books scattered on the desk, which was too large for the room but Mr Paige had worked at it almost all of his life and it was unthinkable to get rid of it.

He looked up as she went in. 'Matilda? Ah, coffee. Thank you, my dear.' He took off his spectacles. 'You went out this morning?'

'Yes, Father, for an interview with Lovell who has the practice here. I'm going to work for him part-time.'

'Good, good; you will meet some young people and get some sort of a social life, I dare say. It will not entail too much hard work?'

'No, no. Just seeing to patients and their notes and writing letters. I shall enjoy it.'

'And of course you will be paid; you must get yourself some pretty things, my dear.'

She glanced down at the desk; the gas bill was lying on it and there was a reminder from the plumber that the kitchen taps had been attended to.

'Oh, I shall, Father,' she said in an over-bright voice.

On Monday morning Matilda got up earlier than usual, took tea to her parents and retired to her room. She couldn't turn herself into a beauty but at least she could be immaculate. She studied her face as she powdered it and put on some lipstick. She wiped it off again, though. She hadn't worn it at the interview, and although she didn't think that Dr Lovell had noticed her at all there was always the chance that he had. She suspected that she had got the job because she was as near alike to Miss Brimble as her youth allowed.

She had met that lady once: plain, bespectacled, clad in something dust-coloured. There had been nothing about her to distract the eye of Dr Lovell, and Matilda, unable to find anything in her wardrobe of that dreary colour, had prudently chosen navy blue with a prim white collar. Such a pity, she reflected, dragging her hair back into its French pleat, that circumstances forced her to make the least of herself.

She pulled a face at her reflection. Not that it mattered. She had as much chance of attracting him as the proverbial pig had of flying. Falling in love with a man who hadn't even looked at you for more than a moment had been a stupid thing to do.

The surgery was at one side of the house and a narrow path led to the side door. It was already unlocked when she got there and a woman was dusting the row of chairs. Matilda bade her good morning and, obeying the instructions she had been given, went into the surgery beyond. The doctor wasn't there; she hadn't expected him to be for it was not yet eight o'clock.

She opened a window, checked the desk to make sure that there was all that he might need there, and went back to the waiting room where her desk stood in one corner. The appointments book was on it—he must have put it there ready for her and she set to, collecting patients' notes from the filing cabinet by the desk. She had arranged them to her satisfaction when the first patient arrived—old Mr Trimble, the pub owner's father. He was a silent man with a nasty cough and, from his copious notes, a frequent visitor to the surgery. He grunted a greeting and sat down, to be joined presently by a young woman with a baby. Neither the mother nor the baby looked well, and Matilda wondered which one was the patient.

The room filled up then and she was kept busy, aware of the curious looks and whispers. Miss Brimble had been there for so many years that a newcomer was a bit of a novelty and perhaps not very welcome.

Dr Lovell opened his surgery door then, bade everyone a brisk good morning, took Mr Trimble's notes from Matilda and ushered his patient inside. He ushered him out again after ten minutes, took the next lot of notes from her and left her to deal with Mr Trimble's next appointment.

It wasn't hard work but she was kept busy, for the phone rang from time to time, and some of the patients took their time deciding whether the appointments offered them were convenient, but by the time the last person had gone into the surgery Matilda was quite enjoying herself. True, Dr Lovell had taken no notice of her at all, but at least she'd had glimpses of him from time to time…

She dealt patiently with the elderly woman who was the last to go for she was rather deaf and, moreover, worried about catching the local bus.

'My cats,' she explained. 'I don't like to leave them for more than an hour or two.'

'Oh, I know how you feel,' said Matilda. 'I have a cat; he's called Rastus…'

The door behind her opened and Dr Lovell said, with well-concealed impatience, 'Miss Paige…'

She turned and smiled at him. 'Mrs Trim has a cat, and so have I. We were just having a chat about them.'

She bade Mrs Trim goodbye, shut the door behind her and said cheerfully, 'I'll tidy up, shall I?'

He didn't answer, merely stood aside for her to follow him back into the surgery. As they went in, the door leading to the house opened and a tall, bony woman came in with a tray of coffee.

Matilda bade her good morning. 'How nice—coffee, and it smells delicious.'

The doctor eyed her with an inscrutable face. Matilda had seemed so meek and quiet during her interview. He said firmly, 'While you drink your coffee, please make a note of various instructions I wish to give you.'

She didn't need to look at him to know that she had annoyed him. She said, 'I talk too much,' and opened her notebook, her nose quivering a bit at the aroma from the coffee pot.

'Be good enough to pour our coffee, Miss Paige. I should point out that, more frequently than not, you may not have time for coffee. This morning was a very small surgery and normally I depart the moment the last patient has gone, leaving you to clear up and lock the door and the cabinets. I should warn you that the evening surgery is almost always busy.'

He opened a drawer and handed her a small bunch of keys. 'If I am held up then I rely upon you to admit the patients and have everything ready, or as ready as possible, for me. Miss Brimble was most efficient; I hope that you will be the same.'

Matilda took a sip of coffee. Strange, she mused, that, of all the millions of men in the world, she should have

fallen in love with this coldly polite man with cold blue
eyes and, for all she knew, a cold heart as well.

'I shall do my best to be as like Miss Brimble as possible,' she told him, and after he had given her a list of instructions she asked, 'Do you want me for anything else,
Doctor? Then I'll just tidy the waiting room and lock up.'

He nodded, not looking up from the pile of notes on
his desk. 'I shall see you this evening, Miss Paige.' He
glanced up then. 'This is not a job where one can watch
the clock too closely.'

She got up and went to the door, where she said in a
quiet little voice, 'I expect you miss Miss Brimble. We
must hope for the best, mustn't we?'

She closed the door quietly behind her and the doctor
stared at it, surprise on his handsome face. But presently
he allowed himself to smile. Only fleetingly, though.
Miss Paige must conform to his ways or find another job.

Matilda went home, donned an apron and began to
load the washing machine. Her father was in the study;
her mother was getting coffee in the kitchen.

'Well, how did you get on?' she asked. 'I don't suppose
it was hard work. Is he nice? Your father has to see him
within the next few days. Such a nuisance that he has to
see the doctor so often; I should have thought that once he
had got over his heart attack he would have been cured.'

'Well, he is cured, Mother, but it's possible to have
another attack unless a doctor keeps an eye on him. He's
feeling fine, though, isn't he? This is the ideal life for
him...'

Mrs Paige said fiercely, 'Oh, it's perfect for him but
what about me? There's nothing to do here in this poky
little village...'

'It's not poky. It's really quite large and Mrs Simpkins was telling me that there's always something going on. There's amateur theatricals in the winter, and bridge parties, and tennis in the summer and cricket. Once you get to know the people living here—'

'And how do I do that? Knock on people's doors? We've been here almost two weeks.'

'If you went to the village more often...' began Matilda. 'Everyone goes to the village shop...'

'Everyone? Who's everyone? No one I can make a friend of. When I think of the pleasant life we had at the vicarage—my friends, the interesting people who came to see your father...'

'I'm sure there are interesting people here, too,' said Matilda. 'Are you going to have coffee with Father? I had some at the surgery. Shall I make a macaroni cheese for lunch?'

Her mother shrugged. 'What is he like? Dr Lovell? A typical country GP, I suppose.'

Matilda didn't answer that; she didn't think that Dr Lovell was typical of anyone, but then, of course, she was in love with him.

She took care to be at the surgery well before five o'clock. She had the patients' notes ready on his desk and was sitting at her own desk in the waiting room when the first patient arrived. The doctor had been right; there was a steady stream of patients—several nasty coughs, a clutch of peevish children and two young men with bandaged hands. She had seen from the notes that most of them had come from outlying farms, and since they all appeared to know each other the room was full of cheerful voices interspersed with coughing fits and whining small voices.

There was no sign of the doctor and it was already well

after five o'clock. Matilda left her desk to hold a fractious toddler while its mother took an older child to the loo. She was still holding it when the surgery door opened and the doctor invited his first patient, an old man with a cough, to come into the surgery.

He looked at Matilda with raised eyebrows but made no comment and by the time he called for his second patient she was back at her desk, busy with the appointments book, very aware that she was being looked over by everyone there. After all, she was a newcomer to the village, and although Mrs Simpkins had given her opinion that Matilda was a nice young lady—a bit quiet, like, but polite—the village had no intention of making up its mind in a hurry.

Parson's daughter, they told each other—well, Miss Brimble had been that, too, but twice this one's age. They bade her a lot of cheerful good evenings as they went home and over their suppers gave their varied opinions: a nice enough young lady, not much to look at but with a ready smile.

As for the doctor, dining at the Reverend Mr Milton's table that evening, he professed himself satisfied with his new receptionist. He had no more to say about her than that, though.

The week progressed. Tuesday was an evening surgery only for he held the post of anaesthetist at Taunton Hospital and spent the day there. On Wednesday the surgery bulged with victims of the first serious chills of winter and on Thursday there was no surgery in the evening. Matilda enjoyed her work although she wished it could have been conducted in a clearer atmosphere than the surgery, redolent of damp coats and the earthy smells clinging to farm workers who came in straight from their work. But she had found her sensible feet by now and she was happy despite the doctor's chilly politeness towards her. At least she saw him each day and sooner or later he would stop comparing her with Miss Brimble and decide that she was quite nice, really...

And, Matilda being Matilda, she already had a few plans. A potted plant for the waiting room, a small vase of flowers for the doctor's desk, a chamber pot for the small children—she wondered why Miss Brimble hadn't thought of that—and some container where people could put their dripping umbrellas. There were still a lot of odds and ends her mother had consigned to the garden shed; there might be something suitable there...

After the first morning she had politely refused coffee after the morning surgery, standing by his desk, listening to whatever it was he needed to tell her and then bidding him a cheerful good morning, shutting the door quietly behind her.

There was no point in sitting there drinking coffee when he was so obviously unaware of her. She would then tidy the waiting room, lock up and go home.

There was an envelope on her desk on Friday morning. She had asked at her interview if she could be paid each week and in cash, and he had agreed without comment. She put it in her handbag and bade the first patient good morning. Her father had taught her that money was no easy path to happiness but she couldn't help feeling rich...

There was a small branch of her father's bank in the village, open on three days a week for a few hours. Matilda paid most of the money into his account, bought sausages from Mrs Simpkins and went home, treading on air.

There was a car parked outside the gate when she reached it: an elderly Rover, immaculately kept. It belonged to the Reverend Mr Milton and she was pleased to see it for it meant that that gentleman had come to visit her parents. He had called briefly a day or so after they had moved in but the place had been in chaos and he hadn't stayed.

He was in the living room and his wife was with him. Mrs Milton was a small, placid lady with a kind face, and according to Mrs Simpkins was very well liked in the village.

Matilda shook hands and, bidden by her mother, went to fetch more coffee, sorry that she hadn't brought some biscuits with her. She handed around second cups and sat down to answer Mrs Milton's gentle questions.

She liked her job with Dr Lovell? Such a dear, good man but very overworked; so fortunate that he had found Matilda to replace Miss Brimble. And did Matilda play tennis? In the summer there was a flourishing club—and amateur theatricals in the winter. 'You must meet some of the younger ones here,' said Mrs Milton.

Mrs Paige interrupted her in the nicest possible way. 'Matilda isn't a very sociable girl,' she said. 'Quite a homebird in fact, which is so fortunate for I'm not very strong and all the worry of my husband's illness has upset my nerves.'

Mrs Milton said that she was sorry to hear it. 'I was hoping you would enjoy meeting a few people here and perhaps join me on one or two of our committees. We do a good deal for charity in a quiet way. And the Mother's Union flourishes. Lady Truscott is our president and we meet each month at her house. The Manor, you know...'

'I shall be delighted to do that and give what help I

can.' Mrs Paige had become quite animated. 'And any-thing else that I can do in my small way.' She gave a rue-ful little laugh. 'This is all so strange. And I do miss the house—and the social life attached to the church. And, of course, the ease with which one could obtain things. It seems I must go all the way to Taunton to a hairdresser.'

'There's Miss Wright in the village; she is really not at all bad. I must confess that I go to Tessa's in Taunton. If you would like it I'll give you her phone number and if you mention my name I'm sure she will fit you in.'

'That's most kind. It would have to be on the day the bus goes to Taunton; I'm told that there is one.'

'You don't drive?'

'No, unfortunately not, and, of course, Jeffrey isn't allowed to, so we sold the car.'

Mrs Milton turned to Matilda. 'You don't drive, my dear?'

Matilda just had time to say yes, before her mother said quickly, 'There seemed no point in keeping the car just for Matilda's use. She enjoys walking and there is a bicycle she can use.'

'In that case,' said Mrs Milton, 'I'll be glad to offer you a lift the next time I go to Taunton. Matilda, too...'

'One of us has to stay home just in case Jeffrey isn't well, but I'd be glad of a lift; it's most kind of you to offer. Perhaps I could fit it in with the hairdresser and have time for a quick shop. I'm sure the shop in the vil-lage is excellent but there are several things I need which I'm sure aren't stocked there.'

'We will arrange something soon and I'll let you know about joining our committee.' Mrs Milton got to her feet. 'I'm glad you have come here to live and I'm sure you will be happy once you have settled in.'

She caught her husband's eye and he rose reluctantly from the earnest talk he was enjoying with Mr Paige. Goodbyes were said and Matilda saw them out of the gate and into their car, waving them away with a friendly hand.

'A very nice girl,' said Mrs Milton, 'but I don't imagine she has much of a life. Her mother…'

'Now, my dear, don't be too hasty in your judgement, although I do see what you mean. We must endeavour to find Matilda some friends.'

'I wonder how she gets on with Henry?'

'Presumably well enough; I don't imagine he's a hard taskmaster. Once they have got used to each other I'm sure she will prove every bit as efficient as Miss Brimble.'

Which wasn't what Mrs Milton had meant at all, although she didn't say so.

Mrs Paige followed Matilda into the kitchen. 'Did you get paid?'

Matilda stacked cups and saucers by the sink. 'Yes, Mother.'

'Good. If Mrs Milton phones I can go to Taunton. I need one or two things as well as having my hair done. If you'd let me have twenty-five pounds? You must see that if I'm to meet all these women I must look my best, and you'll have the rest of your money…'

'I've paid it into Father's account at the bank.'

'Matilda—are you out of your mind? His pension will be paid in a week or so and we can open an account at the shop.'

'There's a gas bill overdue and the plumber to be paid…'

Mrs Paige said tearfully, 'I can't believe that my own

daughter could be so mean.' She started to cry. 'I hate it here; can't you understand that? This poky little house and no shops and nothing to do all day. There was always something at the vicarage—people calling, wanting advice or help; things happening.' She added, 'Of course you don't care; I don't suppose you miss your friends and it isn't as if there were any men keen on you. It's just as well, for I doubt if you'll meet anyone here who'll want to marry you.'

Matilda said quietly, 'No, I don't suppose I will. I'm sorry you're unhappy, Mother, but perhaps you will meet some people you will like when you see Mrs Milton again.'

She took some notes out of her handbag. 'Here is twenty-five pounds.' She laid the money on the table. 'I'll get lunch, shall I?'

Her mother said something but she didn't hear it, for she was fighting a strong wish to run out of the house, go somewhere where she wasn't reminded that she was dull and plain and mean. Life would have been so different if she had been pretty...

She gave herself a shake. Self-pity was a waste of time; and life wasn't all that bad. She had a job, she liked the village and the people she had met were friendly, and there was Dr Lovell. If they hadn't come here to live she would never have met him. The fact that he didn't like her overmuch made no difference to the fact that she was in love with him. That coloured her dull days and perhaps in time, if she could be more like Miss Brimble, he would like her after all. She didn't expect more than that; her mother had made it plain that there was nothing about her to attract a man such as he.

She got the lunch, listened to her father's cheerful

comments about their visitors and her mother's plans to go to Taunton and then, with Rastus for company, Matilda went into the garden. It had once been very pretty but was now woefully overgrown. She began raking the leaves which covered the patch of grass in front of the house.

It was chilly and there was a fresh wind, so that her hair blew free from its tidy pleat, and she had tied a sack over her skirt. The doctor, driving past, thought she looked very untidy, obviously not bothering about her appearance. He dismissed her from his mind and was vaguely irritated to find himself remembering all that pale brown hair, tossed about by the wind.

Chapter 2

There was nothing about Matilda's appearance on Monday morning to remind him of her scruffy appearance in the garden. The picture of neatness, she dealt with the patients with good-humoured patience and real pleasure, for she felt that she had been accepted by the village, included in their gossip as they waited their turn. It was to be hoped, she reflected, that Dr Lovell would accept her, too...

It was a chilly, drizzly morning and she was glad that she had lugged the chimney pot she had found in the garden shed down to the doctor's house and installed it in the waiting room. It wasn't ideal but at least it was somewhere to put the umbrellas. She was sure that the doctor hadn't noticed it; hopefully he wouldn't notice if she brought some of the neglected chrysanthemums from the back garden and put them on the table in the waiting room—and on his desk; they might cheer him up...!

The surgery over, she tidied up, received a few instructions about the evening surgery, refused his offer of coffee and went down the street to the shop. Mrs Simpkins sold everything, or such was her proud boast and sure enough from the depths of her shop she produced a small plastic pot.

'That's what I call sensible,' she declared. 'Miss Brimble never thought of it. Well, a maiden lady such as she were wouldn't 'ave, would she? A real blessing it'll be for all the mums with little 'uns.'

She peered across the counter through the shop window. 'Doctor's just gone past so you can pop across with it.'

Which Matilda did.

At home she found her mother in the best of good spirits. Mrs Milton would be going to Taunton on Wednesday and had offered her a lift. 'You only work in the morning,' she reminded Matilda, 'so you can be here with your father. I don't know how long I shall be gone; perhaps Mrs Milton will ask me to tea. Will you make some coffee? Your father has a headache; a cup might make him feel better. I must iron a few things—perhaps you would get a fire going in the sitting room? It's such a miserable day.'

After lunch Matilda, in an old mac and headscarf, went into the garden. The back garden was quite large and so overgrown it was hard to see what it was once like. But almost hidden against the end fence were the chrysanthemums, deep pink and a bit bedraggled. She picked the best of them, filled a vase for the living room and put the rest in a plastic bag to take with her to the surgery that evening. And while she was about it she rooted round in the garden shed and found two vases. No longer neglected, the chrysanthemums perked up, in one vase on the waiting-room table, and the other on the windowsill in the surgery. Several patients remarked upon them but if the doctor noticed he didn't choose to say anything...

In fact, he had seen them the moment he entered the surgery, given them a quick glance and turned his attention to his first patient. He hoped that Matilda wasn't going to strew cushions around the place or nurture pot plants on the windowsills. Perhaps he had better nip any such ideas in the bud…

But he had no chance to do so that evening; a farm worker on one of the outlying farms had fallen off a ladder and he was needed there. He left with a brisk goodnight, leaving Matilda to pack up and lock the doors. And, of course, the next day there was no surgery until the evening.

When she got there he was already at his desk, writing, and she made haste to get out the patients' notes, and when the phone rang, which it did continuously, answered it. It wasn't until she ushered out the last patient that Dr Lovell came into the waiting room.

Matilda was on her knees, grovelling under the row of chairs collecting the toys the smaller patients had been playing with, so she was not at her best.

His cool, 'Miss Paige,' brought her to her feet, pleased to see him but unhappily aware that she wasn't looking her best.

'I see that you have introduced one or two—er—innovations. And while I appreciate your efforts I must beg you not to make too many drastic alterations.'

Matilda tucked a wisp of hair behind an ear. 'Well, I won't,' she assured him. 'Only the umbrellas dripping all over the floor are nasty and you can't expect a toddler to perch on a loo, you know. And I thought a few flowers would cheer the place up a bit. A potted plant or two?' she added hopefully.

'If you have set your heart on that, by all means, but I must make it clear that I do not wish for a plant in my surgery.'

She said warmly, 'Oh, do they give you hay fever or something?'

The doctor, self-assured and used to being treated with a certain amount of respect, found himself at a loss for a reply. Being in the habit of advising others as to their various illnesses, he hardly expected to hear an opinion passed as to his own health.

When Matilda got back from the Wednesday morning clinic her mother had already left with Mrs Milton.

'Most fortunate,' her father observed as they drank their coffee together, 'that your mother has the opportunity to enjoy a day out; she has so few pleasures.'

'Well,' said Matilda, 'Mrs Milton is going to introduce Mother to her friends and I'm sure she will be asked to join in the social life around here. I suppose there is some...'

'Oh, I believe so. Lady Truscott has a large circle of friends; your mother will enjoy meeting them.' He added, 'Perhaps there will be some young people for you, my dear.'

She agreed cheerfully. She would have dearly liked to go dancing, play tennis, and even venture into amateur theatricals, but only if the doctor was there too, and somehow she couldn't imagine him as an actor. Tennis, yes—he would be a good tennis player and a good dancer—a bit on the conservative side, perhaps. She allowed herself a few moments of daydreaming, waltzing around some magnificent ballroom in his arms. She would, of course, be exquisitely dressed and so very pretty that she was the object of all eyes... But only Dr Lovell's eyes mattered.

Not that he showed any signs of interest in her at the surgery; indeed, she had the strong feeling that as a person she just wasn't there—a pair of hands, yes, and a voice for the telephone and someone to find old notes.

He was engaged to be married, she reminded herself, and quite rightly didn't notice any female other than his betrothed...

Later in the day Mrs Paige came back from Taunton, bubbling over with the delights of her day.

'A marvellous hairdresser, Matilda, worth every penny, and the shops are excellent. Of course I had no money but next time there are several things I simply must have.' She gave a little laugh. 'I'm to go with Mrs Milton to Lady Truscott's—the next committee meeting for some charity or other—so I must smarten up a little. You wouldn't want your mother to look shabby, would you?'

Her father said, 'My dear, I'm sure I can let you have a little extra. Matilda should have her own money to spend how she likes.'

Matilda slipped out of the room. She had heard her father's mild remonstrance often enough but it went unheeded. Once the outstanding bills had been paid she would go to Taunton herself and buy some new clothes, have her hair done, a manicure, new cosmetics... Dr Lovell hadn't noticed her yet; perhaps he never would. He was going to marry, she reminded herself then, and remembered that Mrs Simpkins hadn't liked his fiancée.

Matilda, peeling potatoes, made up her mind to find out more about her.

After morning surgery next day, since it was a fine day with a strong wind blowing, she filled the washing machine and went into the garden and began to sweep up the leaves lying thick on the neglected grass, suitably but unglamorously dressed in an elderly sweater and skirt and wellies. Since there was no one to see, she had tied her hair back with a bit of string from the garden shed.

She had found a rake there and set to with a will, for the moment happy; her small worries were forgotten as she planned just how the garden would look once she had tamed its wildness and cared for it. She paused to lean on the rake.

'Roses,' she decided, 'and lavender and peonies and lupins and hollyhocks.'

She had been talking to herself, something she quite often did even if Rastus wasn't there to listen. 'It'll look lovely, I promise you.'

She flung an arm wide and nearly fell over when the doctor said, an inch or so from her ear, 'Do you often talk to yourself?'

She shot round to face him and he thought that she looked quite pretty with colour in her cheeks and her hair hanging loose.

'Of course not.' She sounded tart. 'I was talking to the garden. Flowers like being talked to. The Prince of Wales talks to his...'

'So he does.' The doctor sounded mild. 'I've never found the time.'

'No—well, of course I don't suppose you would. Anyway, you would want to spend it with your...'

She paused, not liking the cold look he gave her. She went on quickly. 'Is it me you want to see about something? Or Father...?'

'Your father.' He watched her idly. The shabby clothes she was wearing did nothing for her but he had to admit that he liked her hair—and he was intrigued by her naturalness. Not his type, of course...

He said briskly, 'Your father is home?'

'Oh, yes. He'll be in his study—he's writing a book.'

She led the way to the front door, kicked off her

wellies and ushered him into the narrow hall. 'Mother's in the sitting room...'

'I'll see your father first if I may.'

Matilda put her head round the study door. 'Father, here's Dr Lovell to see you.'

He went past her with a brief nod and closed the door gently behind him, and as he did so her mother came out of the sitting room. 'Who is that?' She frowned. 'You should have fetched me, Matilda...'

'Dr Lovell said he'd see Father first.'

'Well, you go back into the garden; I'll have a talk with him.'

Mrs Paige went back to the sitting room and had a look in the old-fashioned mirror over the fireplace. She looked all right, she decided, but it wouldn't harm her to add a little lipstick. And perhaps a touch more powder...

Dr Lovell shook hands with his patient and drew up a chair. He said easily, 'I've had all your notes from your previous doctor—Dr Grant, wasn't it? I've met him; you couldn't have been in better hands. But I'd like you to tell me how you feel now and then perhaps I might take a look at you?'

He took his time, listening patiently to Mr Paige's vague recital of how he felt. 'Of course, I'm aware that I may have another heart attack at any time, but I feel well; I find it most restful living here and I have my writing, and possibly later on I shall be able to assist Mr Milton from time to time should he wish it.'

Dr Lovell listened gravely and said presently, 'Well, if I might take a look?'

That done, he sat back in his chair. 'As far as I can judge you are in excellent shape. I shall write you up for some different pills and I advise you to take a walk each day. Well wrapped up and for half an hour. Taking reasonable precautions you should be able to enjoy a normal life.'

'Splendid. I feel a fraud that you should visit me; I could quite well come to your surgery.'

'Better that I look in on you from time to time, but let me know if you are worried about anything.'

'Indeed I will; Matilda can always take a message. I hope she is proving satisfactory? She seems very happy working at your surgery. Perhaps she will meet some young people once she gets to know the village. She leads a quiet life and, of course, she is indispensable to my wife here in the house.' Mr Paige nodded contentedly. 'We are indeed lucky to have such a caring daughter.'

The doctor, who almost never thought of Matilda, felt a sudden pang of pity for her, destined to play the role of dutiful daughter—and why was she indispensable to her mother?

'Your wife is an invalid?'

'No, no, nothing like that, but she has always been delicate—her nerves.'

So the doctor was forewarned when he found Mrs Paige waiting for him in the sitting-room doorway.

She held out a hand. 'Dr Lovell, so good of you to come. I do worry so much about my husband; it upsets me so. My wretched nerves…' She smiled up at him. 'I'm not at all strong and having to move here to this poky little house has upset me, too. My husband loves it and so does Matilda, so I suppose I must learn to make a new life. They are both content with so little.'

He said blandly, 'I'm sure you will be glad to know

that Mr Paige is doing well. I've advised him to go out for a short time each day for a brisk walk.'

'Such a pity we gave up the car. But, of course, he doesn't drive any more and I have never learned.' She gave a little laugh. 'Silly me.'

'Your daughter drives?'

'Matilda? Oh, yes, but there was no point in keeping the car just for her. Won't you come and sit down for a while?'

'I'm afraid I can't stay; I'm on my afternoon round.' He smiled—a professional smile with no warmth—and shook hands and went out of the open door into the garden.

Matilda was still raking leaves but when she saw him she went to meet him. 'Father? He's all right? I won't keep you; you are on your visits, aren't you?'

She went with him to his car and he said, 'He's pretty fit. I'll give you some pills for him and please see that he walks for a while each day. Let me know if you are worried.' His smile was kind.

He got in and drove away with a casual nod and she watched the grey Bentley slide away down the lane. She thought about the smile; he had looked quite different for a moment. She wondered what he was really like beneath his calm, professional face. Would she ever find out? He was courteous towards her but in a cool, offhand way which daunted her; quite obviously he had no wish to add warmth to their relationship.

And quite right too, reflected Matilda that evening, nodding her sensible head. If I were engaged to marry someone I wouldn't bother with anyone else. She wished very much that she could meet his fiancée, for, loving him as she did, it was important to her that he should be happy.

'I am a fool,' said Matilda, addressing Rastus, making the pastry for a steak and kidney pie. The butcher's van called twice a week in the village and it was a meal that her father enjoyed. Rastus gave her a long, considering look and turned his back.

There was always pay day to cheer her up. She prudently paid most of her wages into the bank and crossed the street to the shop, intent on buying one or two extras for the larder. She also needed tights and toothpaste, and Mrs Simpkins stocked a certain shampoo guaranteed to bring out the highlights on one's hair.

The shop was quite full. Matilda wasn't the only one to be paid on a Friday, and Mrs Simpkins was doing a brisk trade, enjoying a good gossip at the same time. Matilda, waiting her turn, listened to the odd snippets of gossip. Bill Gates up at Hill Farm had had to have the vet out to one of his cows. Triplets, doing well. Time he had a bit of luck. There had been a small fire out at Pike's place—a chip pan left on the stove. 'And what do you expect from that Maisie Coffin? She bain't no housewife...' There were matronly nods all round in agreement and Matilda felt a pang of sympathy for Maisie.

'Coming this weekend, so I hear?' said a stout matron, waiting for her bacon to be sliced. 'Staying with Dr Lovell, of course, bringing that brother of hers with her.'

Matilda edged a little nearer, anxious not to miss anything.

'Time they married,' said another voice. 'Though she is not to my liking, mind you. A real town lady; don't want nothing to do with the likes of us.'

There was a murmur of agreement. 'But pretty as a picture,' said another voice.

Mrs Simpkins spoke up. 'Men don't want a pretty picture for a wife; they wants a wife to make an 'ome for 'im and kiddies. And 'im such a good man, too.'

There was a collective sigh of regret and Matilda wondered what the doctor would say if he could hear the gossip about him. She didn't think that he would mind; he would be amused. And he had no need to worry; he was well liked and respected. In the eyes of the village he was on a par with the Reverend Mr Milton.

Matilda bought her tights and toothpaste and a hand cream Mrs Simpkins assured her was just the thing if she was going to do a lot of gardening. She added back bacon, a cauliflower, cooking apples and a packet of chocolate biscuits to her purchases, answered Mrs Simpkins' questions as to life at the surgery and how her mother and father were.

'If the weather's all right, I hope Father will be able to come to church on Sunday,' said Matilda. 'And, of course, Mother will be with him. Mr Milton has kindly offered to drive them to church.'

'You too?'

'Well, yes, I hope so…'

Mrs Simpkins nodded. 'Time you got around a bit and met a few of us. Church is as good a place as any.'

Matilda said that, yes, she was quite right, and went off home. It was a dry day and she would be able to get into the garden. Her mother, with the prospect of going to church on Sunday, was happy. She would meet some of the people Mrs Milton had mentioned and it was a splendid opportunity for people in the village to get to know them. She fell to wondering what she should wear until

Mr Paige said gently, 'My dear, we are going to church, not a social gathering.' He smiled lovingly at her and turned to Matilda. 'My dear, a man is coming to reconnect the telephone on Monday; your mother—we both feel it is a necessity.'

'Yes, Father. Did you have a letter about it?'

'Yes, it's on my desk, I believe. I should have thought that it could have been done without cost for there has been a telephone here previously, but it seems there is a payment to make.'

Matilda, finding it buried under a pile of books, saw that if she had had any ideas about spending next week's wages on anything she could forget them. And, to be on the safe side, she warned her mother that that particular bill would have to be paid at once. News which Mrs Paige took with some annoyance. 'I was hoping that you could lend me some money; I simply must have a few things. I'll pay you back when your father gets his pension.'

'I'm sorry, Mother; once the bills are paid…'

'Bills, bills, why can't they wait? Really, Matilda, you're nothing but a prig—too good to be true. I suppose you tell everyone that you hand over your money each week because it's your saintly duty to do so.'

Matilda said quietly, 'No, I don't tell anyone, Mother.' She sighed. 'I expect you're right. I'm not quite sure what a prig is exactly, but it sounds like me. I've been a disappointment to myself. I should have liked to have been pretty and clever and well dressed, I should have liked the chance to go dancing and have fun, but there was always some reason why I didn't—helping Father in the parish, taking over most of the household chores so that you had more time to be the vicar's wife and any chance

I might have had to leave home and get a job is finally squashed, isn't it?'

She saw from her mother's face that she wasn't really listening. She said woodenly, 'I'm going into the garden.'

Digging the flowerbeds, cutting back overgrown shrubs, grubbing up weeds helped, and all the while she cried, tears rolling down her cheeks while she sniffed and grizzled. But she felt better presently and when she went indoors she looked very much as usual.

On Saturday morning she walked down to the village armed with the grocery list. It was a long one and she saw that she would have to supplement the housekeeping with some of her own money.

'Let me know how much you spent,' her mother had said. 'I'll let you have it back when your father gives me the month's housekeeping.'

Matilda was walking back, with two plastic shopping bags weighing her down, and had reached the doctor's house when its handsome door was opened and three people emerged—the doctor, a short, thick-set man, a good deal younger than he, and a young woman. A very handsome one, too, Matilda saw out of the corner of her eye. She was tall and fair and slim and dressed in the height of fashion. Not quite suitable for Much Winterlow, reflected Matilda, allowing herself to be catty, but the woman was distinctly eye-catching.

They came down the short path to the gate set in the iron railings separating the house from the street, and had reached it as Matilda drew level with it. The doctor wished her good morning. 'Been shopping?' he asked.

Well, of course; any idiot could see that, thought Matilda. But he was being polite. She said, 'Yes,' and 'Good morning, Doctor,' and walked on.

She wasn't out of earshot when she heard the young woman's voice—well modulated but carrying. 'What a quaint little thing,' she remarked.

And what had she meant by that? reflected Matilda. She had reached the field and could utter her thoughts out loud. 'I'm plain and a bit dowdy, I suppose, but otherwise I look as normal as anyone else. Well, I shan't let it upset me.'

All the same she dressed carefully for church on Sunday—her good suit of timeless cut, and the small felt hat which went with it. Her gloves and shoes had seen better days but they were good and she didn't need a handbag; she tucked her collection money into her glove.

Mrs Milton came early to fetch them and since Matilda was not quite ready, her mother and father were driven away in the car and she walked to the village, getting to the church just as the bell ceased.

The congregation was quite large and she saw that her mother and father were sitting in one of the front pews with Mrs Milton, but her plan to slip into a pew at the back of the church was frustrated by her mother who had turned round and seen her. When she reached the pew she saw the doctor and his guests sitting on the opposite side of the aisle just behind them. She had only a glimpse as she went past but it was enough to see that the girl with him was the picture of elegance…

Matilda reminded herself that she was in church as she said her prayers and sang the hymns and listened to the sermon, but once the service was over and they were outside in the churchyard, meeting various people kind Mrs Milton was introducing to her mother and father, she allowed her thoughts to dwell on the doctor and his companions, standing close by, talking to Lady Truscott.

She edged away from them and took shelter behind Mrs Milton, only to find the two groups merging.

Mrs Milton said, 'Of course you've met Mr and Mrs Paige, haven't you? And Matilda works for you.'

She looked enquiringly at him and he said easily, 'Two friends of mine, spending the weekend: Lucilla Armstrong and her brother Guy.'

He turned to look at them. 'Mrs Milton, the vicar's wife, and the Reverend Mr Paige and Mrs Paige—and their daughter, Matilda.'

Lucilla acknowledged the introductions with a cool nod. 'We saw you yesterday.' Her eyes roamed over Matilda's person. 'I wondered who you were.'

Matilda said in a matter-of-fact voice, 'I'd been to do the shopping. I'm surprised that you remembered me. I must have looked quaint laden down with plastic bags.' She smiled sweetly and the doctor choked back a laugh. Miss Matilda Paige had revealed an unexpected side of her nature—or was he mistaken? Had her remark been as guileless as her ordinary face?

There was polite talk for a few more minutes before Mrs Milton said, 'We mustn't stand around too long. I'm going to drive Mr and Mrs Paige back home—and you too, of course, Matilda.' She smiled at the circle of faces around her.

'I hope you have a pleasant weekend here. I'm sure it's good for Henry to relax from his work.'

Henry, thought Matilda, taking care not to look at him. A nice old-fashioned English name. She looked at his other guest instead. Guy Armstrong was good-looking, she conceded, but he had a weak chin and he laughed too much; besides, by the time he was forty he would be fat...

She added her polite goodbyes to everyone else's and

got into Mrs Milton's car, sitting in the back with her father because her mother wanted to ask about some extra committee Mrs Milton had suggested that she might like to join.

And back home over lunch, while her mother talked animatedly of the people she had met at church and the prospect of a social life even if limited to the village, Matilda had ample free time to think about Dr Lovell. She thought about Lucilla, too, who would be an ideal wife for him. She was not as young as Matilda had first thought—indeed, Lucilla must be edging very close to thirty—but she was so beautifully cared for that no man would believe that... And, of course, her lovely clothes helped.

I'm jealous, thought Matilda, but I can't help that. I should be glad that he has found someone who will make him happy.

She went to the kitchen to wash up, while her mother, still happily making plans, went with her father to the sitting room.

'Perhaps I should find another job.' Matilda addressed Rastus, who gave her a considering look before tucking into his dinner. 'But if I did I'd not see him, would I? And I couldn't bear that. Of course when they marry she will get me the sack. She doesn't like me, which is silly, for I'm hardly a rival, am I?'

Rastus, nicely full, sat and stared at her. 'You're not much help, are you?' said Matilda.

It was pouring with rain on Monday morning. Matilda, wringing herself dry before she opened the surgery door, mopped her face and tugged her wet hair back into a semblance of tidiness and, still a bit damp, got out the notes for the morning's patients. She then opened the door, casting a quick look round the waiting room as she did so. It was spotlessly clean and the chrysanthemums she had brought from the garden made a cheerful spot of colour beside the tidy pile of magazines on the table; the place was nicely warm too.

The first patients arrived, shedding wet macs, umbrellas and leaving muddy marks on the floor, and punctually at eight o'clock the doctor opened his door and requested the first patient.

By the time the last patient had left it was well past ten o'clock. Matilda started to tidy the place, lock away the notes, rearrange the magazines and collect up forgotten gloves, a scarf or two and a child's plastic toy, and, tucked away in a corner, a shopping bag of groceries. She would take it over to Mrs Simpkins' shop since the surgery door would be locked...

The door opened and the doctor stood looking at her.

'You had better have a cup of coffee before you go,' he said briskly.

Matilda put the shopping bag on the table. 'Thank you, Doctor, but I'd rather not stop.'

'You mustn't allow hurt pride to interfere with common sense,' he observed. 'Far be it from me to send you out into this weather without so much as a warm drink inside you.'

'Hurt pride?' said Matilda, and then added, 'Oh, the first morning when you told me not to watch the clock. Oh, that's all right; I'm not one to bear a grudge!'

She smiled and went past him into the surgery where the coffee tray stood on his desk.

'You are happy working here?' asked Dr Lovell, taking his coffee and offering her a biscuit from the tin.

'Yes, thank you.'

'It is rather a quiet life for you,' went on the doctor. 'Miss Armstrong wondered if you found life here dull.'

'How kind of her to concern herself about me,' said Matilda in a quiet voice which gave away none of the powerful rage engulfing her. The interfering busybody... A first step towards getting her the sack.

'She pointed out that you are very young for such a dull job. Of course Miss Brimble was elderly.'

'As long as you are satisfied with my work,' said Matilda, 'I wish to stay here. And if I stay long enough I'll be elderly like Miss Brimble! Won't I?'

She put down her coffee cup. 'Is there anything you would like me to do before I go?'

'No, I think not.'

'Thank you for the coffee. I'll be here this evening.'

She skipped through the door, locked up and went out into the rain, crossing the road to the shop.

'Someone left their groceries at the surgery,' she told Mrs Simpkins. 'Shall I leave the bag here? Or if you know who the owner is I could take it.'

'Bless you, miss; that's a kind thought. It's old Mrs Harding's weekly shopping. Lives just down the street, number fourteen on the other side. She's that forgetful. If it's not troubling you...'

Mrs Simpkins leaned comfortably across the counter. 'Saw you in church,' she said. 'Very nice you looked, too—a sight better than that madam with our doctor. Mrs Inch—'is 'ousekeeper, you know—told me she acted like she was in an 'otel. Can't think what 'e sees in 'er.'

'She's quite beautiful,' said Matilda. 'I'll have a piece of tasty cheese, Mrs Simpkins, and some of those dry cheese biscuits.'

Mrs Simpkins reached for the cheese. 'Bin inside 'is 'ouse? Lovely, so I'm told—furniture 'anded down from way back in the family. Bin in the village for years and years. 'E don't need to earn 'is living, of course; plenty of family money as you might say. A fine catch for that Miss Armstrong.'

She reached up for a packet of biscuits. 'I hear your mum's going to Lady Truscott's for the charity committee meeting. Don't see much of 'er in the village, though. Poorly, is she, like your dad?'

'No, no, Mother's very well, but you know how it is when you move house. But we've settled in nicely and my father is so much better now that he has retired.'

Matilda said goodbye, and left to deliver the shopping bag, then hurry home in the rain. Mrs Simpkins, watching her go, thought what a dull life she must lead with two elderly parents and no young man.

Another week went by and another pay day, and even after bolstering up the housekeeping purse and paying the small outstanding debts Matilda had some money. True, her mother had wheedled some of it for herself so that she might go to Taunton once again. She must look her best when she went to Lady Truscott's, she'd pointed out; she would make do with the clothes she had but her hair must be trimmed and set and a few highlights added. Surely Matilda could understand that. 'And really you have nothing to spend your money on, Matilda. There's nothing to be done about your hair except bundle it up like you do, and you don't need to look fashionable. No one sees you at the surgery and you've got that winter coat once it gets really cold.'

All of which was perfectly true. Matilda said nothing

for the simple reason that if she did she might say something she would regret afterwards.

But on the following Tuesday, her day free until evening surgery, she took the local bus to Taunton. She
hadn't told her mother or father that she was going until
she'd taken them their early morning tea.

'That's right, my dear,' said her father. 'You go and
have a pleasant day. Have you sufficient money?'

She kissed the top of his head. 'Yes, thank you, Father.'

There was no chance to say more for her mother had
sat bolt upright in bed. 'You're going to Taunton? Why
didn't you tell me? I could have gone with you; I need
several things. How thoughtless of you, Matilda—and
why do you want to go?'

'To shop,' said Matilda, 'and I must go now or I'll miss
the bus. I'll be back before tea.'

'I should feel mean, but I don't,' said Matilda to herself, hurrying down to the bus stop outside Mrs Simpkins'. There were several people there already, and the
doctor, standing at his dining-room window, watched
her join the little group. He thought idly that if he had
known she had wanted to go to Taunton he would have
given her a lift for he would be at the hospital for most
of the day. He turned away and went to eat his breakfast.

Matilda hadn't much money but she knew what she
wanted. The doctor only saw her during surgery hours,
so it made sense to make herself as attractive as possible during that time. Well, not sense, actually, since he
never looked at her, but even if she had no hope that he
would like her that wasn't going to stop her from doing
something about her looks.

Silly, really, thought Matilda, making for the shops.

It would have to be Marks & Spencer; she hadn't enough money for any of the smart boutiques. She would go there first, anyway…

Maybe the doctor would never look at her; she would still find solace in the wearing of the grey jersey dress she found almost at once. It was suitably short but not too much so and it had a white collar and pretty buttons, and since it was jersey it wouldn't crease.

And there was some money left over—enough for a navy sweater to wear with her last year's pleated skirt. She checked the money in her purse then, had a cup of coffee and a roll, and went in search of something tasty for supper, as well as the boiled sweets her father liked to suck while he worked and a tiny bottle of the perfume her mother liked.

By then it was time to get the bus back to Much Winterlow.

Chapter 3

The bus went from the castle buildings and Matilda had overlooked the fact that she had walked some distance from it. She hurried now; there was no other bus; it was a once-weekly event. Much Winterlow was far too isolated to merit more than that and how would she get back if she missed it? She broke into a run, much hampered by her parcels.

Dr Lovell, driving himself home after a day at Trinity Hospital, caught sight of her as he turned the car into East Street from North Street. She was dancing with impatience, waiting for the lights to allow her to cross over to the bus depot, now tantalisingly close. He turned the car into the bus park and stopped by the bus. He opened his door and got out as she came galloping along.

'Cut it rather fine, haven't you?' he asked, took her parcels from her and popped her into the car.

Matilda, too breathless to speak, sat wordless as he drove back into the traffic and took the road home. Presently she said, 'Thank you, Doctor,' and then added, 'I've been shopping...'

'One tends to forget the time,' he observed, and then he said nothing more. So she looked out of the window at the gathering dusk and wished that she could think of something interesting or witty to say.

They were nearly at the village when he spoke again.

'Surgery starts in just over an hour. I suggest that you have your tea at my place. You're on the phone? I'll ring your mother when we get there.'

He added, 'And don't argue; it's the sensible thing to do.'

It was hardly an invitation, more like a command, but it was good sense, too. She would have no time to spare if she went home. She thanked him in a stiff manner and followed him into the house after he'd drawn up at his front door.

The interior, she saw at a glance, bore out the charm of the exterior. The hall was square with panelled walls and a staircase with barley-sugar balusters rising from its centre to the gallery above. There was a long case clock and facing it a pair of cane-backed chairs flanking a side table upon which was a Staffordshire china bowl filled with autumn flowers.

She would have liked to stand and stare but the doctor was urging her across the hall and Mrs Inch had come through the baize door at the back of the hall.

'Ah, Mrs Inch, if we might have tea? It is too late for Miss Paige to go home before surgery.'

'Give me a few minutes, Doctor, and I dare say Miss Paige would like to tidy herself.'

Her long, rather solemn face gave the hint of a smile and she whisked Matilda down the hall and into a charming cloakroom, equipped with everything anyone could possibly want and two mirrors, one full-length, the other over the handbasin. Matilda took a quick look at her reflection and sighed, combed her hair and washed her hands and went back into the hall.

The doctor, waiting for her, flung open a door. 'In here, Miss Paige.'

Very polite, thought Matilda, but not much warmth, and she walked into the room.

It was light and airy by reason of the bay window overlooking the garden at the back of the house. There was an open door beside the window and she could see green lawns and flowerbeds, still colourful with autumn flowers and the last roses. And there was a dog racing around, a large, woolly-coated animal with a feathery tail.

'Oh, you've got a dog…?'

She went to the door and the doctor followed her.

'Yes. Sam. You like dogs?'

'Yes. Once we're settled I'd like to have one.'

'They're good company. Come and have your tea.'

She sat down near the log fire burning in the wide fireplace. Mrs Inch had put the tea tray on a low table and as he sat down in a winged armchair opposite her the doctor said, 'I gave your mother a quick call to let her know you're here. Will you pour out?'

When she had passed him his cup and saucer he said, 'You have had a pleasant time in Taunton?'

'Yes, thank you.' She had been brought up to make conversation and put the numerous visitors to her father's house at their ease; so she embarked on a pleasant conversation now and the doctor, amused, encouraged her.

While she talked she looked around her discreetly. It was a splendid room, she decided. There was a William and Mary tapestry settee which could have graced a museum, tripod tables with piecrust edges, a side table with marquetry decorations and a carved court cupboard. There were flowers and several comfortable chairs which blended in nicely with the antiques. The walls were cov-

ered in a cream striped wallpaper and hung with paintings, and there were silver wall-sconces. A lovely room
but warm and lived in. When offered a second of Mrs
Inch's delicious scones, Matilda accepted it. She was hungry and her lunch had been a meagre affair.

The doctor, watching her eating a slice of sponge cake
and, when pressed, a piece of shortbread, was surprised
to feel a pang of concern. She was enjoying her tea with
the pleasure of a hungry child offered an unexpected
treat. And he had seen her glances around the room. He
had long ago taken it for granted, but she, discovering its
beauty for the first time, positively glowed with delight.

It was almost time for surgery; Matilda bent to stroke
Sam's woolly head and got up. The doctor got up, too, and
listened gravely to her thanks. He was quite disarmed by
her. 'I was hungry and it was a lovely tea, and I'm very
grateful for the lift back.'

He said kindly, 'It was a pleasure to have company,
Miss Paige.' He opened the door, crossed the hall with
her and opened the door leading to the surgery.

There weren't many patients and he left to go to one of
the outlying farms the moment the last patient had gone,
leaving her to lock up and then go home. When she got
there, with supper to get, she found her mother was lying
down with a headache.

'Now you're back I think I shall stay in bed and have
something light on a tray.' Mrs Paige added sharply, 'You
should have come straight home instead of having tea at
Dr Lovell's house. I suppose he felt he had to ask you
out of politeness.'

Matilda said merely, 'It was a nice tea; besides, there
wasn't much time before the evening surgery.'

'Well, what do you expect if you go off for the day?'

Mrs Paige eyed Matilda's shopping bags. 'You spent all your money, I suppose.'

'Yes, Mother.' There was no point in showing her mother what she had bought; it would be the wrong colour, or in poor taste or unfashionable... No one was likely to notice and by no one Matilda meant Dr Lovell. But she reminded herself she would enjoy wearing them.

Whilst getting the supper, she pictured him, back home by now—she hoped—sitting by the fire with Sam at his feet, waiting for Mrs Inch to give him his supper. And, that over, he would return to the comfort of his fireside and read or watch the TV. She hoped he wouldn't sit up too late; he had had a busy day...

He was, in fact, delivering premature twins in an isolated cottage and then driving to Taunton behind the ambulance he had called. He stayed to make sure that the mother and babies were in good shape and then took the father back home before going to his own bed in the small hours.

Matilda heard of this when she arrived at the surgery in the morning—not that the doctor had mentioned it to anyone, but a neighbour had told another neighbour and they had told the boy who brought the milk down to the village. The surgery finished, Matilda wondered if she should mention the news to the doctor and decided against it; he looked as well turned out as usual, his manner as calm as always, but she could see that he was tired.

Only after the evening surgery—a particularly heavy one—as she bade him goodnight, did she say in her sensible way, 'I hope you will be able to get a good night's sleep, Doctor. You must be tired.'

He gave her a look from cold eyes. 'Thank you, Miss Paige, but you have no need to concern yourself about me.'

'Oh, I'm not concerned about you; I'm sure you're well able to look after yourself,' said Matilda kindly. She went on chattily, 'Of course, being a clergyman's daughter, I'm in the habit of concerning myself about people. Some people call it being a Nosy Parker.'

She made for the door. 'Goodnight, Doctor. You'll feel more yourself after a good night's sleep.'

The doctor stared at the closed door for a few moments. Then he laughed. There had been something different about Matilda although he had no idea what it might be.

Matilda, hanging the grey dress in the wardrobe ready for the morning, would have been pleased to know that; he might not have noticed the new dress but at least he had been aware that there was something unusual...

Her mother hadn't thought much of it. 'Though I suppose it's suitable for your work. I mean, no one would notice it, would they?' She had added crossly, 'I hope you don't intend to spend all your money on clothes for yourself, Matilda?'

Which was such an unfair remark that Matilda hadn't answered it.

It was fortunate that Mrs Paige was beginning to be invited out to coffee or tea by the various ladies of Mrs Milton's acquaintance, so beyond complaining that she had nothing fit to wear she began to find that life in a small village wasn't so bad after all. She left the shopping to Matilda, of course, and a good deal of the housework. As she pointed out, Mr Paige was now so much better, he could be left for a few hours. After all, he spent so much time in his study, he was seldom aware of anyone else being in the house.

Matilda was uneasy about this, for frequently she left home to go to the surgery in the late afternoon and her mother had not returned. But her father was happy, working away at his book, taking the short walks Dr Lovell had suggested, and glad to see that his wife was becoming content with their new way of life. He was happily oblivious of the mundane problems which Matilda dealt with.

She had no reason to be dissatisfied with life, reflected Matilda. They were managing nicely now; there was even enough money over for her mother to have her trips to Taunton, although Matilda could see that they might have to be curtailed once the winter set in properly and the gas and coal bills mounted...

She enjoyed her job; by now she knew everyone in the village, and although she doubted if the doctor had anything other than a detached acceptance of her presence at least they were on speaking terms.

And that was all she could ever expect of him, she supposed.

She was wrong.

It was a casual traveller, having lost his way and stopping to enquire at Mrs Simpkins' shop, who brought the flu to Much Winterlow. The shop was full at the time, since it was Friday afternoon and housewives, armed with a weekly pay packet, were intent on stocking up for the weekend. The man lingered while several voices told him which road to take, and since he was coughing a good deal Mrs Simpkins sold him some lozenges and several ladies offered advice as to the best way to treat a bad cold such as he had...

It was the following week when the first victims came to the surgery. Matilda, viewing the steadily increasing ranks of miserable, coughing patients, decided to keep the surgery doors open for a little longer each day. She didn't think the doctor would notice; in any case he would never go away before he had seen the last patient.

But he did notice, of course. After a morning surgery which had overshot its length by half an hour he observed that since the surgery seemed to have lengthened its hours it might be as well if the morning surgery was kept open for half an hour longer. 'And an hour longer in the evening. If this flu gets worse, we shall have to tackle it as best we can. We can't expect much outside help; the hospitals in Taunton and Yeovil are already full. Ideally patients should stay at home and be nursed there. I've asked for nursing help but there is a shortage there too.'

'I've got my first aid certificate,' said Matilda. 'I'll help.'

He looked up from his desk. 'An offer which I accept but which I hope you won't come to regret, Miss Paige.'

Towards the end of the week it became obvious that the flu was getting a firm grip on the village. It was difficult to keep it in check, for people still had to go about their business, shopping had to be done, and workers taking the bus to the small furniture factory some miles away coughed and sneezed and spread their germs. That they would have preferred to stay at home in bed was a foregone conclusion, but most of them were on piece work and needed the money.

Matilda, explaining to her mother and father, met with instant opposition from Mrs Paige.

'You mean to say you offered to work longer hours?

You're bound to catch this flu, and what if you give it to us? How very selfish of you, Matilda.'

Her father said, 'You do what you think is right, my dear. Your mother and I will be perfectly all right...'

Matilda gave him a grateful smile. 'Well, I thought it might be a good idea if I got a room in the village, just while this epidemic lasts. I'll be working longer hours and going to and fro might get difficult. I'll come home whenever I can and bring whatever you need, but I won't see you. Luckily you're on the outskirts of the village.'

'Where will you get a room? And who is to pay for it?' asked her mother.

'Mrs Simpkins knows several people who let rooms in the summer. And I'm to be paid for the extra hours.'

'I should hope so. When will you go?'

'I'll see Mrs Simpkins in the morning and ask her to help.'

The morning surgery was packed and afterwards Dr Lovell went away at once to visit his more seriously ill patients in their homes. Matilda tidied up, drank the coffee Mrs Inch brought her, locked up and went across the street to the shop.

There were several customers, buying what they needed briskly, not stopping for the comfortable gossip which was their habit, and when the shop was empty Matilda asked, 'I wonder if you would help me, Mrs Simpkins?'

Mrs Simpkins, deprived of her cosy chats, was all eagerness.

''Course I will, love. What d'yer want?'

'A room,' said Matilda, 'and meals, just till this flu is over. I'm working longer hours and I need to be near the surgery and I don't want to give the flu to my mother and father.'

'Quite right, my dear. And I know just the person— Mrs Trickett, three doors down. She's 'ad it, so she won't be afraid of you giving it to her. She'll be glad of the money. You go along and see her; say I sent you.' She eyed Matilda. ''Aving to work 'ard, I'll be bound. And the doctor out all hours. Can't get 'elp, I'm told. 'Ospitals all full to bursting. 'E 'ad to drive old Mrs Crouch to Bridgewater to get 'er into a bed. Pneumonia and very poorly. You're not scared at getting it?'

Matilda said that, no, she wasn't. Indeed she hadn't thought much about it; all she could really think about was seeing more of Dr Lovell and being able to help him.

Mrs Trickett lived in a very small thatched cottage. Its front door opened onto the street and inside it was crammed with furniture and an enormous number of china ornaments and knick-knacks. But the little bedroom she was shown was spotlessly clean. There was no bathroom. She could go across to the Lovell Arms, said Mrs Trickett, and have a bath there.

'There's a lovely bathroom. There's a jug and basin in the room for a wash and I'll give you your meals.' She looked uncertain. 'It's not much...'

'It's fine,' said Matilda. 'Just what I want. I can nip to and from the surgery. I have to be there well before eight o'clock in the morning and perhaps I may get held up and not get back on time. Would you mind?'

'Lor' bess you, miss, no. You'll come?'

'Please. Shall I pay you each week? I don't suppose it will be for long, and I'll pay in advance. And I'll go and see the landlord at the pub about a bath.'

He was a large, jolly man, although a little downcast

for the time being, since only the foolhardy and those who had had the flu and felt safe spent their evenings in the bar. 'But things will get better, miss; bound to. You come across whenever you want. I'll show you where to go. Bring your own towel and soap, will you?'

He named a modest sum and Matilda, pleased with her arrangements, went home to pack a bag and promise to go home whenever she could. 'But I'll phone you each evening,' she assured her parents.

She decided to say nothing to the doctor; he had enough to worry about without bothering about her plans. And indeed she was right; he scarcely gave her a thought; his days were long and his nights short and frequently disturbed. True, he showed no signs of tiredness, he ate the meals put before him and his manner never varied from his usual calm. When he had occasion to speak to her it was in his usual polite, detached manner.

Matilda, aware that she was, as it were, invisible to him, didn't mind; just going there, helping him, was enough to go on with...

Mrs Trickett's cottage was lacking in mod cons but it was warm and Mrs Trickett herself was just as warm in her manner. Matilda, installed there by lunchtime, took stock of her small bedroom and decided that she had been lucky. True, the room was very small but there was a thick old-fashioned quilt on the bed and, after all, she was only going to sleep there. She ate her midday dinner with Mrs Trickett in the kitchen, a nice piping hot stew and a pot of strong tea, and then went to the shop to buy groceries to take home with her on the following day. While Mrs Simpkins sliced bacon and weighed out the cheese, Matilda impressed upon her the need not to tell anyone that she was lodging with Mrs Trickett.

'You see, the doctor has so much to worry about at the moment, it would only bother him that I wasn't going home each day, but it's much easier for me to be close to the surgery now that it's so busy.'

Mrs Simpkins agreed. 'I'll not tell, miss. Reckon you're right not to bother the doctor more than he's bothered now.'

The flu was at its height; the very ill and elderly were taken to hospital whenever there was a bed but everyone else depended on Dr Lovell for antibiotics as well as resorting to old-fashioned remedies their grannies had used—the syrup from a Swede turnip sprinkled with sugar, camphorated oil, an old sock wrapped round the throat...!

It hadn't entered Matilda's head that she might get the flu too. In any case she was far too busy to think about it. A week went by and she went home twice with groceries, but not to stop. Her father she didn't see, judging it prudent in case she harboured germs, merely handing over what she had brought to her mother and going back to the village again. It was a blessing that they were on the phone and could keep in touch.

It was on Friday evening, after surgery, that Dr Lovell asked her if she would open the surgery on Saturday evening. It would give those who worked on the more distant farms a chance to come to the surgery, he explained, and he scarcely waited for her to agree. And really, she reflected, she might just as well be there as sitting in Mrs Trickett's kitchen.

Saturday morning was as busy as usual for there were still the cut fingers, sprained ankles and aches and pains as well as the flu patients. Matilda closed the waiting-room door thankfully and, told to go into the surgery and have her coffee, went and sat down on the opposite side of the desk and lifted her mug of the fragrant brew. She put it down again as the door to the house was flung open.

Lucilla Armstrong stood there for a moment to allow any onlookers the chance to admire her. And indeed she was worth admiration; she was wearing a leather jacket, a very short skirt, suede boots to die for, and her fair hair was hanging in fashionable untidiness around her subtly made up face...

She said in a thrilling voice, 'Henry, darling, I knew you would be longing to see me so I drove straight from Heathrow.'

The doctor had got to his feet, and if he was surprised he didn't show it.

'Lucilla, this is unexpected...'

She came into the room, ignoring Matilda. 'I meant it to be. I didn't stop for anything, just got into the car and came here. I've had such a wonderful time.'

The doctor said quietly, 'Did you know that there's a flu epidemic in most of the country?'

'Flu? I haven't bothered with newspapers or the radio. Oh, Henry, it was delightful lying around in the sun all day...' She frowned. 'But there's no flu here?'

'Half the village is down with it. You should go home, Lucilla, and stay there until the epidemic is over.'

She was suddenly furious. 'Why didn't someone tell me? I suppose this place is full of germs; I might even catch it just talking to you.'

'Possibly,' said Dr Lovell.

'And what is she doing here?' Lucilla nodded at Matilda.

Matilda answered before the doctor had a chance. 'She works here.'

She picked up her mug, went back into the waiting room and sat down at her desk, finishing her coffee. She took a look at the appointments book; the evening surgery would be full to overflowing. She hoped that the doctor would be back from his visits in time to open it promptly. It was likely to be a busy evening. She would go across to the pub and have a bath after her dinner and have tea with Mrs Trickett before coming back to work.

It was quiet and cold in the waiting room and although she couldn't hear voices she didn't like to go back into the surgery. When the doctor opened the door she looked up enquiringly.

'I'm off on my rounds. Mrs Inch doesn't feel well, so I've sent her to bed. Will you stay and take any messages? I've left my mobile phone number on my desk and I'll be back as soon as I can.'

He had gone before she could reply.

How like a man, thought Matilda, to walk out of his house and presently return to expect a cooked meal on the table, his slippers warmed by the fire, Sam taken for a walk and fed. She had to admit that wasn't quite fair; of course, he couldn't be expected to do otherwise and he had never spared himself. He must be tired, she thought lovingly, and went in search of Mrs Inch, who was lying on her bed and feeling very under the weather. She was fretting about who would get the doctor's meals and what about Sam and who was to answer the phone.

'Well, I will,' Matilda said cheerfully. 'You get into bed and I'll bring you a hot drink and you can tell me what must be done. Dr Lovell has asked me to stay until he gets back.'

'There's soup on the Aga,' said Mrs Inch as Matilda popped her nightgown over her head, 'and a chicken ready to go into the oven and an apple pie. Sam's food is in the cupboard by the door leading to the larder.'

She got gratefully into her bed. 'Doctor gave me some pills; I'll be on my feet in no time.'

'I'll bring you a drink and perhaps you'll be able to sleep. I won't bother you unless I must.'

Matilda sped downstairs and found the kitchen where Sam snoozed in his basket and a tabby cat was curled up on a chair by the Aga. Presently, when she had time, she would take a look round but now she was intent on finding milk and lemons and a small tray and glasses. That wasn't too difficult; it was the kind of kitchen where everything had a place and was in it.

Mrs Inch drank the hot milk, watched Matilda put the jug of lemonade within reach and closed her eyes thankfully, declaring again that she would be up and about in no time.

Matilda went back downstairs, let Sam into the garden, lunched hurriedly on soup and bread and butter and phoned Mrs Simpkins to ask her if she could let Mrs Trickett know that she wouldn't be back until the evening and then possibly late. 'Mrs Inch isn't well and I'm staying here to answer the phone until Dr Lovell gets back for evening surgery,' she explained.

There were several calls from those too ill to come to the surgery; she took names and addresses and hoped that the doctor wouldn't be too long away. Mrs Inch was asleep but she didn't look well, so Matilda went back downstairs and made a pot of tea and sat at the table drinking it. It was too early to put the chicken in the oven but she laid a tray with tea things, buttered some scones she found in the fridge, found bread and butter and a pot of Marmite and put them out ready to make sandwiches.

Both Sam and the cat were looking at her expectantly so she fed them. If they were going to be busy later they might be forgotten...

She glanced at the clock; there was still half an hour or so before evening surgery. She left the kitchen and went to explore the drawing room; she hadn't liked to stare too much when she had had her tea there, but now she could look her fill. She sat for a moment in a chair by the dying fire, allowing her thoughts to dissolve into daydreams. But not for long. She saw to the fire, put the fire guard back and went to the kitchen where she made the sandwiches, warmed the teapot and made sure that the kettle would boil in a moment. And by then it was time to open the surgery doors...

They were going to have a specially busy evening, she realised, explaining to the patients who came hurrying in that the doctor wasn't back. She got out their cards, wrote up her book and begged them to have patience before going back to the house to take a quick peep at Mrs Inch.

She had reached the hall when the doctor let himself in.

'Tea in a couple of minutes,' said Matilda briskly. 'I'm just going to take a look at Mrs Inch; there's a tray ready in the kitchen. The waiting room's full.'

She whisked herself upstairs and found Mrs Inch still asleep and raced down again. The doctor was in the kitchen, eating the sandwiches, and she told him to sit down, made the tea, and while he was drinking it popped the chicken into the Aga. They didn't talk, for she saw that he was tired and hungry and he still had the surgery to cope with...

The doctor ate the last of the sandwiches and watched Matilda arranging saucepans on the Aga. She did it as though she had done it all her life and without any attempt to draw attention to herself. Strange to think that he hadn't been too keen on employing her; she was turning out to be a treasure. He had a fleeting vision of Lucilla dealing with the Aga with such efficiency and dismissed the idea as ludicrous; Lucilla was born to be a beautiful ornament for everyone to admire, to be cherished, spoilt, shielded from unpleasantness…

Matilda tucked a wisp of brown hair behind an ear. 'I'll check the waiting room,' she said, and left him alone.

The surgery ran well over its usual time but it had been a good idea; no one was seriously ill, and with good luck they would recover in their own homes provided they took care of themselves and took the antibiotics the doctor gave them.

Matilda locked the surgery door, tidied the room and after a moment's thought went into the surgery. The doctor was at his desk, coping with paperwork.

'I'll see to Mrs Inch,' said Matilda, 'and dish up your supper. Is anyone coming to help you in the morning?'

'No, I'll be quite all right, thank you, Miss Paige.'

'I dare say you will but Mrs Inch won't be. I'll come over about nine o'clock and see to her. Make the bed and so on. She won't want you to do it and she is not well enough to manage by herself.'

He looked at her then. She was quite right, of course.

'You must be needed at home. Your father is keeping well? Keeping away from the village?'

'Yes, he is very well. If you don't wish me to come in the morning then may I ask Mrs Simpkins to pop over? Mrs Inch would be upset…'

'Ah, yes, of course. Stupid of me. If your mother and father can spare you please come yourself, Miss Paige. I can manage very well now; you must wish to go home?'

'I'll just go up to Mrs Inch. Goodnight, Doctor.'

He was writing again. 'Goodnight, Miss Paige, and thank you.'

He didn't look up.

Mrs Inch was feeling more herself but she was glad of a little help, and to have her bed remade, more lemonade, and a bowl of soup after a refreshing wash. Matilda had put the potatoes in the oven with the chicken and the parsnips and carrots were almost ready by the time she got downstairs. She set the kitchen table, put everything ready in the warm oven and found pencil and paper.

'Dinner ready to eat in the oven. Mrs Inch has had some soup and her pill. I hope you sleep well.'

She didn't sign it. Matilda was too familiar in the face of the doctor's detached coolness, Miss Paige sounded Gothic, so she scribbled her initials.

She would have to go out through the surgery; she knocked on the door and when there was no answer went in. He wasn't there. She went out through the waiting-room door, locking up after her.

Mrs Trickett had a hot meal ready for her, and then, since it was a dark and cold evening, the good soul boiled up several kettles of hot water and left Matilda to have a good wash at the sink. It wasn't very satisfactory but she felt all the better for it, and presently, in her dressing gown, she went and sat in the kitchen with Mrs Trickett and dried her washed hair. It had been a long day and, pleasantly sleepy and further warmed by a cup of hot cocoa, Matilda went to bed. Before she slept she hoped that the doctor had eaten his supper and gone to bed too.

* * *

He had eaten his supper; he had gone to his study when Matilda had gone up to see Mrs Inch, but before long his splendid nose had caught an appetising whiff of something from the kitchen. Sam had got up from his place under the desk and gone to the door, and so had the doctor...

He had read Matilda's note first and then gone to the Aga. He'd been carving the chicken when he'd put down the carving knife and addressed Sam.

'I should have invited her to supper, driven her home at the very least; she must be asleep on her feet...'

He went upstairs to his housekeeper's room and found her awake.

'Mrs Inch, did Miss Paige say that she was going home? She left the house while I was in my study.'

'Not home, sir. She's lodging with Mrs Trickett just across the street, so's to be on hand. Didn't want to take this nasty old flu home and Mrs Trickett's had it. Been there a couple of days. Don't say much about it—she's not one to do that—but Mrs Simpkins told me she's quite happy there. Mrs Trickett feeds her well and she nips across to the Lovell Arms for a bath.' She stopped to cough. 'Don't you worry about her, sir. A very capable young lady and everyone who knows her would help her.'

'Save myself, Mrs Inch,' said the doctor heavily.

'Lor' bless you, sir, you've enough on your plate keeping the rest of us on our feet. You go down and eat your supper and let's hope you'll get a good night's sleep.'

The chicken and everything that went with it was delicious; he tidied the kitchen and took Sam for an evening walk. He passed Mrs Trickett's house, suppressing an urge to knock on its door and ask to see Matilda. She was probably in bed and wouldn't thank him for a visit. Presently he went back home, and, tired though he was, dealt with the paperwork and the conditions of his ill patients. Then he went to bed and a kindly Providence allowed him to sleep all night.

Chapter 4

It was a wet and cold Sunday morning. The pub wouldn't open until midday so there was no chance of going over for a bath. Matilda shared breakfast with Mrs Trickett, helped with the washing-up and then, well wrapped in her elderly mac, went across to the doctor's house.

She let herself in through the surgery waiting room and entered the hall, to be met by Sam and, a moment later, the doctor, coming out of the kitchen. She was happy to see that he looked rested and somehow much younger in cords and a thick sweater.

She wished him good morning and added, 'I've come to see to Mrs Inch if you don't mind?'

'Mind? My dear girl, I am beginning to think that I would be lost without you. Mrs Inch has told me that you have moved in with Mrs Trickett. You should have told me... And you cooked my supper.'

'No trouble,' said Matilda matter-of-factly. 'Everything was ready to put into the oven, and I'm very comfortable with Mrs Trickett. I didn't want to take the flu germs home and she's so handy, just across the street.'

'I'm grateful, Miss Paige. When you have seen Mrs Inch perhaps you will have coffee with me?'

'That'll be nice,' said Matilda, and nipped up the staircase.

Mrs Inch was no worse, but neither was she feeling much better. Matilda helped her to the bathroom leading from her bed-sitting room, put her into a clean nightie, brushed her hair and tucked her into the freshly made bed. 'A nice hot drink and some more lemonade, then perhaps you can have a nap. Shall I pop over this evening?'

'Would you? Just to freshen me up… Kitty will be here in the morning. She's a good girl and quite a good cook, and Mrs Squires will be in to do the rough.'

Matilda nipped downstairs, fetched the cup of tea Mrs Inch craved and carried it back with the lemonade, resisted the urge to tidy herself up before joining the doctor—a waste of time anyway, she told herself, for he wouldn't notice—and went back to the kitchen. He was there and the coffee smelled delicious. He put their mugs on the table, offered her a biscuit, gave one to Sam and sat down opposite her.

'I am hopeful that we are over the worst,' he observed, 'with no new cases yesterday evening.'

'Oh, good; you must be very thankful. You won't mind if I come this evening and see to Mrs Inch? She's better, isn't she? But she doesn't feel up to doing much.'

'I have not the least objection, Miss Paige. Perhaps you will come in the late afternoon and share my tea?'

'All right,' said Matilda. 'If you want me to. Can you manage to get your own lunch?'

'Thank you, yes.' He sounded so frosty that she didn't ask about his supper. He had friends for that, she was sure. They could be coming to get his supper for him, and eat it with him too, no doubt. She finished her coffee, put their mugs in the sink, bade him a civil goodbye and started for the front door.

She reached the door, but he'd got there first.

'Just a moment, Miss Paige. Mrs Inch told me that you go to the Lovell Arms for a bath. Not a very satisfactory arrangement. There are three bathrooms in this house and an abundance of hot water. May I suggest you take advantage of that and have a bath here?'

Matilda eyed him thoughtfully. 'Now?'

'Why not? I shall be working in my study, Mrs Inch appears to be comfortable and there is no one to hurry you. If you go upstairs you will find a bathroom on the right, the second door. Take as long as you like. No need to tell me when you are ready to leave; the front door is unlocked, so let yourself out.'

His offer had been made in a detached manner and with the air of a man doing his duty, and Matilda, who had been doubtful, allowed common sense to rule the day.

'Thank you. That would be nice. I won't disturb anyone, Doctor.'

He watched her go, wondering why on earth he had suggested it. He went to his study, telling himself it was an offer he would have made to anyone in similar circumstances.

The bathroom was large, warm and well equipped. Matilda lay in a steaming hot bath, lavishly scented with something heavenly out of a bottle, and thought about the doctor. She came to the conclusion that she would never know what he was really like. She suspected that behind his austere manner there was quite a different man lurking.

She washed her hair and then, swathed in a huge soft bath towel, sat drying it. It was pleasant to sit there in the lap of luxury, thinking about the doctor, and she could have spent the rest of the morning doing just that, but that, she felt sure, would be outstaying her welcome. She dressed and went quietly downstairs and let herself out into the quiet street.

She phoned her mother from the telephone box outside Mrs Simpkins' shop, assured her that she was well and hoped that she would be coming home as soon as the flu subsided. As she left the box Mrs Simpkins stuck her head out of an upstairs window.

'Bin over to the doctor's, love?'

'Yes, Mrs Simpkins, just to see to Mrs Inch. She's feeling a little better but doesn't feel like doing much; in fact, she's still in her bed. I'm going over again this afternoon, just to settle her. She said that someone called Kitty would be back tomorrow to look after her.'

'That'll be Kitty Tapper—housemaid, you might say. Going back to Mrs Trickett for your dinner?'

'Yes, Mrs Simpkins, and a nice quiet afternoon!'

Mrs Simpkins, thought Matilda, was a dear soul but did like to know everyone's business.

She ate her dinner with Mrs Trickett and then sat with her by the old-fashioned kitchen stove, reading the newspaper her companion shared with her. She had never read this particular tabloid before and its contents were startling enough to keep her engrossed.

She judged that half past four was the right time to go back to see to Mrs Inch, and the doctor opened the door to her, looking, for a moment, surprised to see her. He had his reading glasses on and held a sheaf of papers and she guessed that he had forgotten all about her.

'Shall I go and see how Mrs Inch is?' she suggested, sounding businesslike. 'And give her her tea before I see to her comfort?'

'Yes, yes, please do; you know where everything is.'
He was already on his way back to his study.

Mrs Inch was awake, rather cross and longing for a
cup of tea.

'I'll get it straight away,' Matilda promised, 'and then
I'll make you comfortable. Do you feel a little better?'

'I suppose so. Dr Lovell has been in and out during
the day. He says I'm on the mend. Very kind and thoughtful, he's been, and I know he's busy and men don't think
about a cup of tea and suchlike, do they?'

'Well no,' agreed Matilda. 'I'll bring up a big pot and
perhaps I can find a Thermos jug and leave it filled for
you if you fancy a drink later on.'

'You're a very thoughtful young lady,' said Mrs Inch,
'and I believe I could manage a morsel of bread and butter cut thin.'

There was no sign of the doctor as she made tea and
some wafer-thin slices of bread and butter, arranged everything neatly on a tray and took it back upstairs.

Mrs Inch, propped up on pillows, sipped her tea.
'That's a treat,' she observed. 'Now just you go down
and have your tea with the doctor.'

A bit of a problem, decided Matilda, going down to
a quiet house. Had he forgotten that he had asked her to
tea? Or was she expected to get it for them both?

She found a tray and tea things, boiled the kettle and
poked around the cupboards looking for cake or biscuits.
There was a cake, or half of one. She put it on a plate
and cut more bread and butter and went into the hall and
looked doubtfully at the closed doors. Finally she tapped
on the study door and went in.

The doctor was at his desk, writing, Sam at his feet.

He looked up as she went in, staring at her over his spectacles.

'Yes?' He sounded testy.

'Mrs Inch is quite comfortable until suppertime,' said Matilda baldly. 'Your tea is waiting for you in the kitchen.'

He frowned. 'Presently, presently. I have a good deal of writing to do.'

'I dare say you have. Go and have your tea now while it's still hot.'

She closed the door quietly after her and got into her coat and let herself out of the house. She was suddenly tired and dispirited. And, at the same time, cross. 'I hope he goes hungry to bed,' she muttered as she crossed the road to Mrs Trickett's cottage.

Even if the doctor didn't want his tea, Sam wanted his. He got up and wandered back and forth in doggy impatience until his master put down his pen and got up.

'All right, old fellow; we'll have tea and go for a walk. And I'd better look in on Mrs Inch.'

He ate all the bread and butter and most of the cake and drained the teapot while Sam ate a biscuit, then they both went up to Mrs Inch.

Mrs Inch assured him that she was feeling better. 'That Miss Paige made a lovely pot of tea and bread and butter; I couldn't have cut it thinner myself. Had your tea, have you, sir?'

'Yes, thank you, Mrs Inch. Miss Paige left it ready for me.' He stopped. 'Oh, God...'

Mrs Inch said severely, 'It's not like you to call upon the Lord, sir.'

'Mrs Inch, I asked Miss Paige to have tea with me when she came over this afternoon and I forgot. That's no excuse——I was working but I should have remembered. She got the tea and told me it was ready and left the house. Why didn't she remind me?'

Mrs Inch gave him an old-fashioned look. 'She'd rather go without her tea; she's not the pushy sort,' she said dryly.

'Mrs Inch, will you be all right if I go across and see her? Sam can have a quick run at the same time.'

'You do that, Doctor; I'm fine.'

It was drizzling as he let himself out of the house with Sam. It was Mrs Trickett who answered his knock.

'Doctor? Is something wrong? Do you want Miss Paige? Come in——and Sam…'

'Nothing is wrong, Mrs Trickett. If I might have a word with Miss Paige? You're keeping well? Quite recovered from the flu?'

Mrs Trickett led the way into the kitchen. 'Yes, thank you, Doctor. You don't mind the kitchen? It's warmer, and with just the two of us…'

'I think that the kitchen is sometimes the most cosy place in the house,' said the doctor. He paused in the doorway to look at Matilda, standing at the small sink, clasping a cabbage to her bosom like a shield.

She didn't put it down. She didn't say anything either, only looked at him unsmiling.

'Miss Paige, I've come to apologise. I invited you to have tea with me and forgot about you. Please forgive me?'

'Well, of course I do. I dare say you were too busy to think about it. Besides, I am the sort of person people forget.'

She spoke in a matter-of-fact voice with no trace of self-pity. It was merely a statement of a fact she had been aware of for years, first pointed out to her by her mother. She had accepted it as gospel truth without rancour but with regret.

Mrs Trickett had slipped away and the doctor came further into the small room, his head inches from the ceiling, his large person making it even smaller than it was.

'That's not true; take my word for it. Don't hide your light under a bushel, Miss Paige; I have come to regard you as indispensable.'

'I've done my best to follow in Miss Brimble's footsteps,' said Matilda.

He stared at her. She looked small and rather pale in the dim light of the single bulb, but not in the least sorry for herself. Indeed, she said tartly, 'There was no need for you to have come out...'

'Sam needed a run,' said the doctor meekly. 'I'll bid you goodnight and see you in the morning at the surgery.'

She went with him into the tiny hall and opened the door for him. It was a tight squeeze—him, her and Sam. At the door he turned to say, 'Please use my place for a bath; I'll tell Kitty you may be over during the day.'

'Thank you. Goodnight, Doctor.' She had a nice voice, he reflected, but still tart. There was more to Miss Matilda Paige than one would suppose.

The surgery was crowded in the morning; it was always the same on a Monday. The waiting room filled up, the air redolent of wet coats and a strong whiff of manure from the two farm workers, badly bruised by a slight mishap with a tractor. But it was heartening to find that there were no new flu patients.

The surgery ended late and the doctor went away immediately. He had wished Matilda good morning in his

usual detached manner, left her a couple of letters to answer and made no mention of a bath. She tidied up and
got ready to leave, to be stopped by Kitty coming into
the waiting room.

'If you don't mind coming into the kitchen, miss,
there's coffee ready there. And Mrs Inch says could you
look in on her before you have your bath. I've put out
fresh towels for you.'

The coffee was hot and fragrant and Kitty was a
friendly girl. Matilda drank it thankfully with Sam at
her feet and Kitty sitting opposite her at the table. And
presently she went to see Mrs Inch, who was sitting in a
chair by the gas fire in her room.

'I'm better,' she declared, 'fit for work, but the doctor
won't hear of it. Says I must take things easy for a day
or two. I'm obliged to you, miss; you've been that good
to me! Going to have a bath now? No one will disturb
you so take your time; it's a sight better here than going
over to the pub.'

Matilda agreed, listened to Mrs Inch's mild gossip for
a few minutes then took herself off to the bathroom again.
Sheer luxury, she reflected, lying in a foam-filled bath...

It was obvious that the worst of the flu epidemic was
over; there were no new cases during the next few days
and those who had been laid low were back on their
feet. Matilda phoned home to say that she would be returning in a few days' time, and spent happy moments
doing sums on any bit of paper handy. She had been paid
overtime—the doctor had waved aside her objections
to that—and she had had little chance to spend much
money. Her mother would expect to have some of it and
there were always unexpected or forgotten bills which

her father had mislaid. Still, there would be enough over for her to go to Taunton again. A new mac, she decided, looking out of the window at the cold drizzle...

The waiting room was almost back to normal with its contingent of patients the next morning, for which Matilda felt thankful; she wasn't feeling as energetic as usual. A bit of a headache and a wish to climb into a warm bed somewhere and sleep. There wasn't time to think much about it, though; the doctor came punctually and the first of the patients went in. For once she found the surgery hours dragged; it seemed to her that he was being very slow that morning, which as it happened wasn't the case at all. It was only a short while after ten o'clock when she closed the door on the last patient and the doctor put his head round the surgery door.

'I'll see you this evening, Miss Paige,' he said, and nodded in a perfunctory manner and was gone.

Matilda sat down at the desk and began sorting patients' notes, but presently she laid her head down and closed her eyes. She really felt rather peculiar—hot and cold and aching. She sat up. This wouldn't do at all; she would go over to Mrs Trickett's and lie down for a while. She had a list of things her mother had asked her to bring with her and she would have to go to Mrs Simpkins' shop later.

She got to her feet, took a couple of steps and fell in an untidy heap.

Dr Lovell, back from his morning visits, returned Sam's enthusiastic greeting and went into the drawing room to open the doors so that they might both go into the garden. It was a chilly day but dry and he stood for a moment, enjoying the quiet and peace of it all. The last few weeks had been tiring. Perhaps Miss Paige would like a few days off; she had worked hard without a single grumble.

He whistled to Sam and went to have his lunch, paid a brief visit to Mrs Inch and got into his car again. The flu epidemic might be on the wane but his practice was wide-flung and with winter approaching there was always more illness.

He went to his study when he got back at around four o'clock and then went to the surgery. And the first thing he saw was the light shining under the waiting-room door.

Matilda had woken up several times, aware that she should get up, call for help, make some kind of a noise, but it was too much trouble; she closed her eyes again and prayed for her headache to go away. She had fallen into another uneasy doze when the doctor opened the door, but she roused at the sound of his voice.

She said weakly, 'Watch your language, Doctor,' and then, 'I should like to sit down for a while—with a hot-water bottle and a cup of tea.'

He didn't waste time on talk but scooped her up and carried her out into the hall and up the staircase and into one of the bedrooms, where he laid her on the bed, took off her shoes and covered her with the quilt.

She lay looking at him, shivering, and he said gently, 'It's all right, Matilda; you've got the flu. Kitty will come and help you to bed and I'll give you something for that head.'

She stared at him with bright, feverish eyes; she felt terrible but everything would be all right now. She croaked an answer but he had already gone.

When she opened her eyes again Kitty was there, undressing her and shrouding her in one of Mrs Inch's nightgowns, and then it was the doctor again, bending over her, listening to her chest and sitting her up against her pillows while Kitty held her and told her to say ninety-nine.

She dozed then until Kitty came again with a cup of tea and a jug of lemonade. The doctor was there too; it was he who lifted her up again and held the cup to her mouth so that she could drink, and then, with a nod to Kitty, turned her gently and plunged a needle into her behind.

'Ow,' said Matilda, and two tears crept down her cheeks. He wiped them away and told her to go to sleep in a kind voice, and since staying awake wasn't too pleasant she closed her eyes.

They flew open again almost at once. 'You called me Matilda.'

'So I did,' said Dr Lovell, and laughed. A gentle, friendly laugh which sent her to sleep at once.

He stood looking down at her, half hidden in Mrs Inch's old-fashioned nightie. She was very pale and her hair was all over the pillow in an untidy tangle. Studying her face, he saw the delicately arched eyebrows and the curling eyelashes and felt surprise that he had never noticed them before. But of course he had never really looked at her. He had accepted her as a second Miss Brimble...

He went to see Mrs Inch then, and that lady tut-tutted and observed severely, 'Only to be expected, sir; the poor young lady's been on the go for two weeks or more and never a grumble from her. I shall come down tomorrow and sit in the kitchen. Kitty can manage if I'm there to tell her what's what and it's Mrs Murch's day for the rough cleaning. And who's to manage the surgery for you?'

'Oh, I can see to myself, Mrs Inch. If you come downstairs I must insist that you stay in the kitchen and do nothing. You think that Kitty can manage?'

'Lor' bless you, sir, of course she can, and she'll look after Miss Paige a treat.'

'Thank you, Mrs Inch. I'm going to phone Mrs Paige; she might have some suggestions of her own.'

But when presently he suggested to Matilda's mother that she might like to visit her daughter—stay in his house for a few days and look after her if she wished— he was met with a flurry of excuses.

'But I might get the flu,' objected Mrs Paige. 'I am so delicate, Doctor, that the least breath of infection would have severe consequences. Matilda will be on her feet again in no time; she is really very healthy. I know she doesn't look much…' When the doctor said nothing, she went on hurriedly, 'What I mean is that she's small and doesn't look strong… Should she go to hospital? I really can't have her home.'

'No, Mrs Paige.' His voice was detached, professional. 'She isn't well enough to move and in any case I wouldn't think of doing that. Mrs Inch will look after her and I shall of course treat her with antibiotics and make sure that she is fit for work again.'

'Oh, Doctor, that would be splendid. Give her my love, please, and we shall be glad to have her home once she is well again.'

He put down the phone and stood thinking for a moment then dialled another number.

'Mother? I have a small problem; is Aunt Kate still with you? She is? Do you suppose she would care to stay for a few days here with me? It's like this…'

He put the phone down presently and went in search of Mrs Inch.

She listened to what he had to say and nodded with approval. 'Miss Paige is a clergyman's daughter and a proper young lady. We don't want her worrying, do we? When will Miss Lovell be coming?'

'Some time tomorrow afternoon; she will drive over.'

'Well, that's settled, sir. Miss Paige isn't one to lie about doing nothing. I dare say she'll be on her feet and away the moment she's fit.'

'But not before I say she may,' said Dr Lovell.

Later that evening he went to see how Matilda was and found her awake and not well enough to care two pins where she was or why. Which saved a great deal of explaining. He dosed her with an antibiotic, gave her a drink and turned her pillow. She said in a small, hoarse voice, 'Thank you, I'm very comfortable now,' and dozed off.

But last thing that night as he was going to bed he took another look at her and found her hot and restless. Mrs Inch was long a-bed and so was Kitty; he bathed her hot face, gave her a drink, pulled a chair up to the bed and took a hand in his.

'Don't go,' said Matilda. 'I don't feel very well...'

'I know, but I promise you will feel much better tomorrow. Close your eyes and go to sleep and if you wake in the night just call out. I shall hear.'

'You're a different you!' said Matilda, voicing a thought from the chaos inside her poor head and presently falling into a deep sleep.

She woke early and the doctor was there giving her a pill and a long cool drink, then she slept again. When she woke for the second time it was to find Kitty, murmuring in a comforting voice and proffering tea. And it was Kitty who washed her face and hands and put her into another of Mrs Inch's nightgowns.

She was asleep again when the doctor came to see her after the morning surgery but later, when she roused, it was to find Mrs Inch, dressed in a dressing gown but looking almost her normal self, bending over her.

'I'm being a great nuisance,' said Matilda. She would have said more but her headache was still troublesome. She drank the lemonade she was offered and closed her eyes again. But not to sleep; she hadn't felt well enough to bother about being where she was, but now the thought that she was in the doctor's house, making a nuisance of herself, began to bother her. A few tears crawled down her cheeks but she couldn't be bothered to wipe them away and presently she dozed off.

When she opened her eyes again the doctor was looming over her, to be replaced by an elderly face with a beaky nose and crowned by white hair.

'I'm Aunt Kate,' said the owner of the hair, 'come to stay with my nephew Henry. And you, child, are Matilda?'

Matilda nodded. 'But please go away. I've had the flu and you mustn't get it.'

'Bless the child, I never catch anything—ask Henry.'

The idea of asking the doctor any such thing struck Matilda as amusing. She said in a polite, tired little voice, 'I hope you will enjoy your stay with the doctor.' She allowed her thoughts to spin into words. 'He must be glad to have you; he's been so busy—he must be very tired and he never complains, you know.' She rambled on, 'He's kind and he makes you feel safe, if you see what I mean, even if he doesn't like you very much.'

Aunt Kate's blue eyes narrowed but all she said was,

'Yes, you're so right. Now I'm going away to have my tea and presently someone will bring you tea and some bread and butter. You're feeling better, child.'

She spoke with such conviction that Matilda indeed felt better.

Aunt Kate found the doctor in his study, on the phone. She sat down and listened to the one-sided conversation and when he put the phone down said, 'Who was that, Henry? You sounded very smooth.'

'Mrs Paige—Matilda's mother.'

'Indeed—then why isn't she here with her daughter?'

'She is anxious not to get the flu.' The doctor sounded bland. 'She has told me that she has a delicate constitution.'

'Pooh,' said Aunt Kate. 'I mustn't ask any questions, must I, if she's one of your patients? Has the child a father?'

'Oh, yes, a delightful man, retired after a severe heart attack, has to take life easily. A clergyman.'

'And Matilda?'

'Their only child and I know very little about her, Aunt Kate; she is a quiet girl with a sharp tongue at times. Very efficient and hard-working.'

'And certainly no beauty,' said Aunt Kate. 'No boy-friend?'

'I have no idea.' The doctor frowned. The idea of Matilda having a boyfriend rankled.

It was two days before Matilda felt better but by no means well. She had taken her pills, swallowed drinks and done her best to eat the tasty small dishes Mrs Inch cooked for her, dimly aware of the doctor's visits and the frequent visits from Aunt Kate, urging her to drink this or eat that, or go to sleep. And sometimes it was Mrs Inch or Kitty bending over her, washing her, changing her nightie. She should be worrying about something, she thought fretfully, but it was too wearying to do so.

On the third morning, though, she woke with a clear head, aware that she really was feeling better. She told the doctor so when he came to see her before he went to the surgery and he studied her pale face and agreed that of course she was; another day or two and she would be out of bed, feeling quite her old self. She ate her breakfast with the beginnings of a good appetite, sitting up in bed so that she could see out of the window. For November it was a fine day, with a washed-out blue sky and thin sunshine.

'It's going to be a lovely day,' said Matilda when Aunt Kate came to visit her.

And it was until Kitty went to answer the door after lunch and Lucilla swept past her.

She was in a rage and prepared to vent it upon anyone. It was a pity that Mrs Simpkins, enjoying a gossip with her sister who lived in the village of North Curry where Lucilla's family lived, should have mentioned Matilda's illness and that she was being cared for at the doctor's home. The news had reached Lucilla's ears quickly enough and she'd lost no time in driving to Much Winterlow to see for herself.

She addressed Kitty in peremptory tones. 'What's all this talk of that girl staying here in the house? Where's the doctor? Why wasn't I told?'

Kitty backed away. 'The doctor's away on his rounds, miss, and Miss Paige is lying sick upstairs…'

'Of all the nonsense—she should be sent to hospital. Why hasn't she gone home? She has one, presumably? I shall wait for the doctor.'

She pushed past Kitty and flung open the drawing-room door.

'Come in—Lucilla, isn't it?—and sit down,' said Aunt Kate. 'You seem upset. Henry won't be back for some time but I'm sure you will stay a little while and have a cup of tea with me presently.'

Lucilla said, 'Miss Lovell—I didn't expect to find you here. I heard some tale about Henry's receptionist being here…'

'Indeed she is—very ill with flu; too ill to move. How fortunate that I was visiting Henry and have been able to look after her. There has been such a lot of flu about, hasn't there? It is most kind of you to come all this way to ask after her.'

'Yes, well…has she no home to go to?'

'Her parents live in the village but she has a semi-invalid father and I understand that her mother is very delicate.'

Aunt Kate fell silent, knitted a row of the garment she was working on and added gently, 'Such a hard worker; I'm told that she was a great help to Henry during these last difficult weeks. Such a pity that after helping so many people she should have been struck down herself.'

Lucilla said, 'Oh, yes,' in an insincere voice and Aunt Kate, glancing at her with bright blue eyes, decided that she definitely didn't like the girl. Beautiful, but no heart, she decided silently, and began a series of polite enquiries about Lucilla's family. She didn't much care for her family either; it would be a disastrous marriage if she managed to get Henry to the altar. Aunt Kate reflected thankfully that Henry was no fool; he had been attracted to Lucilla—after all, she was a beautiful young woman—

but he would want more than beauty in the girl he chose to marry.

Aunt Kate heaved a sigh and hoped that Kitty would have the good sense to bring the tea tray without being asked to do so. Mrs Inch would still be having her afternoon nap and Kitty might be busy in the kitchen and not notice the time.

The door opened and Kitty came in, set the tray down on the small table by Aunt Kate and assured her that she would take tea upstairs to Miss Paige when she went to rouse Mrs Inch.

Aunt Kate poured tea, offered cake, and polite small talk, and wished that Henry would return. But there was no sign of him and presently Lucilla said, 'I won't stay; Henry will probably be late and the evenings are so dark for driving. May I go and tidy myself…?'

'Of course, Lucilla. You know where the cloakroom is, don't you?'

Lucilla smiled and went out of the room but not to the cloakroom. She ran silently up the staircase and opened doors just as silently until she opened the door into the dimly lit room where Matilda was in bed. She had been asleep but turned her head and half sat up as the door opened to stare at Lucilla. She said in a still hoarse voice, 'Hello. It's Miss Armstrong, isn't it?'

Lucilla came and stood by the bed. She said in a satisfied voice, 'You look frightful; you're not exactly eye-catching when you are on your feet but now you look like a washed-out hag.' She laughed. 'And to think I was worried…!'

She had gone again before Matilda could say anything. But what was there to say anyway? She didn't cry often but now the tears welled up and she let them trickle down her cheeks. If she was a washed-out hag what would a few tears matter?

Chapter 5

Lucilla reached the hall just as the doctor let himself into his house. 'Lucilla—what brings you here?' If she had expected delighted surprise she was to be disappointed. He glanced at the staircase behind her, his eyebrows raised in an unspoken question. 'Aunt Kate is in the drawing room?'

Lucilla said hurriedly, 'Yes, I've had tea with her—just a passing visit; I hoped you might be here.'

He said quietly, 'You went to see Matilda?'

'Is that her name? Yes. The poor thing, she does look ill. She must be so thankful to be well looked after.'

He didn't answer her, merely opened the drawing-room door for her to go in then closed it behind her and went up the staircase, two at a time.

Tears hardly added to Matilda's wan looks. When she saw who it was she blew her small red nose, mopped her eyes and said politely, 'Good evening, Doctor.'

He ignored this poor attempt at polite small talk. 'You are upset. Lucilla came to see you, did she not? And what had she to say?'

Matilda sniffed. 'Just—well, you know, the usual things you say to someone when they're not well.'

'No. I don't know, Matilda. Enlighten me?'

He sat down on the side of the bed and took one of

her hands in his. It was large and cool and comforting. 'Well?'

She gulped. 'I expect I look awful.' And then she added, 'It was very kind of Miss Armstrong to come and see me. I hope I haven't given her any germs.'

'No, no. The worst is over; you'll be on your feet in a couple of days.' Which wasn't quite true but she needed bolstering up. 'Several people have asked how you are; you have any number of friends in the village, you know.'

'Have I? I'm happy here...' She tugged gently at her hand and he let it go at once. 'I expect you want to go downstairs and talk to Miss Armstrong; she came specially to see you.'

He got up, looking down at her with a faint smile. 'Yes, she and I will have a talk. Are you quite comfortable? Do you want Kitty for anything?'

She shook her head. 'I've everything I want,' she told him, reflecting that she would never have that for everything was the doctor, wasn't it?

Aunt Kate looked up as he went into the drawing room and Sam went to greet him with a waving tail and a happy bark or two. Only Lucilla avoided his look and said nothing.

The doctor sat down, accepted the tea Kitty had brought in and began to talk pleasantly about nothing in particular until Lucilla, at first uncertain as to what he might say about her visit to Matilda, joined in and, sure of her charm and attraction, began to talk about their various friends and acquaintances. She was a clever talker and amusing, but not always kind in her comments. Her companions listened with polite interest and presently the doctor got up.

'Time for surgery,' he observed, and thought what a

very handsome young woman Lucilla was, sitting there, smiling and now completely at her ease. She was looking at him with smiling expectancy and he had a sudden remembrance of Matilda's tear-stained face. He went to the door. His, 'Goodbye, Lucilla,' was cool and he made no mention of further meetings.

Aunt Kate picked up her knitting once more, looking composed. Henry, she reflected, was no more in love with Lucilla than she herself was. He might have been attracted to her when they'd first met and on the surface she seemed to have everything a man would want in a wife. And she had been clever, saying all the right things at the right time, a pleasant companion, a good-looking, elegant young woman, apparently interested in his work, allowing him to know that she more than liked him but never demonstrating it. Henry wasn't a man to be hurried but she was content to bide her time. He was a man worth waiting for: from a deeply respected family, with wealth, good looks, a splendid home and a host of influential friends. That he was also a highly qualified medical man was only of secondary interest. Quite unsuitable, decided Aunt Kate.

She went up to see Matilda presently, took one look at her unhappy face, pulled up a chair close to the bed and observed, 'You're upset. I dare say Lucilla said something to make you so downcast?'

'I'm sure she didn't mean to,' said Matilda, who, being a clergyman's daughter, did her best to see good in everybody. 'And it was quite true.'

'What was?' said Aunt Kate, and her beaky nose quivered slightly but her voice was gentle.

'Well, I'm sure that I do look like a washed-out hag, only I'd rather not be told.' She was silent for a moment then said, 'Miss Lovell, I would like to go home. I'm really much better and I'll be quite all right—if I just have a few days off I could come back to work again quite soon.'

Aunt Kate said decisively, 'Henry won't allow that.'

'No, well, I didn't think he would, but if you could persuade him? He told me that I would be well in a couple of days.'

'There is a difference between being well and being fit for work,' said Aunt Kate. 'I understand that your mother is delicate. Would she be able to cosset you? Breakfast in bed and making sure that you spent your days being lazy?'

'Oh, but I shall be fine once I'm home,' said Matilda in a cheerful voice which belied her seedy appearance. 'Please, Miss Lovell.'

'I will promise nothing, my dear, but if Henry should mention the matter I will see what I can do.'

An answer which hardly held much promise but which Matilda found reassuring enough.

Aunt Kate went down to the drawing room presently and when the doctor joined her after the surgery was finished she voiced the thoughts she had been mulling over.

'Matilda wishes to go home, Henry.'

He had gone to pour their drinks. 'Well, she can't; she's not fit.'

He sat down in his great chair with Sam at his feet. 'Why?'

His aunt took a sip of sherry. 'I hesitate to say this, Henry, for I am sure from what Lucilla says that you and she… Anyway, she upset Matilda so that the child feels she must go away.'

'What did she say? Lucilla is sometimes a little sharp.

I know that you wouldn't tell me unless you thought it might help the matter.'

'She told Matilda that she was a washed-out hag. You may not know this, but Matilda knows that she is a plain girl and a remark such as that, even if it were meant jokingly, is discouraging to someone not in the best of health.' Aunt Kate gave him a thoughtful look. 'And I think, from what she has told me, that there is little chance of her being looked after adequately at home. She is very loyal towards her mother but it is obvious that she can expect very little attention.'

'Then she must stay here until she is quite well.'

'I have an idea,' said Aunt Kate briskly. 'I shall be delighted to take her home with me for a few days, and when she is quite her usual self she can come back to work. I shall leave it to you to speak to her parents but I imagine her mother will agree without a moment's hesitation.'

'Oh, without doubt. You are sure that Matilda wishes to go away from here?' He frowned. 'Why?'

'Yes, dear, and I will tell you why. She neither feels nor looks her best—she wants to go somewhere and hide until she is once more your efficient receptionist.'

He said slowly, 'If you think that is what she would like we will get her on her feet in a few days and you can take her home with you. Indeed, it is a most sensible idea provided you won't find it too much of a bother?'

'No. I shall enjoy her company. You will take her back?'

The doctor looked astonished. 'Of course. She is a splendid worker; I don't know how I would have managed without her.' He smiled suddenly. 'Besides, she is very restful in her ways and always there when I want her. One hardly notices her and yet she is always there when she is needed.'

Aunt Kate was glad to know that Matilda couldn't hear him say that...

Matilda, much encouraged by the prospect of going to stay with Aunt Kate, began to recover, and two days later the doctor declared that she was fit enough to leave his house. Something she was glad to do; shut away in a bedroom with only his two official visits each day had been one thing, but on her feet once more, sitting with Aunt Kate, sharing their meals, she was seeing too much of him for her own peace of mind. She had phoned her mother and since Mrs Paige had declared herself to be feeling poorly Kitty had gone to fetch Matilda some more clothes. She had no idea where Aunt Kate lived but wherever it was it must merit her tweed suit and the blue wool crêpe dress, out of date and seldom worn but entirely suitable in a faceless kind of way for most occasions.

She was surprised to discover that Aunt Kate had her own car, an elderly Jaguar, beautifully maintained and, to Matilda's eye, hardly suitable for someone of her advanced years to drive. But the doctor, seeing them off after morning surgery, seemed to find nothing strange about it; he even forbore from telling his aunt to drive carefully.

Apart from telling her that she lived near Somerton, Aunt Kate hadn't volunteered any more information and Matilda didn't wish to appear inquisitive. That part of Somerset was more or less new to her and she saw quickly enough that they were taking narrow lanes across country and that Aunt Kate drove with the nonchalant ease of a young man. They reached Hatch Beauchamp, drove on to Langport and then turned off the main road to Somerton, into another narrow lane bearing the sign-post to High Ham.

The village, a mile or so ahead, was easy to see, perched on top of a hill, queening it over the surrounding flat countryside. And the village itself, when they reached it, was a delight to the eye with old houses gathered round a green and a splendid church alongside. There were one or two shops, a butcher, baker, village stores and post office, and Aunt Kate said as she swept past, 'We can get all we want here but there are shops at Somerton, only a few miles away.'

She drove down a lane between the houses and stopped before a handsome wrought-iron gate. 'The garage is at the end of the lane; we'll go into the cottage first.'

It was a very different cottage from Matilda's home, built of honey-coloured stone, its slate roof overgrown with moss. The last of the Virginia creeper which covered its walls had long since lost its leaves; in the summer it would be a picture. The windows were small and diamond-paned and its solid wood door would withstand a siege.

Aunt Kate produced a large old-fashioned key from her handbag and opened the door and urged Matilda past her into the hall. It was delightfully warm and through an open door she could see a bright fire burning.

'Mrs Chubb?' called Aunt Kate, and an elderly woman came through the door at the back of the hall.

'There you are, ma'am.' She shot a glance at Matilda. 'And the young lady. There's a good fire burning in the sitting room and there'll be lunch in half an hour. I'll fetch in the bags…'

'Later will do, Mrs Chubb. You'll be going home presently so wait until you've got your coat on. It's cold this morning.'

'I've put out the sherry and Taffy's by the fire,' said Mrs Chubb comfortably, and withdrew to the kitchen.

'I'll show you your room,' said Aunt Kate. 'Come down again without waste of time, Matilda; we can unpack later on.'

She led the way up a narrow straight staircase to the square landing above and opened one of the doors there. The room was a fair size with a sloping roof and a pretty flowery paper on its walls. The furniture was painted white and there was a thick carpet underfoot and a patchwork quilt on the bed; the bedside lamps had pink shades and there were books, a biscuit tin and a tiny nosegay of violets on one of the bedside tables.

'The bathroom is next door, my dear, but do come down as soon as you're ready.'

Matilda, left alone, stood looking around her. The room was delightful; she knew that she would sleep peacefully in it and getting up in the morning would be a joy. And perhaps here she would be able to come to terms with herself, face the fact that to the doctor she was no more than someone who worked for him, someone whom he had considered it his duty to look after when she got the flu. He had been kind and concerned for her but it was Lucilla he intended to marry and she could quite understand why—any man would fall in love with those blonde good looks.

'But she won't make him happy,' Matilda told her pasty reflection as she powdered her nose. 'She's spiteful and most unkind. Not to him, of course...'

She went downstairs and went rather shyly into the

sitting room. Aunt Kate was there, sitting by the fire, a large ginger cat curled up on her lap.

'Come in, child. As you can see I can't get up with Taffy already asleep. He is so glad to have me home again. Will you pour us both a sherry? Come and sit down by the fire. You like your room?'

'It's charming, and what a big garden you have—I looked out of the window.'

'I enjoy gardening. Bob from the village does all the hard work, of course. And whenever Henry comes he advises me. He has rather a splendid garden behind his house. I dare say you've seen it?'

'Only briefly. I usually go in through the waiting-room door and leave the same way.'

'A lovely old place; you must get him to show you round it some time.'

A remark which needed only a polite murmur in response.

They lunched together presently: homemade vegetable soup, cheese omelettes, warm rolls and farm butter. Aunt Kate drank mineral water but Matilda was given a glass of milk.

'You need fattening up, child,' said Aunt Kate.

'That she does,' observed Mrs Chubb, removing plates. 'Thin as a sparrow and washed out. Nasty thing, this flu.' She beamed at them both. 'Send you back with colour in your cheeks, we will, won't we?'

'We will indeed, Mrs Chubb.'

It was impossible not to get better, reflected Matilda a few days later. On the one hand there was Aunt Kate, taking her for brisk walks, well wrapped up so that she went back to the house glowing, to spend happy hours going round the cottage with her hostess, looking at its treasures: its antique furniture, the silver displayed in the little bow-fronted cabinet, the paintings of long-dead Lovells on the walls.

'Of course Henry has most of them,' said Aunt Kate, 'and his mother has a very nice collection.'

Matilda wondered where that lady lived but didn't like to ask.

And on the other hand Mrs Chubb was determined to do her part in sending Matilda back a credit to her splendid cooking. Between the two ladies Matilda blossomed into pink-cheeked plumpness. She had been there for five happy days when she said, 'Miss Lovell, I love being here but I'm quite well again and I ought to go back to work. And Mother must be needing me at home; she's had to manage by herself for too long.'

Aunt Kate's beaky nose quivered—another woman would have sniffed.

'I am loath to let you go, Matilda. Henry suggested that you should stay a week and I respect his judgement. So we will enjoy another two days together, my dear. And now that you feel quite recovered I thought that we might go to Somerton tomorrow—there are one or two shops there and you have had no chance to spend your money. We might see a pretty dress. You always look nice, but one can never have enough clothes at your age.'

There was money in Matilda's purse: two weeks' wages and the overtime money that the doctor had insisted on paying her. She said now, 'I need a new raincoat...'

'No, Matilda,' said Aunt Kate decisively, 'you need a pretty dress. Sooner or later Mr Right, as my nanny always called him, will come along, and although he will certainly love you in a shabby mackintosh you will want to look your best.'

'I don't know any Mr Right!' said Matilda.

'That's what makes life so exciting—never knowing if he may be round the next corner.'

'Well,' said Matilda, 'if I see something I like…'

They went the next morning and after they had had coffee in a stylish little café Aunt Kate led the way to a boutique in a lane just off the main street.

'Henry's sisters often go here,' she told Matilda. 'Don't look at the prices in the window; there's a splendid selection of clothes inside at most reasonable prices.'

She led the way in and was met by a stout little woman who wished them good morning. She and Aunt Kate had had an interesting conversation already that morning and since Aunt Kate was a good customer she had agreed to alter the price tickets if the young lady decided to buy anything.

And, taking a look at Matilda's good tweed suit, not only out of date but not warm enough for the time of year, she could see that new clothes were a necessity.

'I want a dress,' said Matilda. 'Something that won't go out of date too soon, something I could wear for a formal occasion.' Was meeting Mr Right a formal occasion? she wondered, and smiled at the thought so that the sales lady decided that, properly dressed, she would look pretty…

There was a splendid choice and well within her budget. She chose a silk jersey top and skirt in a deep pink which gave her mundane features a glow, and, since she was assured that it was half price as it was a small size and unlikely to sell easily, she allowed herself to be helped into a winter coat. It was grey and of a slightly

military cut, and had, said the sales lady, been bought by
a customer who had decided that she didn't like it once
she got it home. Since it had been worn once, it would
have to be sold at a very reduced price or go into the January sale. So if the young lady didn't mind?

The young lady was delighted. True, she was almost
penniless, but she had been paying in most of her wages
into her father's account and as far as she knew there
were no big bills outstanding.

They left the shop presently and took the dress boxes
to the car.

'What marvellous luck,' said Matilda. 'It's like a mir-
acle, Miss Lovell.'

And worth every penny, reflected Aunt Kate, looking
at Matilda's happy face.

They had lunch at a hotel in the main street and then
spent a short time looking in the shop windows. And in
one of the small shops there was exactly the hat to go with
the new coat. And that accounted for the last money in
Matilda's purse. But there would be another pay day in a
week's time, and if her mother needed anything Christmas wasn't so far off; there would be presents to buy...

They went back to the cottage for tea and Matilda displayed her new clothes to Mrs Chubb, delighted to be told
that she looked a fair treat.

They went for a walk the next morning because she
wanted one more look at the country round her. It was
unlikely that she would visit Miss Lovell again; she had
loved every minute of her stay with the two elderly ladies, and their kindness and gentle spoiling and cheerful
talk. She would miss Taffy too, for after a cautious day
or so he had become her firm friend.

They spent the afternoon round the fire after Matilda

had phoned her mother to tell her that she would be home the next day. Mrs Paige had sounded peevish and expressed the hope that Matilda would settle down to a normal life once more. Matilda had gone to her room to pack then, wishing with all her heart that she weren't leaving in the morning.

She had asked hesitantly how she was to return and when Aunt Kate had said that she would take her Matilda had suggested that she might get a bus. It would be an awkward journey as she would have to change at Taunton but that was preferable to Aunt Kate wasting a morning taking her back. But Aunt Kate shook her head at the idea. 'Besides, I want to see Henry again.'

So after breakfast Matilda put on the new coat and hat and went along to the kitchen to say goodbye to Mrs Chubb and give her the scarf she had bought for her. She was hugged and kissed for it and told to be a good girl and not to work too hard. She went in search of Aunt Kate and gave her the little china figure they had both admired in a shop at Somerton; she made her thank-you speech too because there might not be a chance to do that once they got back to Much Winterlow. She was hugged and kissed once more and only then noticed that Aunt Kate was still without her hat and coat, but before she had time to ask about that the door opened and Dr Lovell came in.

His good morning was genial; he kissed his aunt and then turned to study Matilda.

'Ah—our Miss Paige, fully restored to good health,' he observed. 'You feel quite well?'

So she was to be Miss Paige once more. The warm friendliness while she had been ill had been temporary. She said woodenly, 'Yes, thank you, Doctor; I feel quite well again.'

As indeed she was, nicely plumped out and with a pretty colour in her cheeks. The doctor had seen the coat and the fetching little hat too. She looked pretty, but not as pretty as when she had been sweeping up leaves in some shapeless garment with her hair blowing all over the place.

'You must have coffee before you go,' said Aunt Kate into the silence, and expertly on cue Mrs Chubb came in with the coffee tray.

'Oh,' said Matilda, 'but I thought I was going back with you, Miss Lovell?'

She sounded so disappointed that the doctor said quickly, 'I'm afraid you will have to put up with me. You would like to go straight home, I expect?'

'Yes, please. It's very kind of you to take me.' She added anxiously, 'I'm not wasting your morning?'

'Not at all.' He sounded casually polite. His morning, he reflected, was something he had been looking forward to.

'Have you seen anything of Lucilla?' asked Aunt Kate.

'No. No, I haven't.' He hadn't thought about her either. 'I've been quite busy; the flu's over but it is quite a busy time of year. I've been lucky enough to borrow a nurse from the Taunton health centre but she can't wait to get back there.' He smiled at Matilda. 'We have all missed you and I'm sure your mother and father will be delighted to have you home again.'

Matilda said politely, 'Yes, I think they will,' and fell silent for lack of anything else to say. Then, after a pause, she added, 'I shall be glad to come back to work.'

'And we shall all be glad to see you again.'

They left presently and since the doctor didn't seem disposed to talk Matilda sat beside him and didn't utter a word. It didn't take long to reach Much Winterlow, which in the circumstances was a good thing.

He drove straight through the village and along the road to the cottage, and if Matilda had expected a warm welcome she didn't get it.

Her mother met them at the door. 'You didn't do any shopping on the way?' she asked crossly. 'There's nothing much in the house. You'll have to go this afternoon.'

Mrs Paige became all at once charming. 'Forgive me, Doctor, but my nerves are quite shattered. I've struggled along somehow but I'm exhausted.'

She led the way into the sitting room. 'Your father's in the study. You had better go and see him, Matilda. Doctor, come and sit down. It will be a treat for me to have someone to talk to.'

He followed her into the room and sat down. A tiresome woman, selfish to the bone; he had seen Matilda's face and it had left him strangely disquieted.

'Mr Paige keeps well?' he asked.

'Oh, yes. As long as he has his books and his writing he is happy.' Mrs Paige gave a sigh. 'He is a good deal older than I.' Her smile held a calculated wistfulness. 'I do miss the busy social life I had…'

'You will find that there is plenty of social life in the village. And you can safely go there now the flu is over.'

He stood up as Matilda came into the room. 'If your mother needs some shopping done you had better come back with me.'

Which made sense. Matilda nodded. 'Thank you. What do you want me to buy, Mother?'

Her mother said peevishly, 'Everything. There's almost nothing in the house; I knew you would be back

today.' She added, 'You'll have enough money with
you...'

'No, I haven't.'

Matilda looked guilty, thinking of the coat and dress
she had bought, and as though her mother had read her
thoughts she said, 'Well, not surprising, I suppose. You've
spent it all on yourself.'

Matilda had gone very pink in the face, aware of the
doctor standing there. She said, 'If you could give me a
list and some money, Mother.'

She didn't look higher than the doctor's waistcoat.
'Please don't wait; the walk to the shop will be pleasant
after sitting in the car.'

The pink got deeper. 'What I mean is—the car's most
comfortable, I enjoyed the drive and thank you for bringing me, but I'm sure you must want to get home...'

He took pity on her. 'It's my day off and I have nothing
to do but please myself. So we will go back to the village
and if your mother can spare you for an hour or so you
must have a word with Mrs Inch and Kitty.'

'I've no time to make a list,' said Mrs Paige crossly.
'You'll have to bring whatever you can think of.'

She took money from her handbag. 'And bring the
receipt back.'

Matilda could think of nothing to say as they drove
back to Mrs Simpkins' shop. The doctor had got out and
opened the door before she had a chance to do it. He went
into the shop with her too and wandered around looking at the shelves while she made her purchases. The
money her mother had given her wouldn't go far—tea
and sugar, butter, streaky bacon and eggs, a tin of the
cheapest salmon, cheese, macaroni. Matilda, after tot-

ting everything up in her head, added a packet of biscuits.
There was just enough money over for three lamb chops.

Mrs Simpkins kept up a cheerful flow of talk as she
assembled the food, but that didn't prevent the doctor,
who had excellent hearing, from knowing exactly what
Matilda had bought.

There was something wrong somewhere, he reflected.
Mr Paige would have a pension, surely, and he must have
received some kind of financial assistance when he'd retired, or at least had capital of some sort. Obviously it
was necessary for Matilda to get a job so that she might
be independent of her parents, but it looked as though she
was the breadwinner. And, now he came to think about
it, Mrs Milton had mentioned one day that Mrs Paige put
them all to shame at the bridge afternoons. 'So smart,'
she had explained in her kind voice. 'But of course she
has good clothes—I admire a woman who takes such
pains with her appearance. And that costs money but
her husband is devoted to her and she lacks for nothing.
So nice to see in a middle-aged couple, don't you think?'

He hadn't thought much about it at the time but now
he frowned down at a stack of washing powder. It was
none of his business, of course, but it seemed to him that
Matilda was entitled to spend every penny she earned
on herself if she wished to do so. And heaven knows, he
thought wryly, the girl's got no looks to speak of and a
little pampering would be an improvement.

He looked at her now, stowing groceries into plastic
bags. There was no sign of the happiness he had seen on
her face that morning at Aunt Kate's. But neither was
there discontent. She might not be a beauty but he had
to admit there was something very restful about Matilda.

He took the bags from her, bade Mrs Simpkins good day and led the way across the street to his house.

As he ushered her into the hall Matilda said, 'I'll only stay for a minute. I should get home and I'm sure you have things to do...'

He didn't answer and Mrs Inch came into the hall then.

'Bless me, miss, you're a sight for sore eyes, to be sure, and it's a pleasure to see you looking so well.' And when Kitty followed her the pair of them hovered over her, beaming.

Presently the doctor said, 'Could we have lunch earlier than usual, Mrs Inch? Miss Paige has to get back to her home.'

'Give me ten minutes,' declared Mrs Inch. 'Let Kitty take your coat and hat, miss, and you and the doctor can have a cosy chat until I'm ready.'

Mrs Inch bustled off and Matilda gave her things to the waiting Kitty. It was only when they were in the drawing room, sitting by the fire with Sam between them, that she said quietly, 'I would rather not have stayed. If I had known...'

Sitting in his chair, completely at ease, he smiled at her.

'We have been working together for some weeks now, haven't we? Isn't it time we got to know each other a little?'

'Why?' asked Matilda.

'I think that we might like each other better if we made the effort.'

Which wasn't the answer she had expected and one which she found difficult to reply to. What would he say, she reflected, if she were to tell him that she loved him, had fallen in love with him right from the start? Probably give her the sack, she thought ruefully.

'Why are you smiling?' he wanted to know.

She shook her head. 'I'm glad the flu epidemic is over. It was all a bit of a rush, wasn't it? Have all your patients recovered?'

He accepted the change in conversation without comment.

'Yes, I'm glad to say. You'll find the surgery pretty busy, though. I take it you will come in on Monday morning?'

'Yes, of course. It will be very nice to see everyone again.'

'You enjoyed your stay with Aunt Kate?'

Her smile was enchanting. 'Oh, yes. It was a most wonderful week. She is so kind, and so is Mrs Chubb. They spoilt me dreadfully.'

A little spoiling wouldn't hurt, thought the doctor. He felt concern for her for it seemed that life at home wasn't all it should be. A pretty woman, he thought, with a plain daughter and taking out her disappointment about that on the girl.

He took his phone from his pocket. 'I'll tell your mother you will be home shortly,' he said. She heard the kindness in his voice and winced at it. His pity was the last thing she wanted; it was a pity that he had been there when she'd got home. She hoped that her mother would be nice on the phone, but it was difficult to tell for he spoke briefly and watching his face gave her no clue.

They had lunch presently: chicken soup not out of a tin; a vast ham on the bone which the doctor carved with a practised skill; a winter salad followed by a mincemeat tart and cream and then coffee.

Matilda enjoyed it all for she was hungry and saw no

reason to pretend that she wasn't. And the good food and the glass of wine he poured for her loosened her tongue so that she forgot to be shy and stiff.

The doctor, watching her and listening to her quiet voice, felt a vague stirring of something he had never felt before. He told himself that it was pity and knew that to be wrong. Matilda wasn't to be pitied, nor would she ever accept it.

Chapter 6

Matilda was driven home by the doctor, but he didn't stop this time. Which was a good thing for her mother was waiting for her, brimming over with ill temper. She held it in check while the doctor carried the groceries into the kitchen, thanking him with a charming smile which turned to thin-lipped annoyance the moment he had gone.

'You should have come straight back here, Matilda. How can you be so selfish, knowing that your father and I were depending on you to bring the groceries?'

'Dr Lovell did say that he was taking me to see Mrs Inch and Kitty, Mother. Haven't you been to Mrs Simpkins' while I've been away?'

'I phoned—a boy brought my order. You didn't expect me to go into the village with all this flu about? I told her I would settle the bills later.'

Matilda started to unpack the bags. 'Mother, Father gives you housekeeping money; what has happened to it?'

Mrs Paige rounded on her. 'Don't you dare to criticise me, Matilda. There are three mouths to feed on a pittance.'

'But, Mother, I pay my share so it's two mouths, isn't it? And we both know that there isn't a lot of money but there is enough if we're careful.'

'Am I not to be considered? Living in this dull little place with no friends and nothing to do, nowhere to go...'

'Well, you go to play bridge with Mrs Milton and her friends, Mother, and she did invite you to help out with the church flowers and the Christmas bazaar. You'll meet lots of people if only you would go to the village sometimes—not just the people you meet at bridge.'

'I shall go and lie down,' declared Mrs Paige. 'You've given me a headache; I quite wish you hadn't come home.'

Matilda put away the food and went to see her father. He looked up from his writing, pleased to see her.

'It is very pleasant to have you home again, my dear. Your mother will be so relieved. She has had so much to do; I only wish that I could do more for her. She deserves a holiday; I must see if I can manage to send her to stay with one of her friends for a few days. She misses them so much.'

He sighed. 'She still thinks of the vicarage as home...'

'Well, perhaps we could manage it between us, Father; it would only be the train fare and the bus to Taunton.'

'She would need money in her purse; I couldn't send her away empty-handed.'

He shuffled the papers on his desk. 'There is a bill which I must pay then perhaps she could go in a week or so.' He said worriedly, 'I don't know where the money goes, my dear. I must be a bad manager.'

'No, you're not, Father; it's just taking time to adjust to living on your pension.'

He had found the bill and she took it from him and said cheerfully, 'Well, we could see to this; are there any more?'

He sifted through the muddle. There were. Her mother had made no bones about owing the milkman, the newsagent's, the butcher who came twice a week to the village. She had phoned the orders and now, after a month, the bills were coming in. They didn't add up to a great deal but Matilda thought unhappily that they could have been paid with the money she had spent on her coat and dress. Common sense told her that she had no need to feel guilty, but she did.

'If you will see to these, Father,' said Matilda, 'there will be enough money for Mother to go away for a few days.' And when he looked doubtful she said, 'I don't need next week's pay packet...'

Christmas was coming, she reflected; there would be presents to buy, cards to send, extra food. Perhaps if her mother had a few days away she would settle down.

Although the flu epidemic was over, the waiting room was quickly filled on Monday morning: nasty coughs, bad chests, earache—all the minor ailments which made life harder than it needed to be. But everyone was glad to see Matilda, glad to see her well again, anxious to know if she felt really better.

Not quite everyone, though. The doctor, arriving punctually, wished her a cool good morning and made no mention of her health. She was back on her feet again and that was that. And when the last patient had gone he put his head round the door to tell her that he was going to Taunton.

'The answering machine's on and I should be back by early afternoon. Mrs Inch will bring you coffee. Lock up, if you will.'

At least he hadn't called her Miss Paige—he hadn't called her anything.

Mrs Inch had a cup of coffee with her.

'Rushing off like that,' she grumbled, and offered Matilda a biscuit. 'Swallowing his coffee in the kitchen in such a rush. Give himself an ulcer he will. He had a phone call from that Miss Armstrong quite early this morning. I dare say he's going to see her on his way to Taunton.'

Matilda said, 'Quite likely, I dare say. She lives at North Curry, doesn't she? And that's only a mile or two away from Taunton.'

He would be there by now, she thought, and shut her mind to the thought. Being in love with someone was most unsatisfactory when they didn't care a row of pins for you. Possibly one got used to that just as one got used to the small nagging pain of a corn. Not that she knew what that was like; she had pretty feet which gave her no trouble at all…

She called at Mrs Simpkins' for some eggs, listened to that lady's vivid description of her varicose veins with patient sympathy and then went home.

Her mother greeted her coldly; she wasn't to be allowed to feel that she was forgiven, but her father, already busy at his desk, was delighted to see her.

'I have been thinking of our little talk, my dear, and I think your suggestion concerning a little holiday for your mother is most acceptable. Needless to say, I am deeply grateful for your help. I promise you that once we have got our financial situation settled you will be repaid tenfold.'

'Don't worry about that, Father. Mother will be pleased—you must tell her.' She looked at her father; he looked tired and pale. 'You feel all right?'

'Splendid, my dear. I shall talk to your mother presently. I've no doubt that she will lose no time in writing to one of our friends.'

Mrs Paige was mollified by the prospect of a visit with old friends. She grumbled too; she would need money to spend while she was there, she pointed out, and there were bound to be small expenses...

Matilda handed over almost all of her pay packet at the end of the week and hoped it would be enough, although she doubted that. But the visit was to be a short one—five or six days—and if her mother was careful...

So Mrs Paige packed the elegant clothes she had had little opportunity of wearing at Much Winterlow and was put on the bus to Taunton on Saturday afternoon. She would have liked a taxi but, as Matilda explained, there really wasn't enough money for that and since her mother was to be met at Taunton by her friend the journey would be an easy one for her.

Mrs Milton came to drive her father to church on Sunday and Matilda went too, in the new hat and coat, and of course she was thankful that she was wearing them when she saw Lucilla sitting beside the doctor. They were sitting on the other side of the aisle to Mrs Milton and she was careful not to look across to their pew.

After the service she would have slipped out of the church but her father wouldn't be hurried. Even though he didn't go to the village he had friends there—older men who came to see him from time to time—and what better time to exchange a few words than after morning church? Mrs Milton was never in a hurry; they dawdled towards the church door and found the Reverend Mr Milton talking to the doctor. Lucilla was there too, looking bored, and Matilda said quickly to Mrs Milton, 'I'll walk home and have lunch ready for Father. You don't mind? He does so enjoy his weekly chat.'

Which meant that she needed only to bid a general good morning as she passed them. Out of the corner of her eye she saw Lucilla's nasty little smile.

She was up early on Monday morning. It was too soon for her father to get up but she took him a cup of tea and left his breakfast ready for him. 'I'll be back soon after ten o'clock,' she assured him. 'If it's not too cold we could go for a short walk before lunch. You won't be too lonely?'

He was looking tired again, she thought, although he assured her that he had had a good night's sleep.

It was a fine morning, still dark and frosty, and once in the waiting room, not yet warmed by the radiators, she thought longingly of Aunt Kate's cosy cottage. 'Which won't do at all,' said Matilda, addressing the empty room. 'You're back here now, Miss Paige.'

The waiting room filled up rapidly—mostly mothers with small snuffling children who were peevish with colds and coughs. Mrs Trim was there with what she described as a nasty chest and old Mr Trimble was short-tempered by reason of his persistent cough. There was a good deal of talk; Christmas was the main topic: the carol singers and Mrs Simpkins' splendid display of Christmas goods, the play the amateur theatrical society would be putting on, the schoolchildren's concert.

They fell silent when the doctor put his head round the door with a general good morning and the first patient went into the surgery. The hubbub started up again immediately until he returned, often enough to give a highly coloured version of what was wrong with him

and give a good deal of good-natured advice to the following patient.

Matilda, sitting in her corner, in her sober dress, sometimes felt like a schoolteacher with an unruly class. But
it was all so good-natured and she quite understood that
for people living some distance from the village it was a
splendid chance to have a good gossip.

The last patient seen, the doctor opened the surgery
door.

'Have your coffee before you go, Miss Paige,' he said
and went back to sit at his desk, spectacles perched on
his handsome nose, a pile of forms before him. He didn't
look up as she sat down on the other side of the desk and
poured the coffee. He nodded his thanks when she put
his cup down at his elbow, and without looking up said,
'Just let me finish these...'

Just as though I was making a nuisance of myself,
thought Matilda indignantly, but then he looked up and
smiled.

'Would you come with me to Duckett's Farm? I've bad
news for Mr Duckett and his wife. There's a small child;
I thought that you might come in handy—playing with
him and so on so that I can talk to them quietly. Tell me
if it's not possible; perhaps you had already arranged to
go home. You might like to phone your mother...'

'Mother is staying with friends, Father's alone. If I
could let him know that I might be a little late for lunch,
of course I'll come. Now?'

'Please. The phone's in the hall if you would like to
use it.' He looked at her over his specs and smiled again
and her heart turned over.

Duckett's Farm was three miles from the village,
rather isolated, with ploughed fields surrounding it and

a muddy track leading to the farmyard from a narrow country lane. The house was a fair size but, on this winter day, bleak, huddled in a circle of farm buildings. Matilda wondered if anyone living there could be happy and, as the doctor pushed open the door and she went past him into a warm, low-ceilinged hall, saw that they could. Another door gave her a glimpse of a large room, a roaring fire in the hearth, bright curtains at the small windows. Whoever lived here, she reflected, had made a home.

A voice answered the doctor's hello. 'In the kitchen; I'm just coming.'

A young woman pushed open another door and came towards them, smiling. A small boy toddled beside her and went straight to the doctor, who picked him up and tucked him under an arm.

'Is Rob around, Mrs Duckett?'

She said quickly, 'You've got the results of those tests, Doctor?' When he nodded she said, 'He's in the barn; I'll give him a shout—or do you want to see him alone?'

'I think we must have a talk, Mrs Duckett.' His voice was very kind. 'I've brought my receptionist with me— Matilda Paige; I thought that she might keep an eye on Tom while we go somewhere quiet.'

Mrs Duckett nodded, not trusting herself to speak. But she smiled at Matilda as she went to the door and shouted for her husband. The doctor handed over small Tom to Matilda and he went willingly enough, pleased to see a new face. She hoisted him up and carried him over to a chair by the fire and sat down, talking in her quiet voice, a gentle trickle of sound which took his attention so that he hardly noticed when the doctor told her that they would be back presently and the three of them left the room.

He had told her something of Rob Duckett, a young man still, ignoring a cough and malaise, putting off seeing the doctor until he could no longer ignore the fact that something was wrong. He had been sent for tests and X-rays and the results were what the doctor had expected. And he had the task of telling Rob, knowing that although an operation might be successful Rob might refuse, for who could run the farm while he was away?

Matilda, reciting nursery rhymes, hoped that there would be a solution. The look on Mrs Duckett's face had wrung her heart. She began on 'A Frog he would a-wooing go' and reminded herself that if there was a solution the doctor would find it.

Little Tom liked hearing about the frog, so she recited it again and then again. They came back into the room then but she stayed where she was and since the little boy was quiet on her lap she began on the frog rhyme once more.

Presently Mrs Duckett came across the room to her. She had been crying but her voice was quite steady.

'It's kind of you, miss; he's quite taken to you.'

'He's a darling, isn't he? And do please call me Matilda. Would you like me to do anything for you? Make some tea?'

'I've put the kettle on if you'd like to come into the kitchen?'

Matilda, still cuddling Tom, went with her into the nice old-fashioned kitchen with its scrubbed table and elderly Aga. There was a cat with kittens in a basket and a sheepdog snoozing.

'Do you know,' asked Mrs Duckett, 'about my Rob?'

'Dr Lovell told me a little. I'm so sorry, Mrs Duckett,

but Dr Lovell will know what's best to be done and Mr Duckett is young and strong.'

Mrs Duckett put tea in a vast pot. 'He wants Rob to have an operation; says it's got a good chance of being successful. But Rob isn't wanting that. He's worried about the farm.'

'You want him to have the operation?'

'Me? Yes, of course. But finding someone to come here and help on the farm, just before Christmas, too...'

'But if your husband has the operation soon he might be home by Christmas. He couldn't do anything much, but he'd be here to see to everything, wouldn't he?'

Mrs Duckett was pouring tea into four mugs. 'He's a good man, our doctor.'

'Yes,' said Matilda, 'and I think you could trust him to the ends of the earth.' Something in her voice made her companion look at her sharply.

Driving back presently, Matilda asked, 'What has Mr Duckett decided? It's a terrible thing to happen and he's a young man.'

'He's agreed to an operation and since he is a young man he has an excellent chance of recovery.'

'Good. But he was worried about the farm.'

'I think that can be sorted out.'

Not exactly a snub but she had the strong feeling that he thought she was being nosy. But even if he did he was going to make use of her.

'I shall drive him to hospital the day after tomorrow. Mrs Duckett will go with us. I would be glad if you would stay at the farm with Tom. I shall be bringing back her mother who will look after the place while he is away.'

'Alone? Me, I mean, with Tom.'

'John who helps with the milking will be there. You're not a nervous girl, are you?'

'No,' said Matilda in a voice positive enough to convince herself as well as him.

'Good. I'll drive you home.'

She hadn't expected him to get out of the car when they reached the cottage, but he did, following her into the hall just as though she had invited him.

She said pointedly, 'Do come in, Doctor.'

'Well, I am in, aren't I? I'd like to take a look at your father.'

The reasonable remark made her feel a fool. She offered coffee and when he accepted flounced off to the kitchen, her face red.

She took the coffee to her father's study when it was ready and the doctor took the tray from her with the air of a man who expected her to go away again at once.

It was high time to prepare their lunch. She had laid the table, and the soup was on the stove and eggs beaten for an omelette when he came into the kitchen. He had the coffee tray with him and set it tidily by the sink.

'When will your mother be back?' he asked.

'Well, she was coming back on Thursday but she phoned yesterday evening to say that she might stay a day or two longer. Is Father all right? Should she come back? I mean, he has to spend a good part of the day alone.'

'There's nothing to worry about at the moment and there is no reason why he shouldn't be alone for a few hours at a time. But if you will allow me to do so I'll get Kitty or Mrs Inch to come here on Wednesday while you are at Duckett's Farm. Your father has no objection and they can see to lunch and give him tea before they go. I should be back by five o'clock at the latest. I'm sorry I didn't think of this earlier but little Tom likes you and they live in too isolated a place for anyone to be prepared to go there at short notice.' And at her look he added, 'I regard you as a sensible young woman able to cope.'

Should she tell him that she was terrified of meeting a bull, or a large herd of cows, for that matter, and that the idea of spending the day miles from anywhere with a small boy and an unknown farmhand really didn't appeal?

She looked up at his calm face and decided to say nothing. With her loving him so much it was a foregone conclusion that she would, if necessary, go through fire and water for him, so why boggle at a bull or two?

She said sedately, 'You have arranged things very well, Doctor. It will be nice for Father to have company.' She remembered something then. 'You said that there was nothing to worry about for the moment. Will you explain that?'

'Your father is well; I examined him thoroughly. I have no wish to alarm you but you should know that someone with his heart condition could be taken ill at any time, probably without warning. You are sensible enough to realise that there is no point in anticipating something which may never happen. All the same you should know, and I think your mother should understand that too.'

He studied her quiet face, smiled and went to the door. She went with him and he paused as he reached it and bent and kissed her. A gentle kiss and somehow reassuring.

She watched him get into the car and drive away and then went back into the kitchen and got out the frying pan, wondering about the kiss. He would have no idea what it had done to her, of course; probably he had bestowed it with the same kindly intent with which he would have stroked a kitten or indeed comforted a crying child. But it mustn't happen again.

He was his usual remote self at the evening surgery; beyond wishing her goodnight when it was finished, he had nothing to say.

She got her father's breakfast ready before she left on Wednesday morning, reassured by his obvious pleasure at the prospect of company for lunch. He told her to go and enjoy herself. She hoped she would but she was doubtful about it.

There was a mercifully short surgery; they drank their coffee in silence while the doctor wrote then went out to the car. It was a cold, blustery day and she shivered as they got out of the car at the farm.

There were lights on in the downstairs rooms and Mr and Mrs Duckett were waiting in the kitchen. There was a youngish man there too—John, who grinned and ducked his head at them.

'There's been no time,' began Mrs Duckett rather wildly. 'There's soup ready and a milk pudding in the oven. You'll manage?'

'Don't worry, Mrs Duckett, we'll be fine. And good luck, Mr Duckett.' And, because Mrs Duckett looked so forlorn, Matilda kissed her cheek and picked up little Tom so that he could say goodbye.

They didn't waste time. 'See you around five o'clock,' said the doctor, and drove his passengers away without a backward glance.

Beyond a faint whimper, Tom didn't cry. Matilda sat

him in his high chair, offered him a rusk and turned to
John.

'You won't be far away?' she asked.

'Got to turn the cows out into the lower field, then I
muck out the barn, come in for a mug of tea and then
see to the feed. I'll be around if you need me, miss. I'll
be off now—a bit behind already.'

By five o'clock Matilda was tired. She'd been busy
finding her way around the house, peering into cupboards, hunting for the tea, sugar, salt—all the day-to-
day things which were never where she expected them to
be, as well as feeding Tom and John, the dog and a family
of cats. She'd played with Tom, and while he had a nap
after their midday meal she'd ironed the pile of washing
which she was sure Mrs Duckett wouldn't feel like doing.

John had been a great help, but he had his work to do:
the milking and the feeding, the small flock of sheep to
check, coming indoors from time to time for a mug of tea.

'Good thing the missus 'as got 'er ma coming back
with 'er—lives at 'Atch Beauchamp. She'll stay a while
until things are sorted.'

'And you'll be here to run the farm, John?'

'Yup.'

'Shouldn't you be going home about now?'

'Yup—but I'll stay till the doctor comes. 'E said five
o'clock and 'e's a man of 'is word.'

Matilda, sitting at the kitchen table and coaxing a
sleepy Tom to eat his supper, hoped that he was right.

And he was. She saw the car's headlights as it entered
the yard and a moment later Mrs Duckett and an older
woman came in, followed by the doctor.

He nodded at Matilda, greeted John and said cheerfully, 'Sorry we are a bit late. Everything all right?'

John said, 'Yup,' and Matilda nodded. Mrs Duckett had gone at once to Tom and her mother was taking off her coat and hat.

'The kettle is boiling,' said Matilda. 'Shall I make tea?'

'You'll want to go on home, miss,' said Mrs Duckett. 'I'm grateful. Has Tom been good?'

'As gold. We've had a lovely day together and John's been a marvellous help.'

She wanted to ask about Mr Duckett but hesitated. Supposing it was bad news? But Mrs Duckett forestalled her. 'Rob's having his operation in the morning. Doctor's fixed someone to take me to the hospital in the afternoon and I can stay if I need to now Mother's here.'

She managed a smile. 'He says everything will be all right…'

'And it will be,' said Matilda, 'if he said so.'

The doctor, talking to John, heard that and allowed himself a little smile.

He drove her home then, stopping briefly at his own home on the way. And at the cottage he went in with her, spent a few moments with her father, thanked her briefly and went away again, and this time he didn't kiss her.

Her father had had a pleasant day. Mrs Inch had come at lunchtime and cooked a delicious meal and stayed for an early cup of tea.

'And she told me to tell you that she had left our supper on the stove.'

And when Matilda went to look there was a casserole only needing to be heated up. It looked delicious and her mouth watered.

The week resumed its normal sober pattern. The waiting room filled and emptied, the doctor bade her good morning and good evening, took himself off to Taunton and his far-flung patients, and although he invited her to share his coffee in the mornings she found some excuse not to accept. He showed no sign of minding this but he did keep her informed about Rob Duckett. The operation had been successful; he was still in Intensive Care and would be in hospital for some time yet, but there was a good chance that he would be home for Christmas.

The doctor gave her this information in a business-like way, told her that he had been out to the farm and that Mrs Duckett and Tom sent their love. 'Tom's a nice child...'

'He's a darling,' said Matilda warmly.

'You like children?'

'Yes,' said Matilda. Especially if they were her own and the doctor was their father. Only she didn't say that.

She was glad when it was Friday and she had some money. Her mother had phoned again; friends of the friends she was staying with intended to drive to their daughter's home at Wellington and had offered her a lift, on Sunday.

'It's not too far out of their way,' she had explained. 'I've asked them to stay for tea. We should be home about three o'clock, so have tea ready for four o'clock, Matilda. Get scones and make a cake and see that there's a good fire in the sitting room. Don't fetch your father to the phone; we're just going out to dinner and there's no time. Give him my love.'

So Matilda walked down to Mrs Simpkins' on Saturday morning and presently emerged with two plastic bags and a lighter purse. The doctor, standing at his window, watched her going off home, frowning. It was no concern of his, of course, but Matilda didn't appear to have much fun in her life. No sign of a boyfriend, drab clothes except for the new coat and hat. He might suggest that she might like a few days' holiday before Christmas. Aunt Kate would be delighted to have her again. He might even go over and take her out—dinner perhaps?

He turned away to answer the telephone. It was Lucilla, inviting him in a coaxing voice to take her out to lunch. And since it was his day off he agreed. But later, sitting opposite her at the Castle Hotel in Taunton, he found himself wishing that it were Matilda sitting there and not Lucilla.

Mr Paige, warmly wrapped up, was fetched to church on Sunday morning by Mrs Milton, leaving Matilda free to get lunch and do some baking. While the cake was in the oven she hoovered and dusted, arranged the very last of the chrysanthemums in a vase, and lit the fire in the sitting room. She got out the best china too, and the silver teaspoons, and put everything out ready for tea. Rastus, watching her from his chair in the kitchen, yawned and went to sleep, but, having no one else to talk to, Matilda went on talking to him.

'It will be nice to see Mother again,' she told him, 'and I dare say that now she's had a holiday she will feel much more settled. And there's Christmas to look forward to.'

Mrs Milton had mentioned several social events in the village; perhaps they could all go. Her father, once he could be prised from his books and writing, enjoyed meeting people...

Her mother arrived home soon after three o'clock and two people came with her—a large red-faced man, middle-aged and with a loud voice, and a very thin woman of about the same age, most elegantly dressed and with a voice almost as loud as her husband's. Mrs Paige, wearing a new hat, Matilda saw with a sinking heart, ushered her guests in with little cries of apology.

'Come in, come in. Our funny little cottage—only temporary of course. And this is our daughter, Matilda.'

She didn't wait for Matilda to do more than shake hands. 'Fetch your father, Matilda. Take off your coats and come into the sitting room. At least it will be warm there.'

Matilda fetched her father and they went together to the sitting room where Mrs Paige greeted him effusively and then caught Matilda's eye.

'We'll have tea now. I hope it's quite ready.'

Their guests made a splendid tea and, taking a second slice of cake, pronounced it delicious.

'Oh, Matilda cooks quite well. Such a help to me. It seems so strange that someone as delicate as I am should have such a sensible, practical daughter.'

Two pairs of eyes studied Matilda. From their expressions she guessed that they agreed with her mother, dismissing her as plain and uninteresting but handy to have around. Well, thought Matilda, I am, and smiled at them so that for the moment she wasn't plain at all.

They left presently and her mother embarked on an excited account of the visit. 'I felt so well while I was there; I feel I can face life here once more, and I found a marvellous book for you, dear.' She smiled at Mr Paige. 'I hope it's what you will enjoy.

'And I've something for you, Matilda: gloves—woolly gloves. To keep your hands warm when you go out in the mornings.' She added, 'And I have bought one or two things for myself—the shops were so tempting.'

'That's a pretty hat,' said Matilda.

'Isn't it? I felt rather naughty buying it—it was rather

more than I usually pay—but I couldn't resist it. I've spent every penny…'

And when Mr Paige looked worried she said, 'Don't worry, dear; I know Matilda will help out until your pension is paid into the bank.'

Matilda wondered just what would happen if she said that she wasn't going to help out. Something she would never do because of her father. A quiet life and no worries, the doctor had said.

She presented her usual quiet face at the surgery on Monday morning, presided over the waiting room with her habitual good nature and, when bidden to drink coffee with the doctor when the surgery was closed, politely refused.

A waste of breath. 'I have something to say to you,' said the doctor in a voice which wasn't going to take no for an answer.

But it wasn't until she had almost drunk her coffee that he spoke.

'I think it might be a good idea if you were to have a few days' holiday.'

'But I've just had one with Miss Lovell. Aren't I being satisfactory?'

'You are perfectly satisfactory, Matilda. And that wasn't a holiday, that was convalescence after flu. You may tell me that it is none of my business if you wish, but it seems to me that you have very little opportunity to enjoy life. Have you no young friends of your own age? Men friends? You should be thinking about marriage, a home of your own. Your mother depends upon you, doesn't she? But she has no need to do so. She is able to run her home and look after your father without your

Chapter 7

Mrs Paige welcomed Matilda's news that she was to take a brief holiday with unexpected enthusiasm.

'But how fortunate. As you will be home all day for a few days I shall be able to go to Taunton. We must start to think of Christmas; there will be presents to buy and cards—and you will be home to help me write them. Lady Truscott is giving a dinner party; we are sure to be invited. And I really must return the hospitality I have received—a coffee morning, perhaps.'

Matilda didn't say anything. The doctor had mentioned Aunt Kate but she thought that he had done so in order to persuade her to have some days off. She didn't want them but she couldn't tell him that they would be spent at home for the most part.

All that nonsense about men friends... In bed that night she cried about that, making Rastus, curled up beside her, very damp.

On Wednesday morning, when the surgery was over, she asked him when he would like her to have her days off.

He looked at her, as neat as a new pin, sitting opposite him, drinking the coffee he'd insisted that she should have.

help. Have you ever considered leaving home? You are perfectly capable of earning your own living.'

'You think I should go away from here?' And never see you again? she added silently.

'See something of the world, meet people, travel, perhaps?'

He found himself disliking that idea even as he uttered it. It was all very well suggesting that she should go and make a life for herself, but only if there was someone with her to look after her. She might be sensible and practical but she knew nothing of the world.

'Anyway, take a few days off before Christmas. Go shopping and pay Aunt Kate a visit.'

'I'll have to talk it over with Mother and Father—they may have planned something.'

'Just as you wish. I may be a little late this evening. Will you let the patients know?'

He had called her Matilda but now they were back at the beginning again. It was never going to be any different. She went quietly away and he didn't look up from his desk.

She was pale and there were shadows under her eyes. Lovely eyes, he conceded. There was a good deal he would have liked to say but Matilda could be contrary and tart and withdraw into her shell…

He said pleasantly, 'Are you going to the annual dance at the village hall on Saturday?' He didn't give her time to answer. 'Because if you haven't already made arrangements, will you come with me? Everyone goes—and I mean everyone.'

'Me? Go with you?' said Matilda. 'But what about Miss Armstrong?'

'What about Miss Armstrong?' asked the doctor silkily. 'I wasn't aware we were talking about her.'

'Well, of course we weren't,' said Matilda sharply, 'but ought you not to invite her?' She added, 'She might mind.'

'Lucilla is in the South of France and I hardly think she would have any objection to our more or less obligatory appearance together at a village function.'

'Oh, well,' said Matilda, 'in that case I'll come. Thank you for asking me. What should I wear?'

It would be a pleasure, reflected the doctor, to pop Matilda into his car and take her to a boutique and buy her the prettiest dress there. The thought surprised him so that he didn't answer at once.

'Not black tie,' he assured her, and saw her small sigh of relief. 'The women wear pretty dresses—you know, the kind of thing they wear to weddings and christenings. The dancing is a bit old-fashioned and there's a local band. This is a friendly village—but you have discovered that, haven't you?'

'Yes, it sounds fun.'

'Oh, it is; the vicar gives prizes and there's beer and ham sandwiches.'

She smiled then and a little colour came into her cheeks and he went on, 'I'm having a few days off myself next week. Will that suit you? And Aunt Kate wants you to go and stay, even if it's only for a day or so. She's writing to you.'

'I'd like to see her again but I'm not sure... Mother would like to go to Taunton and if I'm at home she can leave Father all day. And she is going to have a coffee morning.'

'That still leaves three or four days. Aunt Kate declared that she will drive over and fetch you.'

'Oh—I should very much like to see her again. I'll—I'll talk to Mother.'

'Good. I'm going to the Ducketts'. Rob is making excellent progress; he should be home for Christmas. Tom wants to see you again.'

'Does he? I'll borrow Mrs Simpkins' bike and go one afternoon. Mrs Duckett wouldn't mind?'

'Mrs Duckett happens to think you are a very nice young lady.' He got up to go. 'As indeed you are, Matilda.'

Matilda, pink in the face, wished him a muttered good morning and whisked herself back into the waiting room.

The postman drove up just as she reached the cottage. There was a letter for her from Aunt Kate—easily identified by the fine spidery writing and expensive notepaper. Matilda dawdled up the garden path, reading it.

Aunt Kate was inviting her to stay for the last two days of her holiday. She would drive over and fetch her and she would not take no for an answer.

Armed with that, Matilda went indoors to find her mother. Who wasn't pleased. 'How tiresome. It won't

do to offend the old lady, I suppose. I shall have to do
my shopping at the beginning of the week and have my
coffee morning on the Thursday. Really, people are most
inconsiderate.'

'And Dr Lovell has asked me to go to the annual dance
at the village hall.'

'Asked *you*? Whatever for? He's more or less engaged
to that Armstrong girl.'

'She's in France...'

'Oh, well, I suppose he has to show up at those village functions and take someone with him. Farm labour-
ers, I suppose...'

It was hard to like her mother sometimes. 'Yes, I expect so,' said Matilda.

If the doctor was looking forward to their Saturday
outing he gave no sign of it. The patients waiting their
turn at the surgery were full of it. Everyone was going, it
seemed. It was an event not to be missed. Matilda, asked
countless times if she was going, said yes, she was, but
she didn't say who with. The doctor might have invited
her but anything could happen before Saturday...

It wasn't until Friday evening, as she was clearing up
after the last patient had left, that he opened the waiting-
room door to speak to her about it.

'I'll call for you about half past seven,' he told her. 'It
starts at seven o'clock and everyone makes a point of getting there as early as possible.' He stood looking at her.
'You're going to Aunt Kate's at the end of next week?'

'Yes, Friday and Saturday. I'm looking forward to
that.'

He nodded. 'Good. I shall be away most of the week
myself. Dr Ross will come over each day and bring his

nurse with him. He'll be on call for emergencies. I hope everyone read the notice in the waiting room?'

'Yes, they did, and I told Mrs Simpkins.'

'Ah, yes. A wise move. Goodnight, Miss Paige.'

Miss Paige again, thought Matilda. He would be going to the South of France to be with Lucilla, of course. They would go together to the dance and he would dance the first dance with her and then hand her over politely to whoever was nearest.

'For two pins I won't go,' said Matilda, knowing that nothing on earth would stop her.

She was ready long before half past seven on Saturday; she had been afraid that some last-minute thing would hinder her and now she was in the sitting room with her mother and father. She had spent a long time on her hair and face but the result was exactly as usual. Only the new dress was a success. Even her mother had admired it, adding that it was a pity that Matilda couldn't do anything about her hair. 'You need to go to a good hairdresser and have a good cut and highlights.' But she hadn't said any more in case Matilda took her advice and spent money on the hairdresser Mrs Paige intended to visit if she could wheedle some money out of Matilda's purse...

Mr Paige said mildly, 'You look very pretty, my dear. I dare say you will have a delightful evening. I expect you will know many of the people there.'

Mrs Paige said impatiently, 'It is a village dance, dear; no one I know will be there. I suppose Dr Lovell feels that he must make an appearance.'

Matilda put on her coat; she had heard the squeak of the garden gate and a moment later came a knock on the door. She went to let the doctor in and he spent a moment or so with her father and mother before saying briskly, 'Shall we go? Have you a key? I don't suppose we shall be back before midnight.'

'Oh, I'll stay up,' said Mrs Paige. 'I usually keep early hours but I can always have a doze during the day. I do get so tired...'

'In that case there is no need for you to stay up, Mrs Paige. I'm sure Matilda is old enough to have a key.'

'Certainly she is,' said Mr Paige. 'Let her have yours, my dear.'

Matilda kissed him goodnight, received the key from her mother, who turned her cheek away, and went out to the car with the doctor. She wished that she could think of something light-hearted to say but her mother had cast a blight over the evening; she hadn't said much but somehow she had managed to cast a damper...

However, it seemed that the doctor hadn't noticed; he talked cheerfully about nothing much until they reached the village hall where he parked the car and ushered her inside. It was crowded and so noisy that the band could scarcely be heard. It was quite a large hall and it had been decorated with balloons and old-fashioned paper chains and it was evident that everyone was having a good time.

Matilda took off her coat and added it to the pile inside the door, then the doctor took her arm and swung her onto the dance floor.

'I like the dress,' he said to the top of her head. He sounded as though he meant it, too.

He danced well, she discovered, and although she hadn't had much opportunity to go dancing she was a good dancer. He would see friends—people she didn't know—and dance with them presently, she supposed, but just for the moment she was happy.

The crush was terrific and after a minute or two she began to pick out people she knew: Mrs Simpkins in red velvet dancing with a small man, presumably her husband; the pub owner, who shouted greetings to her; several patients, not easily recognised in their best clothes; the Reverend Mr and Mrs Milton; Lady Truscott and several of the ladies her mother had introduced her to from the bridge circle. And they were all enjoying themselves…

Presently the band leader announced an excuse-me dance and she was swept away from the doctor's arms into the jovial embrace of the milkman and then to a succession of partners—Mr Milton, the postman, the pub owner, and then, thankfully, the doctor once more.

'Enjoying yourself?' he wanted to know, and when the band stopped playing he found a quiet corner for her and then fetched ham sandwiches and a fizzy drink for her and beer for himself.

They danced again and Matilda, in his arms, had never been so happy. And the doctor, his arm encircling her small person, knew a deep contentment, as though he had found something he had been looking for and had found unexpectedly.

It was almost midnight when Lady Truscott, standing breathless beside them after a rousing quick-step, suggested that they should go back to her place for hot drinks. 'I'll collect the rest of us,' she told them. She smiled at Matilda. 'It's the done thing,' she confided. 'We slip away about now, and so do some of the older ones here, so that the younger ones can finish the evening with a disco.'

Before Matilda could say anything the doctor said,

'We would like that,' and then, to her, 'Don't worry; I'll take you home whenever you want to go.'

Lady Truscott's house was ablaze with lights and her housekeeper was waiting with hot coffee, tiny sausage rolls and hot mince pies. Matilda, looking round her, saw that as well as her own friends Lady Truscott had gathered several people from the village—Mrs Simpkins and her husband, several of the farmers and their wives from the local farms, the Reverend Mr and Mrs Milton, the peppery old colonel who lived opposite the church, and the pub owner and milkman. It was going to be difficult to explain to her mother.

She found herself standing beside the colonel, who, once you got to know him, wasn't peppery at all but talked about his garden, and when she told him what she planned to do with the cottage garden he promised her some seedlings in the spring. They were joined presently by Mr Simpkins, who, it appeared, was as keen a gardener as the colonel, and the doctor, watching from the other side of the room, saw Matilda's absorbed face, alight with interest.

How was it that he had considered her plain? She was nothing of the sort; her face was one at which it was a delight to look. He listened with apparent attention to Lady Truscott's descriptions of the various delights in store at the Christmas bazaar, assured her that he would be there, and added, 'This has been a delightful evening, Mary; you always organise things so well...'

Lady Truscott laughed. 'What else can an elderly widow do with her days, Henry? Do you have to go so soon?'

'I'm taking Matilda home.'

'What a dear creature she is, and so pretty in that

dress. A pity she doesn't get out more but her mother assures me that she is a homebird and doesn't care for much social life.'

A remark which he very much doubted.

He went across the room to Matilda and gently prised her away from the milkman and the colonel, watched her as she bade them goodbye and thanked her hostess with pretty manners, found her coat for her and stuffed her into the car.

'What a lovely evening,' declared Matilda. 'I wish it could have gone on for ever!' She glanced sideways at the doctor's calm profile. 'Thank you for inviting me; parties like that make it seem like Christmas, don't you think?'

She chatted on happily. 'Lady Truscott is such a friendly person and I thought the sandwiches at the party were delicious. I'm not sure what I had to drink; it tasted a bit like strong lemonade.'

'A special drink which I believe the committee agreed upon,' said the doctor gravely, knowing it was hardly lemonade and certainly potent enough—despite Lady Truscott's excellent coffee—to loosen Matilda's normally prudent tongue.

'I'm quite sleepy,' volunteered Matilda, and then added, 'We're on holiday next week…'

'Indeed we are.'

'Are you going away?'

'For two or three days.'

He had stopped by the cottage gate and leaned across to undo her safety belt. 'Oh, of course—to the South of France,' said Matilda, and nodded. For a moment the lemonade got the upper hand. 'You're making a mistake!' she told him.

She walked up the garden path with his arm around

her, and waited while he unlocked the door. He pushed her gently inside.

She looked up at him with sleepy eyes. 'I'll never forget,' she told him. He didn't answer, only smiled down at her and closed the door quite quietly.

She had been right, of course, he reflected as he got into the car and sat waiting until he saw a light go on in an upstairs room. He had made a mistake.

In the cold light of early Sunday morning Matilda tried to remember just what she had said to the doctor. She suspected that she had spoken with an unguarded tongue but her recollection was a little vague. He hadn't said much, though, so she couldn't have allowed her tongue to run away with her.

Her mother asked if she had enjoyed herself.

'Very much. The hall was packed and there was a good band. And just before midnight we went to Lady Truscott's and had coffee and sausage rolls and mince pies.'

'Lady Truscott's? Who else was there?'

'Mrs Simpkins and her husband, and the milkman and that nice old colonel—and most of the ladies with whom you play bridge. Oh, and the pub owner and his wife.'

'Not at Lady Truscott's, surely?' Mrs Paige sounded horrified.

'Oh, yes. She was at the dance; so were Mr and Mrs Milton—and that nice man who runs the bank on the opening days.'

'The doctor brought you home?'

'Yes, Mother.'

'If I had known,' said Mrs Paige, 'I could have gone to this dance; I didn't realise that it was for everyone. I could

have got someone to come and give your father an hour
or two's company, or I could have gone with Dr Lovell...'

'But it was me he invited,' said Matilda mildly.

'Only because Lucilla Armstrong is away, so I hear.
He had to take someone, I suppose.' She added crossly,
'I'm not going to church; I've one of my sick headaches
coming on. If anyone enquires about me you can say that
I haven't been very well for the past few days.'

So Matilda went to church with her father and, beyond a few brief remarks at her mother's absence, no one
showed much interest. The congregation, considering
how late most of them had been up the night before, was
large, and beyond a quick good morning she had no need
to say anything to the doctor. However, she couldn't help
hearing him tell the vicar that he was leaving directly
after lunch, and she heard the vicar urging him to drive
carefully—'For you are going quite a distance, Henry.'

All the way to the South of France, reflected Matilda.

She thought about him for the rest of Sunday and all
of Monday—a day given over to the washing and ironing
and rummaging in cupboards in search of the best china
and the silver coffee spoons while her mother sat at the
kitchen table planning her coffee morning.

'Wouldn't coffee and biscuits do?' asked Matilda.

'Certainly not. There had better be hot chocolate and
some of those herb teas. No biscuits—petit fours and tiny
sausage rolls and mince pies and those almond biscuits.
And you needn't look like that,' said Mrs Paige sharply.
'Your father has given me the housekeeping money. The
money you pay me each week will tide us over...'

'Until when?' asked Matilda.

'Well, your next week's wages, of course. Really,

Matilda, you are most ungrateful. I am going to a great deal of trouble to entertain the right people.'

Her mother went to Taunton the next day, grumbling because she had to go by bus, and Matilda took the opportunity to tidy her father's desk and make sure that there weren't any bills tucked in among his books and papers. And since it was a fairly mild day the pair of them took a short walk, talking about the garden and what Matilda hoped to do in the spring.

They ate their lunch in the kitchen because it was the warmest room in the house, and Matilda conjured up an economical supper before she lighted the fire in the sitting room. They sat round it eating buttered toast and doing the *Telegraph* crossword puzzle, very content in each other's company.

Mrs Paige was to return on the afternoon bus, but since by the time it reached Much Winterlow it was dark Matilda walked down to the village to meet her and carry the parcels.

Mrs Paige had had a splendid day having her hair done and shopping, but she was quick to point out that returning on the bus had quite spoilt the day. 'So crowded,' she complained, 'and I had so many parcels. I must talk to your father and persuade him that we must have a car.'

'There isn't enough money, Mother,' said Matilda bleakly. 'Besides, you don't need to go to Taunton every day.'

'If I had a car I could get away from this dull place.'

'Mother, if only you would try and like it—there's so much to do in the village and I don't mean bridge parties.'

She was told not to talk rubbish as her mother went past her into the cottage.

Matilda, unpacking bags and boxes under her mother's

eye, noted with a sinking heart the expensive vol-au-vents, petit fours, tiny buns filled with cream and salmon mousse tartlets. Far too much for a friendly coffee morning and heaven only knew what they had cost.

'I've tired myself out,' declared her mother. 'You must hoover the sitting room and make sure the house is fit to be seen. You'll have all day tomorrow in which to do it...'

As it happened, Matilda found time to go into the garden too. It was a wild day with a cold wind but she was soon glowing, collecting up the last of the fallen leaves, raking the beds clear of debris. The dark sky and wild, scudding clouds suited her mood. Was she to be condemned for ever to her mother's beck and call? she wondered. The plain answer was yes, because of her father.

Matilda, preparing for the coffee morning, hardly noticed what she was doing. Tomorrow she would be going to Aunt Kate's house and she could hardly wait. And because she was so happy about that she did everything she could to please her mother. And Mrs Paige needed a lot of pleasing; her coffee morning was to be an elegant affair not easily forgotten.

Lady Truscott came; so did Mrs Milton and the various acquaintances Mrs Paige had made at bridge parties she had been to. And if they were surprised at the elaborate spread put before them they didn't say so. They were happy living at Much Winterlow and felt sorry for anyone who wasn't. Of course they realised that, after the busy life of committees, meetings and parochial gatherings, Mrs Paige might find village life dull. Dull from her point of view, of course, not theirs. There was more than enough to keep life interesting: Farmer Squire's cow having triplets, Mrs Trim winning a few hundred pounds in the lottery, the Kentons' eldest boy getting a scholarship to Sherborne, and now Christmas looming...

They drank the excellent coffee and ate the dainties they were offered, then told their hostess quite sincerely they had enjoyed themselves, at the same time urging her to join in the village activities.

'I know that you couldn't leave your husband,' said Lady Truscott kindly, 'but you would have enjoyed the dance. How beautifully Matilda dances. She and the doctor made a splendid pair and she never lacked for partners. She is very popular in the village, you know; a charming girl.'

When everyone had gone and they were clearing up Mrs Paige remarked with a little laugh, 'Lady Truscott said you were charming. A pity Dr Lovell is going to marry Lucilla Armstrong; you might have stood a chance with him.'

'Most unlikely,' said Matilda cheerfully. 'I work for him.' Her smile hid the hurtful thought that even with no competition she had no chance of attracting him. She would go on working for him too until she retired, like Miss Brimble, to look after an aged parent.

Then she remembered that she was going to stay with Aunt Kate and life became once more an adventure, for who knew what lay around the next corner?

Miss Lovell, in sensible tweeds and a severe hat, arrived punctually in the morning. She accepted coffee, listening to Mrs Paige's account of her coffee morning and enjoying a brief talk with Mr Paige before putting down her cup and saucer and declaring that they must be off.

'I'll bring Matilda back on Sunday evening,' she told them. 'After supper.'

In the car, driving like Jehu through the country roads, Aunt Kate observed, 'You're looking pale, Matilda. Does Henry work you too hard?'

'Heavens, no! I'm only part-time, you know, and I love the work. It's not at all hard.'

'Done any Christmas shopping yet?'

Aunt Kate avoided a farm trailer by a hair's breadth.

'No—well, I bought my Christmas cards from Mrs Simpkins' shop, and wrapping paper and labels. I must go to Taunton and buy presents.'

'Or you can do some shopping in Somerton. The town shops are exciting but I find I can get all I want in the local shops.'

Matilda, her purse moderately filled for once, agreed happily. She hadn't many presents to get and she knew what she wanted to buy. She had worried about the doctor. Should she give him a present? Something impersonal like a diary? She suspected that he got several from the medical firms who were always sending samples. You couldn't give a man flowers unless he was in bed ill; he didn't smoke. A desk calendar, perhaps.

Miss Lovell stopped with a flourish before her door and Mrs Chubb was there, bidding them to come in from the cold, bustling around them, urging Matilda up the stairs to her room with the warning to go straight downstairs again to drink her coffee before it got cold.

'And I can see you're in need of a bit of cosseting. Been working too hard, I'll be bound. All work and no play…you know what they say!'

'But I went to the annual village dance on Saturday, Mrs Chubb. It was lovely.'

'That's as may be; you could do with a few more pounds on you too.'

Saying which, Mrs Chubb took herself downstairs again.

'She don't look happy, Miss Lovell,' she declared, carrying in the coffee tray. 'Now why is that? In love?'

Aunt Kate picked up the coffee pot. 'I think there is that possibility,' she said thoughtfully. 'We'll know soon enough.'

'If you say so, ma'am.'

A few moments later Matilda uttered a small sigh as she entered the sitting room. There was a splendid fire burning, the coffee smelled delicious and Taffy went to meet her.

'He remembers me,' said Matilda happily. Her small nose wrinkled with pleasure. Life for the moment was everything—well, almost everything—she could wish for.

They lunched presently: one of Mrs Chubb's nourishing soups, a soufflé as light as feathers and a winter salad. And a glass of wine with it.

'And now make your list, child,' said Miss Lovell. 'We will go to Somerton and take a look round the shops.'

There was more than enough choice for Matilda's modest list. A silk scarf for her mother, and after a search around a bookshop just the book her father had mentioned he would like to have. Fine lawn hankies for Mrs Inch and chocolates for Kitty and, after consultation with Aunt Kate, a bead necklace for Mrs Chubb. There was still Aunt Kate, of course, and the doctor, but she was running out of money and their gifts would need a good deal of thought.

They had tea at an elegant little café—toasted teacakes and a dish of mouth-watering cream cakes and a large pot of tea. Aunt Kate wasn't a woman to do things by halves.

It had begun to rain as they left the café and it was already dark, which made Aunt Kate's sitting room a haven of comfort and warmth when they reached it. And presently they sat down to supper: steak and kidney pie, its pastry lid a masterpiece of perfection, Brussels sprouts and potatoes mashed to a creamy smoothness, and then one of Mrs Chubb's trifles. All helped down with a glass of claret.

Matilda, curled up in her pretty bed, slept all night. Her last thoughts were of Dr Lovell, of course, as were her waking ones too.

The rain disappeared during the night and the next day it was chilly with a strong wind. But here and there were patches of pale blue sky.

'Brisk walk,' said Miss Lovell, watching Matilda spooning her porridge. 'Nothing like it. We'll take the footpath to Thors Magna and have coffee at the pub there.'

Which they did—a couple of miles across country with the promised coffee at the end of it. There was time for a quick look round the church before they walked back to another of Mrs Chubb's nourishing meals.

'I shall take a nap after lunch,' declared Aunt Kate. 'Put on a coat and explore the garden if you would like to. There are books and magazines in the garden room, so help yourself. Tea at half past four.'

So presently Matilda got into the elderly hooded cloak which Mrs Chubb offered her and went into the garden. She had been there before but now she explored it thoroughly, admiring the brick paths between the flowerbeds, the little summer house right at the end of the garden and the vegetable patch hidden behind a cunningly planted circle of small fruit trees. She would do something like that, she decided. Once winter was over she could spend more time in the garden. And a little summer house would be just the thing for her father. She went and had another look at it, wondering how much it would cost, poking her head inside to get a better look.

Dr Lovell, coming silently across the lawn, stopped to watch her. There wasn't much of her to be seen for the cloak enveloped her entirely and he smiled as he spoke.

'You are in there under the tent thing?' he asked.

Matilda shot up, got entangled in the cloak and had to be set back on her feet. She said the first thing to enter her head and then bitterly regretted it.

'Why aren't you in the South of France?'

'Am I supposed to be there?'

Matilda wrapped the cloak tightly around her. It was a kind of refuge and she felt in need of one. 'Well, no, I just thought that that was where you would be with Lucilla.'

'I had no idea that you were so interested in my private life, Matilda.'

Matilda said coldly, 'You are mistaken; I am not in the least interested.' And that was a waste of breath for he laughed. She turned her back on him then and wished that he would go away although in her heart she knew she would hate it if he did…

'Let us bury the hatchet,' said the doctor mildly. 'Let us ignore our private lives—yours as well as mine—and I for one am prepared to show a true Christmas spirit and invite you to have dinner with me this evening.'

'Dinner? With you? What about Aunt Kate? I mean, she'll come with us?'

He said silkily, 'Afraid to be alone in my company, Matilda?'

'Of course not. What a very silly thing to say. I'd like to have dinner with you if Aunt Kate wouldn't mind.'

'Then let us go indoors and tell her. Mrs Chubb was rattling the teacups when I arrived.'

He put a vast arm around her shoulders and walked her back into the kitchen, where he unwound her from the cloak, waited while she kicked off the wellies she had borrowed, and urged her into the sitting room.

Miss Lovell had had her nap and was knitting. She looked up as they went in. 'You'll be wanting your tea. What do you think of the garden, Matilda?'

'It's lovely—I was looking at the little summer house.' She blushed, remembering the pure joy she had felt at the sound of the doctor's voice. 'I'd like one in our garden, for Father in the warm weather...'

Which started a pleasant discussion about gardens, and somehow this led to her life before she had come to live at Much Winterlow. The doctor, experienced in extracting information from reluctant patients, listened carefully, putting two and two together, no longer pretending to himself that he wasn't deeply interested and aware at the same time that Matilda was going to be a hard nut to crack...

After tea she went up to her room and got into her pink dress, wondering uneasily if she had talked too much. The doctor was being friendly and dining with him would be delightful. But she mustn't forget that probably he had been prevented in some way from going to Lucilla and was taking her out because he had nothing better to do. He must be vexed at having to waste his holiday...

She went back to the sitting room and he got up as she went in.

'You look nice,' he said. He sounded like an elder brother. 'If you're ready, we'll go.'

Chapter 8

In the car Matilda said, 'You didn't bring Sam with you.'

'No; we went for a long walk and had a late lunch. He wouldn't take kindly to staying with Aunt Kate while we're away and I shall be home to take him for his evening walk.'

She had thought that maybe they were going to the hotel at Somerton but he drove through its main street and presently turned into a narrow country road. After a mile or so he turned in between stone pillars. There was no sign of a dwelling until he rounded a narrow bend, to reveal light from a dozen windows streaming towards them in the dark evening. As they reached it Matilda could see that it was a large house built in the Palladian manner. The doctor came to a silent halt before its imposing front door.

'Rather out of the way,' he observed, getting out and coming round to open her door, 'but I think you will like it.'

Matilda, thankful for the decent coat and the pink dress, said in her sensible voice, 'I would be out of my mind if I didn't. What a splendid house. I expect you've been here before.' And then she added, 'Sorry; that's none of my business.'

'If you mean have I brought Lucilla here, no, but I have brought my mother.'

Matilda paused on the steps leading to the entrance. 'I suppose that's what I did mean. It's the kind of place Lucilla would look right in; she is very lovely.'

'Quite beautiful,' the doctor agreed blandly as they went through the door.

She had often wondered what a country house hotel would be like; she had never expected to see one for herself. They had drinks in a lovely room with a blazing fire and presently went to the restaurant, softly lit with wide windows draped in old rose brocade and tables widely spaced.

Matilda, relieved to see that the rose-coloured dress stood up well to these surroundings, studied the menu.

'I hope you're hungry,' said the doctor—a remark she found encouraging. Vichyssoise, she decided—leek soup but with a difference—grilled trout with a pepper sauce, braised chicory and potato purée.

The doctor shared her wish for soup but settled on fillet of beef with sauce Perigord and turned his attention to the *maître d'* and the hovering wine waiter. Vintage claret for himself and a white burgundy for Matilda and, with the pudding trolley, champagne. Matilda, tucking into chestnut soufflé with chocolate sauce, enjoyed every mouthful, something which the doctor found endearing. Unlike Lucilla she appeared to have no qualms about weight problems. Her shape, he considered, was perfection itself.

The wine loosened her tongue nicely so that the sensible Miss Paige became Matilda—a Matilda he had fallen in love with—and who, most regrettably, showed no signs of falling in love with him.

He was prepared to wait just as he was prepared to tackle the problem of Lucilla. In the meantime he listened to Matilda's quiet voice and watched her happy face and possessed his soul in patience.

They sat a long time over their coffee and then he drove back to Aunt Kate's to find Mrs Chubb, cosy in a red dressing gown, waiting for them in the kitchen.

'Just in case you fancied a hot drink,' she told them. She looked at Matilda's happy face. 'Enjoyed ourselves, I'll be bound.'

'Yes, oh, yes!' said Matilda. She turned to the doctor, beaming up at him. 'Thank you very much for taking me out to dinner.' She sounded like a well-mannered child. 'It was a wonderful evening, you know—the kind of evening one always remembers...'

'Indeed, I shall always remember it too,' said the doctor. 'Sweet dreams, Matilda.' And he bent and kissed her, very much to Mrs Chubb's satisfaction and even more to Matilda's.

And, with a smiling glance at Mrs Chubb, he was gone.

Matilda turned a dreamy face to the housekeeper. 'I'll go to bed,' she said, and kissed her and floated upstairs to her room, for the moment wrapped in a dream world of her own.

But morning made short work of shattering dreams. She got up and showered and dressed and went downstairs to have breakfast with Aunt Kate, willing sensible thoughts to brush away the romantic nonsense of the previous evening. It's not as though he said anything, she told herself. We only talked about this and that; I could have been Aunt Kate or Mrs Chubb or a casual acquaintance. I hope I didn't talk too much...

'Where did you go?' asked Aunt Kate. 'And what did you eat?' Matilda told her at some length and her companion nodded briskly. 'Henry takes his mother there. She went there with his father when he was alive. They were a devoted couple. He has always said that it was exactly the place in which to have a love affair... And theirs was a love affair until his father died.'

She didn't give Matilda time to answer. 'We will go to church this morning; you won't need to go home until after lunch.'

The church, like so many in rural England, was too big for the village; nevertheless it was well filled. And Aunt Kate seemed to know everyone in it. Matilda sang the hymns, said her prayers and listened to the sermon carefully, anxious to dismiss her wandering thoughts, and after some delay while Aunt Kate greeted friends and acquaintances outside the church they walked back to the cottage where Mrs Chubb was waiting to serve roast beef with its traditional accompaniments.

'Mrs Chubb has the afternoon and evening off,' Aunt Kate explained, 'so I have a cold supper.' She added abruptly, 'I shall miss you and so will she.'

'I can never thank you enough for having me to stay. You and Mrs Chubb are so kind and this is a lovely cottage. I wish there was something I could do in return.'

'Bless the child.' Aunt Kate was at her most brisk. 'We enjoy your company and we hope that you will come again and again to cheer up two old women.'

Matilda thought that neither Aunt Kate nor Mrs Chubb needed cheering up; they appeared content with their lot and satisfied with their lives. They shared so many interests and they appeared to know everyone for miles around. Matilda, eating the last of Mrs Chubb's apple pie, wondered about the doctor's mother. Was she as nice as Aunt Kate? Even half as nice…?

They had their coffee in the sitting room and presently Aunt Kate said, 'Go and get your hat and coat, Matilda; it's time you were going.'

Matilda put Taffy on the sofa and went upstairs. Now that it was time to go she wanted to go quickly and without fuss. She put on her hat and coat, gave a lingering look round the pretty room and went downstairs; Aunt Kate didn't approve of hanging about.

She was still sitting in her chair, her knitting in her lap, and leaning his vast person against the mantelpiece was Dr Lovell.

Matilda paused just inside the door. 'I'm just going,' she said stupidly.

'Then say goodbye and we'll be off.'

Aunt Kate said, 'Did I forget to tell you that Henry would drive you back? My memory is getting bad, I'm afraid.'

She put down her knitting and got to her feet. 'Now, child, you are not to work too hard and you must come again—after Christmas, for I'm sure you'll want to be home with your family and friends. Here's Mrs Chubb to say goodbye…'

Matilda was kissed and hugged while the doctor stood patiently waiting, then he kissed the two ladies and swept Matilda out to the car.

Sam was there, spread out on the back seat and pleased to see her. She submitted to his whiskery greeting and he rested his head on her shoulder, blowing gently into her neck.

'How very kind of you to take me home,' began Matilda.

'Sam fancied a drive. You have enjoyed your stay?'

'Oh, yes, very much. I hope you had a nice week.'

'It had its high spots. Mrs Inch will have tea ready—you'll stay? She will be so disappointed if you don't.'

'Oh, yes, please. I didn't tell Mother exactly when I would be home; Aunt Kate wasn't sure.'

'Good. Tomorrow morning after surgery I would like you to come out to Duckett's Farm. Rob is home and he would like to see you.'

'He's going to be all right? I'm so glad, and I'd like to see him and his wife and Tom.'

'Don't forget John.'

'What a lot of nice people there are—and you'd never meet them unless it was by chance.'

He agreed with a brief yes and she made no effort to talk any more, and before long she was being ushered into his house and Mrs Inch was welcoming her with as much warmth as Mrs Chubb.

'There's tea ready, sir; just you take Miss Matilda into the drawing room. Such a nasty cold afternoon; you'll be glad of a cup of tea and a slice of my lardy cake!'

The doctor was careful to keep the talk about nothing much as they ate their tea. Matilda's face had a happy glow which he could have watched for hours, but he had seen her quick glances at the long case clock behind him. She finished her tea and after a polite interval said that if he didn't mind she would like to go home.

His cheerfully brisk agreement was a bit disconcerting.

At the cottage she began on the thank-you speech she had rehearsed in her mind but he cut her short.

'I'll come in with you; I'd like a word with your father.'

Leaving Sam in the car, they trod up the path together and opened the door as Mrs Paige came into the hall.

'Matilda—oh, I'm so glad to have you back. I have had the most wretched time with one of my heads; I was so tempted to ring and ask you to come home on Saturday morning but that would have been selfish. Now you are home I can take things easy.'

She turned to the doctor. 'So good of you to bring Matilda home. Do come in and forgive my bad manners. I get upset so easily.'

He watched the happy glow die away in Matilda's face. 'Thank you; I should like a word with Mr Paige.'

'Oh, I'm sure you will find him very well. He's in the sitting room.'

The doctor didn't stay long; a few minutes' quiet talk with Mr Paige, a courteous exchange of nothing much with Mrs Paige and he had gone, with a brief reminder to Matilda that he would see her at the surgery in the morning.

Mrs Paige complained that his visit had been so short. 'But I dare say he has more interesting things to do with his time; I suppose he felt obliged to bring you back, seeing as he suggested that you should go to his aunt's house in the first place.'

Mrs Paige sat down in the sitting room and picked up a book. 'Your father fancies something light for his supper—there's some soup and eggs...'

Matilda went up to her room. She always hoped that things would be different between her mother and herself but they never were. She went to the window and opened it, letting the cold air in, and then shut it again because Rastus, sleeping on her bed, protested.

It had been a lovely few days; she would remember them for the rest of her life and since there was no one else to tell she told Rastus of their delights.

She got the supper presently and listened to her mother making more plans. She had had another invitation, from old friends she had met while she had been away. 'Curry Rivel,' she explained. 'So handy for Taunton, I can do my shopping while I'm there. You'll let me have some extra money for Christmas, won't you? I'll get everything we shall need and bring it back with me.'

She looked sharply at Matilda. 'You'll have several days off at Christmas, I suppose?'

'I expect so. Dr Lovell will let me know.'

'Well, I plan to go at the end of the week and come back the day before Christmas Eve.'

'We shall be perfectly well here, my dear,' said Mr Paige. 'You go and see to the shopping and see the Gibbs; they have always been great friends of yours, haven't they? Perhaps in the New Year we might invite them back here. I do realise how lonely you are here; you had so many friends and were always so busy.' He sighed. 'I do so regret that I was forced to give up the ministry.'

'It's really nice living here,' said Matilda, 'and it will be lovely in the summer. I'll get the garden in some sort of order; it's full of plants and bushes, if only I could clear them.'

'A delightful prospect,' said her father, 'and so fortunate that you are so strong, my dear, for I am useless and your mother is far too delicate to undertake any but the lightest of tasks.'

Mrs Paige leaned across and patted his arm. 'You are so good to me...'

Matilda sat up late in her bed doing sums. She needed

very little money for herself although she had hoped to buy a skirt and cardigan; now they would have to wait until after Christmas for she still had one or two more presents to buy. If she gave her mother most of her wages on Friday they should be enough to get the extra food and delicacies, the turkey and the Christmas pudding. She would talk to her mother in the morning.

The surgery was busy; with the holidays so near, everyone was intent on getting rid of their ailments as quickly as possible. Bidden to have coffee with the doctor afterwards, Matilda was told not to waste time. 'I've a long round this morning,' he explained, 'and I promised to go the Ducketts'. Can you be ready in ten minutes?'

She swallowed her coffee, got into her outdoor things and ran across the street to Mrs Simpkins' shop.

'I'm going to the Ducketts',' she explained breathlessly, 'and I must take something for little Tom.' She added, 'The doctor won't want to be kept waiting.'

Mrs Simpkins, rather in the manner of a conjuror with a rabbit in a hat, produced a small teddy bear sitting on top of a bag of sweets.

'Just the thing. Pay me later, love; he's getting into his car.'

Moments later he leaned over and opened the door for her and she scrambled in. Sam was in the back and heaved himself over to greet her with a pleased rumble, but the doctor didn't speak. She decided it was one of those days when she was Miss Paige, when it was better to be seen rather than heard.

And indeed he didn't speak until they arrived at the farm.

'Fifteen minutes,' he told her. 'I shall be most of the time with Rob but try and be ready.'

'Well really,' said Matilda coldly. 'When have I ever kept you waiting?'

He smiled but said nothing.

The Ducketts were waiting for them; she shook Rob's hand and told him how well he looked and was led away to the kitchen by Mrs Duckett and Tom. They had coffee and Tom had his teddy bear then John came in.

They were glad to see her again and there was so much to tell her about Rob. She sat with Tom on her lap and drank her coffee with one eye on the clock, and sure enough there was one minute of the fifteen left when the doctor joined them.

Everything was exactly as it should be, he told them; Rob would need to see his surgeon after Christmas and he was to take things very easy until then.

They all went out to the car then, calling Christmas good wishes as he drove out of the farmyard.

'I'll drop you in the village,' said the doctor, 'and see you at five o'clock.'

'Would you mind if I hung up one or two decorations in the waiting room?'

'Not in the least. Get whatever you want from Mrs Simpkins and tell her to put it on my bill.'

'I didn't mean you to pay for them.'

'Of course you didn't, but don't deprive me of that pleasure. I could never get Miss Brimble to do more than arrange a sprig of holly on her desk so let us be lavish.'

'Thank you; if you don't like it you'll say so?'

'Most certainly.'

He got out and opened her door and she turned to pat Sam. 'Thank you for taking me out to Duckett's Farm.'

'They wanted to see you.' He got into the car and drove away. A perfectly sensible answer, she reflected, so why did she feel snubbed?

She had a wonderful time with Mrs Simpkins. Without the worry of having to pay for them, she chose Father Christmas in his sleigh for the table, several jolly Christmas scenes to hang on the walls, and yards of tinsel to fasten round the door. Holly, too, and a red paper shade for the ceiling light. She bore the lot back to the waiting room, let herself in and set about decorating it. It took time but she was pleased with the result. 'And if he doesn't like it it's just too bad,' she said.

She was late home, of course, and her mother was annoyed about that.

'We could have had a macaroni cheese if you had been here to make it.'

'I stayed to decorate the waiting room.'

'You never wasted your money on that?'

'No. Dr Lovell paid for everything.'

'I should hope so; he's rich enough. No wonder that Armstrong girl is anxious to marry him.'

The evening surgery was pretty busy and the doctor was late starting, but no one grumbled; they were too busy admiring the decorations. When he did come she didn't look at him as he opened the surgery door and called the first patient in, but when the last patient had gone and she was clearing up he came and stood in the centre of the room, his hands in his pockets.

'Very nice,' he commented. 'You've done us proud. And my patients loved it.' He stared down at her. 'But please don't attempt to decorate my surgery.'

He put out a hand and tucked a strand of hair behind

her ear. 'Go home; you must be tired.' His voice was gentle.

Matilda, who had taught herself not to cry when she was still quite a small girl, swallowed back the tears. He was being kind, she reminded herself. It meant nothing more than that; she must look an object for his pity. The thought banished the tears and she said quite sharply, 'I am not in the least tired, Doctor. I'm glad you like the decorations.'

She got her coat and put it on. 'I'll see you tomorrow evening.'

He opened the door for her and wished her goodnight, locking the door after her, and then stood at the side window watching her walk down the street, her small back very straight and defiant.

It wasn't possible to avoid him for they saw each other every day but she retreated behind a businesslike manner if they needed to talk and found an excuse not to drink coffee with him after morning surgery.

The doctor, a man of no conceit, was at first puzzled and then resigned. He had every intention of marrying her; he would deal with problems as they arose but first he must wait with all the patience he could muster until she fell in love with him.

Mrs Paige, with most of Matilda's pay packet in her purse, left on Saturday morning, having begged a lift from Mrs Milton. She would be back on Monday, she promised, or Tuesday at the latest. With Christmas only a little more than a week away, she would be needed at home.

'I'll bring you some of that game pâté,' she promised her husband, 'from that delicatessen I told you about.'

They waved as she was driven away in Mrs Milton's car.

'Your dear mother, always so thoughtful of me,' said Mr Paige. Matilda took his arm as they went indoors. She agreed cheerfully because she loved him and her mother made him happy. The trouble is, reflected Matilda, making coffee for them both, they shouldn't have had me.

She went to the village presently and did the weekend shopping, and as she left the shop Lucilla Armstrong and her brother got out of a car and rang the doctor's bell. Her brother carried a weekend case. He turned and waved to Matilda but Lucilla ignored her.

'I hope he has a simply beastly weekend,' Matilda muttered as she went home. 'Oh, how could anyone love a person so horrid as Lucilla?'

There was no one to answer her. The cow leaning over the hedge looked sympathetic but what she really wanted was a shoulder to cry on, preferably the doctor's.

Lucilla and her brother were in church with the doctor on Sunday morning. Matilda wished them an unsmiling good morning, and went back with her father in Mrs Milton's car to cook their dinner.

Her father was quiet and she looked anxiously at him and felt relief when he remarked that he was missing her mother. 'But she will be home again tomorrow. We must make this a happy Christmas, our first in this cottage. I am happy here, my dear, and I believe that your mother will settle down just as happily once the winter is over.'

But there was a phone call while Matilda was at the surgery on Monday morning; her mother hadn't had time to do all her shopping. She would be home on Wednesday afternoon.

It was three o'clock on Wednesday morning when Mr Paige had another heart attack. Matilda would never know why she felt compelled to get out bed and cross the landing to her parents' room. She found her father ashen and sweating and only partly conscious. She choked back her fright, found her voice and told him not to worry, she was getting the doctor, and flew downstairs to the phone.

'Lovell,' said his calm voice in her ear, and she found her voice again.

'It's my father; he's having a heart attack. Do come quickly.' She added, 'It's me, Matilda.'

'Five minutes. Leave the door open and go up and re-assure him.'

He came in quietly, large and reassuring and matter-of-fact. He bent over Mr Paige and then opened his bag.

'Go and get dressed, but first of all call an ambulance. Tell them that you are phoning for me and that it is urgent.'

He turned back to the bed and she went to the phone again and tore into her clothes. If her father had to stay in hospital he would need a bag packed. She did that, even remembering to put in his little bible and his favourite anthology of English verse. And by then the ambulance was at the door and they were carrying her father carefully down the stairs on a stretcher.

'I'll take you with me in the car,' said the doctor, and she hurried to lock doors and windows and leave food and water for Rastus. And all the while she didn't allow herself to think.

She was there as they loaded the stretcher into the ambulance, to peer into her father's unconscious face and hold his hand for a moment; then, obedient to the doctor's hand on her arm, she got into his car beside him.

Waiting for the ambulance to lead the way, she asked in a whisper, 'He'll be all right?'

'I can't tell you that, Matilda. It's a pretty massive heart attack, but once we get him to the hospital everything will be done. He is an excellent patient, quiet and unafraid and otherwise fit for his age. I wish I could tell you more but for the moment it is useless to speculate.'

At the hospital her father was taken to the intensive care unit. The doctor went with him, leaving her in the care of a young nurse in Casualty.

She was given a cup of tea and told kindly that once her father was in his bed she would be able to see him. So she sat quietly while nurses bustled to and fro and she tried not to think.

The doctor came for her after half an hour.

'Come and see your father,' he said, and he sounded very reassuring. 'He's rallied and is responding nicely to treatment. It's early days to say that he's out of the wood but at least we can see daylight through the trees.'

It was quite a long walk to ICU even if you counted the lifts from one floor to the next. And when they reached it she was put into a white gown several sizes too large and taken to her father's bed.

He was conscious and smiled a little as she bent to kiss him.

'Don't worry your mother.' His voice was faint but determined.

'In the morning I'll let her know that you are better,' she told him. 'She will want to know, Father, but I won't alarm her.'

'There's a good girl. Go home now and get some sleep.'

'Yes, Father. I'll come and see you later.'

She kissed him again and stood quietly while a nurse took her gown, and then made the endless journey to the entrance and got into the doctor's car again.

He fastened her seat belt. 'Don't come to surgery,' he told her. 'Go to bed and sleep. Come in the evening if you feel like it. I'll keep you posted about your father.' He glanced at his watch. 'It's almost six o'clock; you should ring your mother when you get home.'

'Yes, I'll do that. Her friends will bring her home. And if you don't mind I'd rather come to work. You see, if I'm busy, I don't think so much.'

'Just as you like.'

He took the key from her when they reached the cottage and went in with her, turned on the lights, put on the kettle and found the teapot.

'We both need a hot drink. I'll make tea while you phone your mother.'

It took a few minutes for Mrs Paige to be roused and fetched to the phone.

'In hospital? And Christmas only a few days away. Oh, dear, this is terrible news. I must go to him at once. Is he very ill? I was going out to lunch.'

'You'll come home today, Mother?'

'I can't think now, Matilda, I'm so upset. I'll phone you later.'

The doctor looked at her as she went into the kitchen. 'Your mother is upset? She will go straight to the hospital, will she not? And then come home. There are several people in the village who will willingly take her to see him whenever she wishes.'

He poured their tea, watching her pale face; she had tied her hair back and her eyes looked huge. She needed a warm bed and someone like Mrs Inch or Aunt Kate to comfort her, but he was too wise to insist on her not coming to the surgery in an hour's time. Hopefully she would be so exhausted by the end of it that she would go home to bed and her mother would be there. Mrs Paige was a selfish, idle woman but she was Matilda's mother...

He went away then with a casual, 'See you shortly,' and she fed Rastus, had a bath and got dressed. There wasn't much time for breakfast but in any case she wasn't hungry; nonetheless she swallowed toast and drank tea and then walked briskly to the surgery.

It was as busy as usual, full of people with minor ailments and all very cheerful because it was Christmas, and there was so much chatter that her unusual silence went unnoticed.

She was tired as the door shut for the last time. She would hurry home and get a meal ready for her mother, light the fire and ring the hospital.

The surgery door opened. 'I've rung the hospital.' His arm swept her into the surgery and into a chair. 'He's making progress; that's good news.'

'Oh, I'm so glad. How soon will they know if he's going to be quite well again? I mean to come home?' She looked away. 'That's a silly question, isn't it?'

'No. A natural one. It may be ten days or more and he will have to lead a careful life for a time.'

Mrs Inch came in then with coffee and a plate piled high with hot buttered toast. 'You'll neither of you have had breakfast,' she said severely, 'and you're to eat every crumb.' She paused by Matilda. 'I'm that sorry, Matilda. We're all hoping for good news.'

The doctor drove her home, saying that he had to pass the cottage anyway, but he didn't stay. Which was just as well as the phone rang as he drove away. Her mother.

'I've seen your father; he seems better. I won't come home; the Gibbs have persuaded me to stay with them. It will be so convenient for them to take me to the hospital each day. I'm terribly upset, of course, but everyone is being so kind. The doctors tell me that your father will have to remain in hospital for a week or ten days...'

'Over Christmas...'

'Yes. Of course I'd like to come home, Matilda, but you can understand that I must stay here so that I can see your father each day. You'll be all right? I dare say Mrs Milton will give you a lift if you ask her. I'll phone tomorrow; I must go now as we're going out to lunch.'

Matilda went into the kitchen, let Rastus out into the back garden and then went and sat down at the kitchen table. Of course her mother was very upset and there had been no time to discuss anything. Perhaps she would go to the Gibbs' and stay over Christmas with her mother? But what about Rastus? Or, if her father was out of danger, perhaps her mother would come home, just for Christmas, and hire a car to take them to the hospital on Christmas Day?

There was no point in worrying about it; first of all her father must recover. She went upstairs and made the bed up with clean linen and opened the windows. A few hours' sleep might be a good idea. She went downstairs and let Rastus in and then, with him for company, undressed and got into bed.

Her alarm clock woke her and she got up and showered and dressed and went to the kitchen to make herself a light meal. Later, after surgery hours, she would cook something. Then it was time for her to leave for the evening surgery but first she phoned the hospital. Her father was holding his own, she was told, and resting comfortably, and, yes, said the brisk voice at the other end of the phone, her love would be conveyed to the patient.

The doctor had a more detailed and reassuring message to give her when surgery was over. 'I won't bother you with all the technical details,' he told her. 'Your father is responding well but he will stay in ICU for the next day or two. You have heard from your mother?'

'Yes, she has been to see him and will go again tomorrow.'

'You are all right on your own until she returns home?'

'Yes. Yes, thanks, I'm fine.'

'I'll drive you to the hospital before surgery tomorrow. It will have to be early—six-thirty?'

'Six-thirty will be fine. Thank you.'

'Will your mother's friends bring her back home?'

'Yes, I'm sure they will...'

'Then why not give them a ring and get them to pick you up at the hospital? I expect your mother will be there.'

She said too quickly, 'Yes, of course I can do that. They're very old friends.'

'Good. I'll drive you home; get your coat.'

'There's no need. I always walk home...'

'But there is usually someone there when you get there. Come along.'

When they arrived he went into the cottage with her, turning on the lights, and as she went to the door with him he said, 'Phone me if you need me. Goodnight, Matilda.'

He didn't like leaving her there on her own, but her mother would be back tomorrow. He stood in the doorway looking down at her, small and matter-of-fact and independent. He bent and kissed her hard then went back to his car and drove away.

Chapter 9

Matilda, being a sensible girl, cooked herself some supper, had a bath, attended to Rastus and went to bed early, not sure if she would sleep. But she did, soundly, until her alarm clock woke her the next morning. The day was going to be a long one so breakfast had to be eaten in case she had to miss lunch, Rastus had to be seen to, the cottage locked up and what money she had stowed away in her handbag. The doctor hadn't said that he would pick her up so she locked the door and started down the path. She got to the gate as he drew up and got out. His good morning held a question.

'I was going to walk to the surgery,' she told him, not quite meeting his eye, the memory of his kiss very vivid in her mind. Perhaps he had forgotten it; his greeting had sounded businesslike.

He hadn't forgotten it; indeed, he wondered for one mad moment if he would kiss her again. But he didn't; he opened the car door for her and she got in, to be welcomed by Sam's pleased rumble.

The hospital's day was already under way. They went together to see her father and Matilda thought that he looked much better. He was pleased to see her. 'I shall be home again quite soon,' he assured her. 'Your mother spends much of each day with me. You are all right at the cottage?'

She assured him that she was and slipped away to allow the doctor to take her place. She waited quietly while he talked to the elderly doctor who had joined him and then went back with him to the car.

He took her back to the surgery, patiently answering her questions. Her father was making an excellent recovery but there was no question of him going home before Christmas.

'Your mother will be coming home today? There is no need for her to stay at the hospital each day.'

He wasn't looking at her so it was easier to assure him that she would be home very shortly. He said, 'Good. I know Mrs Milton will take either of you in at any time. Your father is out of danger and there is no reason why he shouldn't be perfectly well for years yet.'

He got out of the car, unlocked the door and went in with her. 'See you later,' he said, and, with a casual nod, disappeared into his room.

It was quiet and rather cold in the cottage, but there didn't seem much point in lighting the sitting-room fire. She went around the house, hoovering and dusting quite unnecessarily, until it was time to get her lunch. She sat at the kitchen table with Rastus beside her, eating scrambled eggs, fighting self-pity.

It was a dreary, cold day but there was plenty to do in the garden. In an old mac, her hair tied into a scarf, she worked until the early dusk, raking up dead twigs, leaves and all the debris of a neglected garden. She went indoors then, feeling better, glowing from the exercise, and made tea and phoned the hospital.

'A continued improvement,' said the voice at the other

end, 'and your mother left a message for you. She will ring you tomorrow morning after you get home.'

It was a dark night and the cottage seemed forlorn and very empty. Supper and bed seemed a good idea. She wasn't a nervous girl but she couldn't help thinking of the empty fields between her and the village. Rastus, sensing her unease, crept close to her, and presently, lulled by his warmth and purr, she slept.

A few minutes after she had left the surgery the doctor had put down the phone. Lucilla had demanded that he should drive over to her home that evening.

'I don't want to spend Christmas at your house,' she had told him. 'I can't think why I ever agreed to it. Guy said I'd been a fool to agree. He's going to a hotel at Cheltenham with the Fergusons—remember them? He suggests we both join him there. I think it's a splendid idea...'

'Why don't you want to come here?'

'Oh, Henry, it'll be so dull—church and carols and just us and your mother and aunt and family. When we are married I intend to change your lifestyle—we might even move to Taunton or Cheltenham, or even Gloucester.'

'No,' the doctor had said.

'What do you mean, no? You don't intend to spend the rest of your life and mine in that old house?'

He'd said evenly, 'My family have spent their lives here for two hundred years or more; I intend to do the same.'

'Well, I don't.'

'If you wish to break our engagement I shall understand. I shan't change my mind, Lucilla.'

'Nor shall I, so you can forget that we were going to marry.'

She had slammed the receiver down and he'd sat for a long time at his desk. Kindly fate had offered him a helping hand...

The next day, Matilda, with the plea of urgent shopping to be done as soon as surgery was over, gave him no chance to do more than bid her good morning. She spent some of her pay packet on groceries and went home. Perhaps her mother would change her mind now that her father was no longer in danger and come home.

But Mrs Paige had no intention of doing that. 'What would I do if I came home?' she wanted to know. 'Oh, I know someone would give me a lift in to the hospital if I asked, but you're not home much and I'd just sit in that cottage and be bored out of my mind.'

When Matilda didn't speak she added, 'Christmas would have been a very dull affair with just the two of us and I'm sure you'll find plenty to do. Everyone here is so kind, cheering me up, taking my mind off your father's illness. He'll be coming home soon, the doctor told me, and I've insisted that a nurse comes to attend him; I couldn't possibly manage. But you and she could do whatever has to be done.' And when Matilda still remained silent she said, 'You're still there? I hope you're not sulking?'

'No, Mother. I'm glad Father is so much better. Will you phone me tomorrow?'

'Yes, yes, of course.'

A good burst of tears helped. Matilda mopped her face, ate the lunch she didn't want and, although it was raining, went into the garden and started to clear the overgrown vegetable patch at the end of it.

* * *

Evening surgery over, the doctor came into the waiting room.

'I'll drive you back,' he told her. 'It's a wretched night.'

It's astonishing, reflected Matilda, how quickly one can think up a parcel of lies when desperate.

'Thank you, Doctor. But I'm going across to Mrs Simpkins' and Mr Simpkins will take me home later.'

She gave him a bright smile.

He looked at her thoughtfully. 'Your mother won't mind being alone?'

'Oh, no,' said Matilda airily. 'She doesn't mind at all and it's only for an hour or two.'

Rather mystified, he wished her goodnight and went to his study to work. He would go and see her in the morning, drive her somewhere quiet so that they could talk. He abandoned his writing and sat back in his chair, Sam at his feet, and allowed his thoughts to dwell on Matilda.

She was avoiding him, he was aware of that, but she hadn't drawn back when he had kissed her. And of course she thought that he and Lucilla were engaged. That they were meant for each other was so obvious to him that he had supposed that she must have been aware of that too.

He picked up his pen again and started to fill in forms and make notes. He was interrupted by Mrs Inch, who came in with such an air of urgency that he put his pen down again and asked what had upset her.

'There's something you should know, sir. Mrs Simpkins has just been over. Ben—the milkman, you know— went in for his groceries; she puts them aside for him. His brother works as a porter at the hospital...'

'Sit down, Mrs Inch. He saw or heard something, perhaps, this porter?'

'Indeed he did. That Mrs Paige—begging your pardon, I'm sure—leaving our nice Matilda alone! He was doing a job right by her when she was talking to one of the sisters. She's staying with friends over Christmas, not coming home, and that her daughter would be with friends and her duty was by her husband, though this man heard one of the doctors telling Mrs Paige that there was no need for her to be there each day now. And there's that dear girl all alone, and over Christmas too, and not said a word to anyone.'

Mrs Inch paused for breath. 'I'm that upset, sir. Not that she'll be lonely; there'll be invitations enough from half the village when they know and Mrs Simpkins won't be slow to tell it around.'

The doctor was sitting back in his chair. 'Thank you for telling me, Mrs Inch, and please tell Mrs Simpkins that I shall go and fetch Matilda to stay here—now, this evening. So would you delay dinner for half an hour or so and get a room ready for her? The balcony room at the back of the house, I think; we mustn't forget Rastus.'

Mrs Inch blew her nose and mopped away a stray tear. 'Oh, sir, I knew you would know what to do.' She went to the door. 'We'll all be so pleased.'

The doctor's feelings were a good deal stronger than pleasure but he gave no sign of his rage. He supposed that since Mrs Paige was to be his mother-in-law he would have to make an effort to like her; at the moment he merely felt murderous towards her.

He went through the house and along the little passage which led to the garage, got into his car, and drove away much too fast.

The kitchen window was at the side of the cottage;

he could see that the room was lit as he went up the path and thumped the knocker.

He had to thump again before the hall light was switched on and Matilda's voice wanted to know who it was.

'Let me in,' roared the doctor, 'before I break the door down.'

Which he will surely do, thought Matilda, for my dearest Henry is in a bad temper. So she opened the door. He swept past her, taking her with him.

'How dare you,' he demanded. 'How dare you not tell me? Do you suppose that I would have left you alone for one minute if I had known? I must in time learn to like your mother but for the moment my feelings towards her are unmentionable…'

'You are extremely cross,' observed Matilda in a reasonable voice calculated to make him even crosser. 'Perhaps you will tell me why you are here?'

'Go upstairs and pack a bag. You're coming back to my house and don't argue about it; the entire village knows that's why I have come. Where do you keep the cat basket?'

Matilda said, 'On the bottom shelf of the cupboard by the sink.' And added, 'I won't pack a bag…'

'Please yourself; come as you are. Mrs Inch will have a nightie for you.'

He looked at her across the little room and smiled. 'This isn't the right time to tell you but Lucilla has decided not to marry me.'

'Well,' said Matilda, 'I have always known that she is most unsuitable for you but I can quite see why you fell in love with her. Are you unhappy?'

He said gravely, 'I am the happiest man on earth. Now go and pack that bag.'

So she did. And came downstairs again, looking rather untidy. He took the bag from her and thought she was the most beautiful girl in the world.

He turned off the lights, shut the windows and, with Rastus in his basket, locked the cottage door behind them then popped her into the car. Matilda tried to think of something to say for his silence unnerved her. Her head teemed with snatches of poetry, first lines of hymns and nursery rhymes, none of which were any use as conversation. Perhaps it would be best to remain silent…

The doctor stopped outside his front door, got out to open the car door for her and, under the interested eyes gazing from neighbouring windows, ushered her into his house.

Mrs Inch came to meet them in the hall.

'There you are, Miss Matilda. Just you come with me; I'll take you to your room. Bring the little cat with you; there's a balcony—so handy for him.'

The doctor gave Matilda a little push and she followed Mrs Inch up the staircase, not speaking, only nodding when he said quietly, 'Come down again, Matilda, to the drawing room.'

The room was charming. Not overlarge but furnished with a brass bed covered by a patchwork quilt, a little tulip wood dressing table with a triple mirror, a bow-fronted chest of drawers and a delicate bedside table with a pink-shaded lamp on it. There were rose-pink curtains at the window and a door opening onto a small covered balcony.

'The bathroom is next door,' said Mrs Inch. 'Just you tidy yourself and come down to your dinner.'

So Matilda combed her hair and did things to her rather pale face and went back down the staircase, feeling that she was in a dream and not at all sure what to do next.

That was settled for her as she reached the hall. The drawing-room door was opened and the doctor said, 'In here—have a drink before we have dinner.'

He sounded exactly the same as usual, as though her sudden and unexpected arrival was all part of his day.

She took the chair he offered her and when he handed her a glass of sherry tossed it down so that his eyes widened with hidden laughter. But he refilled her glass and sat down opposite her, Sam, as usual, at his feet.

'I think,' said Matilda, much emboldened by the sherry, 'that you must explain.' She frowned. 'No, perhaps I'd better explain.'

The doctor stretched his long legs and began to enjoy himself. 'Yes?'

'Well, I ought not to be here. I mean, I'm quite all right at the cottage and it's so convenient that Mother can stay with her friends and see Father each day, and I quite see what she means; it would be very dull for her to come home with just me—I mean, at Christmas and all.' She paused. 'Of course I was a bit disappointed but it's a splendid idea.'

'It's nothing of the sort. It's a splendid arrangement for your mother to enjoy Christmas with her friends. Your father is now out of danger; there is no need to visit him each day and he'll have all the care and attention he could possibly need.' He added gently, 'You should have told me, Matilda.'

She took a sip—a large sip—of sherry. 'Well, I would very much have liked to, only I couldn't, could I? You'd have felt sorry for me...'

'I don't feel at all sorry for you despite the fact that I do know. Sorrow is not what I feel, Matilda.'

He took her empty glass from her. 'Here's Mrs Inch to tell us to come to dinner.'

There was soup—Mrs Inch's own version of French onion soup with cream on top and a circle of toasted bread—grilled salmon steaks with tiny new potatoes and salsify, and a mincemeat tart with clotted cream. And a white burgundy to go with it.

They didn't talk much; the doctor had a great deal to say but not yet, and Matilda, fed and warm and nicely vague from the sherry and the wine, was in no state to listen.

They had their coffee at the table and when they had drunk it he suggested that she might like an early night. Mrs Inch, waiting, as it were, in the wings, whisked her upstairs before she could say more than goodnight.

Someone had attended to Rastus's needs. Matilda had a quick bath and tumbled into bed and he joined her, pressed close to her side, smelling strongly of sardines. 'You had a good dinner too,' said Matilda sleepily, and closed her eyes.

In his study the doctor lifted the phone. 'Mother...' He talked at some length and then picked up the phone again and dialled Aunt Kate's number.

There was just one more problem. He looked up a number and dialled it. Having a bishop in the family could be useful...

At breakfast he was casually friendly, giving her no chance to utter her doubts and questions.

'I'll run you back to the cottage.' He saw with satisfaction the instant dismay on her face. 'You'll need a hat

and coat if we're going to church.' It was the morning of
the vicar's special pre-Christmas sermon, traditionally
delivered on the last Saturday before Christmas.

'Very well. Thank you for having me, Dr Lovell; you
have been very kind. Would you mind if Rastus comes
with us? And my bag.'

'Yes, I do mind. Rastus stays here and so does your
bag. I suggest that you pack a few more clothes while
we're at the cottage.'

'Oh, but...'

'Darling girl, will you do as I ask?'

She stared across the table at him, the colour rushing
into her face. 'Darling girl,' he said again, and smiled.
'And Henry is my name!'

'I can't...' she began, and stopped, not knowing how
to go on.

'We had better go if you're finished; Mother and Aunt
Kate will be here by the time we get back. They hadn't
intended to come until Christmas Eve with the rest of the
family—I think you will like my mother.'

'Christmas...' began Matilda.

'You are spending it at my house with my family—
aunts and uncles, cousins—the house will be packed to
the roof.'

'Mother...?'

'We will telephone her later. Your father is making
excellent progress; he—and your mother—should be
home before the New Year.'

Matilda felt that she was being swept away by a raging torrent, only raging wasn't quite the right word. Loving and caring were.

She went with him to the cottage and packed a case—
the pink dress, woollies, a thick skirt, the grey jersey

dress, undies, dressing gown and slippers. Was she to stay with the doctor until her parents came back? She didn't like to ask.

Mrs Lovell and Aunt Kate were placidly drinking coffee when they got back. They turned smiling, composed faces to them as they went into the drawing room. The doctor kissed them in turn. 'And here is Matilda,' he said to his mother, and stood back while that lady embraced Matilda.

There had been no need to be nervous, thought Matilda. This plump little lady had nothing but kindness in her elderly face.

'I've always wanted a daughter,' said Mrs Lovell, and beamed at her as Aunt Kate in her turn kissed Matilda.

Nothing is quite real, thought Matilda, sitting in the Lovells' pew, aware that the congregation were looking at her from under their hats. Mrs Lovell had said that she wanted a daughter but Henry hadn't said that he wanted a wife. She sat, not listening to a word of Mr Milton's sermon, fuming quietly, unaware that her hands were clenched tightly in her lap, until the doctor's large hand picked one up and held it fast. And when she peeped at him he smiled so that she glowed with happiness.

It took a long time to leave the church for so many people stopped to speak to them, talking trivialities, smiling and nodding to themselves as though they had discovered something interesting. Only Lady Truscott voiced the thoughts of the more discreet friends and acquaintances.

'Hear that Armstrong girl has thrown you over. Always thought your heart wasn't in it. But the best of luck this time, eh?'

She laughed heartily and tapped him on the arm, looking at Matilda, who, much to her annoyance, blushed.

Lunch was a cheerful meal; the talk was all of Christmas—the members of the family who would be coming, Christmas cards and presents—and how splendid it was that Mr Paige had recovered so well.

They had coffee in the drawing room and presently the doctor put down his cup. 'Matilda and I are going for a walk with Sam. Mrs Inch will bring the tea about four o'clock but we should be back by then.'

He turned to Matilda. 'Ready? You'll need some sensible shoes.'

She fetched the shoes, put on the coat and tied a scarf round her head. In the hall she said tartly, 'I wasn't asked if I wanted to go for a walk with you.'

He swung her round to face him. 'But you do, don't you? I didn't need to ask you because I know you so well—all of you: your thoughts and feelings, your kindness and delight in life. I'm not going to kiss you now or I shall be unable to stop. Come along.'

They went up the lane by the church, shrouded by trees, bare now, their leaves thick under foot. It was quiet and cold and the air was like wine. The trees thinned presently and the lane lay ahead of them, winding between wintry fields.

The doctor came to a halt and took Matilda in his arms.

'I fell in love with you a long time ago although I didn't know it at the time, and now I love you so deeply that I cannot go on without you, my darling. You are so beautiful...' He ran a gentle finger down her cheek. 'Will you marry me?' And then he added, 'No, don't answer yet; first this...'

He bent to kiss her and Matilda, who had often wondered what heaven was like, knew now that it was a lane between bare winter fields with Henry's arms around her. Presently she said, 'Yes, of course I'll marry you, Henry. I've been in love with you since the day you asked me if I would start work on Monday!'

She smiled up at him and was kissed once more. 'But it's all a bit difficult.' She went on, 'There's Father and Mother. They won't miss me very much but Mother isn't very happy cooking and doing housework and Father forgets to pay the bills.'

'Leave that to me, dear heart. When shall we marry? Don't, I beg of you, talk about June weddings; I'm not prepared to wait.'

'Well, I can't see just what to do—and I haven't any clothes…'

The doctor tightened his hold. 'My love, I said leave it to me. We'll have the banns read next Sunday. I'm prepared to wait a month but not a moment longer.' He kissed the tip of her nose. 'You may have all the clothes you want once we're married but you must be the loveliest bride the village has ever seen. I want the whole world to see you—the village, at least—I want the church full of friends and family, the organ and the choir and you coming towards me down the aisle with your father.'

Later, much later, they went back and found Mrs Lovell and Aunt Kate sitting over the remains of the tea tray.

'Matilda and I are to be married,' said the doctor.

Mrs Inch, coming in with fresh tea and more cakes, so far forgot herself as to say, 'I saw you going up the lane and I said to myself, He'll pop the question, and I was right.' She arranged the tray just so. 'I'll just pop across and tell Mrs Simpkins; the village will be that glad...'

The doctor rang the hospital then. Mrs Paige would be in in the morning, he was told, and Mr Paige was sitting up in a chair.

'Then be kind enough to ask Mrs Paige to wait at the hospital until we come tomorrow morning, around eleven o'clock.'

'I'll still be your receptionist?' asked Matilda.

'Of course. Until I can find someone else. Mother, we intend to have a village wedding in a month's time.'

Mrs Lovell was unperturbed. 'Quite right, dear. A white wedding after the first dull weeks of January is just what we all need. Kate and I will be entirely at your disposal. Morning coats and wedding hats and a large reception?'

'Yes. As soon as the Paiges are back we can perhaps talk things over with them.'

Matilda said in her sensible voice, 'We couldn't possibly have a reception at the cottage.'

'I'm quite sure that Lady Truscott is longing to lend you her house,' said Aunt Kate. 'You have no need to worry about anything, Matilda.'

She went to bed that night with her head in a whirl, only certain of one thing: Henry loved her and they were to be married.

The next morning he drove her to Taunton. They went to the ward where her father was and found him in a chair and Mrs Paige walking to and fro impatiently.

'Dr Lovell, Matilda, I've been waiting for hours. Couldn't you have phoned?'

Matilda went to kiss her father and the doctor said nothing but went to greet his patient.

'You are to return home very shortly,' he said, 'and there is no reason why you shouldn't resume a quiet life again. We shall all be glad to see you back in the village.'

'Why do you want to see me?' asked her mother.

'Matilda and I are to be married.' He took Matilda's hand as he spoke and smiled at her. 'In a month's time at the village church. When you return home after Christmas you can discuss things with Matilda. She is, of course, staying with me. My mother and family are with me for Christmas.'

Her father was the first to speak. 'Matilda, my dear, what happy news. I am delighted for you both and wish you both every happiness.'

Mrs Paige said slowly, 'But how will I manage? I'm sure it's splendid news but you can't marry so soon. I must have help. Besides, there's no money for a wedding. You could have a very quiet one, of course.'

The doctor said blandly, 'We are having a big wedding; I have a large family and many friends and I want them all to come and see us married. As for the reception, I believe that Lady Truscott will have it at her house.'

'Oh, well, in that case—I must say I'm very surprised.'

Mrs Paige went to Matilda and kissed her cheek. 'At least you will be living near enough to see us frequently.'

'As to that,' said the doctor pleasantly, 'that may not be possible.' He turned to Mr Paige. 'Quite by chance an uncle of mine has asked me if I know of a scholar who would consider taking the post of curator of the ecclesiastical library and museum housed in a large country property near Cheltenham. There is a house with the job, a very fair salary and a fairly lively social life. I'm sure Mrs Paige could deal with that side of the job. It is a permanent position and they prefer an older man. I wondered if you would be interested? You would have plenty of leisure to continue your own writing.'

Mr Paige said slowly, 'It sounds a most promising offer. But will this recent illness be a deterrent?'

'Most unlikely. The work involved will be well within your capabilities.'

'Well, this is indeed a happy day for me. My dear, what do you think? Would you feel strong enough to undertake some social duties?'

Mrs Paige was smiling. 'Of course, my dear. It sounds ideal for you. When are you to go?'

The doctor said, 'I'll drive Mr Paige over after Christmas and if everything is satisfactory I imagine you can move there whenever it is convenient. But not before our wedding; you will want to help Matilda with that, will you not?'

Matilda listened to this in silence. Henry had told her not to worry, to leave everything to him, but all the same she had been worrying. And there had been no need; he was arranging everything exactly as he wanted it to be.

They went soon after, leaving a quietly contented Mr Paige and an excited Mrs Paige. Most of her excitement was at the idea of leaving the village but she spared a few thoughts about Matilda. She was going to lose someone who had always been on hand to help her, with money and time and a willing pair of hands; on the other hand dear Henry—he was already dear Henry—was well off and well connected. Very desirable in a son-in-law.

'You've made Father very happy,' said Matilda as they

drove back. 'Do you suppose they'll accept him? It's exactly what he would like.'

'He'll be accepted, sweetheart. Have we any more problems?'

She had one—the wedding dress—but she wasn't going to bother him with that.

The next day it was work as usual. There would be a surgery tomorrow and then hopefully it would close down until after Boxing Day except for emergencies. The family would start to arrive tomorrow evening; Matilda inspected the pink dress and hoped that it would do, and while she was doing that Mrs Inch came to see her.

'I dare say you've got plans of your own, miss. But you might like to know that Mrs Vickery—she dressmakes, you know—has a length of white silk crêpe going begging. A customer decided not to use it and Mrs Vickery bought it off her. She was wondering if you'd like her to make you a wedding dress from it? She makes nicely...'

'Mrs Inch, that's exactly what I would like. Could I go and see her after Christmas? Would you tell her if you see her? I'll go the day after Boxing Day.'

There was another small problem: she had some presents but still nothing for Henry and his mother. She nipped across to Mrs Simpkins', who, full of enthusiasm at the turn of events, delved into various boxes and drawers. She had a little water colour of the village, painted by a visiting artist and put away ready for the tourists in the summer, and a silver pencil which Matilda thought Henry might never use; but there was nothing else...

It was Christmas Eve, and the family had all arrived by now—pleased to see each other, delighted to meet

Matilda and make much of her. Going down in the pink dress for dinner, she found the doctor waiting for her.

The hall was empty and he held her close and kissed her. 'Come into the study; I've something for you.'

A ring: sapphires in an old-fashioned gold setting. He slipped it onto her finger. 'It was my grandmother's; she left it to me to give to my bride.'

Matilda said, 'It fits and it's beautiful. Thank you, Henry.' And she thanked him suitably, which meant that she had to tidy her hair before they went to join everyone else.

And Christmas Day was a day never to be forgotten. Everyone went to church, even Mrs Inch and Kitty, although Mrs Inch did slip off halfway through the service to baste the turkey. And there was coffee for anyone who wanted it after the service, although the doctor left his mother to act as hostess while he drove Matilda to the hospital. She sat close to him and Sam had his head pressed against her. She was almost too happy to talk.

Mr Paige looked to be almost his old self and Mrs Paige, with the prospect of a future more to her liking, was prepared to like everyone. Her friends were coming for her presently; she told Matilda that she would stay until Mr Paige had had his Christmas dinner.

The doctor had left them briefly and when he returned it was to tell them that Mr Paige could go home in a week.

'I must pull myself together,' said Mrs Paige, 'for there will be a great deal to do if you are determined to marry so soon.'

The doctor was a splendid host. Nothing had been overlooked: there was a tree, presents, a magnificent dinner table, champagne. Matilda, sitting beside him as he carved the turkey, wondered how he had found time to plan it all. She caught his eye and they smiled at each other—two people very much in love.

They had just finished breakfast on Boxing Day when the doctor was called to a small farm some miles from the village. One of the boys in the family had cut himself badly.

'I'll come with you,' said Matilda.

It wasn't very serious, only needing a few stitches, an injection and instructions to go to the surgery in a few days' time. They stopped in a lay-by to talk on the way back.

'I shall have to go home to get ready for Mother and Father.' She tucked a hand in his. 'I can go on working for you?'

'Yes, until I can find someone to take over. And you have no need to go home until the day before their return.'

'But Mother will want to start packing up...'

'They won't move until after our wedding and I've no doubt that there will be some help available.'

So she stayed at his house and part of the day she was Miss Paige in the waiting room and part of the day she was Matilda in her future home.

But she was home to welcome her parents and almost the first thing her mother said was, 'Your wedding dress, Matilda; you had better hire it—there's a shop in Taunton.'

Mrs Vickery was making a splendid job of the white silk crêpe. Matilda said, 'There's no need, Mother. I have my dress.'

'Well, really; am I to have no say in the matter?'

A question which Matilda prudently didn't answer.

The year was a month old. It was a still day with the pale sun shining on early morning frost. Matilda got up

early, made tea, got the breakfast and found her father's
spectacles and zipped her mother into her dress, then she
went to her room.

She took her wedding dress from the empty wardrobe and put it on, fastened the little buttons on its long
sleeves, fastened Henry's pearls around the modest neck-
line and then sat down to arrange her veil before the mirror. A simple one lent to her by his mother.

When her mother came in, she was standing by the
open window listening to the church bells already ringing.

Mrs Paige stopped short at the door. 'Matilda—why,
you look so pretty.' And just for a moment she forgot
to be selfish and thoughtless. 'I hope you will both be
very happy.'

Matilda kissed her mother's cheek. 'We shall be,
Mother. We love each other.'

The drive to church with her father in the be-ribboned
car was short. There was a small crowd outside the church
gates, calling out to her and wishing her well, and in the
porch the two small bridesmaids, Henry's nieces, waited.
Through the open door she glimpsed a packed church.
Henry had told her that he wanted the whole world to
see them wed and he had achieved his wish; the village
had turned out to a man, mingling with his family and
friends.

She saw grey waistcoats and top hats in the pews,
splendid creations on the ladies' heads, early spring flowers, old Miss Clarke thumping away at the organ and the
choir ready to burst into 'The Voice that Breathed o'er
Eden'. Not one single embellishment of their day had
been forgotten.

Miss Clarke allowed the organ to dwindle to a few
soft notes and the choir opened their mouths as the con-

gregation rose to its feet, every head turned to see the bride. All except Henry.

Matilda tweaked her father's sleeve and they started down the aisle. When they were almost at the altar steps the doctor looked round. And such was the look of love on his face that she wanted to break into a run and feel his arms around her. But she didn't; she paced slowly to his side and smiled up at him as he took her hand in his.

Mr Milton opened his prayer book. He began, 'Dearly beloved, we are gathered together here...'

For Matilda's wedding...!

* * * * *

NANNY BY CHANCE

Chapter 1

Araminta Pomfrey, a basket of groceries over one arm, walked unhurriedly along the brick path to the back door, humming as she went. She was, after all, on holiday, and the morning was fine, the autumn haze slowly lifting to promise a pleasant September day—the first of the days ahead of doing nothing much until she took up her new job.

She paused at the door to scratch the head of the elderly, rather battered cat sitting there. An old warrior if ever there was one, with the inappropriate name of Cherub. He went in with her, following her down the short passage and into the kitchen, where she put her basket on the table, offered him milk and then, still humming, went across the narrow hall to the sitting room.

Her mother and father would be there, waiting for her to return from the village shop so that they might have coffee together. The only child of elderly parents, she had known from an early age that although they loved her dearly, her unexpected late arrival had upset their established way of life. They were clever, both authorities on ancient Celtic history, and had published books on the subject—triumphs of knowledge even if they didn't do much to boost their finances.

Not that either of them cared about that. Her father

had a small private income, which allowed them to live
precariously in the small house his father had left him,
and they had sent Araminta to a good school, confident
that she would follow in their footsteps and become a
literary genius of some sort. She had done her best, but
the handful of qualifications she had managed to get had
been a disappointment to them, so that when she had told
them that she would like to take up some form of nursing, they had agreed with relief.

There had been no question of her leaving home and
training at some big hospital; her parents, their heads in
Celtic clouds, had no time for household chores or cooking. The elderly woman who had coped while Araminta
was at school had been given her notice and Araminta
took over the housekeeping while going each day to a
children's convalescent home at the other end of the village. It hadn't been quite what she had hoped for, but it
had been a start.

And now, five years later, fate had smiled kindly upon
her. An elderly cousin, recently widowed, was coming
to run the house for her mother and father and Araminta
was free to start a proper training. And about time too,
she had reflected, though probably she would be considered too old to start training at twenty-three. But her
luck had held; in two weeks' time she was to start as a
student nurse at a London teaching hospital.

Someone was with her parents. She opened the door
and took a look. Dr Jenkell, a family friend as well as
their doctor for many years.

She bade him good morning and added, 'I'll fetch the
coffee.' She smiled at her mother and went back to the
kitchen, to return presently with a tray laden with cups
and saucers, the coffeepot and a plate of biscuits.

'Dr Jenkell has some splendid news for you, Araminta,' said her mother. 'Not too much milk, dear.' She took the cup Araminta offered her and sat back, looking pleased about something.

Araminta handed out coffee and biscuits. She said, 'Oh?' in a polite voice, drank some coffee and then, since the doctor was looking at her, added, 'Is it something very exciting?'

Dr Jenkell wiped some coffee from his drooping moustache. 'I have a job for you, my dear. A splendid opportunity. Two small boys who are to go and live for a short time with their uncle in Holland while their parents are abroad. You have had a good deal of experience dealing with the young and I hear glowing accounts of you at the children's home. I was able to recommend you with complete sincerity.'

Araminta drew a steadying breath. 'I've been taken as a student nurse at St Jules'. I start in two weeks' time.' She added, 'I told you and you gave me a reference.'

Dr Jenkell waved a dismissive hand. 'That's easily arranged. All you need to do is to write and say that you are unable to start training for the time being. A month or so makes no difference.'

'It does to me,' said Araminta. 'I'm twenty-three, and if I don't start my training now I'll be too old.' She refilled his coffee cup with a steady hand. 'It's very kind of you, and I do appreciate it, but it means a lot to me— training for something I really want to do.'

She glanced at her mother and father and the euphoria of the morning ebbed way; they so obviously sided with Dr Jenkell.

'Of course you must take this post Dr Jenkell has so kindly arranged for you,' said her mother. 'Indeed, you cannot refuse, for I understand that he has already promised that you will do so. As for your training, a few months here or there will make no difference at all. You have all your life before you.'

'You accepted this job for me without telling me?' asked Araminta of the doctor.

Her father spoke then. 'You were not here when the offer was made. Your mother and I agreed that it was a splendid opportunity for you to see something of the world and agreed on your behalf. We acted in your best interests, my dear.'

I'm a grown woman, thought Araminta wildly, and I'm being treated like a child, a mid-Victorian child at that, meekly accepting what her elders and betters have decided was best for her. Well, I won't, she reflected, looking at the three elderly faces in turn.

'I think that, if you don't mind, Dr Jenkell, I'll go and see this uncle.'

Dr Jenkell beamed at her. 'That's right, my dear— get some idea of what is expected of you. You'll find him very sympathetic to any adjustments you may have in mind.'

Araminta thought this unlikely, but she wasn't going to say so. She loved her parents and they loved her, although she suspected that they had never quite got over the surprise of her arrival in their early middle age. She wasn't going to upset them now; she would see this man, explain why she couldn't accept the job and then think of some way of telling her parents which wouldn't worry them. Dr Jenkell might be annoyed; she would think about that later.

Presently the doctor left and she collected the coffee cups and went along to the kitchen to unpack her shopping and prepare the lunch, leaving her mother and father deep in a discussion of the book of Celtic history they were writing together. They hadn't exactly forgotten her. The small matter of her future having been comfortably settled, they felt free to return to their abiding interest...

As she prepared the lunch, Araminta laid her plans. Dr Jenkell had given her the uncle's address, and unless he'd seen fit to tell the man that she intended visiting him she would take him by surprise, explain that she wasn't free to take the job and that would be that. There was nothing like striking while the iron was hot. It would be an easy enough journey; Hambledon was barely three miles from Henley-on-Thames and she could be in London in no time at all. She would go the very next day...

Her mother, apprised of her intention, made no objection. Indeed, she was approving. 'As long as you leave something ready for our lunch, Araminta. You know how impatient your father is if he has to wait for a meal, and if I'm occupied...'

Araminta promised cold meat and a salad and went to her room to brood over her wardrobe. It was early autumn. Too late in the year for a summer outfit and too warm still for her good jacket and skirt. It would have to be the jersey two-piece with the corn silk tee shirt.

Her mother, an old-fashioned woman in many respects, considered it ladylike, which it was. It also did nothing for Araminta, who was a girl with no looks worth glancing at twice. She had mousy hair, long and fine, worn in an untidy pile on top of her head, an unremarkable face—except for large, thickly fringed hazel eyes—and a nicely rounded person, largely unnoticed since her clothes had always been chosen with an eye to their suitability.

They were always in sensible colours, in fabrics not easily spoilt by small sticky fingers which would go to the cleaners or the washing machine time and time again. She studied her reflection in the looking glass and sighed over her small sharp nose and wide mouth. She had a lovely smile, but since she had no reason to smile at her own face she was unaware of that.

Not that that mattered; this uncle would probably be a prosey old bachelor, and, since he was a friend of Dr Jenkell, of a similar age.

She was up early the following morning to take tea to her parents, give Cherub his breakfast and tidy the house, put lunch ready and then catch the bus to Henley.

A little over two hours later she was walking along a narrow street close to Cavendish Square. It was very quiet, with tall Regency houses on either side of it, their paintwork pristine, brass doorknockers gleaming. Whoever uncle was, reflected Araminta, he had done well for himself.

The house she was looking for was at the end of the terrace, with an alley beside it leading to mews behind the houses. Delightful, reflected Araminta, and she banged the knocker.

The man who answered the door was short and thin with sandy hair, small dark eyes and a very sharp nose. Just like a rat, thought Araminta, and added, a nice rat, for he had a friendly smile and the little eyes twinkled.

It was only then that she perceived that she should have made an appointment; uncle was probably out on his rounds—did doctors who lived in grand houses have rounds? She didn't allow herself to be discouraged by the thought.

'I would like to see Dr van der Breugh. I should have

made an appointment but it's really rather urgent. It concerns his two nephews…'

'Ah, yes, miss. If you would wait while I see if the doctor is free.'

He led the way down a narrow hall and opened a door. His smile was friendly. 'I won't be two ticks,' he assured her. 'Make yourself comfortable.'

The moment he had closed the door behind him, she got up from her chair and began a tour of the room. It was at the back of the house and the windows, tall and narrow, overlooked a small walled garden with the mews beyond. It was furnished with a pleasant mixture of antique cabinets, tables and two magnificent sofas on either side of an Adam fireplace. There were easy chairs, too, and a vast mirror over the fireplace. A comfortable room, even if rather grand, and obviously used, for there was a dog basket by one of the windows and a newspaper thrown down on one of the tables.

She studied her person in the mirror, something which brought her no satisfaction. The jersey two-piece, in a sensible brown, did nothing for her, and her hair had become a little ruffled. She poked at it impatiently and then looked round guiltily as the door opened.

'If you will come this way, miss,' said the rat-faced man. 'The boss has got ten minutes to spare.'

Was he the butler? she wondered, following him out of the room. If so, he wasn't very respectful. Perhaps modern butlers had freedom of speech…

They went back down the hall and he opened a door on the other side of it.

'Miss Pomfrey,' he announced, and gave her a friendly shove before shutting the door on her.

It was a fair-sized room, lined with bookshelves, one

corner of it taken up by a large desk. The man sitting at
it got to his feet as Araminta hesitated, staring at him.
This surely couldn't be uncle. He was a giant of a man
with fair hair touched with silver, a handsome man with
a high-bridged nose, a thin, firm mouth and a determined
chin. He took off the glasses he was wearing and smiled
as he came to her and shook hands.

'Miss Pomfrey? Dr Jenkell told me that you might come
and see me. No doubt you would like some details—'

'Look,' said Araminta urgently, 'before you say any
more, I've come to tell you that I can't look after your
nephews. I'm starting as a student nurse in two weeks'
time. I didn't know about this job until Dr Jenkell told
me. I'm sure he meant it kindly, and my parents thought
it was a splendid idea, but they arranged it all while I
wasn't there.'

The doctor pulled up a chair. 'Do sit down and tell
me about it,' he invited. He had a quiet, rather slow way
of speaking, and she felt soothed by it, as was intended.

'Briskett is bringing us coffee...'

Araminta forgot for the moment why she was there.
She felt surprisingly comfortable with the doctor, as
though she had known him for years. She said now, 'Briskett? The little man who answered the door? Is he your
butler? He called you "the boss"—I mean, he doesn't
talk like a butler...'

'He runs the house for me, most efficiently. His rather
unusual way of talking is, I fancy, due to his addiction
to American films; they represent democracy to him.
Every man is an equal. Nevertheless, he is a most trustworthy and hard-working man; I've had him for years.
He didn't upset you?'

'Heavens, no. I liked him. He looks like a friendly rat,'

she explained. 'Beady eyes, you know, and a sharp nose. He has a lovely smile.'

Briskett came in then, with the coffee tray, which he set down on a small table near Araminta's chair. 'You be mother,' he said, and added, 'Don't you forget you've to be at the hospital, sir.'

'Thank you, Briskett, I'll be leaving very shortly.'

Asked to do so, Araminta poured their coffee. 'I'm sorry if I'm being inconvenient,' she said. 'You see, I thought if you didn't expect me it would be easier for me to explain and you wouldn't have time to argue.'

The doctor managed not to smile. He agreed gravely. 'I quite see that the whole thing is a misunderstanding and I'm sorry you have been vexed.' He added smoothly, with just a touch of regret allowed to show, 'You would have done splendidly, I feel sure. They are six years old, the boys, twins and a handful. I must find someone young and patient to cope with them. Their parents— their mother is my sister—are archaeologists and are going to the Middle East for a month or so. It seemed a good idea if the children were to make their home with me while they are away. I leave for Holland in a week's time, and if I can't find someone suitable, I'm afraid their mother will have to stay here in England. A pity, but it can't be helped.'

'If they went to Holland with you, would they live with you? I mean, don't you have a wife?'

'My dear Miss Pomfrey, I am a very busy man. I've no time to look for a wife and certainly no time to marry. I have a housekeeper and her husband, both too elderly to cope with small boys. I intend sending them to morning school and shall spend as much time with them as I can, but they will need someone to look after them.'

He put down his coffee cup. 'I'm sorry you had to come and see me, but I quite understand that you are committed. Though I feel that we should all have got on splendidly together.'

She was being dismissed very nicely. She got up. 'Yes, I think we would too. I'm sorry. I'll go—or you'll be late at the hospital.'

She held out a hand and had it taken in his large, firm clasp. To her utter surprise she heard herself say, 'if I cancelled my place at the hospital, do you suppose they'd let me apply again? It's St Jules'…'

'I have a clinic there. I have no doubt that they would allow that. There is always a shortage of student nurses.'

'And how long would I be in Holland?'

'Oh, a month, six weeks—perhaps a little longer. But you mustn't think of altering your plans just to oblige me, Miss Pomfrey.'

'I'm not obliging you,' said Araminta, not beating about the bush. 'I would like to look after the boys, if you think I'd do.' She studied his face; he looked grave but friendly. 'I've no idea why I've changed my mind,' she told him, 'but I've waited so long to start my training as a nurse, another month or two really won't matter.' She added anxiously, 'I won't be too old, will I? To start training…?'

'I should imagine not. How old are you?'

'Twenty-three.'

'You aren't too old,' he assured her in a kind voice, 'and if it will help you at all, I'll see if I can get you on to the next take-in once you are back in England.'

'Now that would be kind of you. Will you let me know when you want me and how I'm to get to Holland? I'm going now; you'll be late and Briskett will hate me.'

He laughed then. 'Somehow I think not. I'll be in touch.'

He went into the hall with her and Briskett was there, too.

'Cutting it fine,' he observed severely. He opened the door for Araminta. 'Go carefully,' he begged her.

Araminta got on a bus for Oxford Street, found a café and over a cup of coffee sorted out her thoughts. That she was doing something exactly opposite to her intentions was a fact which she bypassed for the moment. She had, with a few impulsive words, rearranged her future. A future about which she knew almost nothing, too.

Where exactly was she to go? How much would she be paid? What about free time? The language question? The doctor had mentioned none of these. Moreover, he had accepted her decision without surprise and in a casual manner which, when she thought about it, annoyed her. He should be suitably grateful that she had delayed her plans to accommodate his. She had another cup of coffee and a bun and thought about clothes.

She had a little money of her own. In theory she kept the small salary she had been getting at the convalescent home to spend as she wished, but in practice she used it to bolster up the housekeeping money her father gave her each month.

Neither he nor her mother were interested in how it was spent. The mundane things of life—gas bills, the plumber, the most economical cuts of meat—meant nothing to them; they lived in their own world of the Celts, who, to them at least, were far more important and interesting.

Now she must spend some of her savings on clothes.

She wouldn't need much: a jacket, which would stand up to rain, a skirt and one or two woollies, and shoes—the sensible pair she wore to the convalescent home were shabby. No need for a new dress; she wasn't likely to go anywhere.

And her parents; someone would have to keep an eye on them if she were to go to Holland in a week's time and if Aunt Millicent, the elderly cousin, was unable to come earlier than they had arranged. Mrs Snow in the village might oblige for a few days, with basic cooking and cleaning. Really, she thought vexedly, she could make no plans until she heard from Dr van der Breugh.

Her parents received her news with mild interest. Her mother nodded her head in a knowledgeable way and observed that both she and Araminta's father knew what was best for her and she was bound to enjoy herself, as well as learn something of a foreign land, even if it was only a very small one like Holland. She added that she was sure that Araminta would arrange everything satisfactorily before she went. 'You'll like looking after the dear little boys.'

Araminta said that, yes, she expected she would. Probably they were as tiresome and grubby as all small boys, but she was fond of children and had no qualms about the job. She would have even less when she knew more about it.

A state of affairs which was put right the next morning, when she received a letter from Dr van der Breugh. It was a long letter, typed, and couched in businesslike language. She would be called for at her home on the following Sunday at eleven o'clock and would spend a few hours with her charges before travelling to Holland on the night ferry from Harwich. She would be good enough to carry a valid passport and anything she might require overnight. It was hoped that her luggage might be confined to no more than two suitcases.

She would have a day off each week, and every evening after eight o'clock, and such free time during the day as could be arranged. Her salary would be paid to her weekly in Dutch guldens... She paused here to do some arithmetic—she considered it a princely sum, which certainly sweetened the somewhat arbitrary tone of the letter. Although there was no reason why it should have been couched in friendlier terms; she scarcely knew the doctor and didn't expect to see much of him while she was in Holland.

She told her mother that the arrangements for her new job seemed quite satisfactory, persuaded Mrs Snow to undertake the housekeeping until Aunt Millicent could come, and then sifted through her wardrobe. The jersey two-piece and the corn silk blouse, an equally sober skirt and an assortment of tops and a warmer woolly or two, a short wool jacket to go over everything and a perfectly plain dress in a soft blue crêpe; an adequate choice of clothes, she considered, adding a raincoat, plain slippers and undies.

She had good shoes and a leather handbag; gloves and stockings and a headscarf or two would fill the odd corners in the one case she intended taking. Her overnight bag would take the rest. She liked clothes, but working in the children's convalescent home had called for sensible skirts and tops in sensible colours, and she had seldom had much of a social life. She was uneasily aware that her clothes were dull, but there was no time to change that, and anyway, she hadn't much money. Perhaps she would get a new outfit in Holland...

The week went quickly. She cleaned and polished, washed and ironed, laid in a stock of food and got a room ready for Aunt Millicent. And she went into Henley and bought new shoes, low-heeled brown leather and expensive, and when she saw a pink angora sweater in a shop window she bought that too. She was in two minds about buying a new jacket, but caution took over then. She had already spent more money than she'd intended. Though caution wasn't quite strong enough to prevent her buying a pretty silk blouse which would render the sober skirt less sober.

On Sunday morning she was ready and waiting by eleven o'clock—waiting with her parents who, despite their wish to get back to researching the Ancient Celts, had come into the hall to see her off. Cherub was there too, looking morose, and she stooped to give him a final hug; they would miss each other.

Exactly on the hour a car drew up outside and Briskett got out, wished them all good morning, stowed her case in the boot and held the rear car door open for her.

'Oh, I'd rather sit in front with you,' said Araminta, and she gave her parents a final kiss before getting into the car, waved them a cheerful goodbye and sat back beside Briskett. It was a comfortable car, a Jaguar, and she could see from the moment Briskett took the wheel that despite his unlikely looks they hid the soul of a born driver.

There wasn't much traffic until they reached Henley and here Briskett took the road to Oxford.

'Aren't I to go to the London address?' asked Araminta.

'No, miss. The doctor thought it wise if you were to make the acquaintance of the boys at their home. They live with their parents at Oxford. The doctor will come for you and them later today and drive to Harwich for the night ferry.'

'Oh, well, I expect that's a good idea. Are you coming to Holland too?'

'No, miss. I'll stay to keep an eye on things here; the boss has adequate help in Holland. He's for ever to-ing and fro-ing—having two homes, as it were.'

'Then why can't the two boys stay here in England?'

'He'll be in Holland for a few weeks, popping over here when he is needed. Much in demand, he is.'

'We won't be expected to pop over, too? Very unsettling for the little boys...'

'Oh, no, miss. That's why you've been engaged; he can come and go without being hampered, as you might say.'

The house he stopped before in Oxford was in a terrace of similar comfortably large houses, standing well back from the road. Araminta got out and stood beside Briskett in the massive porch waiting for someone to answer the bell. She was a self-contained girl, not given to sudden bursts of excitement, but she was feeling nervous now.

Supposing the boys disliked her on sight? It was possible. Or their parents might not like the look of her. After all, they knew nothing about her, and now that she came to think about it, nor did Dr van der Breugh. But she didn't allow these uncertain feelings to show; the door was opened by a girl in a pinafore, looking harassed, and she and Briskett went into the hall.

'Miss Pomfrey,' said Briskett. 'She's expected.'

The girl nodded and led them across the hall and into a large room overlooking a garden at the back of the house. It was comfortably furnished, extremely untidy, and there were four people in it. The man and woman sitting in easy chairs with the Sunday papers strewn around them got up.

The woman was young and pretty, tall and slim, and well dressed in casual clothes. She came to meet Araminta as she hesitated by the door.

'Miss Pomfrey, how nice of you to come all this way. We're so grateful. I'm Lucy Ingram, Marcus's sister—but of course you know that—and this is my husband, Jack.'

Araminta shook hands with her and then with Mr Ingram, a rather short stout man with a pleasant rugged face, while his wife spoke to Briskett, who left the room with a cheerful, 'So long, miss, I'll see you later.'

'Such a reliable man, and so devoted to Marcus,' said his sister. 'Come and meet the boys.'

They were at the other end of the room, sitting at a small table doing a jigsaw puzzle, unnaturally and suspiciously quiet. They were identical twins which, reflected Araminta, wasn't going to make things any easier, and they looked too good to be true.

'Peter and Paul,' said their mother. 'If you look carefully you'll see that Peter has a small scar over his right eye. He fell out of a tree years ago—it makes it easy to tell them apart.'

She beckoned them over and they came at once, two seemingly angelic children. Araminta wondered what kind of a bribe they had been offered to behave so beautifully. She shook their small hands in turn and smiled.

'Hello,' she said. 'You'll have to help me to tell you apart, and you mustn't mind if I muddle you up at first.'

'I'm Peter. What's your name—not Miss Pomfrey, your real name?'

'Araminta.'

The boys looked at each other. 'That's a long name.'

They cast their mother a quick look. 'We'll call you Mintie.'

'That's not very polite,' began Mrs Ingram.

'If you've no objection, I think it's a nice idea. I don't feel a bit like Miss Pomfrey...'

'Well, if you don't mind—go and have your milk, boys, while we have our coffee and then you can show Miss... Mintie your room and get to know each other a bit.'

They went away obediently, eyeing her as they went, and Araminta was led to a sofa and given coffee while she listened to Mrs Ingram's friendly chatter. From time to time her husband spoke, asking her quietly about her work at the children's home and if she had ever been to Holland before.

'The boys,' he told her forthrightly, 'can be little demons, but I dare say you are quite used to that. On the whole they're decent kids, and they dote on their uncle.'

Araminta, considering this remark, thought that probably it would be quite easy to dote on him, although, considering the terseness of his letter to her, not very rewarding. She would have liked to get to know him, but common sense told her that that was unlikely. Besides, once she was back in England again, he would be consigned to an easily forgotten past and she would have embarked on her nursing career...

She dismissed her thoughts and listened carefully to Mrs Ingram's instructions about the boys' clothing and meals.

'I'm telling you all these silly little details,' explained Mrs Ingram, 'because Marcus won't want to be bothered with them.' She looked anxious. 'I hope you won't find it too much...'

Araminta made haste to assure her that that was un-likely. 'At the children's home we had about forty chil-dren, and I'm used to them—two little boys will be delightful. They don't mind going to Holland?'

'No. I expect they'll miss us for a few days, but they've been to their uncle's home before, so they won't feel strange.'

Mrs Ingram began to ask carefully polite questions about Araminta and she answered them readily. If she had been Mrs Ingram she would have done the same, however well recommended she might be. Dr van der Breugh had engaged her on Dr Jenkell's advice, which was very trusting of him. Certainly he hadn't bothered with delving into her personal background.

They had lunch presently and she was pleased to see that the boys behaved nicely at the table and weren't finicky about their food. All the same, she wondered if these angelic manners would last. If they were normal little boys they wouldn't...

The rest of the day she spent with them, being shown their toys and taken into the garden to look at the gold-fish in the small pond there, and their behaviour was al-most too good to be true. There would be a reason for it, she felt sure; time enough to discover that during the new few weeks.

They answered her questions politely but she took care not to ask too many. To them she was a stranger, and she would have to earn their trust and friendship.

They went indoors presently and found Dr van der Breugh in the drawing room with their father and mother. There was no doubt that they were fond of him and that

he returned the affection. Emerging from their boisterous greeting, he looked across at Araminta and bade her
good afternoon.

'We shall be leaving directly after tea, Miss Pomfrey.
My sister won't mind if you wish to phone your mother.'

'Thank you, I should like to do that…'

'She's not Miss Pomfrey,' said Peter. 'She's Mintie.'

'Indeed?' He looked amused. 'You have rechristened
her?'

'Well, of course we have, Uncle. Miss Pomfrey isn't
her, is it? Miss Pomfrey would be tall and thin, with a
sharp nose and a wart and tell us not to get dirty. Mintie's
nice; she's not pretty, but she smiles…'

Araminta had gone a bright pink and his mother said
hastily, 'Hush, dear. Miss Pomfrey, come with me and
I'll show you where you can phone.'

Leading Araminta across the hall, she said apologetically, 'I do apologise. Peter didn't mean to be rude—indeed,
I believe he was paying you a compliment.'

Araminta laughed. 'Well, I'm glad they think of me
as Mintie, and not some tiresome woman with a wart. I
hope we're going to like each other.'

The boys had been taken upstairs to have their hands
washed and the two men were alone.

'Good of you to have the boys,' said Mr Ingram. 'Lucy
was getting in a bit of a fret. And this treasure you've
found for them seems just like an answer to a prayer.
Quiet little thing and, as Peter observed, not pretty, but a
nice calm voice. I fancy she'll do. Know much about her?'

'Almost nothing. Old Jenkell told me of her; he's
known her almost all her life. He told me that she was
entirely trustworthy, patient and kind. They loved her at
the children's home. She didn't want to come—she was

to start her training as a nurse in a week or so—but she changed her mind after refusing the job. I don't know why. I've said I'll help her to get into the next batch of students when we get back.'

The doctor wandered over to the windows. 'You'll miss your garden.' He glanced over his shoulder. 'I'll keep an eye on the boys, Jack. As you say, I think we have found a treasure in Miss Pomfrey. A nice, unassuming girl who won't intrude. Which suits me very well.'

Tea was a proper meal, taken at the table since the boys ate with them, but no time was wasted on it. Farewells were said, the boys were settled by their uncle in the back seat of his Bentley, and Araminta got into the front of the car, composed and very neat. The doctor, turning to ask her if she was comfortable, allowed himself a feeling of satisfaction. She was indeed unassuming, both in manner and appearance.

Chapter 2

Araminta, happily unaware of the doctor's opinion of her, settled back in the comfort of the big car, but she was aware of his voice keeping up a steady flow of talk with his little nephews. He sounded cheerful, and from the occasional words she could hear he was talking about sailing. Would she be expected to take part in this sport? she wondered. She hoped not, but, being a sensible girl, she didn't allow the prospect to worry her. Whatever hazards lay ahead they would be for a mere six weeks or so. The salary was generous and she was enjoying her freedom. She felt guilty about that, although she knew that her parents would be perfectly happy with Aunt Millicent.

The doctor drove through Maidenhead and on to Slough and then, to her surprise, instead of taking the ring road to the north of London, he drove to his house.

Araminta, who hadn't seen Briskett leave the Ingrams', was surprised to see him open the door to them.

'Right on time,' he observed. 'Not been travelling over the limit, I hope, sir. You lads wait there while I see to Miss Pomfrey. There's a couple of phone calls for you, Doc.'

He led Araminta to the cloakroom at the back of the hall. 'You tidy yourself, miss; I'll see to the boys. There's coffee ready in the drawing room.'

Araminta, not in the least untidy, nonetheless did as she was bid. Briskett, for all his free and easy ways, was a gem. He would be a handy man in a crisis.

When she went back into the hall he was there, waiting to usher her into the drawing room. The doctor was already there, leaning over a sofa table with the boys, studying a map. He straightened up as she went in and offered her a chair and asked her to pour their coffee. There was milk for the boys as well as a plate of biscuits and a dish of sausage rolls, which Peter and Paul demolished.

They were excited now, their sadness at leaving their mother and father already fading before the prospect of going to bed on board the ferry. Presently the doctor excused himself with the plea that there were phone calls he must make and Araminta set to work to calm them down, something at which she was adept. By the time their uncle came back they were sitting quietly beside her, listening to her telling them a story.

He paused in the doorway. 'I think it might be a good idea if you sat in the back with the boys in the car, Miss Pomfrey...'

'Mintie,' said Peter. 'Uncle Marcus, she's Mintie.'

'Mintie,' said the doctor gravely. 'If Miss Pomfrey does not object?'

'Not a bit,' said Araminta cheerfully.

They left shortly after that, crossing London in the comparative calm of a Sunday evening, onto the A12, through Brentford, Chelmsford, Colchester and finally to Harwich. Long before they had reached the port the two boys were asleep, curled up against Araminta. She sat, rather warm and cramped, with an arm around each of them, watching the doctor driving. He was a good driver. She reflected that he would be an interesting man to know. It was a pity that the opportunity to do that was improbable. She wondered why he wasn't married and allowed her imagination to roam. A widower? A love affair which had gone wrong and left him with a broken heart and dedicated to his work? Engaged? The last was the most likely. She had a sudden urge to find out.

They were amongst the last to go on board, and the doctor with one small sleeping boy and a porter with the other led the way to their cabins.

Araminta was to share a cabin with the boys; it was roomy and comfortable and well furnished, with a shower room, and once her overnight bag and the boys' luggage had been brought to her she lost no time in undressing them and popping them into their narrow beds. They roused a little, but once tucked up slept again. She unpacked her night things and wondered what she should do. Would the doctor mind if she rang for a pot of tea and a sandwich? It was almost midnight and she was hungry.

A tap on the door sent her to open it and find him outside.

'A stewardess will keep an eye on the boys. Come and have a meal; it will give me the opportunity to outline your day's work.'

She was only too glad to agree to that; she went with him to the restaurant and made a splendid supper while she listened to him quietly describing the days ahead.

'I live in Utrecht. The house is in the centre of the city, but there are several parks close by and I have arranged for the boys to attend school in the mornings. You will be free then, but I must ask you to be with them during the rest of the day. You will know best how to keep them happy and entertained.

'I have a housekeeper and a houseman who will do

all they can to make life easy for you and them. When I am free I will have the boys with me. I am sure that you will want to do some sightseeing. I expect my sister has told you her wishes concerning their clothes and daily routine. I must warn you that they are as naughty as the average small boy…they are also devoted to each other.'

Araminta speared a morsel of grilled sole. 'I'll do the best I can to keep them happy and content, Dr van der Breugh. And I shall come to you if I have any problems. You will be away during the day? Working? Will I know where you are?'

'Yes, I will always leave a phone number for you or a message with Bas. He speaks English of a sort, and is very efficient.' He smiled at her kindly. 'I'm sure everything will be most satisfactory, Miss Pomfrey. And now I expect you would like to go to your bed. You will be called in good time in the morning. We will see how the boys are then. If they're too excited to eat breakfast we will stop on the way and have something, but there should be time for a meal before we go ashore. You can manage them and have them up and ready?'

Araminta assured him that she could. Several years in the convalescent home had made her quite sure about that. She thanked him for her dinner, wished him goodnight, and was surprised when he went back to her cabin with her and saw her into it.

Nice manners, thought Araminta, getting undressed as fast as she could, having a quick shower and jumping into her bed after a last look at the boys—deeply asleep.

The boys woke when the stewardess brought morning tea. They drank the milk in the milk jug and ate all the biscuits. Talking non-stop, they washed and cleaned their teeth and dressed after a fashion. Araminta was tying shoelaces and inspecting fingernails when there was a knock on the door and the doctor came in.

'If anyone is hungry there's plenty of time for breakfast,' he observed. He looked at Araminta. 'You all slept well?'

'Like logs,' she told him, 'and we're quite ready, with everything packed.'

'Splendid. Come along, then.' He sounded briskly cheerful and she wondered if he found this disruption in his ordered life irksome. If he did, he didn't allow it to show. Breakfast was a cheerful meal, eaten without waste of time since they were nearing the Hoek of Holland and the boys wanted to see the ferry dock.

Disembarking took time, but finally they were away from the customs shed, threading their way through the town.

'We'll go straight home,' said the doctor. He had the two boys with him again and spoke to Araminta over his shoulder. 'Less than an hour's drive.' He picked up the car phone and spoke into it. 'I've told them we are on our way.'

There was a great deal of traffic as they neared Rotterdam, where they drove through the long tunnel under the Maas. Once through it, the traffic was even heavier. But presently, as they reached the outskirts of the city and were once more on the motorway, it thinned, and Araminta was able to look about her.

The country was flat, and she had expected that, but it was charming all the same, with farms well away from the highway, small copses of trees already turning to autumn tints, green meadows separated by narrow canals, and cows and horses roaming freely. The motorway bypassed the villages and towns, but she caught tantalising glimpses of them from time to time and promised herself that if she should get any free time, she would explore away from the main roads.

As though he had read her thoughts, the doctor said over his shoulder, 'This is dull, isn't it? But it's the quickest way home. Before you go back we must try and show you some of rural Holland. I think you might like it.'

She murmured her thanks. 'It's a very good road,' she said politely, anxious not to sound disparaging.

'All the motorways are good. Away from them it's a different matter. But you will see for yourself.'

Presently he turned off into a narrow country road between water meadows. 'We're going to drive along the River Vecht. It is the long way round to Utrecht, but well worth it. It will give you a taste of rural Holland.'

He drove north, away from Utrecht, and then turned into another country road running beside a river lined with lovely old houses set in well-kept grounds.

'The East Indies merchants built their houses here— there's rather a splendid castle you'll see presently on your right. There are a number in Utrecht province— most of them privately owned. You must find time to visit one of those open to the public before you go back to England.'

Apparently satisfied that he had given her enough to go on with, he began a lively conversation with the boys, leaving her to study her surroundings. They were certainly charming, but she had the feeling that he had offered the information in much the same manner as a dutiful and well mannered host would offer a drink to an unexpected and tiresome guest.

They were on the outskirts of Utrecht by now, and soon at its heart. Some magnificent buildings, she conceded, and a bewildering number of canals. She glimpsed several streets of shops, squares lined by tall, narrow houses with gabled roofs and brief views of what she supposed were parks.

The boys were talking now, nineteen to the dozen, and in Dutch. Well, of course, they would, reflected Araminta. They had a Dutch mother and uncle. They were both talking at once, interrupted from time to time by the doctor's measured tones, but presently Paul shouted over his shoulder, 'We're here, Mintie. Do look, isn't it splendid?'

She looked. They were in a narrow *gracht*, tree-lined, with houses on either side of the canal in all shapes and sizes: some of them crooked with age, all with a variety of gabled roofs. The car had stopped at the end of the *gracht* before a narrow red-brick house with double steps leading up to its solid door. She craned her neck to see its height—four storeys, each with three windows. The ground floor ones were large, but they got progressively smaller at each storey so that the top ones of all were tucked in between the curve of the gable.

The doctor got out, went around to allow the boys to join him and then opened her door. He said kindly, 'I hope you haven't found the journey too tiring?'

Araminta said, 'Not in the least,' and felt as elderly as his glance indicated. Probably she looked twice her age; her toilet on board had been sketchy...

The boys had run up the steps, talking excitedly to the man who had opened the door, and the doctor, gently urging her up the steps said, 'This is Bas, who runs my home with his wife. As I said, he speaks English, and will do all he can to help you.'

She offered a hand and smiled at the elderly lined face with its thatch of grey hair. Bas shook hands and said gravely, 'We welcome you, miss, and shall do our best to make you happy.'

Which was nice, she thought, and wished that the doctor had said something like that.

What he did say was rather absent-minded. 'Yes, yes, Miss Pomfrey. Make yourself at home and ask Bas for anything you may need.'

Which she supposed was the next best thing to a welcome.

The hall they entered was long and narrow, with a great many doors on either side of it, and halfway along it there was a staircase, curving upwards between the panelled walls. As they reached a pair of magnificent mahogany doors someone came to meet them from the back of the house. It was a short, stout woman in a black dress and wearing a printed pinny over it. She had a round rosy face and grey hair screwed into a bun. Her eyes were very dark and as she reached them she gave Araminta a quick look.

'Jet...' Dr van der Breugh sounded pleased to see her and indeed kissed her cheek and spoke at some length in his own language. His housekeeper smiled then, shook Araminta's hand and bent to hug the boys, talking all the time.

The doctor said in English, 'Go with Jet to the kitchen, both of you, and have milk and biscuits. Miss Pomfrey shall fetch you as soon as she has had a cup of coffee.'

Bas opened the doors and Araminta, invited to enter the room, did so. It was large and lofty, with two windows overlooking the *gracht*, a massive fireplace along one wall and glass doors opening into a room beyond. It was furnished with two vast sofas on either side of the fireplace and a number of comfortable chairs. There was a Pembroke table between the windows and a rosewood sofa table on which a china bowl of late roses glowed.

A walnut and marquetry display cabinet took up most of the wall beside the fireplace on one side, and on the other there was a black and gold laquer cabinet on a gilt stand. Above it was a great *stoel* clock, its quiet tick-tock somehow enhancing the peace of the room. And the furnishings were restful: dull mulberry-red and dark green, the heavy curtains at the windows matching the upholstery of the sofas and chairs. The floor was highly polished oak with Kasham silk rugs, faded with age, scattered on it.

A magnificent room, reflected Araminta, and if it had been anyone other than the doctor she would have said so. She held her tongue, however, sensing that he would give her a polite and chilly stare at her unasked-for praise.

He said, 'Do sit down, Miss Pomfrey. Jet shall take you to your room when you have had coffee and then perhaps you would see to the boys' things and arrange some kind of schedule for their day? We could discuss that later today.'

Bas brought the coffee then, and she poured it for them both and sat drinking it silently as the doctor excused himself while he glanced through the piles of letters laid beside his chair, his spectacles on his handsome nose, oblivious of her presence.

He had indeed forgotten her for the moment, but presently he looked up and said briskly, 'I expect you would like to go to your room. Take the boys with you, will you? I shall be out to lunch and I suggest that you take the boys for a walk this afternoon. They know where the park is and Bas will tell you anything you may wish to know.'

He went to open the door for her and she went past

him into the hall. She would have liked a second cup of coffee…

Bas was waiting for her and took her to the kitchen, a semi-basement room at the back of the house. It was nice to be greeted by cheerful shouts from the boys and Jet's kind smile and the offer of another cup of coffee. She sat down at the old-fashioned scrubbed table while Bas told her that he would serve their lunch at midday and that when they came back from their walk he would have an English afternoon tea waiting for her.

His kind old face crinkled into a smile as he told her, 'And if you should wish to telephone your family, you are to do so—*mijnheer's* orders.'

'Oh, may I? I'll do that now, before I go to my room…'

Her mother answered the phone, expressed relief that Araminta had arrived safely and observed that there were some interesting burial mounds in the north of Holland if she should have the opportunity to see them. 'And enjoy yourself, dear,' said her parent.

Araminta, not sure whether it was the burial mounds or her job which was to give her enjoyment, assured her mother that she would do so and went in search of the boys.

Led upstairs by Jet, with the boys running ahead, she found herself in a charming room on the second floor. It overlooked the street below and was charmingly furnished, with a narrow canopied bed, a dressing table under its window and two small easy chairs flanking a small round table. The colour scheme was a mixture of pastel colours and the furniture was of some pale wood she didn't recognise. There was a large cupboard and a little door led to a bathroom. The house might be old, she thought, but the plumbing was ultra-modern. It had everything one could wish for...

The boys' room was across the narrow passage, with another bathroom, and at the end of the passage was a room which she supposed had been a nursery, for it had a low table and small chairs round it and shelves full of toys.

She was right. The boys, both talking at once, eager to show her everything, told her that some of the toys had belonged to their uncle and his father; even his grand-father.

'We have to be careful of them,' said Paul, 'but Uncle Marcus lets us play with them when we're here.'

'Do you come here often?' asked Araminta.

'Every year with Mummy and Daddy.'

Bas came to tell them that lunch was ready, so they all trooped downstairs and, since breakfast seemed a long time ago, made an excellent meal.

The boys were still excited, and Araminta judged it a good idea to take them for the walk. She could unpack later, when they had tired themselves out.

Advised by Bas and urged on by them, she got her own jacket, buttoned them into light jackets and went out into the street. The park was five minutes' walk away, small and beautifully kept, a green haven in the centre of the city. There was a small pond, with goldfish and seats under the trees, but the boys had no intention of sitting down. When they had tired of the goldfish they insisted on showing her some of the surrounding streets.

'And we'll go to the Dom Tower,' they assured her. 'It's ever so high, and the Domkerk—that's a cathedral—and perhaps Uncle will take us to the university.'

They were all quite tired by the time they got back to

the house, and Araminta was glad of the tea Bas brought
to them in a small room behind the drawing room.

'*Mijnheer* will be home very shortly,' he told her, 'and
will be free to have the boys with him for a while whilst
you unpack. They are to have their supper at half past
six.'

Which reminded her that she should have some kind
of plan ready for him to approve that evening.

'It's all go,' said Araminta crossly, alone for a few
moments while the boys were in the kitchen, admiring
Miep—the kitchen cat—and her kittens.

She had gone to the window to look out onto the narrow garden behind the house. It was a pretty place, with
narrow brick paths and small flowerbeds and a high brick
wall surrounding it.

'I trust you do not find the job too tiresome for you?'
asked the doctor gently.

She spun round. He was standing quite close to her,
looking amused.

She said tartly, 'I was talking to myself, doctor, unaware that anyone was listening. And I do not find the
boys tiresome but it has been a long day.'

'Indeed it has.' He didn't offer sympathy, merely
agreed with her in a civil voice which still held the thread
of amusement.

He glanced at his watch. 'I dare say you wish to unpack for the boys and yourself. I'll have them with me
until half past six.'

He gave her a little nod and held the door open for her.

In her room, she put away her clothes, reflecting that
she must remember not to voice her thoughts out loud.
He could have been nasty about it—he could also have
offered a modicum of sympathy…

She still wasn't sure why she had accepted this job. True, she was to be paid a generous salary, and she supposed that she had felt sorry for him.

Upon reflection she thought that being sorry for him was a waste of time; it was apparent that he lived in some comfort, surrounded by people devoted to him. She supposed, too, that he was a busy man, although she had no idea what he did. A GP, perhaps? But his lifestyle was a bit grand for that. A consultant in one of the hospitals? Or one of those unseen men who specialised in obscure illnesses? She would find out.

She went to the boys' room and unpacked, put everything ready for bedtime and then got out pen and paper and wrote out the rough outline of a routine for the boys' day. Probably the doctor wouldn't approve of it, in which case he could make his own suggestions.

At half past six she went downstairs and found the boys in the small room where they had their tea earlier. The doctor was there, too, and they were all on the floor playing a noisy game of cards. There was a dog there too, a black Labrador, sitting beside his master, watching the cards being flung down and picked up.

They all looked up as she went in and the doctor said, 'Five minutes, Miss Pomfrey.' When the dog got to its feet and came towards her, he added, 'This is Humphrey. You like dogs?'

'Yes.' She offered a fist and then stroked the great head. 'He's lovely.'

She sat down until the game came to an end, with Peter declared the winner.

'Supper?' asked Araminta mildly.

The doctor got on to his feet, towering over them.

'Come and say goodnight when you're ready for bed. Off you go, there's good fellows.'

Bas was waiting in the hall. 'Supper is to be in the day nursery on the first floor,' he explained. 'You know the way, miss.' And they all went upstairs and into the large room, so comfortably furnished with an eye to a child's comfort.

'Uncle Marcus used to have his supper here,' Paul told her, 'and he says one day, when he's got some boys of his own, they'll have their supper here, too.'

Was the doctor about to marry? Araminta wondered. He wasn't all that young—well into his thirties, she supposed. It was high time he settled down. It would be a pity to waste this lovely old house and this cosy nursery...

Bas came in with a tray followed by a strapping girl with a round face and fair hair who grinned at them and set the table. Supper was quickly eaten, milk was drunk and Araminta whisked the boys upstairs, for they were tired now and suddenly a little unhappy.

'Are Mummy and Daddy going a long way away?' asked Peter as she bathed them.

'Well, it would be a long way if you had to walk there,' said Araminta, 'but in an aeroplane it takes no time at all to get there and get back again. Shall we buy postcards tomorrow and write to them?'

She talked cheerfully as she popped them into their pyjamas and dressing gowns and they all went back downstairs, this time to the drawing room, where their uncle was sitting with a pile of papers on the table beside him.

He hugged them, teased them gently, told them he would see them at breakfast in the morning and bade them goodnight. As they went, he reminded Araminta that dinner would be in half an hour.

The boys were asleep within minutes. Araminta had a quick shower and got into another skirt and a pretty blouse, spent the shortest possible time over her face and hair and nipped downstairs again with a few minutes to spare. She suspected that the doctor was a man who invited punctuality.

He was in the drawing room still, but he got up as she went in, offered her a glass of sherry, enquired if the boys were asleep and made small talk until Bas came to tell them that dinner was ready.

Araminta was hungry and Jet was a splendid cook. She made her way through mushrooms in a garlic and cream sauce, roast guinea fowl, and apple tart with whipped cream. Mindful of good manners, she sustained a polite conversation the while.

The doctor, making suitable replies to her painstaking efforts allowed his thoughts to wander.

After this evening he would feel free to spend his evenings with friends or at the hospital; breakfast wasn't a problem, for the boys would be there, and he was almost always out for lunch. Miss Pomfrey was a nice enough girl, but there was nothing about her to arouse his interest. He had no doubt that she would be excellent with the boys, and she was a sensible girl who would know how to amuse herself on her days off.

Dinner over, he suggested that they had their coffee in the drawing room.

'If you don't mind,' said Araminta, 'I'd like to go to bed. I've written down the outlines of a day's schedule, if you would look at it and let me know in the morning if it suits you. Do we have breakfast with you or on our own?'

'With me. At half past seven, since I leave for the hospital soon after eight o'clock.'

Araminta nodded. 'Oh, I wondered where you worked,' she observed, and wished him goodnight.

The doctor, politely opening the door for her, had the distinct feeling that he had been dismissed.

He could find no fault with her schedule for the boys. He could see that if she intended to carry it out to the letter she would be tired by the end of the day, but that, he felt, was no concern of his. She would have an hour or so each morning while the boys were at school and he would tell her that she could have her day off during the week as long as it didn't interfere with his work.

He went back to his chair and began to read the patients' notes that he had brought with him from the hospital. There was a good deal of work waiting for him both at Utrecht and Leiden. He was an acknowledged authority on endocrinology, and there were a number of patients about which he was to be consulted. He didn't give Araminta another thought.

Araminta took her time getting ready for bed. She took a leisurely bath, and spent time searching for lines and wrinkles in her face; someone had told her that once one had turned twenty, one's skin would start to age. But since she had a clear skin, as soft as a peach, she found nothing to worry her. She got into bed, glanced at the book and magazines someone had thoughtfully put on her bedside table and decided that instead of reading she would lie quietly and sort out her thoughts. She was asleep within minutes.

A small, tearful voice woke her an hour later. Paul was standing by her bed, in tears, and a moment later Peter joined him.

Araminta jumped out of bed. 'My dears, have you had a nasty dream? Look, I'll come to your room and sit with you and you can tell me all about it. Bad dreams go away if you talk about them, you know.'

It wasn't bad dreams; they wanted their mother and father, their own home, the cat and her kittens, the gold-fish... She sat down on one of the beds and settled the pair of them, one on each side of her, cuddling them close.

'Well, of course you miss them, my dears, but you'll be home again in a few weeks. Think of seeing them all again and telling them about Holland. And you've got your uncle...'

'And you, Mintie, you won't go away?'

'Gracious me, no. I'm in a foreign country, aren't I? Where would I go? I'm depending on both of you to take me round Utrecht so that I can tell everyone at home all about it.'

'Have you got little boys?' asked Peter.

'No, love, just a mother and father and a few aunts and uncles. I haven't any brothers and sisters, you see.'

Paul said in a watery voice, 'Shall we be your brothers? Just while you're living with us?'

'Oh, yes, please. What a lovely idea...'

'I heard voices,' said the doctor from the doorway. 'Bad dreams?'

Peter piped up, 'We woke up and we wanted to go home, but Mintie has explained so it's all right, Uncle, because she'll be here with you, and she says we can be her little brothers. She hasn't got a brother or a sister.'

The doctor came into the room and sat down on the other bed. 'What a splendid idea. We must think of so many things to do that we shan't have enough days in which to do them.'

He began a soothing monologue, encompassing a visit to some old friends in Friesland, another to the lakes north of Utrecht, where he had a yacht, and a shopping expedition so that they might buy presents to take home...

The boys listened, happy once more and getting sleepy. Araminta listened too, quite forgetting that she was barefoot, somewhere scantily clad in her nightie and that her hair hung round her shoulders and tumbled untidily down her back.

The doctor had given her an all-seeing look and hadn't looked again. He was a kind man, and he knew that the prim Miss Pomfrey, caught unawares in her nightie, would be upset and probably hate him just because he was there to see her looking like a normal girl. She had pretty hair, he reflected.

'Now, how about bed?' he wanted to know. 'I'm going downstairs again but I'll come up in ten minutes, so mind you're asleep by then.'

He ruffled their hair and took himself off without a word or a look for Araminta. It was only as she was tucking the boys up once more that she realised that she hadn't stopped to put on her dressing gown. She kissed the boys goodnight and went away to swathe herself in that garment now, and tie her hair back with a ribbon. She would have to see that man again, she thought vexedly, because the boys had said they wouldn't go to sleep unless she was there, but this time she would be decently covered.

He came presently, to find the boys asleep already and Araminta sitting very upright in a chair by the window.

'They wanted me to stay,' she told him, and he nodded carelessly, barely glancing at her. Perhaps he hadn't noticed, she thought, for he looked at her as though he hadn't really seen her. She gave a relieved sigh. Her, 'Goodnight, doctor,' was uttered in Miss Pomfrey's voice,

and he wished her a quiet goodnight in return, amused at
the sight of her swathed in her sensible, shapeless dressing gown. Old Jenkell had told him that she was the child
of elderly and self-absorbed parents, who hadn't moved
with the times. It seemed likely that they had not allowed
her to move with them either.

Nonetheless, she was good with the boys, and so far
had made no demands concerning herself. Give her a day
or two, he reflected, and she would have settled down and
become nothing but a vague figure in the background
of his busy life.

His hopes were borne out in the morning; at breakfast
she sat between the boys, and after the exchange of good
mornings, neither she nor they tried to distract him from
the perusal of his post.

Presently he said, 'Your schedule seems very satisfactory, Miss Pomfrey. I shall be home around teatime.
I'll take the boys with me when I take Humphrey for
his evening walk. The boys start school today. You will
take them, please, and fetch them at noon each day. I
dare say you will enjoy an hour or so to go shopping or
sightseeing.'

'Yes, thank you,' said Araminta.

Peter said, 'Uncle, why do you call Mintie Miss Pomfrey? She's Mintie.'

'My apologies. It shall be Mintie from now on.' He
smiled, and she thought how it changed his whole handsome face. 'That is, if Mintie has no objection?'

She answered the smile. 'Not in the least.'

That was the second time he had asked her that. She
had the lowering feeling that she had made so little impression upon him that nothing which they had said to
each other had been interesting enough to be remembered.

Chapter 3

The boys had no objection to going to school. It was five minutes' walk from the doctor's house and in a small quiet street which they reached by crossing a bridge over the canal. Araminta handed them over to one of the teachers. Submitting to their hugs, she promised that she would be there at the end of the morning, and walked back to the house, where she told Bas that she would go for a walk and look around.

She found the Domkerk easily enough, but she didn't go inside; the boys had told her that they would take her there. Instead she went into a church close by, St Pieterskerk, which was Gothic with a crypt and frescoes. By the time she had wandered around, looking her fill, it was time to fetch the boys. Tomorrow she promised herself that she would go into one of the museums and remember to have coffee somewhere…

The boys had enjoyed their morning. They told her all about it as they walked back, and then demanded to know what they were going to do that afternoon.

'Well, what about buying postcards and stamps and writing to your mother and father? If you know the way, you can show me where the post office is. If you show me a different bit of Utrecht each day I'll know my way around, so that if ever I should come again…'

'Oh, I 'spect you will, Mintie,' said Paul. 'Uncle Marcus will invite you.'

Araminta thought this highly unlikely, but she didn't say so. 'That would be nice,' she said cheerfully. 'Let's have lunch while you tell me some more about school.'

The afternoon was nicely filled in by their walk to the post office and a further exploration of the neighbouring streets while the boys, puffed up with self-importance, explained about the *grachten* and the variety of gables, only too pleased to air their knowledge. They were back in good time for tea, and when Bas opened the door to them they were making a considerable noise, since Araminta had attempted to imitate the Dutch words they were intent on teaching her.

A door in the hall opened and the doctor came out. He had his spectacles on and a book in his hand and he looked coldly annoyed.

Araminta hushed the boys. 'Oh, dear, we didn't know you were home. If we had we would have been as quiet as mice.'

'I am relieved to hear that, Miss Pomfrey. I hesitate to curtail your enjoyment, but I must ask you to be as quiet as possible in the house. You can, of course, let yourself go once you are in the nursery.'

She gave him a pitying look. He should marry and have a houseful of children and become human again. He was fast becoming a dry-as-dust old bachelor. She said kindly, 'We are really sorry, aren't we, boys? We'll creep around the house and be ourselves in the nursery.' She added, 'Little boys will be little boys, you know, but I dare say you've forgotten over the years.'

She gave him a sweet smile and shooed the boys ahead of her up the stairs.

'Is Uncle Marcus cross?' asked Paul.

'No, no, of course not. You heard what he said—
we may make as much noise as we like in the nursery.
There's a piano there, isn't there? We'll have a concert
after tea...'

The boys liked the sound of that, only Peter said
slowly, 'He must have been a bit cross because he called
you Miss Pomfrey.'

'Oh, he just forgot, I expect. Now, let's wash hands
for tea and go down to the nursery. I dare say we shall
have it there if your uncle is working.'

The doctor had indeed gone back to his study, but he
didn't immediately return to his reading. He was remembering Araminta's words with a feeing of annoyance. She
had implied that he was elderly, or at least middle-aged.
Thirty-six wasn't old, not even middle-aged, and her remark had rankled. True, he was fair enough to concede,
he hadn't the lifestyle of other men of his age, and since
he wasn't married he was free to spend as much time
doing his work as he wished.

As a professor of endocrinology he had an enviable
reputation in his profession already, and he was perfectly
content with his life. He had friends and acquaintances,
his sister, of whom he was fond, and his nephews; his social life was pleasant, and from time to time he thought
of marriage, but he had never met a woman with whom
he wanted to share the rest of his life.

Sooner or later, he supposed, he would have to settle
for second best and marry; he had choice enough. A man
of no conceit, he was still aware that there were several
women of his acquaintance who would be only too delighted to marry him.

He read for a time and then got up and walked through

the house to the kitchen, where he told Bas to put the tea things in the small sitting room. 'And please tell Miss Pomfrey and the boys that I expect them there for tea in ten minutes.'

After tea, he reflected, they would play the noisiest game he could think of!

He smiled then, amused that the tiresome girl should have annoyed him. She hadn't meant to annoy him; he was aware of that. He had seen enough of her to know that she was a kind girl, though perhaps given to uttering thoughts best kept to herself.

Araminta, rather surprised at his message, went downstairs with the boys to find him already sitting in the chair by the open window, Humphrey at his feet. He got up as they went in and said easily, 'I thought we might as well have tea together round the table. I believe Jet has been making cakes and some of those *pofferjes* which really have to be eaten from a plate, don't they?'

He drew out a chair and said pleasantly, 'Do sit down, Miss Pomfrey.'

'Mintie,' Peter reminded him.

'Mintie,' said his uncle meekly, and Araminta gave him a wide smile, relieved that he wasn't annoyed.

Tea poured and Jet's *botorkeok* cut and served, he asked, 'Well, what have you done all day? Was school all right?'

The boys were never at a loss for words, so there was little need for Araminta to say anything, merely to agree to something when appealed to. Doubtless over dinner he would question her more closely. She would be careful to be extra polite, she thought; he was a good-natured man, and his manners were beautiful, but she suspected that he expected life to be as he arranged it and wouldn't

tolerate interference. She really must remember that she
was merely the governess in his employ—and in a temporary capacity. She would have to remember that, too.

They played Monopoly after tea, sitting at the table
after Bas had taken the tea things away. The boys were
surprisingly good at it, and with a little help and a lot of
hints Peter won with Paul a close second. The doctor had
taken care to make mistakes and had even cheated, although Araminta had been the only one to see that. As
for her, she would never, as he had mildly pointed out,
be a financial wizard.

She began to tidy up while the boys said a protracted
goodnight to their uncle. 'You'll come up and say goodnight again?' they begged.

When he agreed they went willingly enough to their
baths, their warm milk drinks with the little sugar biscuits, and bed. Araminta, rather flushed and untidy, was
tucking them in when the doctor came upstairs. He had
changed for the evening and she silently admired him.
Black tie suited him and his clothes had been cut by a
masterly hand. The blue crêpe would be quite inade-
quate...

He bade the boys goodnight and then turned to her. 'I
shall be out for dinner, Miss Pomfrey,' he told her with
a formal politeness which she found chilling. 'Bas will
look after you. Dinner will be at the usual time, otherwise do feel free to do whatever you wish.'

She suppressed an instant wish to go with him. To
some grand house where there would be guests? More
likely he was taking some exquisitely gowned girl to
one of those restaurants where there were little pink-
shaded table lamps and the menus were the size of a
ground map...

And she was right, for Paul asked sleepily, 'Are you going out with a pretty lady, Uncle Marcus?'

The doctor smiled. 'Indeed I am, Paul. Tomorrow I'll tell you what we had for dinner.'

He nodded to Araminta and went away, and she waited, sitting quietly by the window, until she judged that he had left the house. Of course, there was no reason for him to stay at home to dine with her; she had been a fool to imagine that he would do so. Good manners had obliged him to do so yesterday, since it had been her first evening there, but it wasn't as if she was an interesting person to be with. Her mother had pointed out kindly and rather too frequently that she lacked wit and sparkle, and that since she wasn't a clever girl, able to converse upon interesting subjects, then she must be content to be a good listener.

Araminta had taken this advice in good part, knowing that her mother was unaware that she was trampling on her daughter's feelings. Araminta made allowances for her, though; people with brilliant brains were quite often careless of other people's feelings. And it was all quite true. She knew herself to be just what her mother had so succinctly described. And she had taught herself to be a good listener...

She might have had to dine alone, but Bas treated her as though she was an honoured guest and the food was delicious.

'I will put coffee in the drawing room, miss,' said Bas, so she went and sat there, with Humphrey for comfort and companionship, and presently wandered about the room, looking at the portraits on its walls and the silver and china displayed in the cabinet. It was still early—too early to go to bed. She slipped upstairs to make sure that the boys were sleeping and then went back to the drawing room and leafed through the magazines on the sofa table. But she put those down after a few minutes and curled up on one of the sofas and allowed her thoughts to wander.

The day had, on the whole, gone well. The boys liked her and she liked them, the house was beautiful and her room lacked nothing in the way of comfort. Bas and Jet were kindness itself, and Utrecht was undoubtedly a most interesting city. There was one niggling doubt: despite his concern for her comfort and civil manner towards her, she had the uneasy feeling that the doctor didn't like her. And, of course, she had made it worse, answering him back. She must keep a civil tongue in her head and remember that she was there to look after the boys. He was paying her for that, wasn't he?

'And don't forget that, my girl,' said Araminta in a voice loud enough to rouse Humphrey from his snooze.

She went off to bed then, after going to the kitchen to wish Bas and Jet goodnight, suddenly anxious not to be downstairs when the doctor came home.

He wasn't at breakfast the next morning; Bas told them that he had gone early to Amsterdam but hoped to be back in the late afternoon. The boys were disappointed and so, to her surprise, was Araminta.

He was home when they got back from their afternoon walk. The day had gone well and the boys were bursting to tell him about it, so Araminta took their caps and coats from them in the hall, made sure that they had wiped their shoes, washed their hands and combed their hair, and told them to go and find their uncle.

'You'll come, too? It's almost time for tea, Mintie.' Paul sounded anxious.

'I'll come presently, love. I'll take everything upstairs first.'

She didn't hurry downstairs. There was still ten minutes or so before Bas would take in the tea tray. She would go then, stay while the boys had their tea and then leave them with their uncle if he wished. In that way she would need only to hold the briefest of conversations with him. The thought of dining with him later bothered her, so she began to list some suitable subjects about which she could talk…

She arrived in the drawing room as Bas came with the tea things, and the doctor's casual, 'Good afternoon, Miss Pomfrey. You have had a most interesting walk, so the boys tell me,' was the cue for her to enlarge upon that. But after a moment or so she realised that she was boring him.

'The boys will have told you all this already,' she observed in her matter-of-fact way. She gave the boys their milk and handed him a cup of tea. 'I hope you had a good day yourself, doctor?'

He looked surprised. 'Yes—yes, I did. I'll keep the boys with me until their bedtime, if you would fetch them at half past six?'

There was really no need to worry about conversation; the boys had a great deal to say to their uncle, often lapsing into Dutch, and once tea was finished, she slipped away with a quiet, 'I'll be back presently.'

She put everything ready for the boys' bedtime and then went quietly downstairs and out of the kitchen door into the garden. Jet, busy preparing dinner, smiled and nodded as she crossed the kitchen, and Araminta smiled and nodded back. There was really no need to talk, she reflected, they understood each other very well—moreover, they liked each other.

The garden was beautifully kept, full of sweet-smelling shrubs and flowers, and at its end there was a wooden seat against a brick wall, almost hidden by climbing plants. The leaves were already turning and the last of the evening sun was turning them to bronze. It was very quiet, and she sat idly, a small, lonely figure.

The doctor, looking up from the jigsaw puzzle he was working on with the boys, glanced idly out of the window and saw her sitting there. At that distance she appeared forlorn, and he wondered if she was unhappy and then dismissed the idea. Miss Pomfrey was a sensible, matter-of-fact girl with rather too sharp a tongue at times; she had her future nicely mapped out, and no doubt, in due course, she would make a success of her profession.

He doubted if she would marry, for she made no attempt to make herself attractive; her clothes were good, but dowdy, and her hairstyle by no means flattering. She had pretty hair too, he remembered, and there was a great deal of it. Sitting there last night in her cotton nightie she had been Mintie, and not Miss Pomfrey, but she wouldn't thank him for reminding her of that.

The boys took his attention again and he forget her.

The boys in bed, Araminta went to her room and got into the blue crêpe. A nicely judged ten minutes before dinner would be served, she went downstairs. She could see Bas putting the finishing touches to the table through the half-open dining room door as she opened the door into the drawing room. The few minutes before he announced dinner could be nicely filled with a few remarks about the boys and their day...

The doctor wasn't alone. The woman sitting opposite

him was beautiful—quite the most beautiful Araminta
had ever seen; she had golden hair, a straight nose, a
curving mouth and large eyes. Araminta had no doubt
that they were blue. She was wearing a silk trouser suit—
black—and gold jewellery, and she was laughing at something the doctor had said.

Araminta took a step backwards. 'So sorry, I didn't
know that you had a guest...'

The doctor got to his feet. 'Ah, Miss Pomfrey, don't go.
Come and meet Mevrouw Lutyns.' And, as she crossed
the room, 'Christina, this is Miss Pomfrey, who is in
charge of the boys while Lucy and Jack are away.'

Mevrouw Lutyns smiled charmingly, shook hands and
Araminta felt her regarding her with cold blue eyes. 'Ah,
yes, the nanny. I hope you will find Utrecht interesting
during your short stay here.'

Her English was almost perfect, but then she herself
was almost perfect, reflected Araminta, at least to look at.

'I'm sure I shall, *Mevrouw.*' She looked at the doctor,
gave a little nod and the smallest of smiles and went to
the door.

'Don't go, Miss Pomfrey, you must have a drink... I
shall be out this evening, by the way, but I'll leave you
in Bas's good hands.'

'I came down to tell you that the boys were in bed,
Doctor. I'll not stay for a drink, thank you.' She wished
them good evening and a pleasant time, seething quietly.

She closed the door equally quietly, but not before she
heard Mevrouw Lutyns' voice, pitched in a penetrating
whisper. 'What a little dowd, Marcus. Wherever did you
find her?'

She stood in the hall, trembling with rage. It was a
pity she didn't understand the doctor's reply.

'That is an unkind remark, Christina. Miss Pomfrey is a charming girl and the boys are devoted to her already. Her appearance is of no consequence; I find her invaluable.'

They were speaking Dutch now, and Mevrouw Lutyns said prettily, 'Oh, my dear, I had no intention of being unkind. I'm sure she's a treasure.'

They left the house presently and dined at one of Utrecht's fine restaurants, and from time to time, much against his intention, the doctor found himself thinking about Araminta, eating her solitary dinner in the blue dress which he realised she had put on expecting to dine with him.

He drove his companion back later that evening, to her flat in one of the modern blocks away from the centre of the city. He refused her offer of a drink with the excuse that he had to go to the hospital to check on a patient, and, when she suggested that they might spend another evening together, told her that he had a number of other consultations, not only in Utrecht, and he didn't expect to be free.

An answer which didn't please her at all.

It was almost midnight as he let himself into his house. It was very quiet in the dimly lit hall but Humphrey was there, patiently waiting for his evening walk, and the doctor went out again, to walk briskly through the quiet streets with his dog. It was a fine night, but chilly, and when they got back home he took Humphrey to the kitchen, settled him in his basket and poured himself a mug of coffee from the pot keeping hot on the Aga. Presently he took himself off to bed.

The evening, he reflected, had been a waste of time. He had known Christina for some years but had thought of her as an amusing and intelligent friend; to fall in love with her had never entered his head. He supposed, as he had done from time to time, that he *would* marry, but neither she nor the other women of his acquaintance succeeded in capturing his affection. His work meant a great deal to him, and he was wealthy, and served by people he trusted and regarded as friends. He sometimes wondered if he would ever meet a woman he would love to the exclusion of everything else.

He was already at breakfast when Araminta and the two boys joined him the next day. Peter and Paul rushed to him, both talking at once, intent on reminding him that he had promised to take them out for the day at the weekend. He assured them that he hadn't forgotten and wished Araminta good morning in a friendly voice, hoping that she had forgotten the awkwardness of the previous evening.

She replied with her usual composure, settled the boys to their breakfast and poured herself a cup of coffee. She had spent a good deal of the night reminding herself that she was the boys' nanny, just as the hateful Mevrouw Lutyns had said. It had been silly to suppose that he would wish to spend what little spare time he had with her when he had friends of his own.

Probably he was in love with the woman, and Araminta couldn't blame him for that for she was so exactly right for him—all that golden hair and a lovely face, not to mention the clothes. If Mevrouw Lutyns had considered her a dowd in the blue crêpe, what on earth would she think of her in her sensible blouse and skirt? But the doctor wouldn't think of Araminta; he barely glanced at her and she didn't blame him for that.

She replied now to his civil remark about the weather

and buttered a roll. She really must remember her place; she wasn't in Hambledon now, the daughter of highly respected parents, famous for their obscure Celtic learning...

The doctor took off his spectacles and looked at her. There was no sign of pique or hurt feelings, he was relieved to observe. He said pleasantly, 'I shall be taking the boys to Leiden for the day tomorrow. I'm sure you will be glad to have a day to yourself in which to explore. I have a ground map of Utrecht somewhere; I'll let you have it. There is a great deal to see and there are some good shops.'

When she thanked him, he added, 'If you should wish to stay out in the evening, Bas will let you have a key.'

She thanked him again and wondered if that was a polite hint not to return to the house until bedtime.

'What about the boys? Putting them to bed...?'

He said casually, 'Oh, Jet will see to that,' then added, 'I shall be away for most of Sunday, but I'm sure you can cope.'

'Yes, of course. I'm sure the boys will think up something exciting to do.'

The days were falling into a pattern, she reflected: school in the morning, long walks in the afternoon, shopping expeditions for postcards, books or another puzzle, and an hour to herself in the evening when the boys were with their uncle.

She no longer expected the doctor to dine with her in the evening.

All the same, for pride's sake, she got into the blue crêpe and ate her dinner that evening with every appearance of enjoyment. She was living in the lap of comfort, she reminded herself, going back to the drawing room to sit and read the English papers Bas had thoughtfully provided for her until she could go to bed once the long case clock in the hall chimed ten o'clock.

She took a long time getting ready for bed, refusing to admit how lonely she was. Later she heard quiet footsteps in the hall and a door close. The doctor was home.

The doctor and the boys left soon after breakfast on Saturday. Araminta, standing in the hall to bid them goodbye, was hugged fiercely by Peter and Paul.

'You will be here when we get back?' asked Peter.

'Couldn't you come with us now?' Paul added urgently, and turned to his uncle, waiting patiently to usher them into the car. 'You'd like her to come, wouldn't you, Uncle?'

'Miss Pomfrey—' At a look from Peter he changed it. 'Mintie is only here for a few weeks and she wants to see as much of Utrecht as possible. This is the first chance she's had to go exploring and shopping. Women like to look at shops, you know.'

'I'll have a good look round,' promised Araminta, 'and when we go out tomorrow perhaps you can show me some of the places I won't have seen.'

She bent to kiss them and waited at the door as they got into the car, with Humphrey stretched out between them. She didn't look at the doctor.

Bas shut the door as soon as the car had gone. 'You will be in to lunch, miss?' he wanted to know. 'At any time to suit you.'

'Thank you, Bas, but I think I'll get something while I'm out; there's such a lot to see. Are you sure Jet can manage with the boys at bedtime?'

'Oh, yes, miss. The doctor has arranged that he will be out this evening...' He paused and looked awkward.

'So she won't need to cook dinner—just something for the boys.'

He looked relieved. 'I was given to understand that you would be out this evening, miss. I am to give you a key, although I will, of course, remain up until you are back.'

'How kind of you, Bas. I'll take a key, of course, but I expect I shall be back by ten o'clock. When I come in I'll leave the key on the hall table, shall I? Then you'll know that I'm in the house.'

'Thank you, miss. You will have coffee before you go out?'

'Please, Bas, if it's not too much trouble.'

She left the house a little later and began a conscientious exploration of the city. The boys would want to know what she had seen and where she had been... She had been to the Domkerk with them, now she went to the Dom Tower and then through the cloister passage to the University Chapter Hall. The Central Museum was next on her list—costumes, jewellery, some paintings and beautiful furniture. By now it was well after noon, so she looked for a small café and lingered over a *kaas broodje*. She would have liked more but she had no idea when she would be paid and she hadn't a great deal of money.

The day, which had begun with sunshine and gentle wind, had become overcast, and the wind was no longer gentle. She was glad of her jacket over the jersey two-piece as she made her way to the shopping centre. The shops were fine, filled with beautiful things: clothes, of course, and shoes, but as well as these splendid furniture, porcelain, silver and glass... There were bookshops, too, and she spent a long time wandering round them, wishing she could buy some of their contents. It surprised her to find so many English books on sale, and to find a shop selling Burberrys and Harris Tweed. It would be no hardship to live here, she reflected, and took herself off to find the *hofjes* and patrician houses, to stand and admire their age-old beauty.

She found another small coffee shop where she had tea and a cake while she pondered what to do with her evening. She thought she might go back around nine o'clock. By then the boys would be in bed and asleep, and if the doctor was out, Bas and Jet would be in kitchen. A cinema seemed the answer. It would mean that she couldn't afford a meal, but she could buy a sandwich and a cup of coffee before she went back to the house.

There were several cinemas; she chose one in a square in the centre of the city, paid out most of her remaining guldens and sat through an American film. Since she was a little tired by now, she dozed off and woke to see that it was over and that the advertisements were on. After that the lights went up and everyone went out into the street.

It was almost dark now, but it was still barely eight o'clock. She went into a crowded café and had a cup of coffee, then decided that she had better save what guldens she had left. There was a small tin of biscuits by her bed; she could eat those. She couldn't sit for ever over one cup of coffee, though, so she went into the street and started her walk back to the house.

She was crossing the square when she saw the little stall at one corner. *Pommes Frites* was painted across its wooden front.

'Chips,' said Araminta, her mouth watering. 'But why do they have to say so in French when we're in Holland?' She went over to the corner and in exchange for two gulden was handed a little paper cornet filled with crisp golden chips. She bit into one; it was warm and crunchy and delicious…

Dr van der Breugh, on his way to dine with old friends, halting at traffic lights, glanced around him. Being a Saturday evening there were plenty of people about; the cafés and restaurants were doing a good trade and the various stalls had plenty of customers.

He saw Araminta as the light changed, and he had to drive on, but instead of going straight ahead, as he should have done, he turned back towards the square and stopped the car a few feet from her.

She hadn't seen him; he watched her bite into a chip with the eager delight of a child and then choke on it when she looked up and saw him. He was astonished at his feelings of outrage at the sight of her. Outrage at his own behaviour. He should have taken her with them, or at least made some arrangement for her day. He got out of his car, his calm face showing nothing of his feelings.

As for Araminta, if the ground had obligingly opened and allowed her to fall into it, she would have been happy; as it was, she would have to do the best she could. She swallowed the last fragment of chip and said politely, 'Good evening, doctor. What delicious chips you have in Holland…'

He had no intention of wasting time talking about chips. 'Why are you here, Miss Pomfrey? Why are you not at the house, eating your dinner….' He paused, frowning. He hadn't given her a thought when he returned with the boys, hadn't asked Bas if she was back, had forgotten her.

Araminta saw the frown and made haste to explain. 'Well, you see, it's like this. Bas thought that I would be out until late; he gave me a key, too, so I expect there was a misunderstanding. I thought—' she caught his eye '—well, I thought that perhaps you expected me to stay out. I mean, you did say that Jet would put the boys to bed, so you didn't expect me back, did you?' She hesitated. 'Am I making myself clear?'

When he didn't speak, she added, 'I've had a most interesting day, and I went to the cinema this evening. I'm on my way back to the house now, so I'll say good evening, doctor.'

'No, Miss Pomfrey, you will not say good evening. You will come with me and we will have dinner together. I have no doubt that you have eaten nothing much all day and I cannot forgive myself for not seeing that you had adequate money with you and arrangements made for your free day. Please forgive me?'

She stared up at him, towering over her. 'Of course I forgive you. I'm not your guest, you know, and I'm quite used to being by myself. And please don't feel that you have to give me a meal; I've just eaten all those chips.'

'All the same, we will dine together.' He swept her into the car and picked up the car phone. He spoke in Dutch so that she wasn't to know that he was excusing himself from a dinner party.

'Oh, that hospital again,' said his hostess. 'Do you never get a free moment, Marcus?'

He made a laughing rejoinder, promised to dine at some future date, and started the car.

Araminta, still clutching her chips, said in a tight little voice, 'Will you take me back to the house, doctor? It's kind of you to offer me a meal, but I'm not hungry.'

A waste of breath, for all she got in reply was a grunt as he swept the car back into the lighted streets, past shop windows still blazing with light, cafés spilling out onto the pavements, grand hotels… She tried again. 'I'm not suitably dressed…'

He took no notice of that either, but turned into a narrow side street lined with elegant little shops. At its far end there was a small restaurant.

There was a canal on the opposite side of the street, and the doctor parked beside it—dangerously near the edge, from her point of view—and got out. There was no help for it but to get out when he opened her door, to be marched across the street and into the restaurant.

It was a small place: a long, narrow room with tables well apart, most of them occupied. Araminta was relieved to see that although the women there were well dressed, several of them were in suits and dark dresses so that her jacket and skirt weren't too conspicuous.

It seemed the doctor was known there; they were led to a table in one corner, her jacket was taken from her and a smiling waiter drew out her chair.

The doctor sat down opposite to her. 'What will you drink?' he asked. 'Dry sherry?'

When she agreed, he spoke to the waiter, who offered menus. There was choice enough, and she saw at a glance that everything was wildly expensive. She stared down at it; she hadn't wanted to come, and it would be entirely his fault if she chose caviar, plover's eggs and truffles, all of which were on the menu, their cost equivalent to a week's housekeeping money. On the other hand, she had no wish to sample any of these delicacies and, since she must have spoilt his evening, it seemed only fair to choose as economically as possible.

The doctor put down his menu. 'Unless you would like anything special, will you leave it to me to order?'

'Oh, please.' She added, 'There's such a lot to choose from, isn't there?'

'Indeed. How about marinated aubergine to start with? And would you like sea bass to follow?'

She agreed; she wasn't shy, and she was too much her parents' daughter to feel awkward. She had never been in a restaurant such as this one, but she wasn't going to let it intimidate her. When the food came she ate with pleasure and, mindful of manners, made polite conversation. The doctor was at first secretly amused and then found himself interested. Miss Pomfrey might be nothing out of the ordinary, but she had self-assurance and a way of looking him in the eye which he found disquieting. Not a conceited man, but aware of his worth, he wasn't used to being studied in such a manner.

For a moment he regretted his spoilt evening, but told himself that he was being unjust and then suggested that she might like a pudding from the trolley.

She chose sticky toffee pudding and ate it with enjoyment, and he, watching her over his biscuits and cheese, found himself reluctantly liking her.

They had talked in a guarded fashion over their meal—the weather, the boys, her opinion of Utrecht, all safe subjects. It was when they got back to the house and she had thanked him and started for the stairs that he stopped her.

'Miss Pomfrey, we do not need to refer again to the regrettable waste of your free day. Rest assured that I shall see to it that any other free time you have will be well spent.'

'Thank you, but I am quite capable of looking after myself.'

He smiled thinly. 'Allow me to be the best judge of that, Miss Pomfrey.' He turned away. 'Goodnight.'

She paused on the stairs. 'Goodnight, doctor.' And then she added, 'I bought the chips because I was hungry. I dare say you would have done the same,' she told him in a matter-of-fact voice.

The doctor watched her small retreating back and went into his study. Presently he began to laugh.

Chapter 4

Araminta woke early on Sunday morning and remembered that the doctor had said that he would be away all day—moreover, he had remarked that he had no doubt that she and the boys would enjoy their day. Doing what? she wondered, and sat up and worried about it until Jet came in with her morning tea, a concession to her English habit.

They smiled and nodded at each other and exchanged a *'Goeden Morgen'*, and the boys, hearing Jet's voice, came into the room and got onto Araminta's bed to eat the little biscuits which had come with the tea.

'We have to get up and dress,' they told her. 'We go to church with Uncle Marcus at half past nine.'

'Oh, do you? Then back to your room, boys, I'll be along in ten minutes or so.'

Church would last about an hour, she supposed, which meant that a good deal of the morning would be gone; they could go to one of the parks and feed the ducks, then come back for lunch, and by then surely she would have thought of something to fill the afternoon hours. A pity it wasn't raining, then they could have stayed indoors.

Jet had told her that breakfast would be at half past eight—at least, Araminta was almost sure that was what she had said; she knew the word for breakfast by now, and the time of day wasn't too hard to guess at. She dressed and went to help the boys. Not that they needed much help, for they dressed themselves, even if a bit haphazardly. But she brushed hair, tied miniature ties and made sure that their teeth were brushed and their hands clean. She did it without fuss; at the children's convalescent home there had been no time to linger over such tasks.

The doctor wasn't at breakfast, and they had almost finished when he came in with Humphrey. He had been for a walk, he told them. Humphrey had needed to stretch his legs. He sat down and had a cup of coffee, explaining that he had already breakfasted. 'Church at half past nine,' he reminded them, and asked Araminta if she would care to go with them. 'The church is close by—a short walk—you might find it interesting.'

She sensed that he expected her to accept. 'Thank you, I would like to come,' she told him. 'At what time are we to be ready?'

'Ten past nine. The service lasts about an hour.'

They each had a child's hand as they walked to the church, which was small and old, smelling of damp, flowers and age and, to Araminta's mind, rather bleak. They sat right at the front in a high-backed pew with narrow seats and hassocks. The boys sat between them, standing on the hassocks to sing the hymns and then sitting through a lengthy sermon.

Of course, Araminta understood very little of the service, although some of the hymn tunes were the same, but the sermon, preached by an elderly dominee with a flowing beard, sounded as though it was threatening them with severe punishments in the hereafter; she was relieved when it ended with a splendid rolling period of unintelligible words and they all sang a hymn.

It was a tune she knew, but the words in the hymn-book the doctor had thoughtfully provided her with were beyond her understanding. The boys sang lustily, as did the doctor, in a deep rumbling voice, and since they were singing so loudly, she hummed the tune to herself. It was the next best thing.

Back at the house, the doctor asked Bas to bring coffee into the drawing room.

'I shall be leaving in a few minutes,' he told Araminta. 'I expect you intend to take a walk before lunch, but in the afternoon Bas will drive you to Steijner's toy shop. They have an exhibition of toys there today and I have tickets. And next door there is a café where you may have your tea. Bas will come for you at about five o'clock. If you want him earlier, telephone the house.'

The boys were delighted, and so was Araminta, although she didn't allow it to show. The day had been nicely taken care of and the boys were going to enjoy themselves. She had no doubt that she would too.

The doctor stooped to kiss the boys. 'Have fun,' he told them, and to Araminta, 'Enjoy your afternoon, Miss Pomfrey. I leave the boys in your safe hands.'

It was only after he had gone that she realised that she hadn't much money—perhaps not enough to pay for their tea. She need not have worried. The boys showed her the notes their uncle had given to them to spend and a moment later, Bas, coming to collect the coffee cups, told her quietly that there was an envelope for her in the doctor's study if she would be good enough to fetch it.

There was, in her opinion, enough money in it to float a ship. She counted it carefully, determined to account for every cent of it, and went back to collect the boys ready for their walk.

They decided against going to one of the parks but instead they walked to one of the squares, the *'neude'*, and so into the Oudegracht, where there was the fourteenth-century house in which the Treaty of Utrecht had been signed. They admired the patrician house at some length, until Araminta said, 'Are we very far from your uncle's house? We should be getting back.'

They chorused reassurance. 'Look, Mintie, we just go back to the *neude* and Vredeburg Square, and it's only a little way then.'

She had been there the day before, spending hours looking at the windows of the shopping centre. The doctor's house was only a short distance from the Singel, the moat which surrounded the old city—much of its length was lined with attractive promenades backed by impressive houses.

'By the time we go home I shall know quite a lot about Utrecht,' she told the boys. 'Now, let's go back to the house and have lunch; we don't want to miss one moment of the exhibition...'

Steijner's toy shop was vast, housed in a narrow building, several storeys high, each floor reached by a narrow, steep staircase. The front shop was large and opened out into another smaller room which extended, long and narrow, as far as a blank wall. Both rooms were lined with shelves packed with toys of every description, and arranged down their centres were the larger exhibits: miniature motor cars, dolls' houses, minute bicycles, magnificent model boats.

The place was crowded with children, tugging the grown-ups to and fro, and it was some time before Araminta and the boys managed to climb the first flight of stairs to the floor above. The rooms here were mostly given over to dolls, more dolls' houses and miniature

kitchens and furniture, so they stayed only for a few minutes and then, together with a great many other people, made their way to the next floor.

This was very much more to the boys' liking—more cars and bikes, kites of every kind, skates, trumpets and drums, puppets and toy animals. Araminta, with the beginnings of a headache, suggested hopefully that they might go and have their tea and wait for Bas in the café. More and more people were filling the shop, the narrow stairs were packed, but the children were reluctant to move from the displays they fancied.

'There's camping stuff on the next floor,' said Peter, and he tugged at her hand. 'Could we just have a look—a quick peep?' He looked so appealing and since Paul had joined him, raising an excited face to her, she gave in. 'All right. But we won't stay too long, mind.'

The last flight of stairs was very narrow and steep, and the room it led to was low-ceilinged and narrow, with a slit window set in the gable. But it was well lit and the array of camping equipment was impressive. There were only a handful of people there and before long they had gone back down the staircase, leaving the boys alone to examine the tents and camping equipment to their hearts' content.

They must have a tent, they told Araminta excitedly, they would ask Uncle Marcus to buy them one. 'We could live in it in the garden, Mintie. You'd come too, of course.'

They went round and round, trying to decide which tent was the one they liked best. They were still longing to have one and arguing about it when Araminta looked at her watch.

'Time for tea, my dears,' she told them. 'We mustn't keep Bas waiting.'

It was another five minutes before she could prise them away and start down the stairs in single file. Peter was in front and he stopped on the last stair.

'The door's shut,' he said.

Araminta reached over. 'Well, we'll just turn the handle.'

Only there wasn't a handle, only an old-fashioned lock with no key. She changed places with Peter and gave the door a good push. Nothing happened; the door could have been rock. She told the boys to sit on the stairs and knocked hard. There was no reply, nor did anyone answer her 'hello'. The place was quiet, though when she looked at her watch she wondered why. The exhibition was due to close at five o'clock and it was fifteen minutes to that hour. All the same, surely someone would tour the building and make sure that everyone had left. She shouted, uneasily aware of the thickness of the door.

'What an adventure!' she said bracingly. 'Let's all shout...'

Which brought no result whatever.

'Well, we'd better go back to the room. Someone will come presently; it's not quite time for people to have to leave yet.' She spoke in a matter-of-fact voice and hoped that the boys would believe her.

Back upstairs again, she went to the narrow window. The glass was thick and, although it had once opened, it had been long since sealed up. She looked around for something suitable to break it, picked up a tent peg and, urged on by the boys, who were revelling in the whole thing, began to bash the glass.

It didn't break easily, and only some of it fell into

the street below, but anyone passing or standing nearby could have seen it. She shouted hopefully, unaware that there was no one there. The doctor's second car, another Jaguar, was standing close by, but Bas had gone into the café to see if they were there.

Of course, they weren't; he went to the toy shop, where the doors were being locked.

'Everyone has left,' he was told, and when he asked why they had closed a quarter of an hour sooner than expected, he was told that an electrical fault had been found and it was necessary to turn off the current.

'But no one's inside,' he was assured by the owner, who was unaware that the assistant who had checked the place hadn't bothered to go to the top room but had locked the door and gone home.

They could have gone back to the house, thought Bas. Miss Pomfrey was a sensible young woman, and instead of lingering about waiting for him she would have taken the boys home to let him know that they had left earlier than they had planned.

He got into the car and drove back, to find the Bentley parked by the canal and the doctor in his study. He looked up as Bas went in, but before he could speak Bas said urgently, 'You're just this minute back, *mijnheer*? You do not know about the exhibition closing early? I thought Miss Pomfrey and the boys would be here.'

The doctor was out of his chair. 'At the toy shop? It is closed? Why? You're sure? They were not in the café?'

'No one had seen them. I spoke to the man closing the place—there's been an electrical fault, that's why they shut early. He was sure that there was no one left inside.'

The doctor was already at the door. 'They can't be far, and Miss Pomfrey isn't a girl to lose her head. Come

along. We'll find them. You stay in the car, Bas, in case
they turn up.'

With Bas beside him he drove to Steijner's shop. There
were few people about—the proprietor and his assistants
had gone home—but there was a van parked outside and
men unloading equipment.

The doctor parked the car and walked over to them.
'You have keys? I believe there are two boys and a young
woman still inside. I'm not sure of it, but I must check.'

He looked up as a small splattering of glass fell between them. He looked up again and saw what appeared
to be a stocking waving from the gabled window.

The man looked up, too. 'Best get them down, *mijnheer*. I'll open up—you won't need help? I've quite a bit
of work here...'

He opened the door, taking his time over its bolts and
chains, giving the doctor time to allow for his relief,
mingled, for some reason which he didn't understand,
with rising rage. The silly girl. Why didn't she leave the
place with everyone else? There must have been some
other people there, and the boys would have understood
what was said—everyone would have been warned in
good time.

He raced up the stairs, turned the key in the lock of
the last door and went up the staircase two at a time. The
boys rushed to meet him, bubbling about their adventure,
delighted to see him, and he put his great arms around
their small shoulders.

He said, very softly, 'I hope you have a good explana-
tion for this, Miss Pomfrey.' The look he gave her shriv-
elled her bones.

Araminta, ready and eager to explain, bit back the
words. He was furiously angry with her. No doubt any

other man would have sworn at her and called her names, but he had spoken with an icy civility which sent shivers down her spine. A pity he hadn't shouted, she reflected, then she could have shouted back. Instead she said nothing at all, and after a moment he turned to the boys.

'Bas is below with the car. If you haven't had tea we will have it together.'

'Shall we tell you about it, Uncle Marcus?' began Peter.

'Later, Peter, after tea.' He crossed the room and took Araminta's stocking off the glass window. It was hopelessly torn and laddered, but he handed it to her very politely. Her 'thank you' was equally polite, but she didn't look at him. She felt a fool with only one stocking, and he had contrived to make her feel guilty about something which hadn't been her fault. Nor had he asked what had happened, but had condemned her unheard.

At the bottom of the staircase she paused; she would show him that there was no handle on the door. But he was already going down the next stairs with the boys.

She was going to call him back, but his impatient, 'Come along, Miss Pomfrey,' gave her no chance. She followed the three of them out to the car and got in wordlessly. Once back at the house, she tidied up the boys ready for tea, excused herself on account of a headache and went to her room.

The doctor's curled lip at her excuse boded ill for any further conversation he might wish to have with her. And she had no doubt that he would have more to say about feather-brained women who got left behind and locked up while in charge of small boys....

Bas brought in the tea. 'Miss Pomfrey will be with you presently?' he wanted to know. He had seen her pale face and his master's inscrutable features in the car. 'You could have cut the air between them with a pair of scissors,' he had told Jet.

'Miss Pomfrey has a headache. Perhaps you would take her a tray of tea,' suggested the doctor.

'Mintie never has a headache,' declared Peter. 'She said so; she said she's never ill...'

'In that case, I dare say she will be with us again in a short time,' observed his uncle. 'I see that Jet has baked a *boterkeok*, and there are *krentenbollejes*...'

'Currant buns,' said Paul. 'Shall we save one for Mintie?'

'Why not? Now, tell me, did you enjoy the exhibition? Was there anything that you both liked?'

'A tent—that's why we were in the room at the very top. It was full of tents and things for camping. We though we'd like a tent. Mintie said she'd come and live in it with us in the garden. She made us laugh, 'specially when we tried to open the door...'

The doctor put down his teacup. 'And it wouldn't open?'

'It was a real adventure. Mintie supposed that the people who went downstairs before us forgot and shut the door, and of course there wasn't a handle. You would have enjoyed it, too, Uncle. We banged on the door and shouted, and then Mintie broke the glass in the window and took off a stocking and hung it through the hole she'd made. She said it was what those five children in the Enid Blyton books would have done and we were having an adventure. It was real fun, wasn't it, Peter?'

His uncle said, 'It sounds a splendid adventure.'

'I 'spect that's why Mintie's got a headache,' said Peter.

'I believe you may be right, Peter. Have we finished

tea? Would you both like to take Humphrey into the garden? He likes company. I have something to do, so if I'm not here presently, go to Jet in the kitchen, will you?'

The boys ran off, shouting and laughing, throwing a ball for the good-natured Humphrey, and when Bas came to clear away the tea things, the doctor said, 'Bas, would you be good enough to ask Miss Pomfrey to come to my study as soon as she feels better?'

He crossed the hall and shut the study door behind him, and Bas went back to the kitchen. Jet, told of this, pooh-poohed the idea that the doctor was about to send Miss Pomfrey packing. 'More like he's got the wrong end of the stick about what happened this afternoon and wants to know what did happen. You don't know?'

Bas shook his head. 'No idea. But it wasn't anything to upset the boys; they were full of their adventure.'

Araminta had drunk her tea, had a good cry, washed her face and applied powder and lipstick once more, tidied her hair and sat down to think. She had no intention of telling the doctor anything; he was arrogant, ill-tempered and she couldn't bear the sight of him. Anyone else would have asked her what had happened, given her a chance to explain. He had taken it for granted that she had been careless and unreliable. 'I hate him,' said Araminta, not meaning it, but it relieved her feelings.

When Bas came for the tea tray and gave her the message from the doctor she thanked him and said that she would be down presently. When he had gone she went to the gilt edged triple mirror on the dressing table and took a good look. Viewed from all sides, her face looked much as usual. Slightly puffy eyelids could be due to the headache. Perhaps another light dusting of powder on her nose, which was still pink at its tip... She practised one or two calm and dignified expressions and rehearsed several likely answers to the cross questioning she expected, and, thus fortified, went down to the study.

The doctor was sitting at his desk, but he got up as she went in.

He said at once, 'Please sit down, Miss Pomfrey, I owe you an apology. It was unpardonable of me to speak to you in such a fashion, to give you no chance to explain—'

Araminta chipped in, 'It's quite all right, doctor, I quite understand. You must have been very worried.'

'Were you not worried, Mintie?'

He so seldom called her that that she stared at him. His face was as impassive as it always was; he was looking at her over his spectacles, his brows lifted in enquiry.

'Me? Yes, of course I was. I was scared out of my wits, if you must know—so afraid that the boys would suddenly realise that we might be shut up for hours and it wasn't an adventure, after all.' She added matter-of-factly, 'Of course, I knew you'd come sooner or later.'

'Oh, and why should you be so sure of that?'

She frowned. 'I don't know—at least, I suppose... I don't know.'

'I hope you accept my apology, and if there is anything—'

'Of course I accept it,' she interrupted him again. 'And there isn't anything. Thank you.'

'You are happy here? You do not find it too dull?'

'I don't see how anyone could feel dull with Peter and Paul as companions.'

She looked at him and smiled.

'You have been crying, Miss Pomfrey?'

So she was Miss Pomfrey again. 'Certainly not. What have I got to cry about?'

'I can think of several things, and you may be a splendid governess, Miss Pomfrey, but you are a poor liar.'

She went rather red in the face. 'What a nasty thing to say about me,' she snapped, quite forgetting that he was her employer, who expected politeness at all times, no doubt, 'I never tell lies, not the kind which harm people. Besides, my father has always told me that a weeping woman is a thorn in the flesh of any man.'

The doctor kept a straight face. 'A very sensible opinion,' he murmured. 'All the same, if it was I who caused your tears, I'm sorry. I have no wish to upset you or make you unhappy.'

She sought for an answer, but since she couldn't think of one, she stayed silent.

'You behaved with commendable good sense.' He smiled then. 'Dr Jenkell assured me that you were the most level-headed young woman he had ever known. I must be sure and tell him how right he was.'

If that's a compliment, thought Araminta, I'd as soon do without it. She wondered what would have happened if she had been pretty and empty-headed and screamed her head off. Men being men, they would have rushed to her rescue, poured brandy down her throat and offered a shoulder for her to cry into. They would probably have called her poor little girl and made sure that she went to her bed for the rest of the day. And the doctor was very much a man, wasn't he? Being plain had its drawbacks, thought Araminta.

The doctor, watching her expressive face, wondered what she was thinking. How fortunate it was that she was such a sensible girl. The whole episode would be forgotten, but he must remember to make sure that her next free day was a success.

He said now, 'I expect you want to go to the boys. I told them that they might have supper with us this evening, but that they must have their baths and be ready for bed first.'

Dismissed, but with her evening's work already planned, Araminta went in search of the boys and spent the next hour supervising the cleaning of teeth, the brushing of hair and the riotous bath. With the boys looking like two small angels, she led them downstairs presently. There had been little time to do anything to her own person; she had dabbed her nose with powder, brushed her own hair, and sighed into the mirror, aware that the doctor wouldn't notice if she wore a blonde wig and false eyelashes.

'Not that I mind in the least,' she had told her reflection.

Her supposition was regrettably true, he barely glanced at her throughout the meal, and when he did he didn't see anyone other than the dependable Miss Pomfrey, suitably merging into the background of his life.

The next days were uneventful, a pleasant pattern of mornings at school, afternoons spent exploring and evenings playing some game or other. When their uncle was at home, the boys spent their short evenings with him, leaving her free to do whatever she wanted.

She supposed that she could have gone and sat in the little room behind the drawing room and watched the TV, but no one had suggested it and she didn't like to go there uninvited. So she stayed in her room, doing her nails, sewing on buttons and mending holes in small garments.

It was a pleasant room, warm and nicely furnished, but it didn't stop her feeling lonely.

It was towards the end of the week that Paul got up one morning and didn't want his breakfast. Probably a cold, thought Araminta, and kept an eye on him.

He seemed quite his usual self when she fetched them both from school, but by the evening he was feverish, peevish and thoroughly out of sorts. It was a pity that the doctor had gone to the Hague and wouldn't be back until late that evening. Araminta put him to bed and, since the twins didn't like to be separated, Peter had his bath and got ready for bed, too. With Bas's help she carried up their light supper.

But Paul didn't want his; his throat was sore and his head ached and when she took his temperature it was alarmingly high. She sat him on her lap, persuaded him to drink the cold drinks Bas brought and, while Peter finished his supper, embarked on a story. She made it up as she went along, and it was about nothing in particular, but the boys listened and presently Paul went to sleep, his hot little head pressed against her shoulder.

Peter had come to sit beside her, and she put an arm around him, carrying on a cheerful whispered conversation until he, reassured about his brother, slept too.

It was some time later when Bas came in quietly to remind her that dinner was waiting for her.

'I'm sorry, Bas, but I can't come. They're both sound asleep and Paul isn't well. They're bound to wake presently, then I can put them in their beds... Will you apologize to Jet for me? I'm not hungry; I can have some soup later.'

Bas went reluctantly and she was left, her insides rumbling, while she tried not to think of food. Just like the doctor, she thought testily, to be away just when he was wanted. She wouldn't allow herself to panic. She had coped with childish ailments at the children's convalescent home and knew how resilient they were and how quickly they got well once whatever it was which had afflicted them had been diagnosed and dealt with. All the same, she wished that the doctor would come home soon.

Minutes ticked themselves slowly into an hour, but she managed a cheerful smile when Bas put a concerned head round the door.

'They'll wake soon,' she assured him in a whisper. But they slept on: Peter sleeping the deep sleep of a healthy child, Paul deeply asleep too but with a mounting fever, his tousled head still against her shoulder. She longed to changed her position; she longed even more for a cup of tea. It did no good to dwell on that, so she allowed her thoughts free rein and wondered what the doctor was doing and who he was with. She hoped that whoever it was wasn't distracting him from returning home at a reasonable hour.

It was a good thing that she didn't know that on the point of his leaving the hospital in the Hague he had been urgently recalled...

When he did get home it was ten o'clock. Bas came hurrying into the hall to meet him, his nice elderly face worried.

'What's wrong?' asked the doctor.

'Little Paul. He's not well, *mijnheer*. He's asleep, but Miss Pomfrey has him on her lap; he's been there for hours. Peter's there too. Miss Pomfrey asked me to phone the hospital, but you were not available...'

The doctor put a hand on Bas's shoulder. 'I'll go up. Don't worry, Bas.'

Araminta had heard him come home, and the voices in the hall, and relief flooded through her. She peered down into Paul's sleeping face and then looked up as the doctor came quietly into the room.

'Have you had the mumps?' she asked him.

He stopped short. 'Good Lord, yes, decades ago.'

He looked at his nephew's face, showing distinct signs of puffiness, then stopped and lifted him gently off her lap.

'How long have you been sitting there?'

'Since six o'clock. He's got a temperature and a headache and his throat's sore. Peter's all right so far.'

The doctor laid the still sleeping boy in his bed and bent to examine him gently. 'We will let him sleep, poor scrap.' He came and took Peter in his arms and tucked him up in his bed, talking softly to the half-awake child. Only then did he turn to Araminta, sitting, perforce, exactly as she had been doing for the past few hours, so stiff that she didn't dare to move.

The doctor hauled her gently to her feet, put an arm around her and walked her up and down.

'Now, go downstairs, tell Bas to ask Jet to get us something to eat and send Nel up here to sit with the boys for a while.'

And when she hesitated, he added, 'Go along, Miss Pomfrey. I want my supper.'

She gave him a speaking look; she wanted her supper, too, and the unfeeling man hadn't even bothered to ask her if she needed hers.

'So do I,' she snapped, and then added, 'Is Paul all right? It is only mumps?'

He said coolly, 'Yes, Miss Pomfrey. Hopefully only mumps.'

She went downstairs and gave Bas his messages, then went and sat in the small sitting room. She was tired and rather untidy and she could see ahead of her several trying days while the mumps kept their hold on Paul—and possibly Peter.

'Twelve days incubation,' she said, talking to herself, 'and we could wait longer than that until we're sure Peter doesn't get them, too.'

'Inevitable, Miss Pomfrey. Do you often talk to yourself?'

The doctor had come silently into the room. He poured a glass of sherry and gave it to her and didn't wait for her answer. 'It will mean bed for a few days for Paul, and of course Peter can't go to school. Will you be able to manage? Nel can take over in the afternoons while you take Peter for a walk?'

He watched her toss back the sherry and refilled her glass. Perhaps he was expecting too much of her. 'See how you go on,' he told her kindly. 'If necessary, I'll get some more help.'

'If Peter were to get the mumps within the next few days I shall be able to manage very nicely,' she said matter-of-factly.

'It is to be hoped that he will. Let us get them over with, by all means.'

Bas came then, so she finished her second sherry far too quickly and went to the dining room with the doctor.

Jet had conjured up an excellent meal: mushroom soup, a cheese soufflé, salad and a lemon mousse. Araminta, slightly light-headed from the sherry, ate everything put before her, making somewhat muddled conversation as she did so. The doctor watched with faint amusement as she polished off the last of the mousse.

'Now go to bed, Miss Pomfrey. You will be called as usual in the morning.'

'Oh, that won't do at all,' she told him, emboldened by the sherry. 'I'll have a bath and get ready for bed, then I'll go and sit with the boys for a bit. Once I'm sure they are all right, I'll go to bed. I shall hear them if they wake.'

'You will do as I say. I have a good deal of reading to do; I will do it in their room.'

'Aren't you going to the hospital in the morning?'

'Certainly I am.'

'Then you can't do that; you'll be like a wet rag in the morning. You need your sleep.'

'I'm quite capable of knowing how much sleep I need, Miss Pomfrey. Kindly do as I ask. Goodnight.'

She wanted to cry, although she didn't know why, but she held back the tears, wished him a bleak goodnight and went upstairs. She felt better after a hot bath, and, wrapped in her dressing gown, she crept into the boys' room to make sure they were asleep. Nel, the house-maid, had gone downstairs again and they slept peace-fully. Promising herself that she would get up during the night to make sure that they were all right, Araminta took herself off to bed.

She was asleep at once, but woke instantly at a peevish wail from Paul. She tumbled out of bed and crept to the half-open door. Paul was awake and the doctor was sit-ting on his bed, giving him a drink. There were papers scattered all over the floor and the chair was drawn up to the table by the window. She crept back to bed. It was two o'clock in the morning. She lay and worried about the doctor's lack of sleep until she slept once more.

She was up very early, to find the boys sleeping and the doctor gone. She dressed, crept down to the kitchen and made herself tea, filled a jug with cold lemonade and went back to the boys' room. They were still asleep. Paul's face was very swollen but Peter looked normal. She had no idea how she would manage for the next few days; it depended on whether Peter got mumps, too.

She was going silently around the room, getting clean clothes for the boys, when the doctor came in.

She wished him a quiet good morning and saw how tired he was, despite his immaculate appearance. Despite his annoyance the previous evening, she said in her sensible way, 'I hope you'll have the good sense to have a good night's sleep tonight. What would we do if you were to be ill?'

'My dear Miss Pomfrey, stop fussing. I am never ill. If you're worried during the day, tell Bas; he knows where to find me.'

And he had gone again, with a casual nod, hardly looking at her.

Chapter 5

The day was every bit as bad as Araminta had expected it to be. Paul woke up peevish, hot and sorry for himself, and it took a good deal of coaxing to get him washed and into clean pyjamas, his temperature taken and a cold drink swallowed. Bas had produced some coloured straws, which eased the drinking problem, but the mumps had taken hold for the moment and her heart ached for the small swollen face.

Nevertheless, she got through the day, reading to the invalid until she was hoarse, playing games with Peter and then taking him for a walk with Humphrey while Nel sat with Paul. They returned, much refreshed, armed with drawing books, crayons, a jigsaw puzzle and a couple of comics, had their tea with Humphrey in the sitting room and then went to spend the rest of the afternoon with Paul. He still felt ill, but his headache was better, he said, although it still hurt him to swallow.

'You'll feel better tomorrow,' Araminta assured him. 'Not quite well, but better, and when your uncle comes home I expect he'll know what to do to take away the pain in your throat.'

The doctor came home just after six o'clock, coming into the boys' room quietly, his civil good evening to Araminta drowned in the boisterous greeting from Peter and the hoarse voice of Paul. Humphrey, who had been lying on his bed, lumbered up to add his welcome and the doctor stooped to pat him.

Before the doctor could voice any disapproval of dogs on beds, Araminta said firmly, 'I said that Humphrey could get on the bed. He's company for Paul and comforting, too, so if you want to scold anyone, please scold me.'

He looked at her with raised eyebrows and a little smile which held no warmth. 'I was not aware that I had given my opinion on the matter, Miss Pomfrey. I see no reason to scold anyone, either you or Humphrey.'

And, having disposed of the matter, he proceeded to ask her how the day had gone. He sat on the bed while she told him, examining Paul's face and neck, taking his temperature, listening to his small bony chest, looking down his throat.

'You're better,' he declared cheerfully. 'You're going to feel horrible for a few days, and you'll have to stay in bed for a while, but I've no doubt that Miss Pomfrey will keep you amused.'

'Does Miss Pomfrey—well, you mean Mintie, of course—amuse you too, Uncle?' This from Peter.

The doctor glanced across at Araminta. 'Oh, decidedly,' he said, and smiled at her, a warm smile this time, inviting her to share the joke.

It was impossible to resist that smile. She agreed cheerfully and listened to Peter, like all small boys, enlarging upon the idea with gruff chuckles from his twin.

The doctor got up presently. 'Ice cream and yoghurt for supper,' he suggested. 'Miss Pomfrey, if you would come down to my study, I will give you something to ease that sore throat. Peter, I leave you in charge for a few minutes.'

In the study, with Humphrey standing between them, he said, 'You have had a long day. I'm afraid the next few days will be equally long. Paul is picking up nicely, and the swelling should go down in another five or six days. He must stay in bed for another day or so, then he could be allowed to get up, wrapped up warmly and kept in the room. Peter seems all right...'

'Yes, and so good with his brother.'

'I shall be at home this evening. I'll keep an eye on the boys while you have dinner, and then if you would be with them for half an hour or so, I'll take over. You could do with an early night...'

She said, before she could stop her tongue, 'Do I look so awful?'

He surveyed her coolly. 'Let us say you do not look at your best, Miss Pomfrey.'

He took no notice of her glare but went to his case. 'Crush one of these and stir it into Paul's ice cream. Get him to drink as much as possible.' He added, 'You will, of course, be experienced in the treatment of childish ailments?'

'Yes,' said Araminta. The horrible man. What did he expect when she'd been kept busy the whole day with the boys? Not look her best, indeed!

She went to the door and he opened it for her and then made matters worse by observing, 'Never mind, Miss Pomfrey, as soon as the mumps have been routed, you shall have all the time you want for beauty treatment and shopping.'

She spun round to face him, looking up into his bland face. 'Why bother? And how dare you mock me? You are an exceedingly tiresome man, but I don't suppose anyone has dared to tell you so!'

He stared down at her, not speaking.

'Oh, dear, I shouldn't have said that,' said Araminta. 'I'm sorry if I've hurt your feelings, although I don't see why I should be, for you have no regard for mine. Anyway,' she added defiantly, 'it's a free world and I can say what I like.'

'Indeed you can, Miss Pomfrey. Feel free to express your feelings whenever you have the need.'

He held the door wide and she flounced through. Back with the boys once more, she wondered if he would give her the sack. He was entitled to do so; she had been more than a little outspoken. On the other hand, he would have to get someone to replace her pretty smartly, someone willing to cope with two small boys and the mumps…

Apparently he had no such intention. Paul was soon readied for the night and Peter was prancing round in his pyjamas, demanding that he should have his supper with his brother.

'Well, I don't see why not,' said Araminta. 'Put on your dressing gown, there's a good boy, and I'll see what Bas says…'

'And what should Bas say?' asked the doctor, coming in in his usual quiet fashion.

'That he won't mind helping me bring supper up here for Peter as well as Paul.'

'By all means. Ask him to do so, Miss Pomfrey, and then have your dinner—a little early, but I dare say you will enjoy a long evening to yourself.'

There was nothing to say to that, so she went in search of Bas.

Peter said, 'You must say Mintie, Uncle. Why do you always call her Miss Pomfrey?'

'I have a shocking memory. How about a game of Spillikins after supper?'

Araminta still felt annoyed, and apprehensive as well, but that didn't prevent her from enjoying her meal. Jet sent in garlic mushrooms, chicken à la king with braised celery, and then a chocolate mousse. It would be a pity to miss these delights, reflected Araminta, relishing the last of the mousse. She must keep a curb on her tongue in future.

She went back to sit with the boys and the doctor went away to eat his dinner, urged to be quick so that there would be time for one more game of Spillikins before their bedtime.

'It's already past your bedtime,' said Araminta.

'Just for once shall we bend the rules?' said the doctor as he went out of the room.

He was back within half an hour, and another half an hour saw the end of their game. He got up from Paul's bed.

'I'll be back in five minutes,' he told them, 'and you'll both be asleep.'

When he came back he said, 'Thank you, Miss Pomfrey, goodnight.'

She had already tucked the boys in, so she wished him a quiet goodnight and left him there.

A faint grizzling sound wakened her around midnight. Peter had woken up with a headache and a sore throat…

She went down to breakfast in the morning feeling rather the worse for wear. The doctor glanced up briefly from his post, wished her good morning and resumed his reading. Araminta sat down, poured her coffee, and, since he had nothing further to say, observed, 'Peter has the mumps.'

The doctor took off his spectacles, the better to look at her.

'To be expected. I'll go and have a look at him. He had a bad night?'

'Yes,' said Araminta, and stopped herself just in time from adding, And so did I.

'And so did you,' said the doctor, reading her peevish face like an open book. He passed her the basket of rolls and offered butter. 'You'll feel better when you've had your breakfast.'

Araminta buttered a roll savagely. She might have known better than to have expected any sympathy. She thought of several nasty remarks to make, but he was watching her from his end of the table and for once she decided that prudence might be the best thing.

She bit into her roll with her splendid teeth, choked on a crumb and had to be thumped on the back while she whooped and spluttered. Rather red in the face, she resumed her breakfast and the doctor his seat.

He said mildly, 'You don't appear to be your usual calm self, Miss Pomfrey. Perhaps I should get extra help while the boys are sick.'

'Quite unnecessary,' said Araminta. 'With both of them in bed there will be very little to do.'

She was aware that she was being optimistic; there would be a great deal to do. By the end of the day she would probably be at her wits' end, cross-eyed and sore-throated from reading aloud, headachey from jigsaw puzzles and worn out by coaxing two small fractious boys to swallow food and drink which they didn't want...

'Just as you wish,' observed the doctor, and gathered up his letters. 'I'll go and have a look at Peter. Did Paul sleep?'

'For most of the night.'

He nodded and left her to finish her breakfast, and presently, when he had seen Paul, he returned to tell her that Peter was likely to be peevish and out of sorts. 'I'll give you something before I leave to relieve his sore throat. Paul is getting on nicely. Bas will know how to get hold of me if you are worried. Don't hesitate if you are. I'll be home around six.'

The day seemed endless, but away from the doctor's inimical eye Araminta was her practical, unflappable self, full of sympathy for the two small boys. Naturally they were cross, given to bursts of crying, and unwilling to swallow drinks and the ice cream she offered. Still, towards teatime she could see that Paul was feeling better, and although Peter's temperature was still too high, he was less peevish.

She hardly left them; Nel relieved her when she had a meal, and offered to sit with them while she went out for a while, but Araminta, with Bas translating, assured her that she was fine and that when the doctor came home she would have an hour or two off.

She was reading *The Lion, the Witch and the Wardrobe* when he walked into the room. He sat down on Paul's bed and didn't speak for a moment.

'I see Paul's feeling better; what about Peter?'

He could at least have wished her good evening or even said hello.

'He's feeling off colour, and he's been very good— they both have—and they've taken their drinks like Trojans. Jet is making them jelly for supper.'

'Splendid. Go and have a stroll round the garden, Miss Pomfrey, and then have dinner.'

'I'm perfectly...' she began.

'Yes, I know you are, but kindly do as I say.' He said something in Dutch to the boys, and they managed to giggle despite the mumps.

Araminta went. First to her room to get a cardigan, and to take a dispirited look at her reflection. There seemed no point in doing more than brushing her hair into tidiness and powdering her nose; she went downstairs and passed Humphrey on his way up to join his master. She would have liked his company as she wandered to and fro in the garden.

It was growing chilly and she was glad of the cardigan and even more glad when Bas came to tell her that dinner would be ready in five minutes.

It was a delicious meal, but she didn't linger over it. The doctor would need his dinner, too, and probably he had plans for his evening. It was Bas who insisted that she went to the drawing room to have her coffee.

Sitting by the cheerful fire presently, with the tray on a table beside her, she felt at peace with everyone...

She was pouring her second cup when she heard Bas admit someone. A minute later the door was thrust open and Christina Lutyns pushed past him and came into the room.

Araminta put the coffeepot down carefully. Her polite 'Good evening, *Mevrouw*,' went unanswered, though.

'Why are you sitting here in the drawing room? Where is Dr van der Breugh? Why aren't you looking after the children?'

Araminta didn't need to answer, for the doctor had come into the room. His '*Dag*, Christina,' was uttered quietly, and he smiled a little. 'Miss Pomfrey is taking a well-earned hour or so from her duties. The reason she is not with the children is because she has been with them almost constantly since the early hours of today. They both have the mumps.'

Christina gave a small shriek. She lapsed into Dutch. 'Don't come near me; I might get them too. And that girl sitting there, she shouldn't be here; she should stay with the boys. I shall go away at once.' She contrived to look tearful. 'And I was looking forward to our evening together. How long will they be ill?'

'Oh, quite a while yet,' said the doctor cheerfully. 'But both Miss Pomfrey and I have had mumps as children, so we aren't likely to get them again.'

'I shall go,' said Christina. 'When there is no more infection you will tell me and we will enjoy ourselves together.'

She went then, ignoring Araminta, escorted to the door by the doctor who showed her out, taking care, at her urgent request, not to get too near to her.

When he went back into the drawing room Araminta had drunk her coffee and was on her feet. She said politely, 'I enjoyed my dinner, thank you. I'll see to the boys now.'

He nodded in an absent-minded manner. 'Yes, yes, by all means. I'll be back later on.'

'There is no need—' began Araminta, then she caught his eye and ended lamely, 'Very well, doctor,' and went meekly upstairs.

She had the boys ready for bed when he came back upstairs, bade her a civil goodnight, waited while she tucked the boys up and hugged them and then held the door open for her. As she went past him, he told her that he would be away from home for the next two days.

'Unavoidable, I'm afraid, but I have asked a colleague of mine to call in each day. The boys have met him on previous visits and they like him. Don't hesitate to call upon him if you need advice.'

Getting ready for bed, Araminta supposed that she should be glad that the doctor would be away from home. They didn't get on and he was indifferent to her, although she had to admit that he was thoughtful for her comfort, while at the same time indifferent to her as a person.

'Not that I mind,' said Araminta, talking to herself, lying half-sleep in the bath. She said it again to convince herself.

Paul was much better in the morning and Peter, although still sorry for himself, was amenable to swallowing his breakfast. The doctor had left very early, Bas told her, but Dr van Vleet would be calling at about ten o'clock to see the boys.

They were sitting up in their beds, well enough now to talk while Araminta tidied the room, when the doctor came.

He was young, thickset and of middle height with a rugged face which just missed being handsome, but he had bright blue eyes and a wide smile. He shook hands with her, said something to the boys which made them laugh and added in English, 'Van Vleet—I expect Marcus told you that I would look in.'

'Yes, he did. They're both much better. Peter's still got a slight temperature, but the swellings have gone down since yesterday.'

'I'll take a look…'

Which he did, sitting on their beds while he examined them in turn, talking all the time, making them laugh.

'They're fine. I should think they might get up tomorrow. Though they must stay in a warm room…'

'There's a nursery close by. They could spend the day there.'

'Don't let them get tired.' He smiled nicely at her. 'Marcus told me that you were very experienced with small children, so I don't have to bother you with a great many instructions.'

He closed his bag just as Bas came in. 'Coffee is in the drawing room, Miss Pomfrey, Doctor... Nel will come and stay with the boys while you drink it.'

And when Araminta hesitated, he added, 'Dr van der Breugh instructed me.'

So they went downstairs together and spent a short time over their coffee. Too short, thought Araminta, bidding him goodbye. She liked Dr van Vleet and he seemed to like her. It had been delightful to talk to someone who didn't treat her with indifference, who actually appeared to like talking to her. She was glad that he would be coming again in the morning.

The boys were so much better the next day that there was really no need for Dr van Vleet to call, but he came, looked down their throats, peered into their ears, examined the receding mumps and pronounced himself satisfied.

'Marcus will be back tonight,' he told her. 'I'll phone him in the morning, but will you tell him that the boys are both fine.'

They had coffee together again, and when he got up he asked, 'Do you get time off? I'd like to show you something of Utrecht while you're here.'

Araminta beamed at him. 'I'd like that. I get time off, of course, but it has to fit in with Dr van der Breugh.'

He took out his pocketbook and wrote in it. 'Here's

my phone number. When you are free, will you phone me? Perhaps we could arrange something.'

'Thank you, I'll let you know.'

She smiled at him, her eyes sparkling at the prospect of a day out with someone with whom she felt so completely at ease.

The pleasant feeling that she had met someone who liked her—enough to ask her out for a whole day—made the day suddenly become perfect, her chores no trouble at all, the boys little angels...

The glow of her pleasure was still in her face when the doctor came home. He had come silently into the house as he so often did, to be welcomed by Humphrey. Bas hurried to greet him, offered tea or coffee, and took his overnight bag. The doctor went into his study, put away his bag, tossed his jacket on a chair and went upstairs two at a time, to pause in the open doorway of the nursery where the two boys and Araminta were crouched on the floor before a cheerful fire playing Happy Families.

They looked round as he went in and the boys rushed to greet him. Araminta got to her feet and he stared at her for a long moment. He had thought about her while he had been away, unwillingly, aware that she disturbed him in some way, and he had returned home determined to relegate her to where she belonged—the vague background, which he didn't allow to interfere with his work.

But the face she turned to him wasn't easily dismissed; she looked happy. He was so accustomed to her quiet face and self-effacing manner that he was taken aback. Surely that look wasn't for him? He dismissed the idea as absurd and knew it to be so as he watched the glow fade and her features assume their usual calm.

He wished her good evening, listened while she gave

him a report on the boys' progress, expressed himself
satisfied and, when Bas came to tell him that he had
taken his coffee to the drawing room, bore the two boys
downstairs with him.

'Fetch them in an hour, if you will, Miss Pomfrey.
When they are in bed we can discuss their progress.'

Left alone, she tidied up the room, got everything
ready for bedtime and sat down by the fire. Why was
a fire so comforting? she wondered. The house was already warm but there were handsome fireplaces in the
rooms in which fires were lighted if a room was in use.
She had got used to living in comfort and she wondered
now how she would like hospital life.

In a few weeks now they would be returning to England.
She thought of that with regret now that she had met Dr
van Vleet. She wondered if she should ask for a day off—
she was certainly entitled to one—but Dr van der Breugh
hadn't looked very friendly—indeed, the look he had given
her had made her vaguely uncomfortable...

She fetched the boys presently, and once they were
finally in their beds went to her room to change for the
evening. The skirt and one of the blouses, she decided.
There seemed little point in dressing up each evening,
for the doctor was almost never home. But she felt that
if Bas took the trouble to set the table with such care,
and Jet cooked such delicious dinners for her, the least
she could do was to live up to that. She heard the doctor come upstairs and go into the boys' room, and presently, making sure that they were on the verge of sleep,
and with a few minutes so spare before Bas came to tell
her dinner was ready, she went downstairs.

There was no sign of the doctor, but she hadn't expected to see him. He would probably tell her at breakfast

of any plans for the boys. Bas, crossing the hall, opened the drawing room door for her and she went in.

The doctor was sitting in his chair, with Humphrey at his feet. He got up as she went in, offered her a chair, offered sherry and when he sat down again, observed, 'I think we may regard Peter and Paul as being almost back to normal. I think we should keep them from school for another few days, but I see no reason why they shouldn't have a short brisk walk tomorrow if the weather is fine. Children have astonishing powers of recovery.'

Araminta agreed pleasantly and sipped her sherry. She hoped he wasn't going to keep her for too long; she was hungry and it was already past the dinner hour.

'You must have a day to yourself,' said the doctor. 'I'm booked up for the next two days, but after that I will be at home, if you care to avail yourself of a day. And this time I promise to make sure that you enjoy yourself. You may have the Jaguar and a driver, and if you will let me know where you would like to go, I will arrange a suitable tour for you.'

Araminta took another sip of sherry. So she was to be given a treat, was she? Parcelled up and put in a car and driven around like a poor old relative who deserved a nice day out.

She tossed back the rest of the sherry and sat up straight. 'How kind,' she said in a voice brittle with indignation, 'but there is no need of your thoughtful offer. I have other plans.'

The doctor asked carelessly, 'Such as?' and when she gave him a chilly look he said, 'I do stand, as it were, *in loco parentis.*'

'I am twenty-three years old, doctor,' said Araminta in a voice which should have chilled him to the bone.

He appeared untouched. 'You don't look it. Had I not known, I would have guessed nineteen, twenty at the most.' He smiled, and she knew that she would have to tell him.

'Dr van Vleet has asked me to spend the day with him.'

She had gone rather red, so that she frowned as she spoke.

'Ah, a most satisfactory arrangement. And it absolves me from the need to concern myself over you. Telephone him and make any arrangements you like; I am sure you will enjoy yourself with him.' He put down his glass. 'Shall we go in to dinner?'

'Oh, are you going to be here?' Araminta paused; she had put that rather badly. 'What I meant was, you're dining at home this evening?'

The doctor said gravely, 'That is my intention, Miss Pomfrey.' She didn't see his smile, for she was looking at her feet and wondering if she should apologise.

He, aware of that, maintained a steady flow of small talk throughout the meal so that by the time they had finished she felt quite her normal calm self again.

Getting ready for bed later, she even decided that the doctor could, if he chose, be a pleasant companion.

The next few days went well. The boys, making the most of their last free days before going back to school, took her about the city, spending their pocket money, feeding the ducks in the park, taking her to the Oude-gracht to look at the ancient stone—a legendary edifice which, they told her, with suitable embellishments, had to do with the devil.

She saw little of the doctor, just briefly at breakfast, with occasional glimpses as he came and went during the

day, but never in the evenings. Somehow he made time
to be with his nephews before their bedtime, when she
was politely told that she might do whatever she wished
for a couple of hours, but they didn't dine together again.

Not that Araminta minded. She had phoned Dr van
Vleet and, after gaining the doctor's indifferent consent,
had agreed to spend the day with him on the following
Saturday.

She worried as to what she should wear. It was too
chilly for the two-piece; it would have to be a blouse and
skirt and the jacket. A pity, she reflected crossly, that
she never had the time to go shopping. In the meantime
she would have to make do with whatever her meagre
wardrobe could produce. She had money, the doctor was
punctilious about that, so the very first morning she had
an hour or two to herself she would go shopping.

The sun was shining when Dr van Vleet came for her;
the doctor had already breakfasted, spent a brief time in
his study and was in the garden with the boys, but they
all came to see her off, the boys noisily begging her to
come back soon. 'As long as you're here in the morning
when we wake up,' said Peter.

Dr van Vleet drove a Fiat and she quickly discovered
that he liked driving fast. 'Where are we going?' she
wanted to know.

'To Arnhem first. We go through the Veluwe—that's
pretty wooded country—and at Arnhem there's an open-
air village museum you might like to see. You've seen
nothing of Holland yet?'

'Well, no, though I've explored Utrecht pretty thoroughly. With the boys.'

'Nice little chaps, aren't they?' He gave her a smiling

glance. 'My name's Piet, by the way. And what is it the boys call you?'

'Mintie. Short for Araminta.'

'Then I shall call you Mintie.'

He was right, the Veluwe was beautiful: its trees glowing with autumn colours, the secluded villas half hidden from the road. They stopped for coffee and, after touring the village at Arnhem, had lunch there.

After lunch he drove to Nijmegen and on to Culemborg, and then north to Amersfoort and on to Soestdijk so that she could see the royal palace.

They had tea in Soest and then drove back to Appeldoorn to look at the palace there. Piet finally took the Utrecht road, and she said, 'You've given me a lovely day. I can't begin to thank you; I've loved every minute of it...'

'It's not over yet. I hope you'll have dinner with me. There's rather a nice hotel near Utrecht—Auberge de Hoefslag. Very pretty surroundings, woods all round and excellent food.'

'It sounds lovely, but I'm not dressed...' began Araminta.

'You look all right to me.'

And she need not have worried; the restaurant was spread over two rooms, one modern, the other delightfully old-fashioned, and in both there was a fair sprinkling of obvious tourists.

The food was delicious and they didn't hurry over it. By the time they had driven the ten kilometres to Utrecht it was almost eleven o'clock.

Piet got out of the car with her and went with her to the door, waiting while she rang the bell, rather worried as it was later than she had intended. Bas opened the door, beamed a greeting at her and ushered her in-

side. He wished Dr van Vleet a civil goodnight and shut
the door, and just for a moment Araminta stood in the
hall, remembering her happy day and smiling because
before they had said goodnight he had asked her to go
out with him again.

'A happy day, miss?' asked Bas. 'You would like coffee or tea?'

'A lovely day, Bas.' Her eyes shone just thinking about
it. 'I don't want anything, thank you. I do hope I haven't
kept you up?'

'No, miss. Goodnight.'

She crossed the hall to the staircase. The doctor's
study door was half open and she could see him at his
desk. He didn't look up, and after a moment's pause she
went on up the stairs. He must have heard her come in
but he had given no sign. She wouldn't admit it, but her
lovely day was a little spoilt by that.

At breakfast he asked her if she had enjoyed her day
out, and, quite carried away by the pleasure, she assured
him that she had and embarked on a brief description of
where they had been, only to realise very quickly that
he wasn't in the least interested. So she stopped in mid-
sentence, applied herself to attending to the boys' wants
and her own breakfast, and when he got up from the table
with a muttered excuse took no notice.

He turned back at the door to say, 'I see no reason why
the boys shouldn't attend church this morning. Kindly
have them ready in good time, Miss Pomfrey. And, of
course, yourself.'

So they went to church, the boys delighted to be with
their uncle, she at her most staid. The sermon seemed
longer than ever, but she didn't mind, she was planning

her new clothes. Piet had said he would take her to Amsterdam, a city worthy of a new outfit.

The doctor, sitting so that he could watch her face, wondered why he had considered her so plain—something, someone had brought her to life. He frowned; he must remember to warn her...

There was a general upsurge of the congregation and presently they were walking home again.

They had just finished lunch and were full of ideas as to how they might spend their afternoon when Christina Lutyns was ushered in.

She kissed the doctor on both cheeks, nodded to the boys and ignored Araminta, breaking into a torrent of Dutch.

The doctor had got up as she entered, and stood smiling as she talked. When she paused he said something to make her smile, and then said in English, 'I shall be out for the rest of the day, Miss Pomfrey.' When the boys protested, he promised that when he came home he would be sure to wish them goodnight. 'Although you may be asleep,' he warned them.

They had been asleep for hours when he came home. He went to their room and bent to kiss them and tuck the bedclothes in, and Araminta, who had had a difficult time getting them to go to sleep, hoped that he would have a good excuse in the morning.

Whatever it was, it satisfied the boys, but not her, for he spoke Dutch.

That evening he asked her when she would like her free day. Piet had suggested Thursday, but she felt uncertain of having it. If the doctor had work to do he wouldn't change that to accommodate her. But it seemed that Thursday was possible. 'Going out with van Vleet again?' asked the doctor casually.

'Yes, to Amsterdam.' She added, in a voice which dared him to disagree with her, 'I hear it is a delightful city. I am looking forward to seeing it.'

'Miss Pomfrey, there is something I should warn you about…'

'Is there? Could it wait, Doctor? The boys will be late for school if I don't take them now.'

'Just as you like, Miss Pomfrey.' And somehow she contrived not to be alone with him for the rest of the day; she felt sure he was going to tell her that they would be returning to England sooner than he had expected, and she didn't want to hear that. Not now that she had met Piet.

Rather recklessly she went shopping during the morning hours while the boys were in school. Clothes, good clothes, she discovered, were expensive, but she couldn't resist buying a dress and loose jacket in a fine wool. It was in pale amber, an impractical colour and probably she wouldn't have much chance to wear it, but it gave her mousy hair an added glint and it was a perfect fit. She bought shoes, too, and a handbag and a pretty scarf.

Thursday came and, much admired by the boys, she went downstairs to meet Piet. He was in the hall talking to the doctor and turned to watch her as she came towards them. His hello was friendly. 'How smart you look—I like the colour; it suits you.'

'We told her that she looks beautiful,' said Peter.

'She does, doesn't she, Uncle?' Paul added.

The doctor, appealed to, observed that indeed Miss Pomfrey looked charming. But his eyes when he glanced at her were cold.

Amsterdam was everything that she had hoped for, and Piet took her from one museum to the other, for a trip on the canals, a visit to the Rijksmusee and there they had a quick look at the shops. They had coffee and had a snack lunch and, later, tea. And in the evening, as the lights came on, they strolled along the *grachten*, looking at the old houses and the half-hidden antique shops.

He took her to the Hotel de L'Europe for dinner, and it was while they drank their coffee that he told her that he was to marry in the New Year.

'Anna is in Canada, visiting her grandparents,' he told her. 'I miss her very much, but soon she will be home again. You would like each other. She is like you, I think, rather quiet—I think you say in English, a home bird? She is a splendid cook and she is fond of children. We shall be very happy.'

He beamed at her across the table and she smiled back while the half-formed daydreams tumbled down into her new shoes. She had been a fool, but, thank heaven, he had no idea...

'Tell me about her,' said Araminta. Which he did at some length, so that it was late by the time they reached the doctor's house.

'We must go out together again,' said Piet eagerly.

'Well, I'm not sure about that. I believe we're going back to England very shortly. Shall I let you know?' She offered a hand. 'It's been a lovely day, and thank you so very much for giving me dinner. If we don't see each other again, I hope that you and your Anna will be very happy.'

'Oh, we shall,' he assured her.

'Don't get out of the car,' said Araminta. 'There's Bas at the door.'

It was quiet in the hall, and dimly lit. Bas wished her goodnight and went away, and she stood there feeling very alone. She had only herself to thank, of course. Had she really imagined that someone as uninteresting as herself could attract a man? He had asked her out of kindness—she hoped he hadn't pitied her…

She was aware that the study door was open and the doctor was standing there watching her. She made for the stairs, muttering goodnight, but he put out an arm and stopped her.

'You look as though you are about to burst into tears. You'll feel better if you talk about it.'

'I haven't anything to talk about…'

He put a vast arm round her shoulders. 'Oh, yes, you have. I did try to warn you, but you wouldn't allow me to.'

He sounded quite different: kind, gentle and understanding.

'I've been such a fool,' began Araminta as she laid her head against his shoulder and allowed herself the luxury of a good cry.

Chapter 6

The doctor, waiting patiently while Araminta snivelled and snorted into his shoulder, became aware of several things: the faint scent of clean mousy hair under his chin, the slender softness of her person and a wholly unexpected concern for her. Presently he gave her a large white handkerchief.

'Better?' he asked. 'Mop up and give a good blow and tell me about it.'

She did as she was told, but said in a watery voice, 'I don't want to talk about it, thank you.' And then she added, 'So sorry...' She had slipped from his arm. 'You've been very kind. I'll wash your hanky...'

He sat her down in a small chair away from the brightness of his desk lamp.

'You don't need to tell me if you don't wish to.' He had gone to a small table under the window and come back with a glass. 'Drink that; it will make you feel better.'

She sniffed it. 'Brandy? I've never had any...'

'There's always a first time. Of course, van Vleet told you that he was going to be married shortly.' He watched her sip the brandy and draw a sharp breath at its strength. 'And you had thought that he was interested in you. He should have told you when you first met him, but I imagine that it hadn't entered his head.' He sighed. 'He's a very decent young man.'

Araminta took another sip, a big one, for the brandy was warming her insides. She felt a little sick and at the same time reckless.

She said, in a voice still a little thick from her tears, 'I have been very silly. I should know by now that there is nothing about me to—to make a man interested. I'm plain and I have no conversation, and I wear sensible clothes.'

The doctor hid a smile. 'I can assure you that when you meet a man who will love you, none of these things will matter.'

She said in her matter-of-fact way, 'But I don't meet men—young men. Father and Mother have friends I've known for years. They're all old and mostly married.' She tossed back the rest of the brandy, feeling light-headed. Vaguely she realised that in the morning she was going to feel awful about having had this conversation. 'I shall, of course, make nursing my career and be very success-ful.' She got to her feet. 'I'll go to bed now.' She made for the door. 'I feel a little sick.'

He crossed the hall with her and stood watching while she made her way upstairs. She looked forlorn and he ig-nored a wish to help her. Her pride had been shattered; he wouldn't make it worse.

Thanks to the brandy, Araminta slept all night, but everything came rushing back into her head when she woke up. She remembered only too clearly the talk she had had with the doctor. To weep all over him had been bad enough, but she had said a great deal too much. She got up, went to call the boys and prayed that he would have left the house before they went down to breakfast.

Her prayers weren't answered; he was sitting at the

table just as usual, reading his letters, his spectacles perched on his splendid nose.

He got up as they went in, received the boys' hugs and wished her good morning with his usual cool politeness. She gave him a quick look as she sat down; there was no sign of the gentle man who had comforted her last night. He was as he always was: indifferent, polite and totally uninterested in her. Her rather high colour subsided; it was clear their conversation was to be a closed book. Well, she had learned her lesson; if ever a man fell in love with her—and she doubted that—he would have to prove it to her in no uncertain fashion. And she would take care to stay heartwhole.

The day passed in its well-ordered fashion; there was plenty to keep her occupied. The boys, fit again, were full of energy, noisy, demanding her attention and time. She welcomed that, just as she welcomed the routine, with their uncle's return in the evening and the hour of leisure while they were with him. He went out again as soon as they were in bed, wishing her a cool goodnight as he went.

Araminta, eating her dinner under Bas's kindly eye, wondered where he was. Probably with Christina Lutyns, she supposed. Much as she disliked the woman there was no doubt that she would make a suitable wife for the doctor. Suitable, but not the right one. There was a side to him which she had only glimpsed from time to time—not the cool, bland man with his beautiful manners and ease; there was a different man behind that impassive face and she wished she could know that man. A wish not likely to be granted.

The following week wore on, and there had been no mention of her free day. Perhaps he thought she wouldn't want one. It was on Friday evening, when she went to collect the boys at bedtime that he asked her to stay for a moment.

'I don't know if you had any plans of your own, Miss Pomfrey, but on Sunday I'm taking the boys up to Friesland to visit their aunt and uncle. I should say their great-aunt and great-uncle. They live near Leeuwarden, in the lake district, and I think we might make time to take you on a quick tour of the capital. The boys and I would be delighted to have you with us, and my aunt and uncle will welcome you.' His smile was kind. 'You may, of course, wish to be well rid of us!'

It was a thoughtful kindness she hadn't expected. 'I wouldn't be in the way?'

'No. No, on the contrary. I promise you the boys won't bother you, and if you feel like exploring on your own you have only to say so. It would give you the opportunity of seeing a little more of Holland before we go back to England.'

'Then I'd like to come. Thank you for asking me. Is it a long drive?'

'Just over a hundred miles. We shall need to leave soon after eight o'clock; that will give us an hour or so at Huis Breugh and then after lunch we can spend an hour in Leeuwarden before going back for tea. The boys can have their supper when we get back and go straight to bed.'

Even if she hadn't wanted to go, she would never have been able to resist the boys' eager little faces. She agreed that it all sounded great fun and presently urged them upstairs to baths and bed. When she went down later it was to find the doctor had gone out. She hadn't expected anything else, but all the same she was disappointed.

Which is silly of me, said Araminta to herself, for he

must be scared that I'll weep all over him again. He must have hated it, and want to forget it as quickly as possible.

In this she was mistaken. The doctor had admitted to himself that he had found nothing disagreeable in Araminta's outburst of crying. True, she had made his jacket damp, and she had cried like a child, uncaring of sniffs and snivels, but he hadn't forgotten any moment of it. Indeed, he had a vivid memory of the entire episode.

He reminded himself that she would leave his household in a short while now, and doubtless in a short time he would have forgotten all about her. In the meantime, however, there was no reason why he shouldn't try and make up for her unhappy little episode with van Vleet.

He reminded himself that he had always kept her at arm's length and would continue to do so. On no account must she be allowed to disrupt his life. His work was his life; he had a wide circle of friends and some day he would marry. The thought of Christina flashed through his mind and he frowned—she would be ideal, of course, for she would allow him to work without trying to alter his life.

He picked up his pen and began making notes for the lecture he was to give that evening.

Araminta, getting up early on Sunday morning, was relieved to see that it was a clear day with a pale blue sky and mild sunshine. She would wear the new dress and jacket and take her short coat with her. That important problem solved, she got the boys dressed and, on going down to breakfast, found the doctor already there.

'It's a splendid day,' he assured them. 'I've been out with Humphrey. The wind is chilly.' He glanced at Araminta. 'Bring a coat with you, Miss Pomfrey.'

'Yes, I will. The boys have their thick jerseys on, but I'll put their jackets in the car. Is Humphrey coming with us?'

'Yes, he'll sit at the back with the boys.'

The boys needed no urging to eat their breakfast, and a few minutes after eight o'clock they were all in the car, with Bas at the door waving them away.

The doctor took the motorway to Amsterdam and then north to Purmerend and Hoorn and so on to the Afsluit-dijk.

'A pity we have no time to stop and look at some of the towns we are passing,' he observed to Araminta. 'Perhaps some other time…'

There wasn't likely to be another time, she reflected, and thrust the thought aside; she was going to enjoy the day and forget everything else. She had told herself sensibly that she must forget about Piet van Vleet. She hadn't been in love with him, but she had been hurt, and was taken by surprise and she was still getting over that. But today's outing was an unexpected treat and she was going to enjoy every minute of it.

Once off the *dijk* the doctor took the road to Leeuwarden and, just past Franeker, took a narrow country road leading south of the city. It ran through farm land: wide fields intersected by narrow canals, grazed by cows and horses. There were prosperous-looking farmhouses and an occasional village.

'It's not at all like the country round Utrecht.'

'No. One has the feeling of wide open spaces here, which in a country as small as Holland seems a solecism. You like it?'

'Yes, very much.'

He drove on without speaking, and when the road

curved through a small copse and emerged on the further side, she could see a lake.

It stretched into the distance, bordered by trees and shrubs. There was a canal running beside it and a narrow waterway leading to a smaller lake. There were sailing boats of every description on it and, here and there, men fishing from its banks, sitting like statues.

The boys were excited now, begging her to look at first one thing, then another. 'Isn't it great?' they wanted to know. 'And it gets better and better. Aren't you glad you came, Mintie?'

She assured them that she was, quite truthfully.

There were houses here and there on the lake's bank, each with its own small jetty, most of them with boats moored there. She didn't like to ask if they were almost there, but she did hope that it might be one of these houses, sitting four-square and solid amongst the sheltering trees around it.

The doctor turned the car into a narrow brick lane beside a narrow inlet, slowed to go through an open gateway and stopped before a white-walled house with a gabled roof. It had a small square tower to one side and tall chimneys, and it was surrounded by a formal garden. The windows were small, with painted shutters. It was an old house, lovingly maintained, and she could hardly wait to see what it was like inside.

The entrance was at the foot of the tower and led into a small lobby which, in turn, opened into a long wide hall. As they went in two people came to meet them. They were elderly, the man tall and spare, with white hair and still handsome, and the woman with him short and rather stout, with hair which had once been fair and was now silver. In her youth she might have been pretty, and she had beautiful eyes, large and blue with finely marked eye-brows. She was dressed in a tweed skirt and a cashmere twinset in a blue to match her eyes. When she spoke her voice was rather high and very clear.

'Marcus—you're here. I told Bep we would answer the door; she's getting deaf, poor dear.' She stood on tip-toe to receive Marcus's kiss on her cheek and then bent to hug the boys.

'And this is Miss Pomfrey,' said the doctor, and the little lady beamed and clasped Araminta's hand.

'You see I speak English, because I am sure you have no time to speak our language, and it is good practice for me.' Her eyes twinkled. 'We are so glad to meet you, Miss Pomfrey, now you must meet my husband…'

The two men had been greeting each other while the boys stood one each side of them, but now her host came to her and shook her hand.

'You are most welcome, Miss Pomfrey. I hear from Marcus that you are a valued member of his household.'

'Thank you. Well, yes, just for a few weeks.' She smiled up into his elderly face and liked him.

He stared back at her and then nodded his head. She wondered what he was thinking, and then forgot about it as his wife reminded them that coffee was waiting for them in the drawing room. Araminta, offered a seat by her hostess, saw that the doctor had the two boys with him and his uncle and relaxed.

'Of course, Marcus did not tell you our name? He is such a clever man, with that nose of his always in his books, and yet he forgets the simplest things. I am his mother's sister—of course, you know that his parents are dead, some years ago now—our name is Nos-Wieringa. My husband was born and brought up in this house and we seldom leave it. But we love to see the family when they come to Holland. You have met the boys' mother?'

Araminta said that, yes, she had.

'And you, my dear? Do you have any brothers and sisters and parents?'

'Parents. No brothers or sisters. I wish I had.'

'A family is important. Marcus is the eldest, of course, and he has two younger brothers and Lucy. Of course you know she lives in England now that she is married, and the two boys are both doctors; one is in Canada and the other in New Zealand. They should be back shortly— some kind of exchange posts.'

Mevrouw Nos-Wieringa paused for breath and Araminta reflected that she had learned more about the doctor in five minutes than in the weeks she had been working for him.

Coffee drunk, the men took the boys down to the home farm, a little distance from the house. There were some very young calves there, explained the doctor, and one of the big shire horses had had a foal.

'And I will show you the house,' said Mevrouw Nos-Wieringa. 'It is very old but we do not wish to alter it. We have central heating and plumbing and electricity, of course, but they are all concealed as far as possible. You like old houses?'

'Yes, I do. My parents live in quite a small house,' said Araminta, anxious not to sail under false pretences. 'It is quite old, early nineteenth-century, but this house is far older than that, isn't it?'

'Part of it is thirteenth-century, the rest seventeenth-century. An ancestor made a great deal of money in the Dutch East Indies and rebuilt the older part.'

The rooms were large and lofty, with vast oak beams and white walls upon which hung a great many paintings.

'Ancestors?' asked Araminta.

'Yes, mine as well as my husband's. All very alike, aren't they? You must have noticed that Marcus has the family nose. Strangely enough, few of the women had it. His mother was rather a plain little thing—the van der Breughs tend to marry plain women. They're a very old family, of course, and his grandfather still lives in the family home. You haven't been there?'

Araminta said that, no, she hadn't, and almost added that it was most unlikely that she ever would. Seeking a change of subject, she admired a large oak pillow cupboard. She mustn't allow her interest in the doctor to swamp common sense.

They lunched presently, sitting at a large oak table on rather uncomfortable chairs; it was a cheerful meal, since the children were allowed to join in the conversation. As they rose from the table Mevrouw Nos-Wieringa said, 'Now, off you go, Marcus, and take Mintie—I may call you Mintie?—with you. We will enjoy having the boys to ourselves for a while, but be back by six o'clock for the evening meal.'

Araminta, taken by surprise, looked at the doctor. He was smiling.

'Ah, yes, it slipped my memory. The boys and I decided that I should take you to Leeuwarden and give you a glimpse of it...'

When she opened her mouth to argue, he said, 'No, don't say you don't want to come; the boys will be disappointed. It was their idea that you should have a treat on your free day.'

The boys chorused agreement. 'We knew you'd like to

go with Uncle Marcus. He'll show you the weigh house and the town hall, and there's a little café by the park where you could have tea.'

In the face of their eager pleasure there was nothing she could say.

'It sounds marvellous,' she told them. 'And what dears you are to have thought of giving me a treat.'

In the car presently, driving along the narrow fields towards Leeuwarden, she said stiffly, 'This is kind of you, but it's disrupting your day. You must wish to spend time with your aunt and uncle.'

He glanced at her rather cross face. 'No, no, Miss Pomfrey, I shall enjoy showing you round. Besides, I can come here as often as I wish, but you are not likely to come to Friesland—Holland—again, are you? What free time you get from hospital you will want to spend at your own home.'

She agreed, at the same time surprised to discover that the prospect of hospital was no longer filling her with happy anticipation. She should never have taken this job, she reflected. It had unsettled her—a foreign country, living in comfort, having to see the doctor each day. She rethought that—he might unsettle her, but she had to admit that he had made life interesting…

She asked suddenly, and then could have bitten out her tongue, 'Do you mean to marry Mevrouw Lutyns?' Before he could reply she added, 'I'm sorry, I can't think why I asked that. It was just—just an idle thought.'

He appeared unsurprised. 'Do you think that I should?' He added pleasantly, 'Feel free to speak your mind, Miss Pomfrey. I value your opinion.'

This astonished her. 'Do you? Do you really? Is it because I'm a stranger—a kind of outside observer? Though I don't suppose you would take any notice of what I say.'

'Very likely not.'

'Well, since you ask… Mevrouw Lutyns is very beautiful, and she wears lovely clothes—you know, they don't look expensive but they are, and they fit. Clothes off the peg have to be taken up or let out or hitched up, and that isn't the same…'

They were on the outskirts of Leeuwarden, and she watched the prosperous houses on either side of the street. 'This looks a nice place.'

'It is. Answer my question, Miss Pomfrey.'

'Well…' Why must she always begin with 'well'? she wondered. Her mother would say it was because she was a poor conversationalist. 'I think that perhaps you wouldn't be happy together. I imagine that she has lots of friends and likes going out and dancing and meeting people, and you always have your nose in a book or are going off to some hospital or other.' She added suddenly, 'I'm sure I don't know why you asked me this; it's none of my business.' She thought for a moment. 'You would make a handsome pair.'

The doctor turned a laugh into a cough. 'I must say that your opinion is refreshing.'

'Yes, but it isn't going to make any difference.'

He didn't answer but drove on into the inner city and parked the car by the weigh house. 'I should have liked to take you to the Friesian Museum, but if I do there will be no time to see anything of the city. We will go to the Grote Kerk first, and then the Oldehove Tower, and then walk around so that you may see some of the townhouses. They are rather fine…'

He took her from here to there, stopping to point out

an interesting house, the canals and bridges, interesting gables, and the town hall. Araminta gazed around, trying to see everything at once, determined to remember it all.

'Now we will do as the boys suggested and have tea— there is the café. They remember it because it has such a variety of cakes. We had better sample some or they will be disappointed.'

It was a charming place, surrounded by a small lawn and flowerbeds which even in autumn were full of co- lour. The tea was delicious, pale and weak, with no milk, but she was thirsty and the dish of cakes put before them were rich with cream and chocolate and crystallised fruit. Araminta ate one with a simple pleasure and, pressed to do so, ate another.

The doctor, watching her enjoyment, thought briefly of Christina, who would have refused for fear of add- ing a few ounces to her slimness. Araminta appeared to have no such fear. She was, he conceded silently, a very nice shape.

'That was a lovely tea,' said Araminta, walking back to the car. 'I've had a marvellous afternoon. Thank you very much. And your aunt and uncle have been very kind.'

He made a vague, casual answer, opened the car door for her and got in beside her. When she made some re- mark about the street they were driving along, he gave a non-commital reply so that she concluded that he didn't want to talk. Perhaps he felt that he had done his duty and could now revert to his usual manner. So she sat silently until they had reached the house, and then there was no need to be silent, for the boys wanted to know if she had enjoyed herself, what she had thought of Leeuwarden and, above all, what kind of cakes she had had for tea.

She was glad of their chatter, for it filled the hour or so before they sat down to their meal. They had had a wonderful afternoon, she was told. They had fished in the lake with their great-uncle, and gone with their great-aunt to see the kitchen cat with her kittens—and did she know that there were swans on the lake and that they had seen a heron?

She made suitable replies to all this and then sat with Mevrouw Nos-Wieringa and listened to that lady's gentle flow of talk. There was no need to say anything to the doctor, and really there was no need even to think of that, for he went away with his uncle for a time to look at something in the study, and when they came back they were bidden to the table.

As a concession to the boys, the meal was very similar to an English high tea, and the food had been chosen to please them, finishing with a plate of *poffertjes*—small balls of choux pastry smothered in fine sugar. Araminta enjoyed them as much as the boys.

They left soon afterwards. The boys eager to come again with their mother and father, the doctor saying that he would spend a weekend with his aunt and uncle when next he came to Holland. Araminta, saying all the right things, wished very much that she would be coming again, too.

The boys were tired by now, and after a few minutes of rather peevish wrangling they dozed off, leaning against Humphrey's bulk. The doctor drove in silence, this time travelling back via Meppel and Zwolle, Hardewijk and Hilversum, so that Araminta might see as much of Holland as possible.

He told her this in a disinterested manner, so that she felt she shouldn't bother him with questions. She sat quietly, watching his large capable hands on the wheel, vaguely aware that she was unhappy.

It was dark by the time they reached Utrecht, and she urged the sleepy boys straight up to bed with the promise of hot milk and a biscuit once they were there. They were still peevish, and it took time and patience to settle them. She was offering the milk when the doctor came to say goodnight, and when he added a goodnight to her, she realised that he didn't expect her to go downstairs again.

She thanked him for her pleasant day in a dampened down voice, since he was obviously impatient to be gone, and when he had, she tucked up the boys and went to her room.

It wasn't late, and she would have liked a cup of tea or a drink of some sort. There was no reason why she shouldn't go down to the kitchen and ask for it, but the thought of encountering him while doing so prevented her. She undressed slowly, had a leisurely bath and got into bed. It had been a lovely day—at least, it would have been lovely if the doctor had been friendly.

She fell asleep presently, still feeling unhappy.

The boys woke early in splendid spirits so that breakfast was a lively meal. The doctor joined in their chatter, but beyond an austere good morning he had nothing to say to Araminta.

It's just as though I'm not here, she reflected, listening to plans being made by the boys to go shopping for presents to take back with them.

'You must buy presents, too,' they told Araminta. 'To take home, you know. We always do. Uncle comes with us so's he can pay when we've chosen.'

'I expect Miss Pomfrey will prefer to do her shopping without us. Let me see, I believe I can spare an afternoon this week.'

'Mintie?' Paul looked anxious.

'Your uncle is quite right; I'd rather shop by myself. But I promise you I'll show you what I've bought and you can help me wrap everything up.'

Suddenly indignant, she suggested that the boys should go and fetch their schoolbooks, and when they had gone she turned her eyes, sparkling with ill temper, on the doctor.

'Presumably we are to return to England shortly?' she enquired in a voice to pulverise a stone. 'It would be convenient for me if you were to be civil enough to tell me when.'

The doctor put down the letter he was reading. 'My dear Miss Pomfrey, you must know by now that I'm often uncivil. If I have ruffled your feelings, I am sorry.' He didn't look in the least sorry, though, merely amused.

'We shall return in five days' time. I have various appointments which I must fulfil but the boys will remain with me until their parents return within the next week or so. I hope that you are agreeable to remain with them until they do? You will, of course, be free to go as soon as their parents are back.'

'You said that you would arrange for me to start my training…'

'Indeed I did, and I will do so. You are prepared to start immediately? Frequently a student nurse drops out within a very short time. If that were the case, you would be able to take her place. I will do what I can for you. You are still determined to take up nursing?'

'Yes. Why do you ask?'

'I'm not sure if the life will suit you.'

'I'm used to hard work,' she told him. 'This kind of life—' she waved a hand around her '—is something I've never experienced before.'

'You don't care for it?'

She gave him an astonished look. 'Of course I like it. I had better go and see if the boys are ready for school.'

That morning she went shopping, buying a scarf for her mother, a book on the history of the Netherlands for her father and a pretty blouse for her cousin, who would probably never wear it. She bought cigars for Bas, too, and another scarf for Jet, and a box of sweets for Nel and the elderly woman who came each day to polish and clean. Mindful of her promise to the boys, she found pretty paper and ribbons. Wrapping everything up would keep them occupied for half an hour at least, after their tea, while they were waiting impatiently for their uncle to come home.

They were still engrossed in this, sitting on the floor in the nursery with Araminta, when the door opened and the doctor and Mevrouw Lutyns came in.

The boys ran to him at once and Araminta got to her feet, feeling at a disadvantage. Mevrouw Lutyns was, as always, beautifully dressed, her face and hair utter perfection. Araminta remembered only too clearly the conversation she had had with the doctor in Leeuwarden and felt the colour creep into her cheeks. How he must have laughed at her. Probably he had shared the joke with the woman.

Mevrouw Lutyns ignored her, greeted the boys in a perfunctory manner and spoke sharply to the doctor. He had hunkered down to tie a particularly awkward piece of ribbon and answered her in a casual way, which Araminta saw annoyed her. He spoke in English, too, which,

for the moment at any rate, made her rather like him. A
tiresome man, she had to admit, but his manners were
beautiful. Unlike Mevrouw Lutyns'.

He glanced at Araminta and said smoothly, 'Mevrouw
Lutyns is thinking of coming to England for a visit.'

'I expect you know England well?' said Araminta politely.

'London, of course. I don't care for the country. Besides, I must remain in London. I need to shop.' Her lip
curled. 'I don't expect you need to bother with clothes.'

Araminta thought of several answers, all of them rude,
so she held her tongue.

The doctor got to his feet. 'Come downstairs to the
drawing room, Christina, and have a drink.' And to the
boys he added, 'I'll be back again presently—we'll have
a card game before bed.'

They went away and Peter whispered, 'We don't like
her; she never talks to us. Why does Uncle like her,
Mintie?'

'Well, she's very pretty, you know, and I expect she's
amusing and makes him laugh, and she wears pretty
dresses.'

Paul flung an arm round her. 'We think you're pretty,
Mintie, and you make us laugh and wear pretty clothes.'

She gave him a hug. 'Do I really? How nice of you to
say so. Ladies like compliments, you know.'

She found a pack of cards. 'How about a game of
Happy Families before your uncle comes?'

They were in the middle of a noisy game when he returned. When she would have stopped playing he squat-
ted down beside her.

'One of my favourite games,' he declared, 'and much
more fun with four.'

'Has Mevrouw Lutyns gone home?' asked Paul.

'Yes, to dress up for the evening. We are going out to dinner.'

He looked at Araminta as he spoke, but she was shuffling her cards and didn't look up.

Two days later the boys went with their uncle to do their shopping, leaving Araminta to start packing. She had been happy in Holland and she would miss the pleasant life, but now she must concentrate on her future. Her mother, in one of her rare letters, had supposed that she would go straight to the hospital when she left the doctor's house. Certainly she wasn't expected to stay home for any length of time. All the same, she would have to go home for a day or so to repack her things.

'We may be away,' her mother had written. 'There is an important lecture tour in Wales. Your cousin will be here, of course.' She had added, as though she had remembered that Araminta was her daughter, whom she loved, 'I am glad you have enjoyed your stay in Holland.'

Neither her mother or her father would be interested in her life there, nor would her cousin, and there would scarcely be time for her to look up her friends. There would be no one to whom she could describe the days she had spent in the doctor's house. Just for a moment she gave way to self-pity, and then reminded herself that she had a worthwhile future before her despite the doctor's doubts.

For the last few days before they left she saw almost nothing of the doctor. The boys, excited at the prospect of going back to England, kept her busy, and they spent the last one or two afternoons walking the, by now, well known streets, pausing at the bridges to stare down into the canals, admiring the boatloads of flowers and, as a treat, eating mountainous ices in one of the cafés.

They were to leave early in the morning, and amidst the bustle of departure Araminta had little time to feel sad at leaving. She bade Jet and Bas goodbye, shook hands with Nel and the daily cleaner, bent to hug Humphrey, saw the boys settled on the back seat and got in beside the doctor.

It was only as he drove away that she allowed herself to remember that she wouldn't be coming again. In just a few weeks she had come to love the doctor's house, and Utrecht, its pleasant streets and small hidden corners where time since the Middle Ages had stood still. I shall miss it, she thought and then, I shall miss the doctor, too. Once she had left his house she wasn't likely to see him again. There was no chance of their lives converging; he would become part of this whole interlude. An important part.

I do wonder, thought Araminta, how one can fall in love with someone who doesn't care a row of pins for one, for that's what I have done. And what a good thing that I shall be leaving soon and never have to see him again.

The thought brought tears to her eyes and the doctor, glancing sideways at her downcast profile, said kindly, 'You are sorry to be leaving Holland, Miss Pomfrey? Fortunately it is not far from England and you will be able to pay it another visit at some time.'

Oh, no, I won't, thought Araminta, but murmured in agreement.

Their journey was uneventful. They arrived back at his London home to be welcomed by Briskett, with tea waiting. It was as though they had never been away.

Chapter 7

Briskett handed the doctor his post, informed him that there were a number of phone calls which needed to be dealt with at once, took the boys' jackets and invited Araminta to go with him so that he might show her to her room.

'The boys are in their usual room. They'd better come with you, miss; the doctor won't want to be bothered for a bit. Had a good time, have you? Hope the boss took time off to show you round a bit.'

'Well, yes, we went to Friesland.'

He turned to smile at her, his cheerful rat face split in a wide smile. 'Nice to have him back again, miss. Here's your room. Make yourself at home.'

It would be difficult not to feel at home in such a delightful room, thought Araminta, with its satinwood bed, tall chest and dressing table. The curtains and bedspread were white and pale yellow chintz, and someone had put a vase of freesias by the bed. The window overlooked the long narrow garden, with a high brick wall and trees screening it from its neighbours.

She would have liked to linger there, but the boys would need to be seen to. They had been good on the journey, but now they were tired and excited. Tea and an early bedtime were indicated, unless the doctor had other plans. She went to their room, tidied them up and took them downstairs.

The study, where she had first been interviewed by the doctor, had its door open. The doctor was at his desk, sitting back in his chair, on the phone, and speaking in Dutch. Araminta's sharp ears heard that. He looked up as they went past.

'Go into the sitting room. Briskett will have tea waiting. I'll join you presently.'

So the boys led her across the hall into quite a small room, very cosy, where Briskett was putting the finishing touches to the tea table.

'I've laid a table,' he told her. 'I don't hold with little nippers balancing plates on their knees. Just you sit down, miss, and I'll give the boss a call.'

The doctor joined them presently, ate a splendid tea and then excused himself with the plea of work. 'I have to go out,' he told the boys, 'and I don't think I'll be back before you go to bed, but I'm not doing anything tomorrow morning; we will go to the park and feed the ducks.' He glanced at Araminta. 'I'm sure Miss Pomfrey will be glad of an hour or two to get your clothes unpacked.' He added casually, 'I expect you would like to let your parents know you are back in England; do ring them if you wish.'

She thanked him. 'And, if you don't mind, I'll go and unpack the boys' night things. I thought an early bedtime...'

'Very wise. I'm sure Briskett will have something extra special for their supper.'

'Perhaps I could have my supper at the same time with them?'

'You would prefer that? Then by all means do so. I'll

let Briskett know. You'll bathe them and have them ready for bed first? Shall I tell him seven o'clock?'

'That would do very well, thank you.' She hesitated. 'Are you going out immediately? If you are, then I'll wait and unpack later.'

He glanced at his watch. 'Half an hour or so, but I need to change first.'

'If I can have ten minutes?'

'Of course.'

She unpacked the overnight bag, put everything ready in the boys' bathroom and whisked herself back downstairs with a minute to spare. The doctor bade the boys goodnight, nodded to her and went away. She was in the boys' room, which overlooked the street, when she heard him in the hall and went to look out of the window. He was getting into his car, wearing black tie, looking remarkably handsome.

'I wonder when he gets any work done,' reflected Araminta. 'Talk about a social whirl.' She knew that wasn't fair, he worked long hours and he was good at it, but it relieved her feelings. She hoped lovingly that he wouldn't stay out too late; he needed his sleep like anyone else...

She sighed; she had managed all day not to think too much about him and it had been made easier by his distant manner towards her, but loving him was something she couldn't alter, even though it was hopeless. No one died of a broken heart; they went on living like everyone else and made a success of their lives. Something which she was going to do. But first she must learn to forget him, once she had left his house. Until then, surely it wouldn't do any harm if she thought about him occasionally?

The boys came tumbling in then, and she allowed stern common sense to take over.

Life in London would be very different from that of Utrecht. For one thing there would be no school in the mornings.

Their parents would be returning in a few days now, and the boys were excited and full of high spirits; she filled the mornings with simple lessons and the afternoons with brisk walks, returning in time for tea and games before bedtime. The doctor was seldom at home; as Briskett put it, 'Up early and home late. No time for anything but his work. Good thing he's got a bit of social life of an evening. You know what they say, miss, "All work and no play"…'

But the doctor still found time to spend an hour with the boys each evening, although it was very evident that he had no time for Araminta. His brief good mornings and good evenings were the extent of his conversations with her. And what else did she expect? she asked herself.

They had been back in England for three days before he told her that the boys' parents would be arriving in two days' time.

'Perhaps you would be good enough to remain for a day or so after their return; my sister is bound to wish to talk to you, and their clothes and so on will need to be packed up. She will be glad of your help.'

Three days, thought Araminta, four at the outside, and after that I shan't see him again. 'Of course I'll stay on, if Mrs Ingram wishes me to,' she told him.

She was surprised when he asked, 'You will go home? Your people expect you?'

'Yes.' She didn't add that they would probably still be

away. Her cousin would be there, of course, and she supposed she would stay there until she heard from the hospital. Which reminded her to add, 'You told me that there was a chance that I might be accepted at the hospital...'

'Ah, yes. It slipped my memory. There is indeed a vacancy; one of the students has left owing to illness. If you can start within a few days and are prepared to work hard in order to catch up with the other students you will be accepted.'

She should have been elated. He had made everything easy for her; she could embark on her plans for a nursing career. And it had been so unimportant to him that he had forgotten to tell her.

'That is what you wanted?' He had spoken so sharply that she hurried to say that, yes, there was nothing she wished for more.

'I'm very grateful,' she added. 'Is there anything that I should do about it?'

'No, no. You will receive a letter within the next day or two. And you have no need to be grateful. You have been of great help while the boys have been with me. They will miss you.'

The doctor spoke with an austere civility which chilled her, but he was aware as he said it that *he* would miss her too: her small cheerful person around the house, her quiet voice which could on occasion become quite sharp with annoyance. He had a sudden memory of her weeping into his shoulder and found himself thinking of it with tenderness...

He chided himself silently for being a sentimental fool. Miss Pomfrey had fulfilled a much needed want for a few weeks, and he was grateful for that, but once she had gone he would forget her.

* * *

Mr and Mrs Ingram duly arrived, late in the afternoon. It was a chilly October day, with a drizzling rain, and Araminta had been hard pushed to keep the boys happy indoors. But at last they shouted to Araminta from their perch by the front windows that their uncle's car had just arrived with their mother and father.

'Then off you go downstairs, my dears. Go carefully.'

She went to the window when they had gone, in time to see Mr and Mrs Ingram enter the house, followed at a more leisurely pace by the doctor. They would all have tea, she supposed, and sat down quietly to wait until Briskett brought her own tea tray. She had sought him out that morning and he had agreed with her that it might be a good idea if she were to have her tea in her room.

'The boys will be so excited, and they will all have so much to talk about that I won't be needed,' she had pointed out.

He came presently with the news that there was a fine lot of talk going on downstairs and she hadn't been missed.

'They'll send for you presently, miss, when they're over the first excitement,' he assured her. 'The boss'll want you there to give a report, as it were.' He gave her a friendly nod. 'Sets great store on you, he does.'

She drank her tea and nibbled at a cake, her usually splendid appetite quite gone. She would start packing this evening, once the boys were in bed, so that when she had done all she could do to help Mrs Ingram, she would be able to leave at once.

She was pouring another cup of tea when the door opened and the doctor came in.

'I didn't hear you knock,' said Araminta in her best Miss Pomfrey voice.

'My apologies. Why did you not come downstairs to tea?'

'It's a family occasion.'

He leaned forward and took a cake and ate it—one of Briskett's light-as-air fairy cakes—and the simple act turned him from a large, self-assured man into a small boy.

Araminta swallowed the surge of love which engulfed her. However would she be able to live without him?

The doctor finished his cake without haste. 'You have finished your tea? Then shall we go downstairs?'

She shot him a look and encountered a bland stare. There was nothing for it but to do as he asked. How is it possible, she thought, to love someone who is so bent on having his own way? She accompanied him downstairs to the drawing room, to be warmly greeted by the boys' parents. Presently Mrs Ingram drew her on one side.

'They were good?' she wanted to know anxiously. 'Peter and Paul can be perfect little horrors…' She said it with love.

'Well, they weren't; they have been really splendid—very obedient and helpful and never bored.'

'Oh, good. I expect you're longing to go home. Could you stay over tomorrow and help me pack their things?'

'Yes, of course. You must be glad to be going home again. I know the boys will be, although they enjoyed living in Utrecht. It seemed like a second home to them.'

'Well, they love Marcus, of course, and since they've both spoken Dutch and English ever since they could utter words they don't feel strange. I'm sure they will have a lot to tell us. You were happy in Holland?'

'Oh, yes. I enjoyed it very much…'

'Marcus tells me that you're to start nursing training very shortly. That's something you want to do?' Mrs Ingram smiled. 'No boyfriend?'

'No, I expect I'm meant to be a career girl!'

If Mrs Ingram had any opinion about that she remained silent, and presently Araminta took the boys off to bed and supper, before slipping away to her room while their parents came to say goodnight. This was a lengthy business, with a great deal of giggling and talk until they consented to lie down and go to sleep. Excitement had tired them out; they slept in the instant manner of children and she was free to go to her room and change her dress.

She excused herself as soon as she decently could after dinner; it had been a pleasant meal, and she had borne her part in the conversation when called upon to do so, but although the talk had been general, she had no doubt that her company hindered the other three from any intimate talk.

She was bidden a friendly goodnight and the doctor got up to open the door for her. She went past him without a look and went off to her room and started to pack her things. Tomorrow she knew that she would be kept busy getting the boys' clothes packed. She felt lonely; Humphrey's company would have been welcome, but of course he was miles away in Utrecht. So she was forced to talk to herself.

'I'm perfectly happy,' she assured herself. 'My future is settled, I have money, I shall make friends with the other nurses, and in a year or two I shall be able to pick and choose where I mean to work.' Not London. The chance of meeting the doctor was remote but, all the same, not to be risked.

There was no one at breakfast when she went down with the boys: the doctor had already left and Mr and Mrs Ingram weren't yet down. They had almost finished when they joined them. Araminta left the boys with them and at Mrs Ingram's suggestion began the task of packing up for the boys. They were to leave that evening but first they were to go shopping with their father and mother. So Araminta had a solitary lunch and spent the afternoon collecting up the boys' toys and tidying them away into various boxes. They were to be driven home by the doctor directly after tea, and she had been asked to have everything ready by then.

Briskett, going round the house retrieving odds and ends for her to pack, was of the opinion that the house would be very dull once they had gone. 'And you'll be leaving, miss—we shall miss you, too. Very quiet, it'll be.'

'I expect the doctor will be quite glad to have the house to himself,' said Araminta.

'Well, now, as to that, I'd venture to disagree, miss. The boss is fond of children and you've fitted in like a glove on a hand.'

She thanked him gravely. He was a kind little man, despite his ratty looks, and he was devoted to the doctor. 'Maybe you'll be back, miss,' said Briskett, to her surprise.

'Me? Oh, I don't think so, Briskett. You mean as a governess when the doctor marries and has children? By then I'll be a trained nurse and probably miles away.'

It took some time for the doctor to get his party settled with their possessions in the car and still longer for them to make their goodbyes. The boys hugged and kissed Araminta and rather silently handed her a parcel, painstakingly wrapped in fancy paper. Seeing the look on their small faces, she begged to be allowed to open it there and then.

'They chose it themselves,' said their mother rather apologetically.

It was a coffret of face cream, powder and lipstick, and a little bottle of scent. When Araminta exclaimed over it, Peter said, 'We know you're not pretty, but these things will make you beautiful. The lady behind the counter said so.'

'It's just exactly what I've always wanted,' declared Araminta, 'and thank you both very much for thinking of such a lovely present. I'll use it every day and I'm sure I'll be beautiful in no time at all.'

She hugged them both, told them to be good boys and then watched with Briskett as they all got into the car, parcels and packages squashed into the back seat with the boys and their mother. They all waved and smiled, but not the doctor, of course; he raised a casual hand as he drove away but he didn't turn his head.

Araminta finished her packing, ate a solitary dinner and decided to go to bed. There was no sign of the doctor; probably he would stay the night at his sister's house. She was halfway up the stairs when he came in and Briskett appeared in the hall to offer supper.

'No, no, I've had a meal, thanks, Briskett, but will you see to the car? I'll be in my study.'

He glanced at Araminta, poised on the stairs. 'Miss Pomfrey, if you would spare me a few minutes…?'

She went with him to his study and sat down in the chair he offered her.

'You've had the letter from the hospital?' And when she said yes, he went on, 'Briskett will drive you to your home in the morning. I expect you are anxious to get back. Is there anything you want to know about your appointment as a student nurse? I presume you have been given instructions?'

'Yes, thank you. There is no need for Briskett to drive me...'

He said in a level voice, 'If you will just tell him when you are ready to leave, Miss Pomfrey. I shall see you in the morning before you go. I won't keep you now; you must be tired.'

She got up quickly. 'Yes, yes, I am. Goodnight, Doctor.'

His goodnight was very quiet.

She went down to breakfast after a wakeful night to find that the doctor had been called away very early in the morning. 'Not knowing when he'll be back, he said not to wait for him, miss. I'll have the car round as soon as you've had breakfast.'

Araminta crumbled toast onto her plate and drank several cups of coffee. Now she would never say goodbye to the doctor. Possibly he had left the house early, so that he might avoid a last meeting. She had no idea what she had expected from it, but at least she had hoped that they would part in a friendly fashion. She went suddenly hot and cold at the idea that he might have guessed that she had fallen in love with him. Now her one thought was to leave his house as quickly as possible...her one regret that Hambledon wasn't thousands of miles away.

It was almost noon when Briskett drew up before her home, took her case from the boot and followed her up the path to the front door.

'Looks empty,' he observed. 'Expecting you, are they?'

'My mother and father are in Wales on a lecture tour. A cousin is staying here, though—housekeeping now that I'm not at home.'

Briskett took the key from her and opened the door. There were letters on the doormat and an open note on the hall table. His sharp eyes had read it before Araminta had seen it. 'Gone with Maud—' Maud was a friend of Millicent, the cousin '—for a couple of days. Good luck with your new job.'

He was bending over her case as she saw it and read it.

'Where will I put this, miss? I'll take it upstairs for you.'

'Thank you, Briskett. It's the room on the left on the landing. Will you stay while I make a cup of tea? I'd offer you lunch, but I'm not quite sure...'

'A cuppa would be fine, miss.'

Briskett hefted the case and went upstairs. Nice little house, he decided, and some nice furniture—good old-fashioned stuff, no modern rubbish. But the whole place looked unlived-in, as though no one much bothered about it. He didn't like leaving Miss Pomfrey alone, but she hadn't said anything about the note so he couldn't do much about that.

He went down to the kitchen, again old-fashioned but well equipped, and found her making the tea.

'I've found some biscuits,' she told him cheerfully. 'Will you get back in time to make lunch for yourself?'

'Easy, miss, there won't be all that much traffic.' He eyed Cherub, who had come in though the kitchen window she had opened and was making much of Araminta.

'Nice cat. Yours, is he?'

'Yes, I found him. Have another biscuit. I shall miss Humphrey in Utrecht...'

Briskett's long thin nose quivered. 'I'm sure he'll miss you. Pity the boss wasn't home. Beats me, it does, him at the top of the tree, so to speak, and still working all the hours God made.'

When he had gone Araminta unpacked. Presently she would sort out her clothes and repack, ready to leave the next day, but for now she went to inspect the fridge. Even those with broken hearts needed to be fed.

As the doctor let himself into his house that evening Briskett came into the hall.

'A bit on the late side, aren't you?' he observed. 'Had a busy day, I'll be bound. I've a nice little dinner ready for you.'

'Thanks, Briskett. You took Miss Pomfrey back to her home?'

Briskett nodded. 'There's a nice young lady for you. I didn't fancy leaving her in that empty house.' He met the doctor's sudden blue stare and went on, 'Her ma and pa are in Wales. There's a cousin or some such looking after the house, but she'd gone off for a few days. Only living thing to greet us was a tatty old cat.'

He watched the doctor's face; he really looked quite ferocious but he didn't speak. Briskett reckoned he was pretty angry...

'Nice house,' he went on. 'Small, some nice stuff though, good and solid, a bit old-fashioned. Nice bits of silver and china too.' He paused to think. 'But it weren't a home.'

And, when the doctor still remained silent, 'We had a

cuppa together—very concerned, she was, about me not having my dinner.'

'Did Miss Pomfrey tell you that this cousin was away?'

'Not a word. I happened to see the note on the table.'

'She seemed quite happy?'

'Now, as to that, Boss, I wouldn't like to venture an opinion.'

He hesitated, cautious of the doctor's set face. 'I'd have brought her back, but that wouldn't have done, would it?'

'No, Briskett, it wouldn't have done at all. You did right. Miss Pomfrey will be going to St Jules' tomorrow, and I dare say this cousin will have returned by then.'

The doctor went into his study and sat down at his desk, staring at the papers on it, not seeing them. I miss her, he thought. I can't think why. She has no looks, she wears drab clothes, she has at times a sharp tongue and yet her voice is delightful and she is kind and patient and sensible. And she has beautiful eyes.

He drew the papers towards him and picked up his pen. This feeling of loss is only temporary, he mused. She has been a member of the household for some weeks; one gets used to a person. I shall forget her completely in a few weeks.

He went to his solitary dinner then, agreeing with Briskett that it was pleasant to have a quiet house once more. Now he would be able to prepare the notes on the learned treatise he was writing without the constant interference of small boys' voices—and Mintie's voice telling them to hush.

He went to his desk after dinner but he didn't write a word, his mind occupied with thoughts of Araminta, alone at her home with only a cat for company. There was no use trying to work, so he took himself for a brisk walk and went to bed—but he didn't sleep.

Araminta had had a boiled egg and some rather stale bread for a late lunch, fed Cherub, put on the washing machine and started packing again. She was to report to the hospital at two o'clock the next day and, since there was no indication as to when her cousin would return, she went down the lane to Mrs Thomas's little cottage and asked her to feed Cherub.

'I'll leave the food out for you in the shed. If you wouldn't mind feeding him twice a day? I've no idea when my cousin will be back...'

Mrs Thomas listened sympathetically. 'Don't you worry, dear, I'll look after him. He's got the cat flap so's he can get into the house, hasn't he?'

'Yes. I hate leaving him, but there's nothing I can do about it.'

'Well, she only went yesterday morning, I saw the car...and your mother and father will be back soon, I dare say?'

'I'm not sure when.'

It wasn't very satisfactory, as she explained to Cherub later, but surely someone would come home soon. Besides, she would have days off. She cheered up at the thought.

Her mother phoned in the evening. 'I thought you might be home,' she said vaguely. 'I expect you're happy to be starting at St Jules'. You see that we were right, my dear. This little job you have had hasn't made any difference at all, just a few weeks' delay. I'm sure you'll have no difficulty in catching up with the other students. Your father and I will be coming home very shortly. I can't say exactly when. The tour is such a success we may extend it. Is your cousin there?'

Araminta started to say that she wasn't, but her mother had already begun to tell her about some remarkable Celtic documents they had been examining. It took a long time to explain them and when she had finished Mrs Pomfrey said a hurried goodbye. 'I have so much to think of,' she explained. 'I'll send a card when we are coming home.'

St Jules' Hospital was old, although it had been added to, patched up and refurbished from time to time. It was a gloomy place, looming over the narrow streets surrounding it, but the entrance hall was handsome enough, with portraits of dead and gone medical men on its panelled walls and the handsome staircase sweeping up one side of it. A staircase which no one except the most senior staff were allowed to tread.

Araminta was bidden to take herself and her case to the nurses' home, reached by a rather dark tunnel at the back of the hall. There was a door at the other end and when she opened it cautiously she found herself in a small hallway with stairs ahead of her and a door marked 'Office' at one side.

It seemed sense to knock, and, bidden to go in, she opened the door.

The woman behind the small desk was middle-aged with a pale face and colourless hair, wearing a dark maroon uniform.

'Araminta Pomfrey? Come in and shut the door. I'll take you to your room presently. You can leave your outdoor things there before you go to see the Principal Nursing Officer.' She shuffled through a pile of papers.

'Here is a list of rules. You are expected to keep them while you live here. When you have completed your first year you will be allowed to live out if you wish. No smoking or drinking, no men visitors unless they visit for some good reason.'

She drew a form from a pile on the desk. 'I'll check your particulars. You are twenty-three? A good deal older than the other students. Unmarried? Parents living? British by birth?' She was ticking off the items as she read them. 'Is that your case? We will go to your room.'

They climbed the stairs, and then another flight to the floor above, and the woman opened a door halfway down a long corridor. 'You'll have your own key, of course. You will make your bed and keep your room tidy.'

The room was small and rather dark, since its window overlooked a wing of the hospital, but it was furnished nicely and the curtains and bedcover were pretty. There was a washbasin in one corner and a built-in wardrobe.

Araminta was handed a key. She asked, 'What should I call you? You are a sister?'

'I am the warden—Miss Jeff.' She looked at her watch. 'Come back to my office in ten minutes and I'll take you for your interview.'

Left alone, Araminta turned her back on the view from the window, took off her jacket and tidied her hair. She hoped she looked suitably dressed; her skirt was too long for fashion, but her blouse was crisply ironed and her shoes were well polished. She went out of the room, locked the door, put the key in her shoulder bag and found her way to Miss Jeff.

The Principal Nursing Officer's office was large, with big windows draped with velvet curtains, a carpet underfoot and a rather splendid desk. She herself was just as elegant. She was a tall woman, still good-looking, dressed in a beautifully tailored suit. She shook Araminta's hand, and told her crisply that she was fortunate that there had been an unexpected vacancy.

'Which I could have filled a dozen times, but Dr van der Breugh is an old friend and very highly thought of here in the hospital. He assured me that you had given up your place in order to cope with an emergency in his family.' She smiled. 'You are a lucky young woman to have such an important sponsor.' She studied Araminta's face. 'I hope that you will be happy here. I see no reason why you shouldn't be. You will work hard, of course, but you will make friends. You are older than the other student nurses, but I don't suppose that will make any difference.'

She nodded a friendly dismissal and Araminta went back to her room, where she unpacked and took a look at the uniform laid out on the bed. It was cotton, in blue and white stripes with a stiff belt, and there was a little badge she was to wear pinned on her chest with her name on it.

The warden had told her to go down to the canteen for her tea at four o'clock. She made her way back down the stairs and into the hospital, down more stairs into the basement. The canteen was large, with a long counter and a great many tables—most of them occupied. Araminta went to the counter, took a tray, loaded it with a plate of bread and butter and a little pot of jam, collected her tea and then stood uncertainly for a moment, not sure where she should sit. There was a variety of uniforms, so she looked for someone wearing blue and white stripes.

Someone gave her a little shove from behind. 'New, are you?'

The speaker was a big girl, wearing, to Araminta's relief, blue and white stripes, and when she nodded, she

said, 'Come with me, we have to sit with our own set—
the dark blue are sisters, the light blue are staff nurses.
Don't go sitting with them.'

She led the way to the far end of the room to where
several girls were sitting round a table. 'Here's our new
girl,' she told them. 'What's your name?'

'Araminta Pomfrey.'

Several of the girls smiled, and one of them said,
'What a mouthful. Sister Tutor isn't going to like that.'

'Everyone calls me Mintie.'

'That's more like it. Sit down and have your tea. Any
idea which ward you are to go to in the morning?'

'No. Whom do I ask?'

'No one. It'll be on the board outside this place; you
can look presently. Have you unpacked? Supper's at eight
o'clock if you're off duty. What room number are you?
I'll fetch you.'

'Thank you.'

The big girl grinned. 'My name's Molly Beckett.' She
waved a hand. 'And this is Jean, and that's Sue in the
corner...' She named the girls one by one.

'We're all on different wards, but not all day, we have
lectures and demonstrations. You'll be run off your feet
on the ward, and heaven help you if Sister doesn't like
you.' She got up. 'We're all on duty now, but I'm off at
six o'clock; I'll see you then. Come with us and we'll
look at the board.'

There was a dismayed murmur as they crowded round
to look for Araminta's name.

'Baxter's,' said Molly. 'That's Sister Spicer. I don't
want to frighten you, but look out for her, Mintie. She's
got a tongue like a razor and if she takes a dislike to you
you might as well leave.'

Araminta went back to her room, put her family photos on the dressing table, arranged her few books on the
little shelf by the bed and sat down to think. She had very
little idea of what hospital life would be like and she had
to admit that Sister Spicer didn't sound very promising.
But she was a sensible girl and it was no use thinking
about it too much until she had found her feet.

The other girls seemed very friendly, and she would
be free for a few hours each day, and she could go home
each week. She allowed her thoughts to wander. What
was the doctor doing? she wondered. Had he missed her
at all? She thought it unlikely. I must forget him, she told
herself firmly. Something which should be easy, for she
would have more than enough to think about.

Molly came presently and, since it wasn't time for supper, took her on a tour of the home, explaining where the
different wards were and explaining the off duty. 'You'll
get a couple of evenings off each week. Trouble is, you're
too tired to do much. Otherwise it's a couple of hours in
the morning or in the afternoon. Days off are a question
of luck. We come bottom of the list, though if you've
got a decent sister she'll listen if you want special days.'

The canteen was full and very noisy at suppertime.
Araminta ate her corned beef and salad and the stewed
apple and custard which followed it, drank a cup of strong
tea and presently went to the sitting room for the more
junior nursing staff. Molly had gone out for the rest of
her free evening and she couldn't see any of the other
girls she had met at tea. She slipped away and went to
her room, had a bath and got into bed.

She told herself that it would be all right in the morning, that it was just the sudden drastic change in her

lifestyle which was making her feel unhappy. She lay thinking about the doctor, telling herself that once she started her training she wouldn't let herself think of him again.

Marcus van der Breugh, dining with friends, bent an apparently attentive ear to his dinner companion while he wondered what Mintie was doing. He had told her that he didn't think she would make a good nurse and he very much feared that he was right. Possibly it was this opinion which caused his thoughts to return to her far too frequently.

Chapter 8

Lying in bed at the end of her first day at St Jules', Araminta tried not to remember all the things which had gone wrong and reminded herself that this was the career she had wished for. Now that she had started upon it, nothing was going to deter her from completing it.

Of course, she had started off on the wrong foot. The hospital was large, and had been built in the days when long corridors and unexpected staircases were the norm. Presumably the nurses then had found nothing unusual in traipsing their length, but to Araminta, who had never encountered anything like them before, they'd spelt disaster. She had gone the wrong way, up the wrong staircase and presented herself at Sister's office only to be told that she had come to Stewart's ward; Baxter's was at the other end of the hospital and up another flight of stairs.

So she had arrived late, to encounter Sister Spicer's basilisk stare.

'You're late,' she was told. 'Why?'

'I got lost,' said Araminta.

'A ridiculous excuse. Punctuality is something I insist upon on my ward. Have you done any nursing before coming here?'

Araminta explained about the children's convalescent home, but decided against mentioning her work for the doctor.

Sister Spicer sighed. 'You will have to catch up with the other students as best you can. I suppose Sister Tutor will do what she can with you. I have no time to molly-coddle you, so you had better learn pretty fast.'

Araminta nodded her head.

'If you don't you might as well leave.'

Once upon a time Sister Spicer had probably been a nice person, reflected Araminta. Perhaps she had been crossed in love. Although she could see little to love in the cold handsome face. Poor soul, thought Araminta, and then jumped at Sister Spicer's voice. 'Well, go and find staff nurse.'

The ward was in the oldest part of the hospital, long, and lighted by a row of windows along one side, with the beds facing each other down its length occupied by women of all ages. There were two nurses making beds, who took no notice of her. At the far end Staff Nurse, identified by her light blue uniform, was bending over a trolley with another nurse beside her.

She was greeted briefly, told to go and make beds with the nurse, and thrown, as it were, to the lions.

Araminta didn't like remembering that rest of the morning. She had made beds, carried bedpans, handed round dinners and helped any number of patients in and out of bed, but never, it seemed, quite quickly enough.

'New, are yer, ducks?' one old lady had asked, with an alarming wheeze and a tendency to go purple in the face when she coughed. 'Don't you mind no one. Always in an 'urry and never no time ter tell yer anything.'

Her dinner hour had been a respite. She had sat at the table with Molly and the other students and they had been sympathetic.

'It's because you're new and no one has had the time

to tell you anything. You're off at six o'clock, aren't you? And you'll come to the lectures this afternoon. Two o'clock, mind. Even Sister Spicer can't stop you.'

She had enjoyed the lectures, although she'd discovered that there was a good deal of catching up to do.

'You must borrow one of the other students' books and copy out the lectures I've already given,' Sister Tutor had said. This was an exercise which would take up several days off duty.

'But it's what I wanted,' said Araminta to herself now.

She had to admit by the end of the week that things weren't quite as she had expected them to be. According to Sister Spicer, she was lazy, slow and wasted far too much time with the patients. There was plenty of work, she had been told, without stopping to find their curlers and carry magazines to and fro, fill water jugs and pause to admire the photos sent from home of children and grandchildren. It was all rather unsatisfactory, and it seemed that she would be on Baxter's ward for three months…

She longed for her days off, and when they came she was up early and out of the hospital, on her way home as quickly as she could manage. She scooted across the forecourt as fast as her legs could carry her, watched, if she had but known, by Dr van der Breugh, who had been called in early and was now enjoying a cup of coffee before he went back home.

The sight of her small scurrying figure sent the thought of her tumbling back into his head and he frowned. He had managed for almost a whole week to think of her only occasionally. Well, perhaps rather more than occasionally! She would be going home for her days off and he toyed with the idea of driving to Hambledon to find out if she had settled in. He squashed the idea and instead, when he encountered one of the medical consultants on his way out of the hospital, asked casually how the new student nurses were shaping.

'I borrowed one of them for a few weeks and she's been accepted late.'

'Oh, yes, I remember hearing about that. They're quite a good bunch, but of course she has to catch up. She's on Baxter's and Sister Spicer is a bit of a martinet. Don't see much of the nurses, though, do we? If I remember she was being told off for getting the wrong patient out of bed when I saw her, something like that. Rather quiet, I thought, but Sister Spicer can take the stuffing out of anyone. Terrifies me occasionally.'

They both laughed and went on their way.

Araminta, home by mid-morning, found her cousin and Cherub to welcome her. Over coffee she made light of her first week at St Jules'.

'Have you heard from your mother?' asked Millicent. 'She phoned, but they were still busy with some new Celtic finds. She said they might not be home yet...'

'They'll be back before Christmas, though?'

'Oh, I'm sure they will! It's still October. Will you get off for the holiday?'

Araminta shook her head. 'I don't think so, I'm very junior, but of course I'll get my days off as near to Christmas Day as possible.'

'You like it? You're happy?'

Araminta assured her that she was.

The two days were soon over, but they had given her a respite, and she went back on the ward determined to make the week a better one than her first had been. It was a pity that Sister Spicer was bent on making that as difficult as possible.

Molly had told her that Sister Spicer, if she took a dislike to anyone, would go to great lengths to make life as unpleasant as possible for her. Araminta hadn't quite believed that, but now she saw that it was true. Nothing she did was quite right; she was too slow, too clumsy, too careless. She tried not to let it worry her and took comfort from the patients, who liked her. Staff Nurse was kind, too, and the two senior student nurses, although the other student nurse who was in the same set as she now was, did nothing to make life easier for her.

Melanie was a small, pretty girl, always ready with the right answers during the lectures they both attended, and, since Sister Spicer liked her, the fact that she sometimes skimped her work and was careless of the patients' comfort, went unnoticed. She was young, barely nineteen, and made it obvious that Araminta need not expect either her friendship or her help on the ward.

When once she came upon Araminta speaking to one of the house doctors she said spitefully, 'Don't you know better than to talk to the housemen? Is that why you're here? To catch yourself a husband? Just you wait and see what happens to you if Sister Spicer catches you.'

Araminta looked at her in blank astonishment. 'He was asking me the way to Outpatients; he's new.'

Melanie giggled. 'That's as good an excuse as any, I suppose, but watch out.'

Thank heavens I've got days off tomorrow, Araminta thought. Since she was off duty at six o'clock that evening, she would be able to catch a train home. She hadn't told her cousin, but she would be home by nine o'clock at the latest...

The afternoon was endless, but she went about getting patients in and out of bed, helping them, getting teas, bedpans, filling water jugs, but it was six o'clock at last and she went to the office, thankful that she could at last ask to go off duty.

Sister Spicer barley glanced up from the report she was writing.

'Have you cleaned and made up the bed in the side ward? And the locker? It may be needed. You should have done it earlier. I told Nurse Jones to tell you. Well, it's your own fault for not listening, Nurse. Go and do it now and then you may go off duty.'

'I wasn't told to do it, Sister,' Araminta said politely, 'and I am off duty at six o'clock.'

Sister Spicer did look up then. 'You'll do as you are told, Nurse—and how dare you answer back in that fashion? I shall see the Principal Nursing Sister in the morning and I shall recommend that you are entirely unsuitable for training. If I can't train you, no one else could.'

She bent her head over her desk and Araminta went back into the ward where there was a third-year nurse and Melanie, who had taken such a dislike to her. Neither of them took any notice of her as she went to the side ward and started on the bed. She very much wanted to speak her mind, but that might upset the patients and, worse, she might burst into tears. She would have her days off and when she came back *she* would go and see the Principal Nursing Officer and ask to be moved to another ward. Unheard of, but worth a try!

It was almost seven o'clock by the time she had finished readying the room and making up the bed. She went down the ward, wishing the patients a cheerful goodnight as she went, ignoring the nurses and ignoring, too, Sister's office, walking past it, out of the ward and along the corridor, then going down the wide stone staircase to the floor below and then another staircase to the ground floor.

She was trying to make up her mind as to whether it was too late to go home, or should she wait for the morning, but she was boiling with rage and misery. Nothing was turning out as she had hoped, not that that mattered now that she would never see Marcus van der Breugh again. The pain of loving him was almost physical. She swallowed the tears she must hold back until she was in her room.

'I shall probably be given the sack,' she said out loud, and jumped the last two steps, straight into the doctor's waistcoat.

'Oh,' said Araminta, as she flung her arms around as much of him as she could reach and burst into tears.

He stood patiently, holding her lightly, and not until her sobs had dwindled into hiccoughs and sniffs did he ask, 'In trouble?'

'Yes, oh, yes. You have no idea.' It seemed the most natural thing in the world to tell him, and, for the moment, the delight of finding him there just when she wanted him so badly had overridden all her good resolutions not to see him again, to forget him…

He said calmly in a voice she wouldn't have dreamt of disobeying, 'Come with me,' and he urged her across the corridor and into a room at its end.

'I can't come in here,' said Araminta. 'It's the consultants' room. I'm not allowed…'

'I'm a consultant and I'm allowing you. Sit down, Mintie, and tell me why you are so upset.'

He handed her a very white handkerchief. 'Mop up your face, stop crying and begin at the beginning.'

She stopped crying and mopped her face, but to begin at the beginning was impossible. She told him everything, muddling its sequence, making no excuses. 'And, of course, I'll be given the sack,' she finished. 'I was so rude to Sister Spicer, and anyway, she said I was no good, that I'd never make a nurse.'

She gave a sniff and blew her nose vigorously. 'It's kind of you to listen; I don't know why I had to behave like that. At least, I do, I had been looking forward to my days off, and I would have been home by now. But it's all my own fault; I'm just not cut out to be a nurse. But that doesn't matter,' she added defiantly. 'There are any number of careers these days.'

The doctor made no comment. All he said was, 'Go and wait in the nurses' sitting room until I send you a message. No, don't start asking questions. I'll explain later.'

He led her back, saw her on her way and went without haste to the Principal Nursing Officer's office. He was there for some time, using his powers of persuasion, cutting ruthlessly through rules and regulations with patience and determination which couldn't be gainsaid.

Araminta found several of her new friends in the sitting room, and it was Molly who asked, 'Not gone yet?' and then, when she saw Araminta's face, added, 'Come and sit down. We were just wondering if we'd go down to the corner and get some chips.'

Araminta said carefully, 'I meant to go home this evening, but I got held up. I—I was rude to Sister Spicer. I expect I'll be dismissed.'

She didn't feel like a grown woman, more like a dis-
obedient schoolgirl and she despised herself for it.

Molly said bracingly, 'It can't be as bad as all that,
Mintie. You'll see, when you come back from your days
off you'll find it will all have blown over.'

Araminta shook her head. 'I don't think so. You see,
Molly, I think Sister Spicer is probably right; I'm not very
efficient, and I'm slow. I like looking after people and
somehow there's never enough time. Oh, you know what
I mean—someone wants a bedpan but I'm not allowed to
give it because the consultant is due in five minutes—
that sort of thing.'

'You've not been happy here, have you, Mintie?'

'No, to be honest I haven't. I think it will be best if I
go and see the Principal Nursing Officer and tell her I'd
like to leave.'

'You don't want to give it another try?' someone
asked, but Araminta didn't answer because the warden
had put her head round the corner.

'Nurse Pomfrey, you're to go to the consultants' room
immediately.'

She went out, banging the door after her.

'Mintie, whatever is happening? Why do you have
to go there?'

Araminta was at the door. 'I'll come back and tell
you,' she promised.

Dr van der Breugh was standing with his vast back to
the room, looking out of the window, when she knocked
and went in. He turned round and gave her a thoughtful
look before he spoke.

'Have you decided what you want to do?'

'Yes, I'll go and ask if I may leave. At once, if that's
allowed. But I don't suppose it is.'

'And what do you intend to do?'

'It's kind of you to ask, doctor,' said Araminta, hoping that her voice wouldn't wobble. 'I shall go home and then look for the kind of job I can do. Probably they will take me back at the convalescent home.'

They wouldn't; someone had taken her place and there was no need of her services there now. But he wasn't to know that.

'I feel responsible for this unfortunate state of affairs,' said the doctor slowly, 'for it was I who persuaded you to look after the twins and then arranged for you to come here. I should have known that it would be difficult for you, having to catch up with the other students. And Sister Spicer...'

He came away from the window. 'Sit down, Mintie, I have a suggestion to make to you. I do so reluctantly, for you must have little faith in my powers to help you. I have a patient whose son is the owner and headmaster of a boys' prep school at Eastbourne. I saw her today and she told me that he is looking urgently for a temporary assistant matron. The previous one left unexpectedly to nurse her mother and doesn't know when she intends to return. I gave no thought to it until I saw you this evening. Would you consider going there? You would need to be interviewed, of course, but it is a job with which you are already familiar.'

'Little boys? But how can I take the job? I am not sure, but I expect I'd have to give some sort of notice.' She added sharply, 'Of course I have faith in you, I'm very grateful that you should have thought of me.'

'But if it could be arranged, you would like the job, provided the interview was satisfactory?'

'Yes. You see, that's something I can do—little boys

and babies and girls.' She paused, then explained, 'It's not like nursing.'

'No, I realise that. So you are prepared to give it a try? I have seen the Principal Nursing Officer. If you go to her office now you may make a request to leave. It is already granted, but you need to go through the motions. I will contact my patient and ask her to arrange things with her son. You should hear shortly.'

He went to the door and opened it for her. 'I will drive you home tomorrow morning. Ten o'clock in the forecourt.'

'There is really no need...' began Araminta. 'I'm perfectly able...'

'Yes, yes, I know, but I have no time in which to argue about it. Kindly do as I ask, Mintie.'

If he had called her Miss Pomfrey in his usually coolly civil way, she would have persisted in arguing, but he had called her Mintie, in a voice kind enough to dispel any wish to argue with him. Besides, she loved him, and when you love someone, she had discovered, you wish to do everything to please them.

She said, 'Very well, doctor,' and added politely, 'Good evening.'

She went off to the office, buoyed up by the knowledge that if Marcus had said that everything was arranged, then that would be so and she had no need to worry. She knocked and, bidden to enter, received a bracing but kind lecture, a recommendation to find work more suited to her capabilities and permission to leave.

'Be sure and hand in your uniform and notify the warden. There is no need for you to see Sister Spicer.' She was offered a hand. 'I have no doubt that you will find exactly what you want, Nurse.'

So Araminta shook hands and got herself out of the office, leaving her superior thoughtful. Really, Dr van der Breugh had gone to great lengths to arrange the girl's departure. After all, he wasn't responsible for her, whatever he said. The Principal Nursing Officer wouldn't have allowed her arm to be twisted by anyone else but him; she liked him and respected him and so did everyone else at the hospital. All the same, he must be interested—such a plain little thing, too.

Araminta went back to the sitting room and half a dozen pairs of eyes fastened on her as she went in.

'Well?' asked Molly. 'Who was it? What's happened? Was Sister Spicer there?'

Araminta shook her head. 'No, just me. I'm leaving in the morning…'

'But you can't. I mean, you have to give notice that you want to, and reasons.'

Araminta decided to explain. 'Well, I didn't come with the rest of you because I was asked to take on a job in an emergency. I did tell you that. But the thing is the person I worked for was Dr van der Breugh—with his nephews— and I went to look after them provided he would do his best to get me a place here as soon as possible. Well, he did, but it hasn't worked out, so now he has arranged for me to leave. The Principal Nursing Officer was very nice about it.'

There was a chorus of voices. 'What will you do? Try another hospital? Find another job?'

'Go home.'

Molly said, 'It's good of Dr van der Breugh to help you. I can quite see that he feels responsible—I mean, you obliged him in the first place, didn't you?'

'Yes. And he did warn me that he didn't think I'd be

any good at nursing. Only I'd set my heart on it. I'll start again, but not just yet.'

'If you're going in the morning you'll have to pack and sort out your uniform. We'll give you a hand.'

So several of them went to Araminta's room and helped her to pack. She went in search of the warden and handed in her uniform, taking no heed of the lecture she was given by that lady, and presently they all went down to supper and then to make tea and talk about it, so that Araminta had no time at all to think or make plans. Which was a good thing, for her head was in a fine muddle. Tomorrow, she told herself, she would sit down quietly and think things out. Quite what she meant by that she didn't know.

She woke very early, her head full of her meeting with the doctor. It was wonderful that he had come into her life once more—surely for the last time. And since he had gone to so much trouble she would take this job at Eastbourne and stay there for as long as they would have her. It was work she could do, she would have some money, she could go home in the holidays and she would take care never to see Marcus again. That shouldn't be difficult, for he had never shown a wish to see more of her. She got up, and dressed, then said goodbye to her friends, and promptly at ten o'clock went down to the entrance with her case. She hadn't been particularly happy at the hospital but all the same she felt regret at leaving it.

The doctor came to meet her, took her case and put it in the boot, and settled her beside him in the car. He had wished her good morning, taken a look at her face and then decided to say nothing more for the moment. Mintie wasn't a girl to cry easily, he was sure, but he suspected that there were plenty more tears from where the last outburst had come, and it would only need a wrong word to start them off.

He drove out of the forecourt into the morning traffic.

'We will go home and have coffee, for Briskett wants to bid you goodbye. You have an appointment to see Mr Gardiner at three o'clock this afternoon. He will be at the Red Lion in Henley. Ask for him at Reception.'

He didn't ask her if she had changed her mind, and he had nothing further to say until he stopped in front of his house.

Briskett had the door open before they reached it, delighted to see her again.

'There's coffee in the small sitting room,' said Briskett, 'and I'll have your coat, Miss Pomfrey.'

They sat opposite each other by the fire, drinking Briskett's delicious coffee and eating his little vanilla biscuits, and the doctor kept up an undemanding conversation: the boys were fine, he had seen them on the previous weekend, they were all going over to Friesland for Christmas. 'They sent their love—they miss you, Mintie.'

He didn't add that he missed her, too. He must go slowly, allow her to find her feet, prove to herself that she could make a success of a job. He had admitted to himself that she had become the one thing that really mattered to him, that he loved her. He had waited a long time to find a woman to love, and now that he had he was willing to wait for her to feel the same way, something which might take time...

He drove her to Hambledon later, and once more found the house empty save for a delighted Cherub. There was another note, too, and, unlike Briskett, the doctor coolly took it from Araminta's hand when she had read it.

The cousin had gone to Kingston to shop and would be

back after tea. He put the note back, ignoring her indignant look, and glanced around him. Briskett had given a faithful description of the house: pleasant, old-fashioned solid furniture and lacking a welcome.

'It's a good thing, really,' said Araminta. 'I've an awful lot to do, especially if I get this job and they want me as soon as possible.'

He rightly took this as a strong hint that he should go. He would have liked to have taken her somewhere for a meal but she would have refused. When she thanked him for the lift and his help in getting her another job, he made a noncommittal reply, evincing no wish to see her again, but wishing her a happy future. And in a month or two he would contrive to see her again…

Araminta, wishing him goodbye and not knowing that, felt as though her heart would break—hearts never did, of course, but it was no longer a meaningless nonsense.

But there was little time to indulge in unhappiness. In three hours' time she would have to be at the Red Lion in Henley, and in the meantime there was a lot to do.

There had been no time to have second thoughts; that evening, washing and ironing, sorting out what clothes she would take with her while she listened to her cousin's chatter, Araminta wondered if she had been too hasty.

Mr Gardiner had been no time-waster. He was a man of early middle age, quiet and taciturn, asking her sensible questions and expecting sensible answers. His need for an assistant matron was urgent, with upwards of fifty little boys and Matron run off her feet. He'd read her credentials, then voiced the opinion that they seemed satisfactory.

'In any case,' he told her, 'my mother tells me that

Dr van der Breugh is a man of integrity and highly respected. He gave you a most satisfactory reference. Now,
as to conditions and salary…'

He dealt with these quite swiftly and asked, 'Are you
prepared to come? As soon as possible?' He smiled suddenly. 'Could you manage tomorrow?'

The sooner she had something to occupy her thoughts
the better, reflected Araminta. She agreed to start on the
following day. 'In the late afternoon? Would that do?
There are several things I must see to…'

'Of course, we'll expect you around teatime. Take
a taxi from the station and put it down to expenses. I
don't suppose you have a uniform? I'll get Matron to
find something.'

He had given her tea and she had come back home
to find her cousin returned. A good thing, for she'd offered to cook them a meal while Araminta began on her
packing. She'd phoned her mother later to tell her that
she had left the hospital and was taking up a job as an
assistant school matron.

'What a good idea,' observed her parent comfortably.
'You liked the convalescent home, didn't you? A pity you
couldn't have stayed with Dr van der Breugh's nephews,
for it seems to me, my love, that you are cut out to be
a homebody. I'm sure you will be very happy at Eastbourne.

'We shall be home very shortly and we must make
plans for Christmas. We still have a good deal of research
to do and the publishers are anxious for us to have our
book ready by the spring, but we shall be home soon,
although we may need to make a trip to Cornwall—
there have been some interesting discoveries made near
Bodmin.'

Araminta was sorry to leave Cherub once again. It was fortunate that he was a self-sufficient cat, content as long as he was fed and could get in and out of the house. Araminta, on her way to Eastbourne the next day, wondered if it would be possible for her to have him with her at the school. There was a flatlet, Mr Gardiner had told her, and Cherub would be happy in her company. She would wait until she had been there for a time and then see what could be done. It depended very much on the matron she would be working with. Araminta, speculating about her, decided that no one could be worse than Sister Spicer...

The school was close to the sea front, a large rambling place surrounded by a high brick wall, but the grounds around it were ample; there were tennis courts and a covered swimming pool and a cricket pitch. And the house looked welcoming.

She was admitted by a friendly girl who took her straight to Mr Gardiner's office. He got up to shake hands, expressed pleasure at her arrival and suggested that she might like to go straight to Matron.

'I'll take you up and leave you to get acquainted. The boys will be at supper very shortly, and then they have half an hour's recreation before bed. Perhaps you could work alongside Matron for a while this evening and get some idea of the work?'

Matron had a sitting room and a bedroom on the first floor next to the sick bay. She was a youngish woman with a round, cheerful face and welcomed Araminta warmly. Over a pot of tea she expressed her relief at getting help.

'It's a good job here,' she observed. 'The Gardiners are very kind and considerate, but it does need two of us. You like small boys? Mr Gardiner told me that you had worked with them.'

She took Araminta along to her room presently, at the other end of the house but on the same floor. It was quite large, with a shower room leading from it, an electric fire, a gas ring and a kettle. It was comfortably furnished and on the bed there was an assortment of blue and white striped dresses.

'I've done the best I could,' said Matron. 'See if any of them fit—the best of them can be altered.' She hesitated. 'Mr Gardiner always calls me Matron—but the name's Pagett, Norma. I should call you Matron as well, when the boys are around, but…' She paused enquiringly.

'Would you call me Mintie? It's Araminta, really, but almost no one calls me that. Do I call you Miss Pagett?'

'Heavens no, call me Norma. I'm sure we shall get on well together.'

Norma went back to her room and left Araminta to try on the dresses. One or two were a tolerable fit, so she changed, unpacked her few things and went back to Norma's room.

There was just time to be given a brief resumé of her work before the boys' suppertime, and presently, presiding over a table of small boys gobbling their suppers, Araminta felt a surge of content. She wasn't happy, but it seemed that she had found the right job at last—and who could be miserable with all these little boys talking and shouting, pushing and shoving and then turning into pious little angels when Mr Gardiner said grace at the end of the meal?

Later that evening, sitting in her dressing gown, drinking cocoa in Norma's room, Araminta reminded herself that this was exactly what she had wanted. She would never be a career girl, but she hoped there would be a secure and pleasant future ahead for her.

Hard on this uplifting thought came another one. She didn't want security and life could be as unpleasant as it liked, if only she could see Marcus again.

The next few days gave her no chance to indulge in self-pity. Accustomed as she was to the care of small children, she still found the day's workload heavy. Norma was well organised, being a trained children's nurse, and efficient. She was kind and patient, too, and the boys liked her. They liked Araminta, too, and once she had learned her day's routine, and her way round the school, she found that life could be pleasant enough even if busy—provided, of course, that she didn't allow herself to think about Marcus.

The following weekend was an exeat, and the boys would have Saturday, Sunday and Monday to go home, save for a handful whose parents were abroad.

'We will split the weekend between us,' Norma told her, 'I'll have Friday evening—you can manage, can't you?—and come back on Sunday at midday. You can have the rest of Sunday and Monday, only be back in the evening, won't you? The boys will come back after tea. Mr Gardiner doesn't mind how we arrange things as long as one of us is here to keep an eye on the boys who are staying—there aren't many; all but half a dozen have family or friends to whom they go.'

'I don't mind if I don't go home,' said Araminta. 'I've only just got here…'

'Nice of you, but fair's fair, and you'll be glad of a couple of days away. This is always a busy term—Christmas and the school play and parents coming and the boys getting excited.'

* * *

Marcus van der Breugh, busy man though he was, still found time to phone Mrs Gardiner senior. 'A happy co-incidence,' he told her, 'that you should have mentioned your son's urgent need for help. I am sure that Miss Pom-frey will be suitable for the work.'

Mrs Gardiner, with time on her hands, was only too glad to chat.

'I heard from him yesterday evening. He is very sat-isfied. She seems a nice girl—the boys like her and the matron likes her. So important that these people should get on well together, don't you agree? And, of course, she is fortunate in that it is an exeat at the weekend and she will be free for part of the time to go home. She and Ma-tron will share the days between them, of course; some-one has to be there for the boys who stay at the school.' She gave a satisfied laugh. 'I feel we must congratulate ourselves on arranging things so successfully.'

The doctor, making suitable replies when it seemed necessary, was already making plans.

Araminta was surprised to get a letter the next morn-ing; her parents were still away and the writing on the envelope wasn't her cousin's. She opened it slowly; her first delighted thought that it was from the doctor was instantly squashed. The writing was a woman's; his writ-ing was almost unreadable.

It was from Lucy Ingram. She had asked her brother where Araminta was, she wrote, and he had given her the school's address. Could Araminta come and stay for a day or two when she was next free? The boys were so anxious to see her again. 'It's an exeat next weekend and I dare say all the schools are the same. So if you are free, do let us know. I'll drive over and fetch you. Do come if you can; it will be just us. Will you give me a ring?'

Araminta phoned that evening. It would be nice to see Peter and Paul again, and perhaps hear something of Marcus from his sister. She accepted with pleasure but wondered if it was worth Mrs Ingram's drive. 'It's only a day and a half,' she pointed out, 'and it's quite a long way.'

'The M4, M25, and a straight run down to Eastbourne. I'll be there on Sunday at noon. And we shall love to see you again.'

The school seemed very empty once most of the boys had gone and Norma had got into her elderly car and driven away. There were eight boys left, and with Mr Gardiner's permission Araminta had planned one or two treats for the next day. The pier was still open and some of the amusements—the slot machines, the games which never yielded up a prize, the fortune-teller—were still there.

After their midday dinner she marshalled her little flock and, armed with a pocket full of tenpenny pieces which she handed out amongst them, she let them try everything and then trotted them along the esplanade and into the town, where they had tea at one of the smartest cafés.

Mr Gardiner had told her to give them a good time, that she would be reimbursed, so they ate an enormous tea and, content with their outing, walked back through the dusk to the school. Since it was a holiday they were allowed to stay up for an hour and watch television after their supper. Araminta, going from bed to bed wishing them goodnight, was almost as tired as they were.

She put everything ready for the morning before she

went to bed, praying that Norma would be as good as her word and return punctually.

She did. Araminta, back from church with the boys and Mr Gardiner and his wife, wished everyone a hurried goodbye and went out of the school gate to find Mrs Ingram waiting there.

'You've not been waiting long?' she asked breathlessly. 'It's been a bit of a scramble.'

'Five minutes. How nice to see you again, Mintie. I thought we'd stop for lunch on the way; we'll be home before three o'clock and then we'll have an early tea with the boys. They can't wait to see you again.'

'It's very kind of you to invite me. I—I didn't expect to see you or the boys again.'

'You like this new job?' Mrs Ingram was driving fast along the almost empty road.

'Yes, very much. I've only been here for a week. I started nursing, but I wasn't any good at it. Dr van der Breugh happened to see me at the hospital and arranged for me to give up training, and he happened to know of this school. He's been very kind.'

Mrs Ingram shot her a quick look. 'Yes, he is. Far too busy, too. We don't see enough of him, so thank heaven for the phone. Now, tell me, what exactly do you do?'

The drive seemed shorter than it was; they found plenty to talk about, and stopped for a snack meal at a service station. The time passed pleasantly and, true to her word, Mrs Ingram stopped the car at her home just before three o'clock.

Chapter 9

Peter and Paul fell upon her with a rapturous welcome. They had missed her, they chorused, and did she still remember the Dutch they had taught her when they were in Holland? And did she remember that lovely toy shop? And why did she have to live so far away? And was she to stay for a long, long time? For they had, assured Peter, an awful lot to tell her. But first she must go into the garden and see the goldfish...

They had a splendid tea presently, and then everyone sat around the table and played Snakes and Ladders, Ludo and the Racing Game, relics from Mr Ingram's childhood. Then it was time for supper, and nothing would do but that Araminta should go upstairs when they were in bed and tell them a story.

'You always did in Uncle Marcus's house,' they reminded her.

The day was nicely rounded off by dinner with the Ingrams and an hour or so round the drawing room fire talking about everything under the sun, except Marcus.

It was still dark when she awoke in the pretty bedroom.

'It's a bit early,' said Peter as the pair of them got onto her bed and pulled the eiderdown around them, 'but you've got to go again at tea time, haven't you? So we thought you might like to wake up so's we can talk.'

The day went too quickly. They didn't go out, for the weather had turned nasty—a damp, misty, chilly November day—but there had been plenty to do indoors. It was mid-afternoon when Mr Ingram took the boys into the garden to make sure that the goldfish were alive and waiting for their food, leaving Mrs Ingram and Araminta sitting in the drawing room, talking idly.

They were discussing clothes. 'It must be delightful—' began Araminta, and stopped speaking as the door opened and the doctor came in.

He nodded, smiling, at his sister, and said, 'Hello, Mintie.'

Nothing could have prevented her glorious smile at the sight of him. He noted it with deep satisfaction and watched her pale cheeks suddenly pinken.

'Good afternoon, Doctor,' said Araminta, replacing the smile with what she hoped was mild interest, bending to examine one of her shoes.

Mrs Ingram got up to kiss him. 'Marcus, how very punctual you are. We're about to have tea. Such a pity that Araminta has to go back this evening.'

The doctor glanced at his watch. 'You have to be back to get the boys settled in again?' he asked Araminta. 'If we leave around four o'clock that should get you there in good time.'

Araminta looked at Mrs Ingram, who said airily, 'Oh, you won't mind if Marcus drives you back, will you, Araminta? After all, you do know each other, and you'll have plenty to talk about.'

'But it's miles out of your way…?'

Araminta, filled with delight at the thought of several hours in Marcus's company, nonetheless felt it her duty to protest.

'I am interested to hear how you are getting on at the school,' he observed blandly. 'I feel sure that there will be no chance to discuss that once the boys have come indoors.'

Which was true enough. They swarmed over their uncle and grown-up conversation of any kind was at a minimum. Tea was eaten at the table: plates of thinly cut bread and butter, crumpets, toasted teacakes, a sponge cake and a chocolate cake.

'The boys chose what we should have for tea—all the things you like most, Araminta,' said Mrs Ingram. 'And, I suspect, all the things they like most, too! We always have an old-fashioned tea with them. I can't say I enjoy milkless tea and one biscuit at four o'clock.'

She glanced at her brother. 'Did you have time for lunch, Marcus?'

'Oh, yes. It's Briskett's day off, but he leaves me something.' He sounded vague. But there was nothing vague about his manner when presently he said that they must leave if Araminta needed to be back at the school by six o'clock. She fetched her overnight bag and got into her coat, then made her farewells—lengthy ones when it came to the boys, who didn't want her to go.

'Araminta must come and see us all again soon,' said Mr Ingram. 'She gets holidays just like you do.'

A remark which served to cheer up the boys so that she and Marcus left followed by a cheerful chorus of goodbyes.

Beyond asking her if she were comfortable, the doctor had nothing to say. It wasn't until they were on the M4, travelling fast through the early dusk, that he began a desultory conversation about nothing in particular. He was intent on putting Araminta at her ease, for she was sitting stiff as a poker beside him, giving him the strong impression that given the opportunity she would jump out of the car.

She had said very little to him at his sister's house, something which no one but himself had noticed, and now she was behaving as though he were a stranger. Driving to Oxford that afternoon, he had decided to ask her to marry him, but now he could see that that was something he must not do. For some reason she was keeping him at arm's length, and yet at St Jules' she had flung those arms around him with every appearance of relief and delight at seeing him. She seemed happy enough at the school. Perhaps she was trying to make it plain that she resented his reappearance now that she had settled into a job that she liked.

They reached the M25 and he was relieved to see that her small stern profile had resolved itself into her usual habitual expression of serenity. He waited until they had left the motorway, going south now towards Eastbourne.

'You are happy at the school?' he asked casually. 'You feel that you can settle there, if permanent job should be offered, or would you prefer to use it as a stop-gap? You can always enrol at another hospital, you know.'

'No. That was a mistake. I hope that I can stay at the school. Matron is thinking of leaving next year; there's always the chance that I might get her job. I would be very happy there for the rest of my life.'

She spoke defiantly, expecting him to disagree about that, but all he did was grunt in what she supposed was agreement, which should have pleased her but left her illogically disappointed.

Presently he said, 'You feel that you have found your niche in life?' He shot past a slow-moving car. 'Have you no wish to marry? Have a home of your own, a husband and children?'

It was on the tip of her tongue to tell him that was exactly what she wished, but what would be the point of wishing? Where was she to find a home and a husband and children? And anyway, the only husband she wanted was beside her, although he might just as well have been on the moon.

She wasn't going to answer that; instead she asked, 'And you, doctor, don't you wish for a wife and children?'

'Indeed I do. What is more, I hope to have both in due course.'

Not Christina, hoped Araminta, he would be unhappy. She said, at her most Miss Pomfrey-ish, 'That will be nice.'

A silly answer, but what else was there to say? She tried to think of a suitable remark which might encourage him to tell her more, but her mind was blank. Only her treacherous tongue took matters into its own hands.

'Is she pretty?' asked Araminta, and went scarlet with shame, thankful that it was too dark for him to see her face.

The doctor managed not to smile. He said in a matter-of-fact way, as though there was nothing unusual in her question, 'I think she is the loveliest girl in the world.'

To make amends, Araminta said, 'I hope you will be very happy.'

'Oh, I am quite certain of that. Paul and Peter are looking very fit, don't you agree?'

Such a pointed change in the conversation couldn't be ignored. She was aware of being snubbed and her reply was uttered in extreme politeness with waspish undertones. It seemed the right moment to introduce that safest of topics, the weather.

She spun it out, making suitable comments at intervals, and the doctor, making equally suitable answers in a casual fashion, was well content. True, his Araminta had shown no sign of love, even liking for him, but she was very much on her guard and anxious to impress him with her plans for her solitary future.

But he had seen her gloved hands clenched together on her lap and the droop of her shoulders. She wasn't happy, despite her assurances. He wished very much to tell her that he loved her, but it was only too obvious that she was holding him at arm's length. Well, he could wait. In a week or so he would find a reason to meet her again...

They were in the outskirts of Eastbourne and he glanced at the clock on the dashboard. 'Ten minutes to six. Do you go on duty straight away?'

'I expect so. There'll be the unpacking to do, and the boys will want their supper.'

He stopped the car by the school entrance and she undid her seat belt. 'Thank you for bringing me back; I have so enjoyed my weekend. Don't get out—you must be anxious to get home.'

He took no notice of that but got out, opened her door, got her case from the boot and walked her to the door.

She held out a hand. 'Goodbye, Dr van der Breugh. I hope you have a lovely time at Christmas.'

He didn't speak. He put her case down in the vestibule and bent and kissed her, slowly and gently. And only by a great effort was she able to keep her arms from flinging themselves round him. He got back into his car then, and drove away, and she stood, a prey to a great many

thoughts and feelings, oblivious of the small boys troop-
ing to and fro in the hall behind her.

Their small voices, piping greetings, brought her to
her senses and back into the busy world of the school.
It was only that night in bed that she had the time to go
over those last few moments.

Had he meant to kiss her like that? she wondered. Or
was it a kind of goodbye kiss? After all, if he intended
to marry, he would have no further interest in her, and
any interest he might have had had been more or less
thrust upon him.

She was glad that she had been so positive about the
future she had planned for herself. She must have convinced him that she had no interest in getting married.
There were hundreds of girls who had made independent lives for themselves and there was no reason why
she shouldn't be one of them.

No one would mind. Her mother and father would
want her to be happy, but it wouldn't worry them if she
didn't marry.

She was too tired to cry and tomorrow morning was
only a few hours away. She went into an uneasy sleep
and dreamed of Marcus.

With Christmas only weeks away there was a good
deal of extra activity at the school: the play, the school
concert, the older boys carol-singing in the town, and
all of the boys making Christmas presents. Model aero-
planes, boats, spacecraft were all in the process of being
glued, nailed and painted, destined for brothers and sisters at home. Cards were designed and painted, drawings
framed for admiring mothers and fathers, calendars cut

out and suitably ornamented for devoted grannies, and, as well as all this, there were lessons as usual.

Araminta, racing round making beds, looking for small lost garments, helping to write letters home, helping with the presents and making suitable costumes for the play, and that on top of her usual chores, had no time to think about her own life. Only at last when she had her free day did she take time to think about the future.

She didn't go home; her parents would be coming back during the following week and she would go then. She wrapped up warmly and walked briskly along the promenade, oblivious of the wind and the rain.

It seemed obvious to her that she wouldn't see Marcus again. It must have been pure chance which led him to visit his sister while she was staying there. Indeed, it was always pure chance when they met. He had had no choice but to offer to drive her back to Eastbourne.

'I must forget him,' said Araminta, shouting it into the wind.

She turned her back on that same wind presently and got blown back the way she had come. In the town she found a small, cosy restaurant and had a meal, then spent the afternoon shopping. Dull items like toothpaste, hand cream and a new comb, some of the ginger nuts Norma liked with her evening cocoa and coloured wrapping paper for some of the boys whose gifts were finished and ready to pack up.

She had an extravagant tea presently, prolonging it as long as possible by making a list of the Christmas presents she must buy. Then, since the shops were still open, she spent a long time choosing cards, but finally that was done and there was nothing for her to do but go back to the school.

The cinema was showing a horror film, which didn't appeal, and besides, she didn't like the idea of going alone. The theatre was shut prior to opening with the yearly pantomime.

She bought a packet of sandwiches and went back to her room; she would make tea on her gas ring and eat her sandwiches and read the paperbacks she had chosen. She had enjoyed her day, she assured herself. All the same she was glad when it was morning and she could plunge headfirst into the ordered chaos of little boys.

At the end of another week she went home for the day. It was a tedious journey, travelling to London by train and then on to Henley where her father met her with the car. He was glad to see her, observed that she looked very well and plunged into an account of his and her mother's tour. It had been an undoubted success, he told her, and they would be returning at a future date. The details of their trip lasted until they reached the house, where her mother was waiting for them.

'You look very well, my dear,' she told Araminta. 'This little job is obviously exactly right for you. Did your father tell you about our success? I'm sure he must have left out a good deal...'

Even if Araminta had wanted to talk to her mother there was no chance; they loved her, but she couldn't compete against the Celts. After all, they had been involved with them long before she was born. Her unexpected late arrival must have interfered with their deep interest in Celtic lore, but only for a short time. Nannies, governesses and school had made her independent at an early age and she had accepted that.

She listened now, made suitable comments and, since her cousin had gone to Henley to the dentist, cooked lunch. It was only later, while they were having tea, that her mother asked, 'You enjoyed your stay with those little boys? Dr Jenkell has told us what a charming man their uncle is. You were well treated?'

'Oh, yes, Mother, and the boys were delightful children. We got on well together and I liked Holland. Utrecht is a lovely old city...'

'I dare say it is. A pity you had no time to explore the *hunebedden* in Drenthe and the *terps* in Friesland; so clever of those primitive people to build their villages on mounds of earth. Your father and I must find the time to visit them. I'm sure something can be arranged; he knows several people at Groningen University.'

Araminta poured second cups and passed the cake. 'You will be home for Christmas?'

'Yes, yes, of course we shall. We are going to Southern Ireland next week, for your father has been invited to give a short lecture tour and there are several places I wish to see—verifying facts before we revise the book. It will be published next year, I hope...'

'I get almost three weeks' holiday,' said Araminta.

Her mother said vaguely, 'Oh, that's nice, dear. You'll come home, of course?'

'Yes.' Araminta looked at her cousin. 'I could take over for a week or so if you wanted to go away.'

An offer which was accepted without hesitation.

Back at school, activities became feverish; the play was to be presented to an audience of parents who could get there, friends who lived locally and the school staff. So costumes had to have last-minute fittings, boys who suddenly lost their nerve had to be encouraged, the school hall had to be suitably decorated, and refreshments dealt with. Everyone was busy and Araminta told herself each night when she went to bed that with no leisure to brood she would soon forget Marcus; he would become a dim figure in her past.

She shut her eyes, willed herself to sleep and there he was, his face behind her lids, every well-remembered line of it; the tiny crow's feet round his eyes when he smiled, the little frown mark where he perched his spectacles, the haughty nose, the thin, firm mouth, the lines when he was tired…

It will take time, thought Araminta, shaking up her pillows, and she tried to ignore the thought that it would take the rest of her life and beyond.

It wasn't only the school play. The carol-singers had to be rounded up and rehearsed, and someone had discovered that she could play the piano, so that each evening for half an hour she played carols, not always correctly but with feeling, sometimes joining in the singing.

The school concert would be held on the very last day, so that parents coming to collect their small sons could applaud their skills. There were to be recitations, duets on the piano, and a shaky rendering of 'Silent Night' by a boy who was learning the violin and a promising pianist. It was a pity that the two boys didn't get on well and rehearsals were often brought to a sudden end while they squabbled.

But it was a happy time for them all and Araminta, sitting up in bed long after she should have been asleep, fashioning suitable costumes for the Three Kings, to be sung by three of the older boys, although she was unhappy, was learning to live with her unhappiness. The answer was work; to be occupied for as many hours as there was daylight and longer than that so that she was too tired to think when she went to bed.

She didn't go home on her next day off, but spent the day buying Christmas presents and writing cards. Her parents had never celebrated Christmas in the traditional way; they exchanged presents and Araminta made Christmas puddings and mince pies, but there was never a tree or decorations in the house. This year, now that she had money to spend, she determined to make it a festive occasion. So she shopped for baubles for the tree, and tinsel, candles in pretty holders, crackers in pretty wrappings.

There was a tree set up in the Assembly Hall at school, too, and the boys were allowed to help decorate it. The nearer the end of term came the more feverish became the activity. End of term examinations were taken, reports made out and the boys' clothes inspected ready for packing. After the concert there would be a prize giving, and then the boys would go home. Araminta was to stay for another day, helping Norma leave the dormitories and recreation rooms tidy, before they, too, would go home.

Before the end of term the Gardiners gave a small party for the staff. Araminta had met them all, of course, but saw very little of them socially. She changed into a pretty dress and went with Norma to drink sherry and nibble savoury biscuits and exchange small talk with the form masters, the little lady who taught music and the French girl who taught French. Mr Gardiner was kind, asking her if she enjoyed her work, wanting to know what she was doing for Christmas, and Mrs Gardiner admired her dress.

The last day came, a round of concert, prize-giving and seeing the boys all safely away. Even those few whose parents were abroad were going to stay with friends or relatives, so that by suppertime the school was empty of boys and several of the staff.

Araminta and Norma began on the task of stripping beds, making sure that the cupboards and lockers were empty, checking the medicine chest and the linen cupboard, and then they spent the next morning sorting bed linen, counting blankets and making sure that everything was just so. They would return two days before the boys to make up beds and get things shipshape.

Norma was ready to leave after lunch. 'I'll go and see Mr Gardiner,' she told Araminta, 'and then go straight out to the car. So I'll say goodbye and a Happy Christmas now. You'll catch the train later? Have a lovely Christmas.'

Araminta finished her own packing, took her case and the bag packed with presents down to the hall and went in search of Mr Gardiner.

He was in his study, sitting at his desk, and looked up as she went in.

'Ah, Miss Pomfrey, you have come to say goodbye. You have done very well and I am more than pleased with you; you certainly helped us through a dodgy period.' He leaned back in his chair and gave her a kind smile.

'I am only sorry that we cannot offer you a permanent position here; I have heard from our assistant matron, who tells me that her mother has died and she has begged for her job back again. She has been with us for a number of years and, given that your position was temporary, I feel it only fair to offer her the post again. I am sure you will have no difficulty in finding another post; I shall be only too glad to recommend you. There is always a shortage of school matrons, you know.'

Araminta didn't say anything; she was dumb with disappointment and surprise, her future crumbling before her eyes just as she had felt sure that she had found security at last. She had really convinced herself that the previous Matron would not return. Mr Gardiner coughed. 'We are really sorry,' he added, 'but I'm sure you will understand.'

She nodded. 'Yes, of course, Mr Gardiner...'

He looked relieved. 'The post was brought to me a short while ago; there is a letter for you.' He handed her an envelope and stood up, offering a hand. 'Your train goes shortly? Stay here as long as you wish. I'm sure they will give you a cup of tea if you would like that before you go.'

'Thank you, there is a taxi coming for me.'

She shook hands and smiled, although smiling was very difficult, and went quickly out of the room.

In the hall she sat down and opened her letter. It was from her mother.

Araminta would understand, she felt sure, that she and her father had been offered a marvellous opportunity to go to Italy, where there had been the most interesting finds. Splendid material for the book, wrote her mother, and an honour for her father. They would return as soon as they could—some time in the New Year. 'You will have your cousin for company,' finished her mother, 'and I'm sure you will be glad of a quiet period.'

Araminta read the letter twice, because she simply hadn't believed it the first time, but it was true, written clearly in ink in her mother's flowing hand. She folded the letter carefully, then crossed the hall to the telephone and dialled her home number.

Her cousin answered. 'I've had a letter from mother,' began Araminta. 'It was a bit of a surprise. I'm catch-

ing the five o'clock train from here, so I'll be home for
supper...'

There was silence for a few minutes. 'Araminta, I
won't be here. Didn't your mother tell you? No, of course,
she would have forgotten. I'm on the point of leaving—
Great Aunt Kate is ill and I'm going to Bristol to nurse
her. I've left food in the fridge and Cherub is being looked
after until you come. I'm sorry, dear. Your mother and
father left in a hurry and I don't suppose they thought...
Could you not stay with friends? I'll come back just as
soon as I can.'

Araminta found her voice; it didn't sound quite like
hers, but she forced it to sound cheerful. 'Don't worry,
I'll be quite glad of a quiet time after rushing round
here. I'll look up some friends in the village. I'm sorry
you won't be at home, and I hope Christmas won't be
too busy for you.'

She must end on a bright note. 'My taxi's just arrived
and I mustn't keep it waiting. Let me know how you get
on. I'll be at home for a couple of weeks, and you may
be back by then.' She added, 'Happy Christmas,' with
false brightness.

The taxi had arrived. It was too early for the train
but she had planned to leave her luggage at the station
and have tea in the town. Now all she wanted was to go
somewhere and sit as far away from people as possible.
She didn't want to think, not yet. First she must come to
terms with disappointment.

She got into the taxi. 'Will you drive me along the
promenade? I'll tell you where I want to be put down.'

It was dusk already, and cold. The promenade was
bare of people and only a handful of cars were on it.
Away from the main street it was quiet, only the sound

of the sea and the wind whistling down a side street. She asked the driver to stop and got out, took her case and bag, then paid him, assuring him that this was where she wished to be, and watched him drive away.

She crossed the road to a shelter facing the sea. It was an old-fashioned edifice, with its benches sheltered from the wind and the rain by a roof and glassed-in walls. She put her luggage down and sat down in one corner facing the sea. It was cold, but she hadn't noticed that; she was arranging her thoughts in some kind of order. Just for a short time she allowed disappointment to engulf her, a disappointment all the more bitter because she hadn't really expected it—nor would it have been as bad if she had gone home to a loving family, waiting to welcome her.

'Wallowing in self-pity will do you no good, my girl,' said Araminta loudly. 'I must weigh the pros and cons.'

She ticked them off on her gloved fingers. 'I have some money, I have a home to go to, I can get another job after Christmas, Mother and Father...' She faltered. 'And there is Cherub waiting for me.'

Those were the pros, and for the moment she refused to think of anything else. But presently she had to, for she couldn't sit there for the rest of the evening and all night. The idea of going home to an empty house was something she couldn't face for the moment, although she could see that there was nothing else that she could do. She had friends in the village, but she had lost contact with them; her parents were liked and respected, but hardly neighbourly. There was no one to whom she could go and beg to stay with, especially at Christmas, when everyone had family and friends staying.

The tears she had been swallowing back crawled slowly down her cheeks.

* * *

The doctor was well aware that school had broken up, and upon which day Araminta would be going home for the holidays; old Mrs Gardiner had been delighted to have another little gossip when she had visited him at his consulting rooms. She had even volunteered the information that the teaching staff and the matrons stayed at the school for an extra day in order to leave everything tidy. And she had added, 'Miriam—my daughter-in-law—told me that the matrons stay until the late afternoon. They have a good deal to see to, but she is always glad when they have gone and the school is empty. I shall be going there for Christmas, of course.'

It took a good deal of planning, but by dint of working early and late the doctor achieved his object. By two o'clock he was driving away from St Jules', on his way to Eastbourne.

Araminta had left the school ten minutes before he stopped before its gates.

'Gone to catch the five o'clock train,' the maid who answered his ring told him. 'I said she was too early, but she was going to have tea somewhere first.'

The doctor thanked her with a civility which quite belied his feelings, then drove into the town, parked the car and began his search. The station first, and then every tea room, café, restaurant and snack bar. Araminta had disappeared into thin air in the space of half an hour or so.

The doctor went back to the station. He was tired, worried and angry, but nothing of his feelings showed on his face. He searched the station again, enquired at the ticket office, questioned the porters and went back to the entrance. There was a row of taxis lined up, waiting for the next train from London, and he went from one to the other, making his enquiries in a calm unhurried manner.

The third cabby, lolling beside his cab, took a cigarette out of his mouth to answer him.

'Young lady? With a case? Booked to go to the station, but changed her mind. Looking for her, are you?'

'Yes, will you tell me where you took her?'

'Well, now, I could do that, but I don't know who you are, do I?'

'You're quite right to ask. My name is van der Breugh. I'm a doctor. The young lady's name is Miss Araminta Pomfrey. She is my future wife. If you will take me to her, you could perhaps wait while we talk and then bring us back here. My car is in the car park.' He smiled. 'If you wish you may accompany me when I meet her.'

The man stared at him. 'I'll take you and I'll wait.'

Araminta, lost in sad thoughts, didn't hear the taxi, and didn't hear the doctor's footsteps. Only when he said quietly, 'Hello, Mintie,' did she look up, her mouth open and her eyes wide. All she said was, 'Oh.'

It was apparently enough for the doctor. He picked up her case and the plastic bag and said in a brisk voice, 'It's rather chilly here. We'll go somewhere and have a cup of tea.'

'No,' said Araminta, then added, 'I'm going home.'

'Well, of course you are. Come along, the taxi's waiting.'

The utter surprise of seeing him had addled her wits. She crossed the road and got into the taxi, and when the cabby asked, 'OK, miss?' she managed to give him a shaky smile. She was cold, her head felt empty, and it was too much trouble to think for the moment. She sat quietly beside Marcus until the taxi stopped before a tea room, its lighted windows welcoming in the dark evening. She stood quietly while the doctor paid the cabby, picked up her luggage, opened the tea room door and sat her down at a table.

The place was half full, for it was barely five o'clock, and it was warm and cosy with elderly waitresses carrying loaded trays. The doctor gave his order, took off his overcoat, then leaned across and unbuttoned her jacket, and in those few minutes Araminta had pulled herself together.

'I do not know why you have brought me here,' she said frostily.

'I was hoping that you would tell me,' said Marcus mildly. 'The school has broken up for the holidays, everyone has gone home but you are still here, sitting in a shelter on the promenade with your luggage. Why are you not at home, Mintie?'

His voice would have melted the Elgin Marbles, and Araminta was flesh and blood.

She said gruffly, 'I've been made redundant—the other girl is coming back. I thought I'd just stay here for a day or two.'

'And why would you wish to do that?' His voice was very quiet—a voice to calm a frightened child…

'Well,' began Araminta, 'there's really no need for me to go home. Mother and father have gone to Italy— the Celts, you know—and my cousin has had to go to an aunt who is ill. There's only Cherub…'

He perceived that Cherub was the only close tie she had with her home. He said nothing, but his silence was comforting, so that she went on, pot-valiant, 'I shall have no trouble in getting another job. I'm well qualified…'

A gross exaggeration, this, in a world of diploma holders and possessors of degrees, but she wouldn't admit that, not even to herself, and certainly not to him.

The doctor remained silent, watching her from under his lids while she drank her tea.

'Well, I must be going.' She had never been so unhappy in her life, but she must get away before she burst into tears. 'I cannot think why I have wasted my time here. I suppose you were just curious?'

'Yes.' He had spent a good deal of time and trouble looking for her, but he found himself smiling. He said in his quiet voice, 'Will you marry me, Mintie?' and watched the colour creep into her pale face as she stared at him across the table. 'I fell in love with you the moment I set eyes on you, although I wasn't aware of that at the time. Now I love you so deeply I find that I cannot live without you, my darling.'

Araminta took a minute to understand this. 'Me? You love me? But I thought you didn't like me—only you always seemed to be there when I had got into a mess. You—you ignored me.'

'I did not know what else to do. I am years older than you; you might have met a younger man.' He smiled suddenly and she felt a warm tide of love sweep over her. 'Besides, you were always Miss Pomfrey, holding me at arm's length, so I have waited patiently, hoping that you might learn to love me. But now I can wait no longer.' He added, 'If you want me to go away, I will, Mintie.'

Her voice came out in a terrified squeak. 'Go away? Don't go—oh, please, don't go. I couldn't bear it, and I want to marry you more than anything else in the world.'

The doctor glanced around him, for those sitting near their table were showing signs of interest. He laid money on the table, got into his overcoat, buttoned her jacket and said, 'Let us leave…'

'Why?' asked Araminta, awash with happiness.

'I want to kiss you.'

They went outside into the dark afternoon, into their own private heaven. The narrow street was almost empty—there were only two women laden with shopping bags, an old man with his dog, and a posse of carol-singers about to start up. Neither the doctor nor Araminta noticed them. He wrapped his great arms round her and held her close, and as the first rousing verse of 'Good King Wenceslas' rang out, he kissed her.

* * * * *

Special excerpt from

H^{TM} **HARLEQUIN**® SPECIAL EDITION

Read on for a sneak preview of
Adding Up to Family, *part of Marie Ferrarella's*
Matchmaking Mamas series!

"Please, Celia, you're a mother. You must know what I'm talking about," Bonnie Reynolds implored, obviously attempting to appeal to her longtime friend's maternal instincts. "For the first twelve years of that girl's life, I felt as if I could barely keep up with her. Even her homework assignments were so far beyond my own understanding, I had a headache every time I tried to check it."

Despite the situation that had brought her to Celia, there was pride echoing in Bonnie's voice as she added, "Rebecca whizzed through her studies like it was child's play—at a time when she was little more than a child herself."

Celia Parnell smiled understandingly at the distraught woman sitting opposite her in her Bedford, California, office.

When Bonnie had come in, looking as if she was at

her wit's end, Celia had closed the door to her small inner office to ensure privacy. Speaking calmly, she had poured them both a cup of vanilla chai tea. She'd urged the trim brunette to take a seat and tell her exactly what was troubling her.

And just like that, the words poured out of Bonnie like a dam whose retaining wall had suddenly cracked in half.

Listening, Celia nodded. It was a story she was more than a little familiar with.

"Rebecca had a wonderful job, Celia. An absolutely wonderful job—for three years. And then one day she decided to just up and leave it. Just like that." Bonnie snapped her fingers. "Don't get me wrong. When you first offered Rebecca a job with your company, I was grateful. I thought that this—this *wrinkle* was something she needed to work out and then she'd be back to herself again. In the interim, she was still earning money. But Celia, that girl is *wasting* her potential. You know she is," Bonnie cried, sitting so close to the edge of her chair that she looked as if she was in danger of falling off it if she so much as took in a big breath.

"Breathe, Bonnie," Celia counseled.

"I *am* breathing—and very nearly hyperventilating," the other woman cried, very close to tears now. "Celia, Rebecca graduated from MIT at eighteen. *Eighteen!*"

"I remember," Celia replied calmly.

But Bonnie only grew more agitated. "And she did it on a full scholarship, because her father, that rat, ran out on us, leaving me with nothing but debts and no way to pay for anything without working two jobs! That meant hardly ever seeing Rebecca, and yet she turned out like a gem."

"I know," Celia said, doing her best to continue to sound calm.

She had a feeling that she knew where this was going, but she allowed the other woman to say her piece, hoping that Bonnie would find a way to calm herself down and not be so hopeless about her daughter's current situation. Because if there was anything she'd learned these last few years, it was that no situation was hopeless.

"When she first got that job at the engineering firm— practically the best aerospace firm in the country—I was in seventh heaven. But after three years, the bottom suddenly dropped out for her. Without any warning, Rebecca decided that she was 'burned out.' Burned out," Bonnie repeated, shaking her head. "What does that even *mean*?"

"That she worked so hard, exceeding all expectations for so long, that she wound up exhausting herself," Celia told her friend. "She just needs to recharge her batteries."

"She's been recharging now for three years," Bonnie lamented. "My brilliant daughter has been *cleaning houses* for three years," the woman cried, looking at Celia for her understanding.

"I know, Bonnie. I'm the one who writes her paychecks," she replied with a smile.

As if worried that she might have insulted her, Bonnie quickly apologized. "Look, Celia, I meant no disrespect—"

"None taken," she replied serenely.

Bonnie let out a shaky breath, then continued. "But I am afraid—no, terrified—that Rebecca is just going to go on cleaning houses forever. That she's never going to be my Rebecca again."

"There is a possibility that she's happier this way," Celia suggested.

Bonnie looked stunned at the mere suggestion that this

could be the case. "No, she's not. I know she's not. And right now, she's so busy cleaning other people's houses that she's not doing anything to put her own life back together again. She lives in a silly little apartment, for heaven's sake."

"How's that again?" Celia asked, slightly confused. She interacted with the young woman under discussion all the time, and from where she stood, Rebecca seemed rather content.

"She's not *dating*," Bonnie complained, verbally underlining the word. "She's cleaning other people's houses and not saving up to buy her own house."

Hiding her amusement, Celia said, "I thought she liked living in an apartment."

Bonnie let out a long sigh. "That's okay for now— but what about later? She's not thinking about later," she complained, clearly irritated with the situation. "Am I making any sense to you?"

"Actually, I think you are. You're not upset that Becky's not working herself into a frazzle in the engineering world. What you're actually upset about is that she's not looking for a husband."

After releasing another long, frustrated breath, she confessed, "I want grandchildren, Celia. Is that such a horrible thing?"

Celia laughed. "No, not at all, Bonnie. Been there, done that. I understand perfectly what you're going through."

The subject was touching on something that she and her two best friends, Maizie and Theresa, had begun doing almost eight years ago. It had started as a spur-of-the-moment undertaking to find a husband for Maizie's daughter, without the young woman suspecting what they were up to. But the venture had turned out to be so successful, all three of them began doing it as a hobby on the side.

The women still maintained their own businesses, but they all agreed that it was matchmaking that afforded them the most satisfaction.

Leaning forward, Celia beamed at the woman. "Bonnie, I think that I just might have a solution for you."

"Oh please, tell me," her friend all but begged. "After waiting three years for this to resolve itself, I'm ready to listen to anything and even make a deal with the devil."

"Luckily," Celia told her with a smile, "it won't have to go that far."

Chapter One

"Mrs. Parnell? This is Steve Holder," the deep male voice on the other end of the phone said.

Celia recognized the name. Steve was one of her sporadic clients, making use of her services whenever he suddenly found himself without a housekeeper. Although she didn't remember all her clients, she remembered the ones who were special, and Steve Holder's case was. A widower, he was struggling to raise a preteen daughter on his own.

And Celia had just been thinking of him.

"Steve," she said with pleasure. "How is everything?"

"Not good, I'm afraid," he replied honestly. "It happened again."

Celia didn't have to guess what he was talking about. The young aerospace engineer wouldn't be calling her just to shoot the breeze or talk aimlessly. He was far too

conscientious about how he used his time—and hers—
for that.

"I take it that you've had another housekeeper quit?"
There was no judgment in Celia's voice, only sympathy.
She knew Steve to be a very personable man. Unfortunately, for one reason or another, the housekeepers he
employed seemed to have no staying power. She suspected that it had to do with his daughter. Incredibly
intelligent, the ten-year-old was becoming increasingly
difficult to handle.

She heard Steve sighing as he answered, "Yes."

Since she needed the information to update her files,
Celia tactfully asked, "May I ask what happened?"

Steve had to admit that at least this housekeeper, who
had lasted longer than the others, had a viable excuse for
leaving. "Mrs. Pritchett's daughter just had a baby and
Mrs. Pritchett is moving to Seattle to help her take care
of the new addition. She already told me that she didn't
think she'd be coming back," he added.

"Was it a girl or boy?" Celia asked.

He wasn't a people person and had to pause and think
for a minute before he could answer the question. "Girl,"
he finally said.

"That's lovely," Celia said with genuine feeling. "But
that does leave you in an immediate bind, doesn't it,
dear?"

He appreciated how direct the woman was. "Well, I
can have you and your company clean my house once
every two weeks, and Stevi's going to school right now,
but I do need someone to cover the hours when she's
home and I'm still at work."

"She's going to school?" Celia repeated, surprised.
"But it's summer."

"I know. Stevi's going to summer school. She wanted to take some classes so she could get ahead. It was her idea, not mine," he added quickly, before Mrs. Parnell could accuse him of robbing his daughter of her childhood. He was pleased she wanted to learn, but had to admit that he was really beginning to miss his little "buddy." Stevi had begun to change on him in the last few months.

"My daughter's suddenly gone serious on me, Mrs. Parnell," he confessed. "She doesn't even want to be called 'Stevi' anymore. She's 'Stephanie' now. And I've got this feeling that those fishing trips we used to take might just be a thing of the past."

Steve took his work very seriously. These outings he used to take with his daughter were what he'd looked forward to, a way to wind down. And now it appeared that this might be changing.

"Not necessarily, Steve. Your daughter could just be broadening her base, not shifting her focus," Celia pointed out. "Ten-year-olds have been known to change their minds a great deal at this age."

He could only hope, Steve thought. "Could I talk *you* into becoming my housekeeper?" he asked wistfully.

If he could put in an order for the perfect grandmother, it would be Mrs. Parnell. He was beginning to feel as if he knew his daughter less and less these days, but he was fairly certain that Stevi—Stephanie, he amended—would get along very well with her.

"I would if I could, Steve," Celia answered kindly. "But I'm afraid my company keeps me very busy these days. Otherwise—"

"I know," Steve said, cutting her short. He didn't want

the woman feeling that he was serious. "I just thought I'd give it a shot."

Celia knew he was attempting to politely extricate himself from the conversation, but she detected an underlying note of bewilderment and even sadness. She didn't think she remembered ever hearing him sound down before.

"Steve, I wouldn't give up on the idea of finding a decent housekeeper just yet." She recalled the visit she'd had with Bonnie Reynolds the other day. An idea began to form. "I just might have the perfect person for you. Let me get back to you—"

"Wait, there's more," he said, wanting to tell her something before she hung up. "I mean, I do need a housekeeper, but she'll need to be more, as well."

"Oh?"

"Well, as you know, it's been Stevi—Stephanie and I for the last six years. Despite the demands of my job, I've been able to manage finding a lot of quality time with my daughter. We've done everything together. Everything from fishing to tea parties to baseball games and 'Aliens and Astronauts'—"

"'Aliens and Astronauts'?" Celia questioned, puzzled. As the grandmother of three, including one teenage boy, she made an effort to keep up with the latest trends in games, but this was a new one.

"It's a video game," Steve explained. "It's Stevi's—Stephanie's favorite. I am having a really hard time remembering to call her that," he complained. "Anyway, suddenly, without any warning, she's switching gears on me."

"By asking you to call her Stephanie," Celia said knowingly.

"That's part of it," Steve admitted. "The other part—
the bigger one—is that she suddenly seems to be growing up right in front of my eyes."

"They have a habit of doing that," Celia told him
wryly. "I think it might have something to do with the
daily watering," she added, tongue in cheek.

Distressed over what was going on in his life, he barely
realized she was trying to lighten the mood.

"What I'm trying to get at is that all of a sudden,
Stevi's got these questions I don't know the answers to. I
mean, I know the answers, but I just can't—I just can't..."
He trailed off helplessly.

"I understand, Steve," Celia told him kindly. "Your
daughter's at a crossroads in her life. It's an admittedly
delicate area and sometimes a young girl just needs to
talk to another woman, no matter how close she is to
her father."

"Yes!" Steve cried, relieved that she understood what
he was attempting to clumsily put into words. "I need
someone who knows how to cook, who's neat, and most
of all, for Stevi—Stephanie's sake, I need someone who
is understanding and sympathetic. Someone who my
daughter can turn to with all her unanswered questions
and be comfortable doing it. I know it's a lot to ask," he
confessed with a sigh. "And I don't mean to be putting
you on the spot like this. To be honest, I've been considering the possibility of perhaps sending Stevi to boarding school."

"Boarding school?" Celia repeated, surprised. "Have
you spoken to her about it?"

"No, not yet," he admitted. "But I thought that it might
be best for her, all things considered."

Celia wanted to tell him how bad she thought that idea

was, but managed to refrain. Instead, she tactfully suggested, "Why don't you hold off on that, Steve? Let me see if I can find someone for you who could fill that bill before you decide to do anything rash." Realizing that he might think she sounded judgmental, Celia softened her words by saying, "I'm assuming that you really don't want to send Stevi away."

"No," Steve confessed, "I don't. But she needs more than me right now. She's got questions about, well—" he dropped his voice "—bras and boys and the changes her body's going through that I can't figure out how to address without embarrassing both of us. Do you understand what I'm trying to say, Mrs. Parnell?"

"Completely," she assured him. "Do me a favor, Steve. Hold off doing anything permanent for now. Don't start calling any boarding schools just yet. If worse comes to worst, I'll fill in as your housekeeper for a few days and be there for Stevi when she comes home after summer school, so you won't have to worry about her. I'm sure we can resolve this situation to everyone's satisfaction."

She could almost hear the weight falling off Steve's shoulders.

"You are a lifesaver, Mrs. Parnell," he told her with genuine enthusiasm and gratitude.

"It's all part of the service, Steve," Celia replied warmly. "One way or the other, I'll be getting back to you," she promised, before hanging up.

The moment she terminated her call to Steve, she was back on the phone, calling first Maizie Sommers, who was the unofficial leader of their informal group, and then Theresa Manetti.

She informed both women that she needed to have an emergency meeting with them.

"Okay, we're here," Maizie announced as she and Theresa walked into Celia's house later that afternoon. Because she spent a good deal of her time driving from place to place, Maizie had swung by Theresa's catering business and picked her up before coming to Celia's. "So, what's the big emergency?"

"I need to run something by you," Celia told her friends.

"Uh-oh, is this something we should be sitting down for?" Theresa asked, taking a seat at the dining room table.

"Maybe you had better sit," Celia said. "It's nothing bad," she added quickly. "But this might take me a little time to explain."

Waiting until Theresa was settled as well, Celia finally started talking. "You know how one of us is usually approached by either a parent or a friend to find someone for their son or their daughter, or maybe even friend, and then we all sit around this table and brainstorm, trying to find the perfect match for that person?"

Maizie studied her friend. "Where are you going with this?"

"I have a friend…" Celia started. "Actually, she's the mother of one of my employees. Anyway, she asked me to find someone for her daughter."

"All right," Maizie said. So far, this sounded no different than anything they normally undertook. "What's the problem?"

"It's not a problem exactly," she replied. "I actually think that I came up with the perfect person for her…" Her eyes swept over her friends. "I just wanted to run this choice by the two of you before I make the introduction."

"So run it by us," Maizie encouraged, waiting for her to get to the heart of the matter.

"He's a single dad and his daughter's at an age where she's starting to ask those kinds of questions," she said. "He told me that he needs a competent housekeeper, as well as someone to field such questions for him."

"And this employee of yours, you think she's a match for this single dad?" Theresa inquired.

"Well," Celia began cautiously, "he's an aerospace engineer and she graduated MIT at age eighteen."

"Wait a minute. I don't understand," Maizie protested, trying to make sense out of the scenario. "She graduated MIT at eighteen? No offense, Celia, but what is she doing working for you?"

Celia smiled. "I know. It sounds strange, doesn't it?"

"Not if she's in the witness protection program," Maizie quipped.

"She's not, she's just kind of conflicted. When Becky first came to me," Celia said, filling her two friends in, "she said she was looking for something 'different.' She felt burned out and she just wanted something that wasn't mentally taxing to do, something that made her feel as if she'd accomplished something basic and simple at the end of the day." Celia smiled. "Like cleaning a bathroom."

"Well, that's basic and simple, all right," Maizie agreed.

"Anyway, my point is that I think they have a lot in common and could help one another," Celia concluded. Again, she looked from Maizie to Theresa, waiting to get their take on the situation.

"Well, if that's what you think, it's good enough for me," Maizie said. "Theresa?"

She nodded. "We've all gotten good at this," she told her friends. "I trust Celia's judgment."

Maizie totally agreed.

"All right then," Celia declared, getting revved up. "I'll call Steve tomorrow and tell him that I have a house-keeper for him."

Don't miss Adding Up to Family *by
Marie Ferrarella, available August 2018 wherever
Harlequin® Special Edition books and
ebooks are sold.*

www.Harlequin.com